THE CIELO

THE CIELO

A Novel of Wartime Tuscany

PAUL SALSINI

iUniverse, Inc.
New York Lincoln Shanghai

The Cielo
A Novel of Wartime Tuscany

Copyright © 2006 by Paul E. Salsini

iUniverse books may be ordered through booksellers or by contacting:

iUniverse
2021 Pine Lake Road, Suite 100
Lincoln, NE 68512
www.iuniverse.com
1-800-Authors (1-800-288-4677)

This is a work of fiction. All of the characters, names, incidents, organizations, and dialogue in this novel are either the products of the author's imagination or are used fictitiously.

ISBN-13: 978-0-595-40697-5 (pbk)
ISBN-13: 978-0-595-85061-7 (ebk)
ISBN-10: 0-595-40697-1 (pbk)
ISBN-10: 0-595-85061-8 (ebk)

Printed in the United States of America

For Barbara,
Jim, Laura and Jack

AUTHOR'S NOTE

When my wife and I visited Tuscany in 2004, we stayed in one of those ubiquitous farmhouses in the hills that now welcome tourists. This one, though, had a special meaning for me. More than a hundred years ago, my grandfather, a tenant farmer, lived there. The place had subsequently been abandoned and restored only recently.

In the village at the base of the hill, my 80-year-old cousin told us the story of the farmhouse. During World War II, she said, Italian partisans were engaged in fierce battles with the Germans in this area, and terrified villagers fled to farmhouses in the hills for safety. We asked if her family had fled. Quietly, she said they did, and then began to recount stories of how people had trouble getting along, how they cowered when they heard the fighting and the bombing and how some of them didn't survive. Back in the farmhouse, I felt surrounded by the ghosts of villagers from sixty years earlier.

When we returned home, I couldn't stop thinking about those brave people and was determined to write a story about them. In the course of my research, I discovered the horrific event that had taken place close by, in a village called Sant'Anna di Stazzema, in August 1944. That required return trips to Italy to talk to the survivors in what remained of Sant'Anna.

This book is a tribute to the gallant people who suffered for so long, and with such courage, under the heat of the Tuscan sun.

—Paul Salsini

THE CHARACTERS

Rosa Tomaselli, 56, a housewife
Marco Tomaselli, 70, her husband

Annabella Sabbatini, 56, a housewife
Francesco Sabbatini, 57, her husband

Dante Silva, 64, a retired schoolteacher

Maria Ruffolo, a widow

Fausta Sanfilippo, a middle-aged working woman

Maddelena and Renata Spinelli, elderly sisters

Gabriella Valentini, The Contessa

Vito Tambini, an elderly man
Giacomo Tassaro, his cousin

Gina Sporenza, the wife of an Italian soldier, Pietro

    Lucia, 16
    Roberto, 12
    Anna, 10
    Adolfo, 8
    Carlotta, three months

Father Luigi, the parish priest

Gavino, an elderly farmer on the adjoining farm

Dino and Paolo, young men fleeing from the army

Fritz Krieger and Konrad Schultz, both 17, members of the SS

Ezio Maffini, a partisan

Colin Richards, an escaped British war prisoner

Angelica Marchetti, daughter of Maria, who lives in Sant'Anna

  Little Carlo, 4
  Nando 2

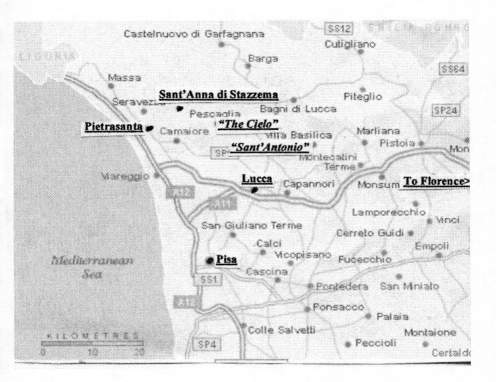

The map shows the locations of the "Cielo" and "Sant'Antonio."

PART ONE

CHAPTER 1

──────────▼──────────

Rosa just happened to glance out the kitchen window when she saw them running across the field toward her house. One stumbled on a fallen branch and she could hear the other two yelling at him. As the shouts came nearer she saw Gatto arch his back and flee behind the shed.

"*Santa Maria!*" she said to herself. "Why are they coming here now?"

She quickly grabbed the broom in the corner and pounded the kitchen ceiling with all her might. Four times.

Just in time. She heard a heavy lid slam shut upstairs just as the soldiers pushed open the door and filled her tiny kitchen. They were sweating, and their shirts clung to their chests.

"*Buongiorno,* Signora," the chubby one said. "We want to…"

"Please close the door," Rosa commanded. "I'm trying to keep the house cool. We've never had such a hot July, just terrible." The shortest soldier dutifully obeyed.

The summer had been horrid. All of her neighbors kept their doors and windows closed. They said they wanted to be protected from the boiling Tuscan sun, but they wanted to keep other dangers out, too.

"Now, what can I do for you?" Rosa said, wiping her sweaty hands on her apron. Flustered, the three soldiers looked at one another, and when Rosa picked up her rolling pin they instinctively reached for the pistols in their holsters. Ignoring them, Rosa calmly began to roll out the dough on the kitchen table. Finally, the tall one spoke. His Italian was at best imperfect.

"We are looking for an army deserter. We know he's in Sant'Antonio and we are searching every house."

Rosa didn't look up. "Why in the world would you want to look for a deserter from the Italian army? Don't you have enough soldiers in your army?"

"Well, of course we have. But we can't let you Italians run away from your army now, can we?"

"As you can see," Rosa said, intent on rolling out the dough, "I'm quite alone here, and I'm trying to make these ravioli. Can't you men see this is a lot of work? I don't imagine you've made ravioli, have you? You've probably never cooked anything in your lives. Now if you would just leave, we can all go about our business."

As much as she tried to speak calmly, Rosa knew that her voice, always high, had climbed higher, and she prayed that the soldiers could not see her heart beating so fast under the top of her apron.

For the last three years, the Wehrmacht soldiers had occupied all of northern Italy. At first, they were simply a presence, and most people tried to ignore them. But in the last months, there had been a growing number of incidents. The soldiers roughed up men who wouldn't answer their questions. They raided houses without warning. They took food and wine from homes. They enforced a 10 o'clock curfew every night. And there were even more convoys of tanks rumbling through the little village, sometimes skidding off the road and barely missing houses and trees.

The Italians had tried to endure all this without complaint but they were getting more impatient as the Allies slowly worked their way north from the heel of the country. Now, the British were bombing cities and villages in the north to flush out the Germans, and more and more Italian partisans, especially here in Tuscany, were sabotaging the Nazis in the hills.

"Well, then," the tall soldier said, "you won't mind if we just take a look around, all right?"

Rosa knew she didn't have a choice. The soldiers went into the living room, looking under the couch and behind the chair.

"*Raus!*" one shouted.

"*Santa Maria!*" Rosa said. "Do you think someone is hiding behind that little chair?"

The tall soldier glared at her. Then they went into the dining room, where they opened the cupboards.

"He would have to be awfully small to fit in there," Rosa said as she watched one of the soldiers pull tablecloths and linens from a shelf in a cupboard.

"Come on. Let's look upstairs." The tall soldier pulled out his pistol.

Rosa froze as the men's heels clattered on the stone stairs. She hadn't wanted to take the young man in when he arrived at their door two days ago, starving and looking desperately for food. He said he was from Montepulciano and he and a friend had jumped from the troop train in the Serchio Valley north of Lucca last month. So she and Marco agreed that he could stay a few days and hide in the sewing room upstairs. He knew that if Germans arrived he would have to crawl into the chest inside the closet and cover himself with blankets.

"Anyone here? *Raus! Raus!*"

Her knuckles white as she gripped the rolling pin, Rosa stood at the bottom of the stairs. She heard the soldiers going into the bedroom and rifling through her and Marco's clothes in the *armadio*. She held her breath when she heard the door to the sewing room open.

"It's dark in here. Open the curtains," one soldier said.

"It's still pretty dark," another one said.

"Look in that closet," the third one said. "Anything there?"

A long silence. Rosa closed her eyes and wiped her brow.

"There's no light in here. Can't see anything."

"All right then. Let's go. It's too hot up here. No one could stay here for long."

Rosa was back at the table rolling out dough when the soldiers came down. Sweat glistened on her forehead and matted her thick hair.

"You see?" she said. "I told you no one was here."

"I bet you know a lot about what's happening in this village, don't you?" the tall soldier said, standing close behind her and breathing on her neck. "Tell us what you know, little *Signora*."

"I don't know anything," Rosa said, squirming away. "I just keep to myself."

The soldier put his pistol on the table, right next to the dough. He leaned back in the chair opposite her, watching as she sprinkled more flour on the dough and rolled it out.

"Are you trying to frighten me?" Rosa asked. "I don't frighten easily." But her heart was still racing. The soldier smirked.

The chubby soldier sat in the chair next to the stove and the short one stood at the door. They pulled out cigarettes from their pockets and didn't look like they were going to leave.

For the next forty-five minutes, the soldiers tried to get information. Rosa ignored their questions or changed the subject.

"Who are the people here supporting the partisans?"

"Do you like ravioli? I don't suppose they have it in Germany. I'm using my mother's recipe. She got it from her mother who probably got it from her mother before that."

"What do you know about the priest?"

"I have a secret ingredient," Rosa said. "I bet you can't guess. I use nutmeg. All the other women here use cinnamon."

"Where are the older men? Where have they gone?"

"The other women use fancy ravioli cutters. I just use a fruit juice glass, see? My mother used a glass. Her ravioli were fat and round, not square and flat like you see in restaurants."

The chubby soldier perked up. "That's how they were in the restaurant in Reboli," he said.

"You mean at Nero's? My husband took me there on our tenth wedding anniversary a year ago. It's a nice restaurant, but I could tell their ravioli weren't as good as mine just by looking at them. So small. I didn't have them. Did you like them?"

Rosa was getting tired of this conversation. Finally, the soldiers stood up, the tall one replaced his pistol, and they all left. Rosa watched as they ran across the back to her neighbor Maria, next door.

"Good. Maria will tell them a thing or two," she said aloud. "*Santa Maria!* I thought they would never leave."

Grabbing a glass of water, she ran upstairs where Dino, the army deserter, was still in the chest in the closet. Rosa pulled up the heavy cover. "Are you all right?"

Dino climbed out. He was drenched with sweat. "A few more minutes in there and I think I would have suffocated."

"Those soldiers just would not leave," Rosa said. *"Bastardi!"*

"Thank you for warning me, Signora. That was close."

"Here, drink this. Are you sure you're all right?"

Dino gulped down the water. "I'm fine. Just hot. Don't worry about me."

"You rest now. That was terrible. Nazi bastards!"

CHAPTER 2

▼

While Dino stretched his arms and legs, Rosa went downstairs, washed her face and hands and scrubbed the back of her neck where the soldier had breathed on her. She picked up the things the soldiers had scattered about and straightened the furniture. Back in the kitchen, she washed the table where the soldier had put his pistol and swept up the cigarette butts they had scrunched on the floor she had just scrubbed.

"Bastardi!" she muttered.

Her hands shaking, she began to make the filling for the ravioli. She beat eggs into the spinach and added ricotta and spices. Fortunately, the chickens were still laying, so she had enough eggs for a while. She had gathered the big brown eggs just this morning.

She had just enough nutmeg for two more batches. Maybe they would have some in Reboli. Like everything else, there wasn't any left here at Leoni's, and even the supplies of prosciutto were dwindling at Manconi's, the butcher. The Germans took whatever they wanted and people had to depend more and more on what they had in their gardens.

Three planes flew overhead, so low that Rosa could see the British insignia on the fuselage and so loud that the little house shook. Rosa held on to the table and wondered when they would start to bomb Sant'Antonio.

More bombings, Rosa thought. More people killed. Now villages were being evacuated. Everything was closing in on them and nobody knew how it would end. Every night the radio brought more bad news. How could she even think about making pasta with the war all around her? But it gave her something to do.

"Basta!"

Rosa smoothed her apron and began to place the filling, spoonful after spoonful, in neat rows on the dough. She folded the dough over and cut the ravioli with the glass.

Seventy, seventy-one, seventy-two. There, enough for the two of them for four meals if she was careful. Marco would have ten, twelve, but Rosa would eat only three or four. Like a bird, Marco would tease her. Rosa would blush.

She put the ravioli on a starched white cloth to dry until tomorrow. She washed the bowl and put it back on the shelf. It was a pretty bowl, orange with red flowers around the rim. She always used it when she made ravioli. It was one of the few pieces left of the set she had from her mother.

Tomorrow she would make the sauce. Marco had shot three wild rabbits yesterday and they hung in the shed.

Marco was going to be very upset when he came home and she told him about the visitors. Well, these Wehrmacht soldiers weren't as bad as what she'd heard about the SS. She didn't want to listen to her neighbors' rumors that an SS division would be coming soon.

Wiping the sweat from her brow with the back of her hand, Rosa smeared flour onto her hair. She had to smile when she looked out the kitchen window at her long line of wash, already dry in the hot Tuscan sun. Marco's red shirt looked so big next to her tiny pink nightgown.

Under the bench, Gatto had found a cool spot and was giving himself yet another bath. Someday, Rosa thought, she should give her cat a real name.

Gatto was such a comfort. Marco didn't want him to come into the house, but when Rosa sat outside, the cat would jump into her lap. And when she stroked his orange and black fur, Gatto purred louder than any cat she had ever known. He was a big cat, maybe twelve pounds, and although he was almost fourteen years old he didn't show his age. He could still chase after lizards and catch mice in the shed and proudly present them to Rosa.

Next door, Maria had her wash on the line, too. Two black housedresses, a white nightgown and a couple of pair of black stockings. As usual, she had her underwear inside a pillow case. Maria would never put her underwear naked on the line.

"Poor Maria," Rosa sighed. "I wonder what she told those soldiers. She probably gave them some biscotti. Poor Maria. All alone."

But she knew she didn't have to feel sorry for Maria. "I'm just fine," Maria would say. "My husband may be dead, and my daughter may have moved away, but God gets me through everything."

Nervous and upset, Rosa thought that perhaps she could keep busy by dusting. She made the rounds of the rooms, adjusting pictures on the walls and dusting the bookcases, the dressers, the couches and chairs. Dust covered the lace doily on the buffet. With tanks roaring by so often now, she couldn't leave the windows open for long because everything would get so dusty.

Near the door, she straightened her parents' picture, heavy in a dark oval frame. Every time a tank went by, it slid to one side. It was their wedding portrait, taken fifty-seven years ago. Her father was seated and wore a dark suit. He looked pained, as if the stiff white collar was choking him. His mustache was thick then, and it drooped over his mouth, but Rosa thought she could see his eyes twinkling. Her mother, standing behind him with her hand on his shoulder, beamed in a white dress with tiny pearls on the bodice.

Rosa still had the dress, wrapped in tissue paper and laying on the bottom of a drawer upstairs. She was the same size as her mother, and could have worn the dress when she got married, but Rosa was forty-five then and thought it was inappropriate.

Rosa put her fingers to her lips and touched her mother and father in the photograph.

"*Cari mei,*" she whispered.

Passing a mirror, Rosa looked at her own figure. She looked good in blue, she thought. At fifty-six, she had only the slightest broadening below her waist and her breasts and hips were still firm. Like her mother's, her hair had remained black, and she wore it in a bun at the back of her neck. Marco liked it when she let her hair fall down her back.

She just wished she was more attractive. Her mouth and chin were too small and her nose too big. "A real Italian nose," her father would say, hugging her when she cried about it. Her eyes were too narrow and her eyebrows too thick. She took after her father, rather than her mother, who had such delicate features. As a child she was aware that other girls were prettier, and even now she compared herself to other women. Maybe someday she would accept herself as she was. Marco didn't seem to mind.

The clock opposite the door chimed three times as Dino came down the stairs. She was surprised to see him carrying his knapsack.

"I was watching from the window," Dino said. "The soldiers went from house to house. They have finally left."

"And you're going, too?"

"*Mille grazie,* Signora. It's safer in the hills than in this village now."

"Are you sure? Aren't you still weak? Do you feel better now?"

"Much better, Signora! Thank you for the wonderful meals!"

"Where will you go?"

"First, I want to find my friend. Paolo's up in the hills somewhere, I think I know where. Then we'll just keep going from place to place. There are farmers who will take us in. We stayed with one up on that hill over there."

"Aren't you afraid?"

The young man grinned. Rosa noticed that the freckles that covered his nose and cheeks seemed brighter when he smiled.

"This is an adventure, Signora! I'm seeing the world!"

Rosa shook her head. She went into the kitchen and put bread, cheese and some apples together for his knapsack.

"War isn't an adventure, Dino," she said when she returned. "Listen to me! Be careful! Be careful in everything!"

"Signora, I'm always careful. Don't worry about me. Maybe we will meet again?"

"Yes, perhaps," she said, though she could not believe that would ever happen.

Rosa kissed him on both cheeks and watched as he ran out the door, through the fields and into the woods. She made the sign of the cross.

Then she went upstairs, rearranged the clothes in the *armadio* and picked up a letter from the dresser. It was crushed and dirty, but it was the last letter they had received from her cousin in Livorno.

"*Cari* Rosa and Marco. Livorno has been blown up and we had to evacuate our lovely home. Imagine, our beautiful home. We have moved to Sant'Anna di Stazzema. It took us so long to get here. It's very high in the hills and everyone says it is the safest place in Tuscany. The British won't bomb us and the Germans won't find us. There are so many evacuees here. We are staying with a family named Pierini. They are very kind, but there are two other families here and we don't have much food. Some people are giving food to the partisans. I don't like that. Please tell Maria that I saw her daughter Angelica in the shop yesterday. Her little boys are so beautiful, but she looked very tired. We are all so sick and frightened. How can we bear this? I can't write any longer now. I will try to write later. Pray for us. Love, your cousin, Lara Andriotti."

The letter was dated April 2, 1944, three months ago.

Poor Lara, Rosa thought. How terrible it would be to be evacuated and live with strangers, no matter how safe Sant'Anna di Stazzema might be. And what would happen to Lara and Rico's lovely house in Livorno? They had such beautiful things.

"I can't imagine being evacuated and living somewhere else," Rosa thought. "No, we're going to stay here no matter what."

Just then, a convoy of tanks went by, rattling every house on the street.

"*Santa Maria!*" she said aloud.

She was pleased her parents weren't here. What would they think about what was going on? She suspected that her father might have been a communist, and if he were alive today perhaps he would have joined the partisans. She saw the books and newspapers that he read. She knew he wouldn't be a Fascist. While everyone else thought Mussolini would do good things for Italy, he kept saying, "Just wait. Just wait and see what he will do."

Her mother wouldn't talk about any of it. When her father got upset after listening to the radio, she would go to bed and hide under the covers.

Her father's predictions had come true. They had to pay higher taxes. They had to obey more laws. They had to watch what they said because anyone could be listening. And now Mussolini had gotten the country into this terrible war.

From the bedroom window, Rosa's eyes searched the top of the distant hill. Yes, there it was, just a yellow speck among the oaks and chestnut trees, the big old farmhouse where she used to live. If they had stayed up at the Cielo, Rosa thought, they wouldn't have to worry about the Germans in this valley. At the Cielo, they would have been safe.

"We're so far up on this hill, no one can get us," her mother used to tell Rosa when she thought that bogeymen lurked in the far corners of the house.

As a child, Rosa loved living there. She played in the olive groves and vineyards and she helped with some of the chores. Another family lived in the farmhouse, too, but there were no other children to play with. So she lived in her own little world, making up stories about wild and wonderful creatures who lived in the woods and came to visit her at night.

The Cielo was part of the old *fattoria* that covered most of the hills above Sant'Antonio. With other families, Rosa's parents worked sixteen-hour days, farming the fields, taking care of the cattle and pigs and chickens and making olive oil and wine. All of this for a British man who owned the entire area, took half of everything they produced and came to visit only once a year, before Christmas.

But the land slowly gave up. The olive trees and the vineyards yielded less and less. After the English man died, the *contadini* families gradually moved to villages in the valley. For the last three years the only peasant living on the land was an ancient farmer who refused to move.

Contadini. How Rosa hated that word. She didn't feel like a peasant. Neither did her parents. But no matter how long they lived in Sant'Antonio, they never felt accepted by those whose families had lived there for generations.

"*Contadina! Contadina!*" the other children would yell when she missed a catch playing ball on the school playground. No wonder Rosa developed a strong heart, strong enough to defy the Germans now.

Rosa's parents would have stayed at the Cielo longer, but her father had a heart attack when he was forty. When Rosa was ten years old, they moved down to Sant'Antonio and bought the house where she lived now.

Then he developed the *brutto male.* No one called it cancer in those days. Rosa and her mother looked on helplessly as he slowly deteriorated. Rosa took care of him for years because her mother was too distraught. Sometimes it was messy, but what could she do? When he died at the age of fifty, her mother decided she didn't want to live any longer, so she stopped eating and died three months later. Every day, Rosa visited her parents' graves in the little cemetery next to the church.

Then Rosa had the house to herself. Until she married Marco Tomaselli. Thank goodness her parents weren't here to see what was happening, she thought. They had lived through the first war, but it wasn't all around them like this one.

Although it was stifling hot, Rosa opened the bedroom window to let in some air. She thought she could hear more rumbling. Yes. Again from the north, but this time a different sound.

An armored car was coming around the corner, followed by a truckload of soldiers, more than ever before. They didn't seem to be heading through the village. Instead they slowed down. They were turning.

These were different kinds of soldiers. Where were they going?

To the church! Why would they be going to the church? Rosa leaned out of the window as far as she could.

The car screeched to a stop in front of the priest's house way up the street. Three soldiers got out. She could see Father Luigi open the door and the soldiers go inside. Then the truck skidded to a stop and a couple dozen soldiers jumped down. These weren't the Wehrmacht soldiers who had been here before. Rosa saw the "SS" symbol on the side of the truck.

They were running all over the grass!

They were running into the cemetery!

They were running across the graves!

"*Bastardi! Bastardi!*" Rosa cried.

Rosa ran downstairs, picked up her rolling pin and ran into the street. "*Bastardi! Bastardi!*"

Only this morning she had brought fresh flowers for her parents' graves.

"*Bastardi!*"

Rosa looked at herself. Her hair was in tangles and covered with flour and her face was flushed. What would the neighbors say?

She ran back into the house and stood by the door. She wished Marco would come home.

CHAPTER 3

▼

Since it was midafternoon, Rosa knew that Marco was playing cards at Leoni's, the tiny *bottega* in the center of Sant'Antonio that almost everyone visited every day. With a green and white striped sign overhead and pots of red geraniums at the door, Leoni's was a warm and inviting place. Barrels just inside the entry contained a few olives, figs and sun-dried tomatoes. Sunflowers from the neighboring hills filled a fat jar nearby. Before the war, Nino Leoni stocked fresh vegetables along one wall, pasta and canned goods in shelves on another and candies and gifts on tables in the middle. Since the Germans arrived, supplies were being quickly depleted, and some shelves were bare.

Although villagers liked to linger at Leoni's to gossip, they spent less time at Manconi's, the butcher shop next door. The bloody carcasses of rabbits and pigs hanging overhead gave off peculiar odors, but that wasn't the only reason. Guido Manconi was not as friendly as Nino Leoni, frightening children as he chopped off the heads of chickens while complaining about the war, the weather, his wife, his sons, his long hours. No, better just to buy the cod for the *baccala* and go next door.

Outside of Leoni's, Franco Deserto, Leandro Magno, Danilo Falone and Renzo Papia, all more than ninety years old, were back in their customary places in their straight-backed chairs. Although the temperature was in the nineties, each wore a black suit, white shirt, black tie, black shoes and a fedora. They gathered here every day, no matter what the weather. Once, they greeted each other and engaged in small conversations. Now, mornings and afternoons, they simply sat, each in his own silent world but sharing the comfort of friends.

Fresh from their afternoon siesta, a small crowd, mostly women, had gathered outside. All of them were talking about the visits from the German soldiers that morning, and each had a story to tell, one more extravagant than the other. By the time the last person told her story, it sounded as though the Germans had destroyed her house.

"They knocked over a chair in the living room," one said.

"They threw clothes off the hangers," another said.

"They broke my lovely vase from Venice," said a third.

They were still telling their stories when two German soldiers came running from the direction of the church. Everyone noticed the SS emblems on their collars. The soldiers forced their way to Leoni's door, nailed a poster with heavy black letters next to the one that declared the 10 o'clock curfew, sneered at the villagers and ran back. A crowd quickly congregated around the poster.

"What does it say?" one cried. "Read it!"

"*Proclamation!*" a woman close to the poster shouted. "*Let it be known that whoever knows where a partisan group is located and does not give the information to the German army will be shot.*"

"*Mamma mia!*" an elderly widow sobbed, smacking her forehead with her hand.

"*Whoever gives shelter or food to a partisan group or a single partisan will be shot.*"

"*O Dio!*" another moaned.

"*Any house in which a bandit is found or had been there will be blown up.*"

"What are we going to do?" a small woman in a delicate yellow dress wailed. "Oh, Maddelena, what are we ever going to do?"

"We're not going to do anything," Maddelena Spinelli told her sister firmly. "We're not harboring partisans. We don't have to worry. Now let's go inside and see what we can't find today."

"Did you see those emblems on their collars?" Renata said, tugging at her sister's sleeve. "Oh, Maddelena, I'm so afraid."

"We're not going to think about it, Renata," Maddelena declared. She dabbed her cheeks with a lacy handkerchief.

Maddelena, tall and thin, wore her glasses on a chain around her neck. Now, she dropped the glasses back on her slender chest and pushed Renata through the crowd and into the shop where Nino was trying to appease some customers. An old woman dressed in black and two younger women were picking over what was still left on the shelves.

"No, we're out of that," Nino told one customer.

"Maybe tomorrow," he told another.

"I don't know when we'll get that," he told a third.

But a few villagers did find what they needed, and after each purchase, Nino wrote down the amount in his little black book. Some people paid at the end of the month, but they were becoming fewer and fewer. Perhaps some day he would be paid.

"I don't suppose you have any black or brown thread," Maddelena said when her turn came. "We could really use more."

"Well, that's one thing nobody asks for anymore." Nino climbed on a stool and began looking in boxes on a high shelf. "Are you still giving sewing lessons?"

"A few," Maddelena called up to him. "Not many girls seem interested nowadays, though. They're more interested in boys."

"And there aren't many boys left around here," her sister piped in. Renata's voice was high and sweet. "They're either in the army or they've joined the partisans. But we do what we can."

"I can't find any thread here, but maybe there is some in the back," Nino said, stepping back down. "Why don't you go on back and look on the shelves there."

Maddelena and Renata made their way to the rear of the shop. Twenty years ago Maddelena had broken her right leg in a fall and she walked with a limp. She was too proud to use a cane. Someone once told her she looked pretty when she wore a lavender dress and now she wore shades of violet all the time. Seventy years ago, when she was a child, she was so thin her father compared her to a strand of spaghetti. She was still thin.

Renata, five years younger and considerably heavier, preferred light, colorful dresses, often trimmed with lace. Her left arm was withered from a childhood sledding accident.

"Put the two of us together and you have a whole person," Maddelena liked to joke. Renata would grimace.

The sisters edged their way between the counters and the little marble tables where the afternoon card games had just started.

"Hey Maddelena! You're looking beautiful today!"

Maddelena ignored the comment. She was tired of Vito Tambini's daily remarks, if not here at Leoni's then from his yard across the street from the sisters' house.

"She heard me, she just doesn't want to answer," Vito told the other card players. The players were the same every day: Marco and his friend Francesco Sabbatini played against Vito and his cousin Giacomo Tassara.

Marco and Francesco were longtime friends and hunting companions, confiding in each other about everything in their lives except for one subject, their wives. Since he was retired, and Rosa didn't mind, Marco could easily come to Leoni's to play cards every afternoon. Francesco stubbornly left his trattoria in Neboli every day to join the group.

Although Vito Tambini and Giacomo Tassara were cousins, they looked so much alike they could have been brothers. Both were in their eighties, with thin wiry bodies, weathered nut-brown skin, thinning white hair, white mustaches and bushy white eyebrows. People could tell them apart by their teeth. Vito had lost most of his on top, Giacomo on the bottom.

They had farmed in the *fattoria*, but when their wives died, they moved to Sant'Antonio. They lived side by side in a double house and since neither of them had children, they spent every day together. Playing cards at Leoni's provided the only entertainment in their lives.

Giacomo shuffled the deck and dealt three cards to each of the others. He put down the next card, the jack of diamonds.

"Diamonds is *briscola* this time," Francesco said.

Vito looked at his cards and distorted the left side of his face, a signal everyone at the table recognized.

No sooner had the game started when it was interrupted by the rumble of Panzers on the street outside. Marco and Francesco put down their cards and went to the window at the front to watch.

"I know what the tanks look like," Vito said. "I don't have to go look."

"More tanks, more tanks," Marco said as they returned to the table.

"These seem to be bigger," Francesco said.

"*Boh!* Play the cards, play the cards," Vito told Giacomo.

"Did you listen to the radio last night?" Marco asked, offering Francesco a cigarette. Vito and Giacomo didn't smoke.

"Thanks," Francesco said. "Yes, there's some good news for a change."

Francesco and Marco were two of the few people in Sant'Antonio who had radios.

"It sounds like the Allies are nearing Livorno. In this moment, they are as far as Cecina," Francesco said. "After Livorno, they'll head to Pisa and then Lucca..."

"And then here!" Marco said.

"It may take days before they get to Livorno, though."

"And what will they find there? Nothing. The British have blown everything up. Rosa has a cousin there and they had to evacuate months ago."

"At least some Allies are in eastern Tuscany now," Francesco said. "Maybe they'll come by way of Siena and then Florence. Then they can get to the Apennines and the Gothic Line. Once they're through that, it's over for the Germans."

"*Boh!* Play the cards, play the cards," Vito said.

Marco dealt more cards. Giacomo looked up at the ceiling. It was such an obvious signal that Francesco and Marco smiled.

Maddelena and Renata passed the table as they edged their way back to the front of the shop. Maddelena carried two small boxes.

"A pretty dress you have on today," Vito said loudly.

"Stupid *contadino*," Maddelena muttered under her breath.

"What did she say?" Vito asked the other card players.

"It's a good thing you don't hear so good any more," Giacomo said.

"*Boh!* Play the cards, play the cards," Marco and Francesco said together, laughing.

The game stopped as three planes roared overhead and the cups on the table rattled.

"The British are going to start bombing here soon, I'm afraid," Francesco said.

Marco dealt another round of cards in the silence that followed. Francesco looked at his card and shrugged a shoulder.

Nino Leoni came over to refill their espresso cups. Nino's head was bald, his black mustache thick and his white apron impeccably clean. He always carried a cigarette over his left ear even though he hadn't smoked in thirty years.

"How is Rosa, Marco?" he said as he put a cup back on the table. "I haven't seen her all day."

"She's at home, making ravioli. She's fine."

Nino and everyone else in the village knew enough not to ask Francesco about Annabella.

"There's a new poster outside," Nino said. "It says anyone who helps the partisans will be shot."

"Oh?" Marco said, looking at his cards. "I don't know anyone who's helping the partisans."

"Neither do I," Francesco said, also intent on his cards.

"*Boh!*" Vito said. "They're just trying to scare us."

"I don't think so," Francesco said, so softly that the others barely heard him.

While Nino watched, the men were silent for several minutes, seemingly intent on playing their cards. Then Vito shouted, "Don't get me started on the partisans! *Ruffiani!*"

Marco, Francesco and Giacomo knew Vito's opinions of the partisans only too well and weren't in a mood to hear them again.

"The soldiers who put up the poster?" Nino said. "They're the SS."

"O *Dio!*" Marco said. "They're finally here."

There had been increasing reports that units from the dreaded SS were replacing the regular soldiers in western Tuscany. Worse were reports that the SS was indiscriminately killing people suspected of helping the partisans and burning their houses. With the British, American and other Allied forces still to the south, newly formed partisan *banda* were the main obstacle for the German occupying forces. Only this summer new partisan bands had been formed, and they were becoming more skilled in sabotaging the German forces.

"Well, that changes everything," Francesco said. "We're going to see Hitler's scorched earth policy around here soon."

"What can we do?" Marco said. "We wait."

The men concentrated on their game again.

"You know," Nino said, "the Germans are planting mines all over the place, the fighting is getting closer, the bombing has started, there are partisans in the hills ready to die, and now the SS are here. And what do you do? You come here and play cards like nothing is happening."

"We're Italian," Vito explained.

"No other explanation needed," Giacomo added.

"Besides, we're good customers," Vito said. "Look at all the espresso we drink."

Nino poured more thick black coffee into their tiny cups.

"What do you think the SS wants to do around here?" Giacomo asked. "Why would they care about this little town?"

"I'll tell you why," Francesco said. "It's the bridge."

Sant'Antonio had only a couple of dozen houses, lined along the street next to the Maggia River, which eventually flowed into the Serchio River. Across the bridge at the end of town was the much bigger town of Reboli. The bridge was one of the main supply routes between the area south of the Maggia and the Tuscan hills to the north.

"The Germans have to control the bridge for supplies," Marco said.

"There's another reason," Francesco said. "When the Allies finally get here, the Nazis can blow up the bridge. That would stop the Allies."

"They'd blow up the bridge?" Vito said.

"Why not? What do they care?"

"It will take a lot of dynamite to blow up that bridge. It's heavy steel and iron," Marco said.

Marco had been part of the construction crew when Mussolini ordered all bridges to be repaired. It was Marco's last job before he retired.

"Then how could we get to Reboli?" Giacomo asked. "People have to go there to shop. Francesco's trattoria is there. People work there. Children go to school there. What are we supposed to do, swim?"

"There aren't that many left here who work there," Marco said.

"Fausta Sanfilippo still works at the thread factory," Vito said. "I see her crossing the bridge every morning on her bicycle."

"And everyone knows that the Messina sisters cross the bridge every night to entertain the German troops," Giacomo said.

"I wouldn't mind if that Anita Messina came over to entertain me," Vito said. "Have you seen her lately? I've never seen such big..." Vito lowered his voice as an elderly widow walked by.

"Nobody goes to Reboli very much any more," Marco said. "Everyone in Sant'Antonio is too old or too young."

Thirteen young men from Sant'Antonio were serving in the Italian army. Another fifteen had disappeared, either joining the partisans or simply hiding out from conscription. The old spent their days alone in their houses or gossiping at Leoni's. The young had learned to grow up very fast.

It was Francesco's turn to deal the cards. Picking his up, Marco showed the tip of his tongue.

"Allora," Francesco sighed. "Sant'Antonio has never been on the map. Now it may never be on a map."

"Wipe us out, who cares anymore?" Giacomo said.

In all of Tuscany, there was no village more nondescript than Sant'Antonio. People from all over the world photographed the hill towns in the southern part and visited the medieval villages all over. No one photographed Sant'Antonio, and no one visited it.

Sant'Antonio had only one real street, the highway that led across the bridge to Reboli, and a few homes were mixed with fields on side roads. Made of concrete and painted yellow, the houses weren't particularly pretty or distinctive, and in an area once inhabited by the Etruscans and then the Romans, some were only a hundred years or so old, others somehow surviving into their third century.

An old well across from Leoni's and Manconi's was the closest thing the village had to a piazza, and in the evening it was the gathering place for young people who weren't walking or riding their bicycles along the river. Lately at night, children had been playing "war" around the fountain, the boys using sticks for guns and the girls pretending to be nurses for the wounded. Shortly after 9 o'clock, mothers and fathers began calling the children home in time for the 10 o'clock curfew.

Not even the church, just to the north, was distinctive. Its facade was vaguely Romanesque, its interior somewhat Gothic. Built long before the village, the church was more than three hundred years old. Its only work of art was a stark painting of Saint Francis shaving the head of Saint Clare.

Once, an art professor from Florence came to visit the church. He had been told that the painting might be the work of a famous artist no one in Sant'Antonio had ever heard of. Everyone got very excited.

"Now people will come to Sant'Antonio," they said.

The professor went away. He said someone else had painted the work and it wasn't important.

In Reboli, on the other hand, there were three churches, including the Chiesa di Sant'Ignazio with its famous ornate golden crucifix that contained a relic of the saint himself. People said it was a toenail. The town hall boasted a clock tower that was a copy of the one in Siena, and the gardens at Palazzo Signorini were the scene of formal dinner parties. People dined in restaurants around the piazza in summer. Fashionable shops lined Via Fiorini and the festival of *Ferragosto* on August 15 brought visitors from as far away as Viareggio and Pistoria. Just west of the city, archeologists had discovered tools and artifacts from the Etruscans, and there was a remnant of a Roman aqueduct nearby.

Sometimes, people from Sant'Antonio felt sad when they crossed the bridge and returned home from Reboli. Then they saw the trees and were heartened. A row of tall ancient oaks lined each side of the street, their branches almost touching at the top to form a protective arch that shielded the town from the midday sun. The trees, the villagers believed, kept Sant'Antonio safe.

"Maybe the SS will force us to evacuate," Francesco said.

"Evacuate? Where would we go?" Giacomo said.

"*Boh!* Play the cards, play the cards," Vito said. "Let's not think about this."

With Marco and Francesco having more cards in their pile, Vito played his Queen of diamonds. Marco put down his King.

"*Briscola!*" Marco said.

"*Stupido,* Giacomo!" Vito suddenly shouted. "Don't you know how to play cards?"

"I know how, it's you who doesn't know how!" Giacomo yelled back. "You've never known how to play!"

"Cretino!"

"Pistolino!"

Marco and Francesco smiled. This happened every day.

Just then an armored car followed by a truckload of soldiers veered around the corner and screeched down the street.

"What the...?" Francesco said, going back to the window. "What are they doing? It looks like they came from the church."

"I'd better go home," Marco said. "Rosa will be very upset."

"I'm going, too," Francesco said. "I need to get back to the trattoria."

"Not home to Annabella?" Marco asked.

"No, Marco," Francesco said slowly, looking his friend in the eyes. "First, I'm going to Reboli and the trattoria. I'm needed there."

"We're going, too," Vito said, and he and Giacomo walked out the door arm in arm.

The four guided the confused elderly men in front of Leoni's to their homes, and it took Marco only a few minutes to reach his own house.

"Did you see that?" Rosa said as he came in the door. She was still holding the rolling pin. "Those soldiers went to the church. They were there about a half hour. Why would they stop at the priest's? And did you see the side of the car? 'SS!' *Santa Maria!* Oh, Marco, what's going to happen to us?"

"I don't know, Rosa. I don't know."

"Maybe we should go somewhere else? But where would we go?"

"There's no place that's safe anymore. No place. Anyway, those soldiers are gone now."

Another plane roared overhead.

Marco took his wife in his arms and leaned down to kiss the top of her head.

"Cara Rosa," he whispered. *"Cara* Rosa."

Rosa didn't want him to see the tears in her eyes. She went to the counter.

"Look, I made ravioli. Tomorrow I'll make the sauce. I'll use the rabbits you shot yesterday."

Rosa bent over the sink, tears falling down her cheeks.

"Rosa, Rosa."

"I have to tell you something else, Marco."

He stroked her hair.

"There were soldiers here a few hours ago"

"Rosa, no!"

"Not those new soldiers, the old ones. Three of them. They asked me a lot of questions but I didn't answer them. They searched the house…"

"Dino?"

"Dino was hiding. They didn't find him."

"Rosa!"

"Now he's run away, back to the hills."

Before she had a chance to tell him more, the bell in the church tower started to ring. It was not the usual sound, but echoed loudly in the hills.

"Now what's going on?" she said, going to the door.

"Maybe somebody died."

"If someone had died the bell would be tolling, not ringing like that."

Rosa pulled off her apron. "I'm going to go look at the cemetery."

"Can't you wait until tomorrow?"

"I want to see what they've done, the bastards."

At that moment, Pietro, the little grandson of the priest's housekeeper, ran up to the door. He was out of breath.

"The priest! The priest wants everybody to come to the church! Now!"

CHAPTER 4

▼

Whenever Father Luigi was nervous, he began to sweat. Not just a trickle here and there, but great streams that ran down his face and the back of his neck. His starched white collar would immediately melt and turn yellow. His hands would become wet and, forgetting, he would wipe them on the front of his cassock, causing large stains to appear.

And when he was very nervous, his voice rose and squeaked, like a bird being throttled. Now fifty-four, he had been the priest at Sant'Antonio for twelve years and so was still considered new.

Sweating on this humid late Monday afternoon, Father Luigi unlocked the doors of his church and opened some windows. Pulling the heavy rope for the bell had only worsened his anxiety, and the papers in his hands were wet and drooping.

With only the red vigil lights burning, the church looked pretty with the sun streaming through the stained glass window. The painting of Saint Francis and Saint Clare shimmered over the side altar and there were still flowers from Signora Vituchi's funeral on Saturday. Some parishioners liked all the statues and candles and votive lights that filled almost every corner of the church. Father Luigi thought it just looked cluttered.

How he wished he hadn't opened the door to those Germans. But his bicycle was outside, so they knew he was home.

Although the Wehrmacht soldiers had been in and out of the village for months, he had never actually talked to them. Now these were the SS, with the jagged letters and death head emblems on their collars. He wondered if they had mothers who prayed for them.

The lieutenant, who must have been in his late twenties, seemed almost as nervous as he was. He talked very fast in his mangled Italian and was sweating, too. He kept a firm hand on the pistol in his holster. The lieutenant kept looking out the window at his men as they trampled through the cemetery, but he didn't give them orders to stop.

The two soldiers with him didn't look more than sixteen. One had thick glasses and stuttered when he talked to the lieutenant. The other spent the time examining the leather books in the bookcase. Was he planning to steal them?

Pacing up and down the aisle, the priest looked around his little church. It had seen so many weddings and baptisms and funerals. And now...And now...So many terrible things were happening and perhaps the church itself would be in danger. But no one would harm a church, would they?

He knelt at the altar and prayed. "Oh, God, please help me in what I must do. Help these people of Sant'Antonio. They have suffered so much. And please protect our country. Amen."

He could hear the first villagers arriving and went to the doors.

"Ah, *buonasera*," the priest squeaked, greeting the first to arrive, Annabella Sabbatini. Annabella was the president of the church ladies society and even though her husband, Francesco, rarely came to church, they were the parish's biggest contributors. Francesco's trattoria in Neboli was very successful.

"*Buonasera*, Father," Annabella said. "Why have you called us here?"

"I'll tell you when everyone is here. Please go inside and take a seat. Hurry."

Behind her came Bruna and Carlo Adolfo, who lived just next door to the church.

"*Buonasera*," the priest said, wiping his forehead. "Please go inside."

At that moment a plane flew low over the church and Father Luigi instinctively ducked.

Rosa and Marco hurried along next with their neighbor Maria Ruffolo. Rosa had rushed a comb through her hair but still had some flour on her cheeks. Since Maria's daughter had married and left home five years ago, Rosa and Marco had become very protective of Maria, stopping in to see if she needed anything and offering to buy her food at Leoni's and Manconi's. Maria always politely refused, saying she was quite capable of walking to the shops.

"*Buonasera*, Father," Rosa said.

"*Buonasera*, Rosa, Marco, Maria," Father Luigi said. "Please take a seat. We'll start as soon as everyone is here."

The others came quickly. Now that old Signora Vituchi had died and some families had fled to stay with relatives in the hills, only ninety-four people lived in Sant'Antonio.

Soon, the little church was filled. In fact, there were almost as many people here this late afternoon as at midnight Mass on Christmas. Even a few men were in the church again, men who usually came only on Christmas and Easter.

Annabella was in her customary first pew on the right. Rosa, Marco and Maria were in their usual pew, too, the third on the left. Rosa noticed that Annabella's hair was, as usual, impeccably in place.

Suddenly, Maria began to sob quietly.

"Maria!" Rosa said, gripping her arm. "What's the matter?"

"Oh, Rosa, I'm so afraid." Maria wiped her eyes with a tiny lace handkerchief.

"We all are, Maria. Let's just hear what Father Luigi has to say."

"It's not that. Did you see that poster in front of Leoni's?"

"Marco told me about it. But we don't have to worry. We know the partisans are in the hills, but we haven't been helping them. You haven't, have you?"

"No..."

"Well, then?"

"Rosa, it's not me, it's..."

"Who, Maria, who?"

Maria fingered the rosary beads she always wore around her wrist. "I can't, Rosa, I can't tell you."

"It's all right then," Rosa said, patting Maria's hand. "I'm sure everything will be fine. There's nothing to worry about."

Rosa wanted to learn more, but Father Luigi hurried up the aisle and climbed the steps to the pulpit. No, he thought, he shouldn't be talking about such things from the place where he spoke the word of God. He came down and stood in front of the Communion rail. Looking out over the crowded pews, he noticed that women who had forgotten their veils in their hurry had put handkerchiefs on their heads. He shuffled the papers and cleared his throat.

"I have some very bad news," he said, knowing that there was no way to lead up to this. Everyone leaned forward.

"Today I was visited by a German officer of the SS. They have decided that they want to set up headquarters here in Sant'Antonio."

"Why?" came a roar from the villagers. "Why here?"

"It's because of the bridge," the priest said nervously. "They want to secure the bridge so they can have a safe route to the south and this is the most convenient location."

He didn't mention the possibility that they could also blow up the bridge.

Marco gripped Rosa's hand.

"We don't want them here," a man said from the back. "Tell them to go to San Giorgio, to someplace else," another said. "What are they going to do here?" "What shall we do?"

"Wait," Father Luigi said, raising his hands so that the stains under his arms were visible. "There is more."

As best as he could, and with his voice squeaking, the priest explained that the Germans had commanded that the village be evacuated. The Germans, he said, were ordering people in all the villages in the valley to take trains to northern Italy.

"No! No!" "Evacuate our homes?" "We can't leave here!"

Women began to cry, men to shout, some with their fists in the air.

Rosa clutched Marco's hand. "This is it, Marco. This is what I worried about most. It's happening. *O Dio!*"

Marco put his arm around his wife. He had no words to comfort her and started to tremble himself.

"Please wait," the priest said. "I have another plan."

Father Luigi may not have been the most intelligent of men, he may not have given the best sermons, and he certainly wouldn't be confused with the saintly Father Angelo who preceded him, but he was extremely well-organized. After the Germans had left this afternoon, he knew what he had to tell his people.

"I don't want you to take the trains. We've all heard the stories of people being sent to work camps in northern Italy or, worse, in Germany. I want you to stay near here."

"Where?" a man said. "Where can we go?"

"As you know, there are five empty farmhouses in the hills that were in the *fattoria*," the priest began. "They have not been used for a few years, but they are generally in good condition. I want you to go there. From all the reports I've heard the Allies will surely be here soon and maybe this fighting will be over. They're already near Livorno on the coast and near Siena in the south. As soon as the Germans retreat you can come back to your homes."

"No! We don't want to leave our homes!" "We won't go!" "What in God's name have we done to deserve this?" "We can't all fit in those farmhouses!"

Father Luigi took out his handkerchief, which was already soggy, and wiped his brow. He held up his arms to silence the crowd.

"Please listen," he said. "There are almost one hundred of you, so there would be about twenty people at each farmhouse. The houses are big. And I'm sure it's just for a few days, a week at most."

He did not sound confident. More men stood up and waved their fists. A woman in the rear fainted and other women rushed to revive her.

Another plane flew overhead and after the echoes of the roar had ended the church was silent for a few minutes. Then everyone demanded answers. How could old women climb the hills to those places? After being empty for so many years, the farmhouses must be dirty. How could young babies live in such a place, even for a few days? And what about their homes here? The Germans would steal things, they'd break things. They might even blow the houses up. Look what happened in Livorno.

Father Luigi could not answer their questions.

"There isn't time to complain," he said. "The Germans are coming back very soon. They want to set up tonight. Please. Let us have some cooperation. We don't have a choice. I don't want you to take the trains."

The sweat was now dripping down his back. The papers in his hands were soggy.

"Here is what I propose to do. I have a list of all your names from our parish records. I want one group to go to the Nero Nube farmhouse, another to Due Stelle, another to Vino Rosso, another to Olivio and another to the Cielo.

Rosa nudged Marco. If she had to go someplace, at least it might be the Cielo. Even though it was not that far away, she hadn't been there in years. What would it be like to actually sleep there again?

"And we don't have time to argue about who is going where," Father Luigi was saying. "We will do this by the letters."

More shouts and cries.

"I want to stay with Leonardo." "…with Sandro." "…with Urbano."

Rosa stood up. "Please! Let Father take care of this. We have to trust him."

"Thank you, Rosa," Father Luigi said. "We must hurry. Please stand up or raise your hand if you are here. This group will go to Nero Nube. Marcus and Maria Angelo…"

Marcus raised his hand.

"The Calavari family."

Angelo Calavari stood up.

The list went on. After the priest had read about twenty names, he stopped. The church was now insufferably hot. Rosa took the handkerchief off her head, wiped her forehead and used it for a fan.

"All right. Those are the people who will go to Nero Nube. Now for those going to Due Stelle."

More names. Gellelli, Germano, Imperatta, Lugano…Another group of about twenty.

"And now for those going to Vino Rosso."

More names. Mafizolli, Manconi, Nigrini, Onofrio…

"Those lucky people will be with Guido Manconi," Rosa whispered. "Can you imagine listening to his complaints all day?"

"Now for Olivio," Father Luigi said.

Again, more names. Pallini, Picco, Reginelli…

"And now for the Cielo."

Rosa sat up straight. She noticed that Annabella did, too.

"You mean the Sabbatinis didn't get in that other group?" she whispered loudly to Marco. "You mean we're going to be with her?"

"Be quiet. Listen."

Father Luigi dropped a sheet of paper and stooped down to pick it up.

"Signora Maria Ruffolo."

Rosa helped Maria to stand. Maria waved to the priest and sat down.

"Francesco and Annabella Sabbatini."

"*O Dio*," Rosa whispered so loudly that the people in front of her turned around.

Annabella stood up. "Francesco is still at the trattoria," she said.

"I'll get word to him," Father Luigi said, putting a mark next to his name on his sheet.

"Fausta Sanfilippo."

There was no answer. "She must still be at work in Reboli," Rosa said loudly.

Father Luigi sighed. "I'll get word to her, too." He found her name again and marked it.

"Dante Silva?"

Everyone recognized the beloved former schoolmaster as he stood up, tall and dignified and with his white hat in his hands.

"Maddelena and Renata Spinelli."

The sisters helped each other up.

"Gina Sporenza and her five children."

Gina, who was holding the baby Carlotta, stood up. Her daughters, Lucia and Anna, stood on one side. Her sons, Roberto and Adolfo, jumped up with their hands in the air. "Here!" they shouted. Rosa could hear the women whisper behind her. "All those children!" "They're going to be so noisy." "Why did she have to have so many?"

Rosa turned around and glared at the women, but then it was her turn.

"Marco and Rosa Tomaselli."

"*O Dio.*" This time it was Annabella's loud whisper.

Rosa and Marco raised their hands.

"Vito Tambini and Giacomo Tassara."

The cousins stood up.

"Signora Gabriella Valentini."

"Who?" Rosa whispered. "I don't know any Signora Gabriella Valentini." And she knew everyone in Sant'Antonio.

A thin jeweled hand was raised in the middle of the right aisle.

"The Contessa! I didn't know that was her name."

Father Luigi folded up his papers and wiped his forehead.

"All right. Everyone is here except Francesco and Fausta. I'll ride my bicycle over to Reboli and tell them. Now hurry. Go home now and then leave right away. Take only what you can carry. I'm sure the Allies will be here in a few days and the Germans will retreat, and then you can come back."

"Do you promise that?" came a voice from the left aisle. Father Luigi said a silent prayer, "Please God."

"And be careful," he said. "You know there are land mines all over the hills now. But the partisans are there, too, and perhaps they'll find you and protect you. But stay on the roads, and stay together. God be with you!"

"But Father," Rosa asked, "shouldn't there be someone in charge at each house? This is going to be chaos."

That was something the priest hadn't considered. But, as always, he came up with a quick answer."

"All right. I will pick a leader for each house. Dante, you will be in charge at the Cielo. Marcus, you take charge of the group at Nero Nube. Paolo for Due Stelle, Giancarlo for Vino Rosso and Stefano for the Olivio. Please come up here so I can tell you some things."

"Well, at least we have a good person in charge of us," Rosa said. She turned and smiled at Dante as he went up to the priest to get further instructions. Father Luigi huddled with the men for a few minutes.

"And what about you, Father?" a woman asked.

"I will stay here and pray for you all," he said. "I will be all right."

He didn't add that the Germans had ordered him to stay in the village.

"We can't come back here for any reason?"

"No, it's just not safe."

"Can you come to see us?"

"I don't know. I will try."

"Another question," Marco said. "How will we know what's going on? Those places don't have electricity and we don't have radio transmitters."

Father Luigi thought about what he should say.

"I will work on that problem," he said finally. "Now, please, go."

As everyone crowded out through the narrow doorway, Rosa found herself next to Annabella. She is wearing that expensive perfume again, Rosa thought.

Neither of them spoke.

CHAPTER 5

▼

Rosa and Marco walked Maria to her home and hurried to their own house next door. Forcing back tears, Rosa rushed around the rooms, putting things out of sight. If the Germans took over her house, she didn't want to leave anything out that they could easily take. She took the big photograph of her mother and father down from the wall and hid it under some blankets in a chest behind a chair.

Then she pulled down the little suitcase they had hardly ever used, put some clothes in for herself and Marco and grabbed some food packages and pasta from the shelves.

"Let's go," Marco said.

"I can't go like this."

Rosa ran back upstairs, took off her housedress and put on the dress she had last worn at Signora Vituchi's funeral. It was also blue. She also took off her slippers and put on some better shoes. She redid the bun at the back of her neck.

"Wait," she called to Marco. "What should I do with the ravioli?"

"Why don't you take them along?"

"And give them to those people?"

Marco knew that Rosa meant Annabella.

"Well, do you want to leave them for the Germans?"

Rosa took the four corners of the white cloth, tied the ends together and put the ravioli in the basket her father had made from birch branches. They had used the basket for years to pick mushrooms.

"I'll need some sauce, too."

She took down three jars from the shelf above the sink. She didn't see Marco take the silver pistol from his dresser drawer and put it in his pocket.

"Ready?" Marco was halfway out the door.

"Wait!"

Rosa ran out the back door. Pulling down her laundry and throwing it in a bin, she cried, "Gatto! Gatto!"

The cat was nowhere in sight. She looked under the bushes and behind the shed. Nowhere. Well, it was only for a few days, and Gatto was good at finding his own food. She filled Gatto's bowl with the scraps of leftover chicken she'd been saving for him and put some water in another bowl.

"All right. I'm ready."

At the door, Rosa grabbed Marco's arm and burst into tears.

"Rosa, you never cry," Marco said, taking her into his arms. She was shaking.

"What's going to happen to us, Marco? What if it's more than a few days? What if they blow up our house? What if we don't come back?"

"We'll come back, Rosa."

"You can't promise that."

"I promise." Marco looked over her head and out the door. A truckload of SS troops roared down the street.

"Marco, I want to tell you something, now before it's too late," Rosa said, still holding him tightly. "I want to thank you for coming into my life. I know I haven't said this often enough, but my life was so lonely before I met you. I never knew what love was. You have made me so happy. I love you so much."

Marco smoothed Rosa's hair. "I love you so much, too, Rosa."

"I have a terrible feeling about what's going to happen now." She reached up to stroke his cheek. "I feel like we're going down a path where we might not return. Promise me we'll be together no matter what, Marco?"

"Of course, Rosa. No matter what." Marco bent down, wiped the tears from her cheeks and held her for a long time. He knew that he could not, should not, make such a promise, but what was he to say? He loved her more than anything in the world.

Then they went next door to help Maria. She was almost ready, having packed an extra black dress and stockings. Although her husband died eight years ago, Maria still wore mourning clothes.

"I wish I could get word to Angelica," she said. "There isn't any way I can get a letter to Sant'Anna di Stazzema now."

"Maria, we'll be back home before she could even get a letter." Rosa's voice was not very confident.

"Look," Maria said, "I'm taking this picture of Angelica with Little Carlo and Nando. Aren't the boys cute? And they are so smart! Nando is almost two and

Carlo is four. I don't know how she takes care of those children with her husband off to war. Angelica wrote that just the other day…"

"The boys are beautiful, Maria, but we'd better go now," Rosa said, helping her tie her satchel together with some rope. "Do you think you can walk that far? Are your legs hurting today?"

Maria's doctor had repeatedly told her she should lose some weight. It would be good for her heart and for her legs. Maria tried, but it was difficult. She liked her pasta.

"Rosa," Maria said, looking her friend in the eye, "don't you remember that last Easter I walked from the train station in Pietrasanta all the way up the hill to Angelica's in Sant'Anna? It took three hours, but I made it. I can certainly climb this hill."

With Marco carrying the suitcase and Rosa clutching her purse and the basket, they walked with Maria down the street to the road leading to the Cielo.

If there had been a straight road from the village to the Cielo, it would have been about two miles. But the hill was so steep that the road was about three times as long. It zigzagged up and around, over and under, and sometimes it was so narrow that a mule wagon could scarcely get through. The first part was paved, and then there was gravel. The last hundred yards were simply dirt, which became thick mud whenever it rained.

A groove had been forged every hundred yards or so to allow water to drain. Despite that, the road became treacherous with ice in winter, and Rosa remembered sliding perilously down on her way to school some days.

The others quickly began to gather at the bottom of the hill. Maddelena and Renata Spinelli had collected the pills for their various ailments, Vito and Giacomo brought a hammer and some tools, the Contessa packed her necklaces and earrings into a velvet bag and Dante held his well-worn copy of *The Divine Comedy*.

Soon, everyone was there. Five men, eight women and five children. Except for a few faint smiles and greetings, the villagers were silent and grim. Some people kept close together while others, like Vito and Giacomo, stood off to the side, waiting. They looked back toward Sant'Antonio but the oaks made it invisible.

Just then, another plane dipped over the hill and there was an argument about whether the people should stay together or climb separately. Dante thought they should stay together.

"*Andiamo!*" he shouted. As they started up the hill the villagers heard the rumble of Panzers arriving in Sant'Antonio.

Dante tried not to walk fast, knowing that some people in the group could not keep up. Fausta Sanfilippo followed. She always walked quickly. When Father Luigi found her in the thread factor she left a note for her employer. At least he would know why she wasn't at work tomorrow.

The Spinelli sisters came next, Renata helping Maddelena along. Forgetting their dispute at the card game, Vito and Giacomo walked arm in arm. Vito made a few half-hearted jibes at Maddelena's back but grew silent when she ignored him.

The Contessa wore a yellow silk dress with pink flowers that hung almost to the ground and she held a pink umbrella over her head. No one knew how old the Contessa was but she walked briskly, her eyes straight ahead. She didn't talk to anyone.

Rosa saw that Annabella followed Francesco by a half dozen paces. Before leaving Reboli, Francesco told his workers at the trattoria that he didn't know when he would be back. Rosa noticed that he carried his violin in a case on his back. That had caused an argument at home.

"Why do you want to take that thing?" Annabella had said. "It's just one more thing to carry."

"I just want to take it," Francesco had replied quietly.

"Do you think people will want to listen to that?"

"I'll play softly," Francesco had said as he put the violin in its case.

The Sporenza family came behind them. Gina wore a low-cut white peasant blouse, a red skirt that hung to the ground and sandals. Her frizzy blond hair hung loosely to her shoulders, revealing big golden loops hanging from her ears. She pushed Carlotta, only three months, in her carriage. Just up from her nap, the baby must have thought her mother was taking her for an outing, and Gina's "coos" and Carlotta's giggles brought smiles to those around her.

Lucia, who was sixteen, sulked and kicked at the pebbles in her path. Anna, who was ten, hopped on stones while clutching her rag doll. Gina's sons, Roberto, who was twelve, and Adolfo, who was eight, chased one another back and forth. Shortly after they started, Roberto and Adolfo went off the road and into the trees.

"You can't catch me!" Roberto taunted his brother.

"Come back here this minute!" their mother shouted. "Hold hands and walk together."

Last came Rosa and Marco and Maria.

"Are we going too fast?" Rosa asked Maria.

"I'm fine," Maria said, "Don't go slow because of me."

As they climbed the hill, the brush turned into woods and finally a thick forest. Chestnut trees mixed with oaks provided so much shade that there was little grass. Every once in a while, starlings swooshed down upon the travelers and the women clutched their hair.

A small shrine to an unknown saint stood on the side of the road. It had recently been cleared of brush. Obviously, people lived somewhere in these woods.

About halfway up the hill a plane flew so low that some of the villagers jumped into the ditch. Maddelena and Renata just bent their heads.

The villagers stopped short when they turned a bend in the road. Marco quickly put his arm around Rosa's shoulders. Francesco was about to do the same with Annabella, but thought better of it. His wife stared straight ahead. Maddelena and Renata looked away. Gina tried to shield her children's eyes. Dante's tanned face turned white. The Contessa bent over and heaved into her handkerchief.

"*Bastardi!*" Vito and Giacomo said together.

"*O Dio,*" Maria said. Even though the path was filled with hard gravel, she fell to her knees and began to say the rosary.

"The partisans are near here," Marco said softly.

"And the Germans," Rosa whispered as they tried to understand the desolate scene before them.

All the trees on the left seemed to have bullet holes in them. Branches and even entire trees littered the ground. The remains of what must have been a small fortress lay crumbled behind deep gashes in the barren soil. Three steel helmets and a rifle were half-buried in a ditch. Shell cases were scattered around. In the distance, a cave was empty except for what appeared to be a blood-stained shirt hanging from a rock. Big black crows swooped to the ground, grappled with what looked like pieces of flesh and then flew off with the booty. And off to the side, a cloud of flies hovered over the bloated carcass of a mule. The stench of smoke and rotting flesh filled the air.

Then the villagers moved forward. No one spoke.

By now, the sun was lower in the west, and a cool breeze rose as the group climbed higher and higher. About two-thirds of the way to the top, Marco suddenly stopped.

"What is it?" Rosa asked.

"I thought I saw something."

He had. Some forty yards from the path, two young men ran from behind a tree and into a grove of chestnut trees.

"It looks like we're going to have neighbors," Marco said, gripping the pistol in his pocket.

As they neared the top of the hill, the land was terraced for olive trees and grape vines. Most were withered.

"Maybe some grapes are good, but look at that mold. The olive trees are long gone," Marco said.

Finally, as they rounded yet another turn, the Cielo loomed ahead. It had taken almost two hours for everyone to make it to the farmhouse. Three stories high, with tall windows and doors, it had survived years of abandonment. Trees and brush had grown close to the house, but there was still a little stone path. With the sun reflecting off its thick golden walls and red tile roof, it seemed to glow.

"Now I know why they call it the Cielo," Rosa said. "It looks like heaven."

"Let's hope it is heaven and not hell," Marco said.

"It will be heaven," Maria said. "I know it will be."

The Cielo also looked smaller than Rosa had remembered.

"How are all of us going to fit in there?" Maddelena shouted to Dante.

"We'll just have to," he shouted back.

Just outside the front door was a magnificent kaki tree, its long dark leaves shining in the sunlight. In winter, it would produce succulent fruit, which some called persimmon. Dante waited for everyone to catch their breath, then he shoved the brush aside and pushed the door open.

It was not as bad as they had feared. With the windows and doors closed for years, the air inside was musty and smelled faintly of burned wood, but it was cool. Dust covered everything, of course, but not too thickly.

Everyone crowded into the main room on the first floor. The children were tired and cranky. Out of breath, Maddelena and Renata collapsed on the bench in front of the fireplace. Lucia found a tall mirror next to the door and put on new lipstick. Gina took Carlotta out of the carriage and let her play with her rattle on a little blanket on the floor. The Contessa folded her umbrella and stood on the first step leading upstairs.

Rosa and Maria immediately went into the kitchen. As it turned out, when the last family left the Cielo a half dozen years ago, it was as if they just walked out the door. There were still dishes on the shelves, pasta and even some jars of sauce in the pantry. Three earthenware jars contained olive oil. And best of all, there were three big barrels of chestnut flour. They were sealed so tightly that two of them had somehow escaped an infestation of insects. If there wasn't cornmeal, at least they could make polenta from chestnut flour. The electricity had been turned off, but there was a pump in the back. Tomorrow they would see if it worked.

"All right," Dante said. "Let me take a look around."

He excused himself and squeezed past the Contessa to see what the second and third floors looked like.

A few years earlier, just out of curiosity, Dante had looked up the history of several farmhouses in the archives in Reboli. He was surprised to find that the records indicated, though not very clearly, that the Cielo dated back to around 1500. That was hard to believe. Had this building, or at least part of it, survived occupations by the Hapsburgs, the Spanish, the French under Napoleon and now, God forbid, the Germans? Who could have lived here during those terrible times?

With countless restorations and additions over four centuries, the Cielo now was vastly different from its beginnings. The main room was originally the stables and made of stone. It probably housed mules, since mules were the main method of transporting goods and supplies up the treacherous hill. Two rings to harness the mules were still hanging on a wall. At some point, the dirt floor was replaced by stones and concrete poured around them. Eventually, a large hayloft was built over the room.

When the farmhouse was made part of the *fattoria*, it was turned into living quarters for two or three farm families. A fireplace was built into the far wall of the main room and its stone hearth extended the width of the room. A kitchen on the right had two *fornelli* for cooking, with space underneath for the charcoal. A small room, perhaps for a child, was built in front of the kitchen. On the left, two bedrooms were added.

Upstairs, the hayloft was converted into four rooms of various sizes, and another floor, with a large unfinished room, was added on top. The most recent addition was a little tower off that room. Legend had it that the English man who owned the *fattoria* wanted to survey his holdings on his annual visits. On a clear day, the tower offered a view of the entire hillside, all the way down to Sant'Antonio.

Outside in the back, a shed extended almost the length of the house. It contained a mule cart, piles of lumber, empty wine barrels and a jumble of heavy tools. The Cielo did not have indoor plumbing but there was a *cesso* about fifteen feet from the back door.

"All right," Dante said, returning to the main room and edging past the Contessa, who smiled brightly at him. "The rooms upstairs look good. There are enough beds, I think, and they even have sheets and blankets. So I have a plan for us."

For safety, he said, the men would stay on the first floor. Marco and Francesco could have one of the rooms on the left and Vito and Giacomo the other. Dante would take the small room in front of the kitchen to the right.

"There are four rooms on the second floor," Dante said. "Maddelena and Renata, you can take the room just above, Maria and Contessa, you can have the room opposite. Then Rosa and Annabella, you can have the room to the rear."

The villagers gasped. Everyone knew that Rosa and Annabella had not spoken to each other in years and suspected that Dante put them together on purpose. Both women knew that everyone was looking at them, but both stared grimly ahead.

"And Fausta, you can have the little room at the right in the back."

The third floor was entirely open, and so the Sporenza family could stay there and hang some sheets for privacy. Lucia made a face. Her mother gave her a threatening look.

It was now almost dark and no one wanted to search for candles at this hour. Moonlight through the two front windows cast ominous shadows on the far wall. The kaki tree's branches rattled against the side of the building.

"Mamma," Adolfo said. "I'm afraid."

"It's all right," Gina said, hugging him. "We're going to be fine."

"Remember," Dante said, "let's hope this is only for a few days. If we all try, we can get along with one another. Maybe we can even make new friends. I know the place needs some cleaning, but it's late. I suggest we use the *cesso* if we have to and then let's just go to bed."

"A *cesso*?" Roberto said. "Mamma, do we have to?"

"We don't have a choice 'Berto," Gina said. "Now come along before it gets too dark."

Exhausted, angry and afraid, the villagers mumbled a few *"buonanottes"* and went silently to their rooms.

Renata helped Maddelena from the bench. "Are you tired, sister?"

"I'll be better in the morning," Maddelena said. "Let's try to get some sleep."

Rosa put her hand on Maria's arm. "Are you all right, Maria?"

"I'm fine, Rosa. Don't worry about me. I know we're all afraid, but I know God will get us through this. I'm going to put the picture of Angelica and the boys out and I'm going to say the rosary and then I'm going to sleep. You do the same."

"I will."

Annabella went to her room with only a glance at Francesco.

"Only a few days," Giacomo said.

"*Boh!*" Vito said, taking his cousin's arm. "I'll believe it when the Allies get here."

Rosa edged past the others and went to the kitchen. She cleared a space on the counter, unwrapped the ravioli and spread them out, putting her shawl on top so they wouldn't get dusty.

Marco came from behind and held her. "I guess this is good night," he said.

They had never slept apart in all the time they were married. She stood on her tiptoes and kissed him.

"I love you so much, Marco. And I'm so afraid."

"I'll be right here, Rosa," he said. "I'll be here all the time."

Marco went to the room he was to share with Francesco.

"Perhaps our wives will finally start talking," he said.

Unpacking his violin, Francesco nodded. Whatever happened between the two women long ago, the men had remained friends over the years.

When Rosa arrived at her appointed room, she realized it was the one she had slept in as a child. She found that Annabella had crawled onto the little bed against the wall with her clothes on. Her eyes were closed, but Rosa knew she wasn't asleep.

Rosa put her purse on the dresser, took off her dress and shoes and got into the bed under the window. Lying there, she could look up at the stars.

How strange, she thought. This morning she woke up next to Marco, the love of her life. Now she was in the room that was hers as a child with a woman who had caused her so much unhappiness. How she wished Marco was at her side. She thought of the scene they had witnessed on the climb up the hill and pulled the coverlet over her head.

CHAPTER 6

▼

As soon as he returned home after finding Francesco and Fausta in Reboli, Father Luigi took off his wilted collar, his cassock and his dirty shoes. It was a little cooler in only his undershirt and trousers, and since all the others in the village were fleeing to the farmhouses, he didn't expect any visitors. He was still sweating profusely, and his undershirt clung to his shoulders and abundant belly.

His housekeeper, Signora Digardi, could take care of his clothes tomorrow. Then he remembered that Signora Digardi would not be here tomorrow. She would be at the Nero Nube.

A little risotto and a glass of red wine felt good after this long day, and the priest looked out the window as he ate. There was no sign of any of the villagers and he could see the Germans moving into the homes far down the road.

"O Dio," he thought, "what's going to happen?"

After washing his dishes, he felt like collapsing into his chair near the window, but he knew he should pray. He took out his breviary and found the date, July 11.

"O God in Heaven…"

Father Luigi had always found it difficult to pray and tonight his mind wandered more than usual as he watched the Germans.

Should he have talked to those soldiers? Were they trying to set a trap? Maybe he should have let the people go on the trains like the Germans said. But from what he had heard he could never trust the SS. He didn't know where the trains would take the people. But then, what if something happened in the farmhouses? They would be up there alone among the partisans and the Germans and the land mines. It would all be his fault.

Those poor villagers up in the hills. At the Cielo alone, such a mix of people. The Spinelli sisters are so old. Gina Sporenza is still nursing a baby and has all those children. Maria Ruffolo won't know how to reach her daughter in Sant'Anna. Those crazy cousins, Vito and Giacomo. How were all those people going to get along together? They would be at each other's throats. They gossiped so much here, they would be even worse there.

"Help us now…"

How was he going to live through this war? He hadn't known this was how it was going to be when he became a priest. When he entered the seminary he thought he would just have to say Mass and baptize babies and officiate at weddings and funerals. That's what the priest in his parish had told him when he was an altar boy. He didn't think he was going to have to be the leader of the village.

He didn't feel like a leader. He got so nervous and he perspired so much. The people must think he was some kind of fool.

"We need your help…"

He liked most parts of being a priest. He liked going to the school in Reboli and talking to the children. He liked helping young couples before they got married. He even liked consoling widows when their husbands died. But confession was the worst part. Every Saturday afternoon, listening to old women talk about their husbands who were long dead, wives who gossiped about other wives, and teenagers who giggled when they talked about the impure thoughts they had. Sometimes he felt like falling asleep in the box.

"We are suffering so much…"

If only he could forget about the war for a time. But it was everywhere, in the newspapers, on the radio. He was tired of sending young men from the village off to die. If this war ever ended, he wanted to go away for a while. Maybe he could make a retreat. He would love to go to Rome, see St. Peter's, maybe even meet the pope. He was the only one of his classmates who had never been to Rome. Florence was the farthest he had ever traveled. He had never even been to the hill towns in southern Tuscany that Dante was always talking about.

All his other classmates were in big parishes. They had beautiful churches and their people gave so much money. Here he was in this little village that wasn't even on the map.

"Help us in our hour of need…"

He was glad that his mother had died six years ago and couldn't see any of this. Like the mothers of most Italian priests, she had come to take care of his house when he was assigned to Sant'Antonio. A widow, with no other children, she was pleased to be with her son. But then she had the heart attack, and now she was buried in the little cemetery next to the church. Father Luigi said a mass for her every Saturday.

No, he couldn't feel sorry for himself. That would be the worst thing. He was the only person left in Sant'Antonio and the Germans said he couldn't leave.

"Oh, God, please help me."

And what if the SS found out he was communicating with the partisans? They'd kill him. He couldn't think about that.

Father Luigi closed his breviary. He looked at the clock and saw that it was 8 o'clock. It was time to get out his radio transmitter.

In a small house in Sant'Antonio, Fritz Krieger and Konrad Schultz unpacked their gear and settled in. They were members of the 5th Company of the 2nd Battalion of the 35th SS Regiment of the 16th SS Panzergrenadier Division *Reichsfuhrer-SS* of the X1V Panzer Corps of the 14th Army. The troops were needed in Italy now that the Allies were moving northward and guerrilla activity by the partisans was rapidly increasing

Fritz and Konrad looked remarkably similar, tall and gangly with short blond hair and fair skin. Friends since they were ten years old and members of Hitler's youth corps, the *Jungvolk,* in Munich, they joined the SS in May as soon as they turned seventeen. Their training had pushed them into adulthood.

"Looks like we're going to be here a while," Fritz said.

Konrad dropped his field equipment on the bed but instead of unpacking began pacing the room. "There's nothing in this town. It's a dung heap."

He looked out the window, took off his thick glasses and began to wipe them. Whenever Konrad was nervous, he found he needed to clean his glasses.

"Maybe we can use the Eytie lingo we learned on the train," Fritz said. "I could understand a few words that priest said."

"He was so nervous I didn't know what he was saying. But I know enough to get by if we find some women," Konrad said.

"Konrad, you wouldn't know what to say to a woman. You wouldn't know what to do with a woman."

"Oh yeah? I'd know what to do. Anyway, I'd learn fast."

Neither Fritz nor Konrad had ever been with a woman.

After hanging up their shirts, the two soldiers unpacked their gear in silence. Luger pistols. Two cartridge pouches each holding thirty rounds of rifle ammunition. An entrenching shovel. A combat pack with mess kit and shelter.

"I wonder where all the Eyties went," Konrad finally said.

"The lieutenant said they should take the trains north. I don't think they did. They know what happens when they take the trains."

"Yeah," Konrad said, slicing a finger across his neck.

"Maybe they fled into the hills with all the communists," Fritz said.

"Fritz," Konrad said, "did you notice there are only two shops in this village? And they don't look like much."

"The lieutenant says we can go there tomorrow and take anything we want from the shelves," Fritz said. "There's probably nothing left."

Fritz made a round of the rooms, opening drawers and cupboards in the kitchen. "It smells good in here. They must have been making pasta before they left. So why didn't they leave some for us?"

"Looks like they left some stuff for the cat," Konrad said.

"Did you see that pussycat?" Fritz said. "Biggest cat I ever saw."

"Yeah," Konrad said, "I threw a big rock at him but he ran away."

Fritz went to a window and looked out at the street. Other soldiers were taking their gear off the truck and going into houses. The red-and-black swastika flags were already hanging next to Leoni's and Manconi's.

Konrad sat on the bed, took out his Luger and started cleaning it. He liked holding the pistol, small and yet strong. Then he walked through the house, aiming the pistol at pictures on the wall, dishes on the shelves.

"Konrad, put that thing down," Fritz said. "Why the hell are you so nervous?"

"I can't wait to see some action, Fritz. We've been in the SS for three months."

"We'll have plenty to do soon enough," Fritz said. "The lieutenant says we're going to plant mines in the hills to kill those communists and we're going to have to mine the bridge."

Fritz returned to his bed, took off his belt and began polishing the buckle. "Isn't this a great buckle, Konrad? Look at this eagle and the swastika." He read the words, "My Honor Is Loyalty."

"We can be proud we're in the SS, Konrad."

Konrad took off his glasses and wiped them again. "When I think about the Führer I'm ready to die, Fritz. I'm ready to die."

The young soldiers were quiet for a long time.

"Do you miss Munich, Konrad?" Fritz asked.

Konrad turned his back and his answer was muffled. "Yes."

Around the village, other soldiers were settling into other houses. One had pulled out a harmonica and some soldiers were singing. Others had opened a keg and were drinking beer. They knew they wouldn't have much longer to relax.

In a cave high in the hills above Sant'Antonio, Ezio Maffini took out his note-book and found the next blank page. The other partisans were cleaning their weapons or had already fallen asleep. At twenty-four, Maffini had graduated from the University of Pisa with honors and had quickly joined a Garibaldi band in the Apuan Alps in Tuscany. Now he was the leader of five partisans, two in their twenties, two of them just boys and one in his late thirties. Ezio planned to write a book about his experiences when the war ended, and he tried to keep a record of each day.

"It looks now like something is going to happen soon. We have had reports from our contact that the SS has stormed into villages and they have been evacuated. Some people have fled to farmhouses in these hills. The SS! We can't wait to fight them!

"We are still waiting for the Allies to send us some supplies. We're still using those old Model 91 rifles that jam all the time. We have had only one drop since we arrived here three weeks ago and what was that? Some Sten guns and ammunition and some hand grenades. Oh, yes, they dropped some chocolate, too. Chocolate? What are we supposed to do with the chocolate, hurl it at the Nazis when they attack us?

"We can't trust the Allies to come through with anything. Churchill and Eden, what fools. They despise us. They call us 'Eyties' and don't think we can fight. The Americans aren't much better. They land in the south and take their time coming north.

"We're the only ones defending Italy now. Today we got messages from other partisan formations. Just in the last two weeks, partisans sabotaged railway lines so the American Eighth Army could move forward. Some other partisans disrupted German supply routes on the Adriatic. They blocked a railroad tunnel to stop a train. And the Nazis say we can't fight? We're going to keep on with this sabotage.

"Our contacts say there are about 100,000 partisans in northern Italy now. We get new recruits every day. Not just Italians but Russians, Slavs, Poles and then the deserters, Americans, British, Indians, from all over. Farmers let us stay in their houses and give us food. They tell us where to go where it's safe.

"There are some bad apples among us, sure. There are in any organization. It's too bad they've done things that make people afraid of all of us. But if we weren't fighting for Italy, who would be?

"Some people say we're fighting a civil war against the Fascists, but we have been doing that since the 1920s, ever since Mussolini came to power. Some people say we're fighting a war of liberation against the Germans, and of course we are. They are occupying our country. And others say that we are poor peasants who are fighting against the rich businessmen and manufacturers. They say we are all communists. Not all of us are, but I'm proud to be one. I'm not a peasant, my father owned a shop. But I have joined the Communist Party because I know what it stands for and I am in full support. I am from Tuscany! We have always been radical.

"At university we learned about the history of Italy and we felt great pride. That is why I am fighting and why I could easily kill if necessary for our country. Every partisan I talk to feels the same way. Thousands of us have been killed already and there will be many more deaths.

"Kesselring has been forcing his German troops on and sending them to their deaths. He doesn't know how tired they are. Now he's sent the SS. He knows they won't give up. Whatever they feel, we will fight them.

"*Viva l'Italia!*"

Ezio closed his notebook and put it back in his pack. He was very tired. Then he took it out again.

"I need to add a personal reflection. I miss my angel so much. She brought me such joy in this terrible world. We had only a couple of months together. She didn't understand why our band had to move, but we couldn't have stayed there longer. The Germans have threatened to kill anyone who helps us. There were people in that village who could have notified the Germans. If they did, my angel's life would be in danger. Maybe it still is. There is another partisan group there now. I think it is more reckless. I hope my angel doesn't help them. Oh, my angel. After this terrible war is over, I will find you again."

Ezio leaned back against the stone wall, placed his rifle on his knees and was soon asleep.

CHAPTER 7

▼

In that voice that made Rosa want to scream, Annabella was taunting her again. Her voice faded in and out and there seemed to be a crashing of thunder in the background, but then the words became sharper, piercing the air.

"I'm getting married, Rosa, I'm getting married!"

Rosa was running ahead of her, on the bank of the river.

"I don't care, Annabella, I don't care. Leave me alone!"

Annabella wouldn't let up. "I'm getting married tomorrow and there's something else, too, Rosa. Do you want to hear?"

"No! Stop it!"

"I'm going to have a baby, Rosa! I'm going to have Francesco's baby!"

"You are not!"

"I am!"

"You are not. How could you have Francesco's baby when you just made love? You're lying!"

Annabella was laughing. "It doesn't take long, you know. It only takes one time, Rosa. I'm going to marry Francesco and we're going to live in a big house and we're going to have lots of children."

"Leave me alone, Annabella!" Rosa crumpled on the stones along the river. Tears ran down her cheeks.

"Don't be angry, Rosa. You can come to the wedding!"

"I'll never come to your wedding, you stupid horse!"

Annabella shouted down at her. "Don't call me a horse, you fat cow!"

"Slut!"

"You, you…*contadina!*"

"Whore!"

"*Contadina!* Ugly *contadina!* Homely ugly *contadina!*"

Annabella's laugh echoed and finally faded. Thrashing in the blankets, Rosa tried to turn over in the tiny bed. Then the force of the sunlight beating down on her coverlet made her realize where she was. That dream again. She hadn't had it for many years. She looked over at the other bed and found that Annabella had already gone downstairs.

She knew she should get up, too, but she needed time to recover from the nightmare. She was still shaking. Besides, it was so warm here in the tiny, soft bed. Through the fog of waking up, she forced herself to have other, more pleasant, memories. Here she was in the Cielo again, in her old room, in her old bed. She tried to relive that time. The smell of hot coffee from the kitchen below. The sounds of rain on the windows. The fireplace crackling in winter. The mounds of snow that sometimes kept her home from school. Her father coming in from the fields, throwing her in the air. Her mother making pasta, the same ravioli she had made just yesterday.

She looked behind her head to see if the picture of the Virgin Mary was still on the wall. It was not, but there was a black mark from the frame. She always hated that picture, the Virgin looking so smug holding the Christ Child.

It was another world then. It was safe, like her mother said. "We're so far up on this hill, no one can get us." She burrowed deeper under the blanket.

The room hadn't changed much in the years since she lived there. The walls were faded now, but the beams on the ceiling gleamed dark and shiny. The dresser where she had stored her dolls and books now looked so small in the corner. The white curtains on the window had turned yellow.

It was strange enough to be back in this house, and here she was with Annabella and Francesco, and even in the same room with Annabella. She greeted Francesco whenever they met, but she had not talked to Annabella for almost forty years.

Rosa was seventeen when she started going out with Francesco. He was the best looking boy in the village, and he knew it. He wore his collar up and his thick black hair slicked back, and he rode his bicycle so fast people thought he would flip into the ditch. Sometimes he did. All the girls wanted to ride with him, but he was particular.

Francesco's parents had always lived in Sant'Antonio and they owned a popular trattoria in Reboli. Rosa's parents had not lived in Sant'Antonio very long, so she was surprised when Francesco started talking to her as they walked home from school. She knew she wasn't pretty. She knew she was a *contadina* and he was a *cittadino*. Why did he like her?

Then they started walking in the town together. They went down the street hand in hand for everyone to see, not just by the river. She was excited when he asked her to ride behind him on the fender of his bike and she clung to him tightly as they rode up and down the hills. He sounded the bell on his bicycle so that everyone could see them and he laughed his crazy laugh. Rosa never saw him laugh now.

It was hard for Rosa to get away with her father so sick, but after he was sleeping at night she met Francesco near the fountain and they talked and walked. Sometimes they spent time in the dark forests up the hill.

She remembered the first time they made love. They had gone up the hill for a picnic in the late summer. The sun was setting and it was cool. Francesco put his arm around her and kissed her. They lay on the blanket and hugged.

"Do you want me to do this?" he asked.

"More than anything in the world."

Francesco was very gentle. Afterwards, she knew she wanted to live with him forever.

"You'll always be with me, right, Rosa?" he said.

"If you want me to."

She had never been so happy.

When she told Annabella the next day, Annabella just laughed. She said Francesco would never marry her, that he was just using her. Rosa couldn't understand that. How could Annabella say something like that? But Rosa knew that she was a *contadina* and Annabella was a *cittadino*.

Annabella had been her best friend. When they were girls, they played together after school and on weekends and when they were older they learned how to sew from the Spinelli sisters. After that, they mostly lay on their beds and talked about boys.

Then suddenly, Annabella began flirting with Francesco. She knew she was prettier than Rosa, and she wore earrings and necklaces and perfume. Soon, Francesco started taking her on walks and then on bike rides. Rosa knew that they did other things, too. Francesco liked to have two girls to play with.

When she confronted him, Francesco got angry. Annabella meant nothing to him, he said. Rosa was his only girl.

"But Annabella is prettier than me," Rosa said.

"But you're nicer," Francesco said. It was small comfort.

A few months later, Rosa heard that Annabella and Francesco were getting married. Francesco came to Rosa's house one night with his face and arms bruised and battered.

"Francesco!" Rosa cried. "What happened to you?"

"It's nothing," he said. "I don't want to talk about it."

"Oh, my dearest."

"Rosa, I have to tell you something. Annabella and I are getting married. But I don't want to marry her."

He started to cry.

"I don't understand," Rosa said.

"I can't tell you any more than that. I'm sorry, Rosa."

She put her arms around him. "This wasn't your decision, was it? Your father?"

Francesco didn't say anything. Rosa kissed him on the cheek and ran up to her room.

The night before the wedding, as they walked along the river, Annabella told Rosa she was pregnant. Rosa didn't believe it. She and Annabella fought bitterly, saying things and using words they would later regret but stubbornly would never retract.

Rosa went to Francesco's house and confronted him.

"Is Annabella pregnant?"

"No!" he shouted. "She's making this up. Don't you see she's jealous of you?"

Rosa believed Francesco. She did not go to the wedding.

A month later, Annabella had a miscarriage, or so she said. Rosa, who had never believed Annabella was pregnant in the first place, stopped talking to her. And even though they lived five houses apart, they never spoke to each other again.

A year later, Rosa's parents died, and she lived alone in the house. People thought that was strange, but Rosa refused to go to live with her aunt in Lucca. She found a job she liked with a dressmaker in Reboli, and she found friends there, too. She wasn't afraid to go there at night. In those days, it was safe.

Yes, Rosa remembered, there was that experience with Sergio. Sergio was the owner of the dress shop. He was married, but everyone knew that he liked to have a girl on the side. Sergio didn't make the first move. Rosa did. He was tall and attractive, and she was young and single and lonely.

One day she volunteered to stay late to finish a dress. He was the only other person in the shop. They worked together on the dress, and Rosa flirted with him. It didn't take long for them to go to the apartment he kept above the dress shop. Their lovemaking was over quickly and Sergio left.

For almost a year they would put a sign on the door saying the shop was closed when they wanted to go upstairs. At first, Rosa found it exciting. Then it was just something to do. Then she got tired of the way he was treating her, always late for their meetings and smelling of garlic.

Sergio fired her, of course, when she broke off the affair. She didn't care.

A few months later, Rosa encountered Sergio and his wife in a cafe.

"Hello, Sergio," she said. "Have you found a new dress to work on?"

"A new dress?" he stammered. She wondered how Sergio explained her question to his wife.

Rosa got a job in another dress shop. In the mid-1920s, Franco, the owner of the flower shop next door, started paying attention to her. He was a widower, considerably older and a little overweight, but there weren't many younger men in Reboli and certainly none in Sant'Antonio.

Franco brought her flowers and took her to dinner. She was flattered, but she soon found that they did not have much in common, One evening he started talking about Mussolini and how Italy was going to be so much different under a Fascist government. Franco said Mussolini would bring many changes and people would have better lives.

"Are you a Fascist?" Rosa asked him.

"Of course," he replied.

Except for what her father had told her, Rosa had never been interested in politics, but she knew she did not like the changes that Mussolini and his Blackshirts were bringing. She told Franco it would be best if they did not see each other again.

After that, her friends noticed that she began to dress in dark colors and no longer wore makeup or jewelry. She wore her hair in a tight bun on the top of her head. They wondered what she did alone at night.

Then Marco became a part of her life. Marco Tomaselli was fourteen years older than she was, but she had known him for years because he did odd jobs around her house.

She liked to look at him working, the muscles in his back, the strength in his arms. Mostly, she liked the way his eyes twinkled when he talked to her. They reminded her of her father. He even told jokes.

In 1931, years after they first met, Marco's wife died. A few months later, after Marco started repairing a door at her house, Rosa invited him in for coffee. They found that they both liked to garden, that they didn't have much use for the church and they both hated Mussolini.

Marco had to make three visits to finish the door, and each time he and Rosa spent longer times talking. Then he asked her to go to a movie with him in Reboli. A few weeks later, they went dancing. Suddenly Rosa was laughing again. She started wearing pretty dresses and fixing her hair.

For three years, they enjoyed one another's company. Sometimes, Marco would stay overnight. Then one night, Rosa made an exceptionally nice dinner and served wine from her father's collection. They were having a good time.

"Marco," she said, "do you miss your wife very much?"

"Of course."

"Marco," she said, "let's get married."

"Married? I didn't think I would ever get married again."

"Why not? You're not going to live in that lonely house for the rest of your life."

"Are you doing this for me?"

"No, I'm doing this for me," she said.

After Francesco, Rosa had thought that she would never get married. For a long time, she wasn't interested, and then she began to look at other women in the village, like Maria next door, and think that she was missing something.

"Marco," Rosa said. "You know I'm not pretty like Emilia was."

"Emilia was Emilia. You are Rosa. You are the most beautiful thing in my life."

Two weeks later, there was a quiet ceremony in the church. Rosa wore a plain blue suit and a little hat with a veil. Marco dug out the suit he had worn for his first wedding and found he could still fit in it. The only others present were his sister from Lucca and Rosa's cousin Lara and her husband from Livorno. Rosa was forty-five and Marco was fifty-nine.

Marco retired from his job as a mason and with a small government pension their life was good. They talked a lot and went for walks. Sometimes they went to movies and even dances in Reboli. Until the war started, they listened to the radio together, but she didn't like to do that any more.

Rosa felt nothing but pity for Francesco now. She was convinced Annabella had tricked him into marriage, and what could he do? She knew he was trying to make the best of it. After his father died, he took over the family trattoria in Reboli and often worked late, she heard. Although he and Marco were good friends, he tried to avoid her eyes whenever he happened to meet Rosa. She also heard that at night, Francesco would have too much wine.

"Does Francesco have a problem with the wine?" she once asked Marco.

"I wouldn't know," Marco replied. Marco would never say anything bad about anyone.

Well, what did she care?

Whenever she saw Francesco now, Rosa had to smile. He had lost his hair and he seemed to have shrunk because Annabella was now taller than he was. But he was still lean and wiry. Marco, on the other hand, was still tall and handsome. If he wasn't as romantic as Francesco or even Sergio or Franco, she knew that he cared for her very much.

Both Francesco and Annabella always seemed sad, Rosa thought. She often wondered about their marriage and why they never had children.

Rosa stretched in her little bed. *Basta!* Enough about the past. She got up, found that she ached all over, and went downstairs to join the others.

CHAPTER 8

▼

By the time Rosa got downstairs, all the others from the village had gathered in the main room. She found Marco standing by the window and hugged and kissed him. She looked around and found that Annabella was watching.

"Did you sleep well?" he asked.

"Not without you there," she said, not wanting to tell him about her nightmare.

Although Sant'Antonio was small, people kept to themselves and some of the villagers didn't know others well. So there was a certain awkwardness as they took the coffee Maria had made and exchanged simple greetings. Clearly, they were trying to make the best of this terrible thing that had happened to them. But since they were sure they would not be together long, they declined to share too much with one another.

"I've always liked the roses in front of your house."

"Aren't you related to the Gallos in Lucca? They are our best friends."

"Do you think we'll get used to the *cesso?* I didn't like the line outside there this morning."

"I wonder when we will be going home."

Rosa, however, was pleased that she knew almost everyone in the room, some of them quite well. Maria was her neighbor and Dante her good friend. The Spinelli sisters had taught her sewing when she was a child. If Vito and Giacomo were a little eccentric, they had good hearts and were always ready to help others. She felt sorry for Gina having to take care of so many children. As for the Contessa, Rosa didn't believe all the stories, although she was pretty certain "Signora

Gabriella Valentini" was not a countess after all. Fausta Sanfilippo was the only person Rosa didn't know well, but no one did. Fausta kept to herself.

"Buongiorno, buongiorno." Rosa went around the room, hugging and kissing most everyone. She bent down and kissed the baby Carlotta in Gina's arms, patted Anna, Roberto and Adolfo on the head and smiled at Lucia. Annabella stayed by herself on the other side of the room.

The main room of the Cielo was large, but it could barely hold all of the villagers and sometimes they bumped into each other. Shelves containing various utensils were along one wall and chests along another. A long heavy table and benches stood in front of the fireplace. When the *fattoria* was active, other farm families came here to eat.

Not all of the greetings that morning were pleasant. Vito could not resist making an elaborate compliment about Maddelena's hair and she grimly turned her back. He knew enough not to continue. When Roberto, who was chasing Adolfo, ran into Fausta, she glared at Gina.

"Well," Dante said after everyone had finished the coffee, "I think we should get to work cleaning in here and doing some repairs outside. At least it will keep our minds off other things."

Because it was Dante, everyone seemed eager to help.

There was no one, not even Father Luigi, who had more respect in Sant'Antonio than Dante Silva. He was now sixty-four years old but looked no older than forty-five.

Dante had been a teacher in the school at Reboli for forty years, so he knew many of the people as pupils or as parents of pupils. The children loved him. He could even make mathematics interesting, and he could talk about astronomy, painting, history, anything with such enthusiasm that they became excited, too.

But his favorite subject was the great Dante Alighieri, only coincidentally because he shared his name. Children would gather round and cling to each other when he read from *The Divine Comedy* in a deep and sonorous voice, "Abandon all hope, ye who enter here."

Like other scholars before and since, Dante was fascinated by the poet's depiction of a corrupt church and the vivid portraits of historical and contemporary figures, but mostly he was interested in the journey to God and peace on earth. And he spent much time reading about Beatrice, the real woman that the poet loved.

Dante was more than six feet tall. His hair was now white and flowing to his shoulders. His mustache and goatee were always trimmed, and his face was deeply tanned. Until today, he always wore a light suit with a red ascot tied around his neck. Whenever he entered a room, women seemed to blush a little more, flutter a little more.

But men liked him, too. Dante didn't play cards at Leoni's very often, but when he did he listened carefully to what the other men were talking about, making only a few comments.

He never went to church, but there was no kinder man in the village. No one else knew that each month he sent a check to the school to buy books.

Dante had never married. There was a widespread rumor that the great love of his life was a beautiful young woman in Florence when he was a student there. But, the story went, she drowned in the Arno. Over the years, a few women in Sant'Antonio had suggested to him that they might help relieve his sorrow. Dante just smiled and changed the subject.

Both men and women remarked that there was often sadness in Dante's eyes. He never talked about his feelings to anyone, not even to Rosa, his best friend in the village.

To the surprise of everyone, Dante had exchanged his light suit for a blue flannel shirt and work pants, although he still had a red scarf around his neck. This made him look even younger.

"Did you see Dante?" Maria whispered to the Contessa. "I didn't recognize him."

The Contessa rolled her eyes and smiled. Maria noticed that the Contessa had put on even more makeup and jewelry this morning.

Dante proved to be just as willing and strong as the rest of the men as they worked out in back. They discovered that the pump still worked, even though it took about an hour for the rusty water to stop running and clear water to start. They brought four pails of water into the house, and everyone used it to wash up a little.

Dante and Francesco straightened the shed while Marco went to work clearing brush. Vito climbed a ladder to nail down some of the loose tiles on the roof.

"If you fall, I'm not going to catch you," Giacomo said, holding the ladder. *"Asino!"*

No one strayed far from the house, however. They did not know what was out there.

Inside, the women turned over the mattresses. They dusted the walls. They washed the dishes. And then they brought in more pails of water, rinsed out the sheets and hung them on the third floor. As usual, Rosa and Maria took charge.

Every once in a while they took turns to play with Carlotta. The baby had awakened early, crying to be fed, but after she was nursed she was her usual sunny self, not even fussing when Maddelena awkwardly held her across her lap like a sausage. Carlotta was a chubby baby, with bright blue eyes and several chins. She had inherited her father's deep dimples. Gina had dressed her in a pretty pink outfit and put a pink ribbon in her yellow curls.

"She's such a dear, Gina," Maria said, finally having her chance to hold the baby. "I remember when Little Carlo and Nando were babies like this. Sometimes they got sick and then they got better. Both of them laughed a lot but both of them cried a lot, too, and poor Angelica..."

Rosa smiled indulgently. "Maria, I think we should get back to work," she said.

In their room upstairs, Maddelena and Renata discovered an *armadio* with dresses still on their hangers. They brought them all down to the main room.

"Look at this," Maddelena told her sister. "Remember when we used to wear dresses like this?"

The sisters had always prided themselves on looking their best, and always dressed up when they went out. With her one good arm, Renata held the dress in front of her. It was made of dark blue velvet with lace embroidery around the collar and wrists.

"It looks like the one you wore to the dance in Lucca," Renata said. "Remember the boys we danced with?"

"And this looks rather like the one you wore," Maddelena said, holding up a frumpy red gown with a high neck and long sleeves.

"Mother gave me her pearls to wear with that."

They were interrupted by a low-flying plane. Here, near the top of the hill, the planes were even closer. Seconds later, they heard an explosion in the valley.

"*O Dio*," Maddelena cried. "Now they're going to start bombing around Sant'Antonio."

The other women raced to the window to look out, but there was nothing to see. It was the first bomb dropped in the valley.

Annabella wiped away some tears. "I'm so afraid it was near our house." She saw Rosa looking at her.

Quietly, they went back to sorting out the dresses they had found and trying them on in front of the mirror. Even Lucia joined in, putting on a fancy nightgown over her dress and wearing it for the rest of the day. At sixteen, she still liked to dress up. Anna put on the blue velvet gown and paraded up and down the room.

As they were putting the dresses back on their hangers, the women froze when the back door suddenly opened and a small grizzly figure appeared. Rosa recognized him at once. It was Gavino, the farmer who had refused to leave the *fattoria* with the others and now lived in the hut on the far end of the property.

"I thought I heard some noise up here," he said, shuffling into the room. "What are all you lovely ladies doing here?"

Rosa went up and kissed him, although he hadn't the slightest idea who she was.

Gavino was not even five feet tall. His thin gray hair hung to his shoulders and his beard fell almost to his belt. His jacket and trousers were worn, and his shoes were made of wood and canvas. A pointed green hat on top of his big ears made him look like an elf.

Gavino sat down on the wooden bench and accepted Maria's offer of biscotti from a package she had forgotten to send to her daughter. He proceeded to tell the women how he wanted to stay in the hills and still had a pig, a half dozen or so rabbits and some chickens. He had a big garden, too, so there was no need to ask anyone else for help. He went down to Sant'Antonio only once or twice a year.

The villagers were full of questions, which they shouted since the old man had trouble hearing.

"Aren't you frightened up here alone?" Rosa asked.

"No, never."

"Don't you think of moving down to Sant'Antonio?"

"Why should I? This is my home."

"What about the partisans, aren't they all over?"

"Yes, but I've gotten to know them. Sometimes I help them out." Gavino smiled a toothless smile.

"How?"

"I tell them where the Germans are."

"How do you know that?"

"I hear things. And I've still got my eyesight."

Now, he said, there were also Allied prisoners of war, mostly British, who had escaped from the Germans.

"They usually stay for a few days and then they move on. They try to get into the Appenines and then north."

There were also more and more young Italian men who were deserting the army. Gavino told of two young men last month who had been traveling for days and had run out of food. Gavino sheltered them in a cave at the back of his property for a week and then they decided to move on. He thought they might still be in the area.

Rosa knew immediately that he was talking about Dino and his friend, but she didn't say anything.

"Don't you know you could be shot if the Germans found that you helped partisans and these deserters?" Fausta asked. It may have been the first time she had spoken since the group arrived.

Gavino just smiled. "I'll take the chance."

The morning rushed by quickly, and it was soon time for *il pranzo*. Even under these conditions, Maria said, they should still try to keep the same life as they did in the village. Gavino was invited to stay for the meal.

"Are we all going to eat together?" Annabella asked.

"Of course," Rosa said.

"But you don't have enough food," Gavino said.

"Rosa brought ravioli!" Renata beamed.

"That won't be enough for everyone. We should make this a real Italian meal. I will be right back." Gavino hurried out the door.

Marco put some charcoal in the *fornelli* and Rosa soon had a pot of water boiling. The long table could seat a dozen people, and the others sat on benches nearby. The children sat on the floor.

Maddelena and Renata set the table with the mismatched plates and bowls from the kitchen shelves. Vito and Giacomo found some wild lettuce in the back, and Maria discovered a couple of bottles of red wine under the stairs. And then Gavino returned, bearing four rabbits, bright red without their skins.

"I killed these yesterday. I have too many rabbits. They won't take long to cook. We will have a *festa*, OK?"

When the ravioli and the rabbits were ready, Dante was asked to give a toast.

"I think we should drink to an end to the war and an end to suffering," he said simply. "May it come very soon."

Rosa went around with the pot and served her ravioli. Since they were unusually large, there was enough for everyone. The Sporenza boys decided that they "tasted funny" and Gina told them that was because of the nutmeg and to eat them anyway. Nursing Carlotta in her arms, she didn't have time to deal with finicky children.

From appearances, it could have been a dinner after a wedding in Sant'Antonio. Vito and Giacomo told jokes and Gavino recounted tales of his errant pig who seemed to have the run of the property.

"Please, no more stories," Renata begged through her tears. "I'm laughing so hard I'm crying."

Maria told stories about her older grandson in Sant'Anna who was just learning to go to the toilet. "Every time, he has to look in and tell his mother what it looks like."

Fausta didn't think this was an appropriate table subject and said she wished she could go back to work in Reboli very soon.

"Your boss will find out soon enough that we've been evacuated," Maria said.

"Please don't use that word," the Contessa said. "I can't bear to think about it."

"That's what we have done, we have evacuated," Rosa said.

The war was still close at hand. Airplanes flew overhead three times as they ate, causing everyone to stop and stare straight ahead, waiting.

After the meal, Dante asked Gavino if he could talk to him privately. They stood just outside the back door for several minutes and then Dante returned and told the group he wanted to have a discussion.

"Come sit by me," the Contessa said.

Dante chose to stand. He said he thought that there should be certain rules for everyone to obey even if they were only at the Cielo for a few days.

"I think we should have a schedule, everyone getting up at the same time," Vito said.

"Then everyone will be standing in line at the *cesso*," Giacomo pointed out.

"I think we should hurry when we're in there so there isn't a line," Annabella said.

"We should be on time for meals."

"We shouldn't waste food. There isn't enough."

"We should be polite to one another."

"We should conserve water. We don't know how much there is in the well."

"I think we should all respect everyone's privacy," Fausta said. "We shouldn't enter other rooms."

"And we shouldn't ask each other personal questions," the Contessa said, looking at Maria.

"We need to talk about another thing, and this is important," Dante said. "We should not go to the *cesso* in the middle of the night. You found a *vaso da notte* under your beds. I am glad that they left them here. Please empty them in the mornings in the *cesso*. We do not want this place to begin to smell."

Everyone agreed. Roberto and Adolfo giggled.

"There's another more important thing," Dante said. "As Gavino said, this area is very dangerous. The partisans are all over and they may get in fights with the Germans. And there are land mines planted in these hills. We should not go out of the Cielo alone farther than the *cesso,* ever."

Everyone seemed to agree until Lucia raised her hand.

"Please!" Lucia said. "This place is so crowded. We have to get out sometime. Can't we just go for short walks?"

"Listen to Dante," Gina said. She put her arm around her daughter. "You can wait until we get back home to take a walk. You'll be home very soon."

"Not soon enough," Lucia said, burying her face in her hands.

"*Allora.* Listen to your mother, Lucia," Rosa said. "She knows what's good for you."

When the women were washing the dishes afterwards, Annabella said loudly, "I thought the ravioli were just wonderful."

Rosa smiled.

In the afternoon, the villagers returned to their rooms for quiet and a rest. Then the men did more work outside and the women found more cleaning to do. They were twice interrupted by planes flying overhead, but there were no more explosions. Since the Cielo had no electricity and candles were scarce, most people prepared to retire early. Besides, Dante warned that if they did light candles they should pull the curtains. The farmhouse should be invisible at night.

"Maybe just a few days more here," Maddelena said, hugging her sister as they went upstairs to their room.

"Let's hope so," Renata said.

In his room Dante took out *The Divine Comedy* and opened a letter he used as a bookmark. After reading it, he wiped tears from his eyes and looked up. He hadn't told the group everything that Gavino had said. They were going to be here more than a few days.

CHAPTER 9

▼

Maria got up early the next morning to make *castagnaccio*, the chestnut bread that everyone in the region had for breakfast. She thought it would be a comforting treat. But when they came downstairs most of the villagers were not as polite as they were the day before and now were more silent and tense. They barely said *buongiorno* to each other, but just sat grimly at the table or looked out the window. It didn't help when thick storm clouds began moving in from the east.

Rosa realized what was happening and asked Dante if he could provide some comfort. But Dante did not have anything encouraging to say.

"If you could listen for a moment," he said, standing up and tapping his cup with a spoon. "As you know, I talked to Gavino for a few minutes yesterday before he left. I'm afraid I didn't tell you everything. It's worse than I said last night. It seems these hills are filled with all sorts of people. Deserters from the Italian army. British soldiers who have escaped from prison. Thugs and ruffians trying to take advantage of the situation. And, of course, the partisans."

"The partisans!" Vito sneered. "Of course the partisans."

"As I said," Dante continued, "it is very dangerous out there. The Germans who are occupying our village will be looking for any of these people and they could come here. The partisans could encounter them and there would be fighting."

"*O Dio,*" Maria cried.

"So I have to tell you again that it is even more important that we stay in this building."

Dante cleared his throat. "There is one more thing. We will be staying here longer than we expected. Gavino's sources told him the SS troops have settled into Sant'Antonio and look like they will be staying there for some time. Besides looking for all these people in the hills, they will probably be mining the bridge at Sant'Antonio. They want to stop the Allies from coming north. So I'm afraid we can't go back there soon."

The villagers looked startled, then angry.

"How long do you think, Dante?" Vito asked

"Vito," Dante sighed, "I don't know. A week? Maybe two? Longer? I just don't know. I'm sorry."

"Oh, Dante," Rosa said. "It's not your fault. You're just telling us what you know."

She put her arm around him. The others in the room now looked even more grim. Maria went around with a coffee pot and a plate of *castagnaccio*.

"Please. We have to eat. We're going to need our strength."

"Don't nag us, Maria," Annabella said. "If we want to eat, we will."

The bread remained untouched, and then the villagers fell silent.

"I wish we had brought more pills," Maddelena finally said.

"I told you to," Renata said.

"Well, I'm sorry!" Maddelena glared at her sister.

Both sisters were perfectly healthy but they liked to complain about the aches in their backs, their arms, their legs. Maddelena could always be counted on to have something worse than her sister.

"And Gina," Maddelena said, turning to the corner of the room where Gina sat surrounded by her children, "can't you keep those boys from running around up there? The pounding last night sounded like the Germans were coming."

"Have you ever had children, Maddelena?" Gina asked sweetly.

"I think you have enough for all of us here," Maddelena said, her voice even lower than usual.

"Now, Maddelena," Maria said.

"Yes, aren't children wonderful," Gina said, pulling up her blouse and taking out an ample breast which Carlotta immediately attacked. The men in the room tried to avert their eyes. "I was so happy when Lucia came along that Pietro and I got married right away. And then Roberto and then Anna and then Adolfo. And now here's little Carlotta. Pietro and I love to have children. And you know what?" Gina smiled broadly. "We love to make babies, too!"

Rosa giggled, but Maddelena put her glasses on her nose and said, "Gina, do you really think you should talk like that in front of your children?

"Why not?" Gina said, patting her nursing baby. "Lucia certainly knows what it's all about and so do the boys and Anna. Don't you, children?"

Lucia, paging through a magazine, and her brothers and sister, playing cards on the floor, seemed not to have heard any of the conversation. At the table, Vito could barely control his laughter.

Before she met Pietro, Gina had gone out with Angelo. Then Gaetano. Then Manfredi. That was before she was eighteen. But then, at a dance in Reboli, she and Pietro bumped into each other, danced some more, went to his home and soon decided to live together. They found a little house at the edge of the village with a big garden and an empty field next door. This, of course, scandalized many of the women in the village.

That was sixteen years ago. Pietro worked odd jobs as a painter and Gina took care of their growing family. They took the children on picnics, walked them along the river and pushed them on swings in the field. They rarely went to church. Some of the women in the village gossiped about the way Gina was raising the children, saying they should wear cleaner clothes and be more respectful. They thought Gina should keep a closer watch on them. And they didn't like her clothes or her makeup.

Then Pietro was called into the army, but he came home on a short leave a year ago. That's when Carlotta happened. Gina didn't know where Pietro was now. But she never looked at another man.

Tensions continued to increase during the morning. When Fausta told the group she should let her boss know where she was, Vito said, "None of us want to be here, Fausta. You're not the only one."

Suddenly Annabella jumped up. "We're never going to get out of here!" she shouted. Francesco put his hand on her shoulder.

"Please, 'Bella, be quiet. We've only been here a day."

Annabella took his hand from her shoulder and turned to a window. Francesco shook his head, went to his room and took his violin out of the case. He adjusted the strings and soon the rich and familiar strains of Corelli's "La Follia" filtered throughout the farmhouse. Francesco had taken lessons as a child, and every day, no matter what, he spent a half hour with his violin. His repertoire was not large and he played the Corelli whenever he felt depressed.

"Ah," Maria said. "I love that piece."

"If you heard it every day you wouldn't like it so much," Annabella said.

It was the first time Rosa had heard Francesco play the violin. She went to the window and stared at the dark clouds approaching from the west.

Only Carlotta helped relieve the tension. Although she had again awakened crying and wanting to be fed, she spent the morning traded from lap to lap. Even Vito and Giacomo took their turns, holding the baby ever so gingerly.

"There's nothing like a baby to make you smile," Maria said, trying to give her over to Lucia. "Do you want to hold your sister for a while?"

"No, thank you," Lucia said. "I don't like babies."

"Why ever not?" Maria asked.

"I just don't," Lucia said, and went up to her room on the third floor.

"Doesn't like babies?" Maria said. "Everyone likes babies."

"I'll hold her!" Anna shouted. "I love holding my sister."

Anna made faces and Carlotta started giggling as soon as she took her. "I'm the only one who can make her laugh," Anna said proudly.

Having put the baby in Anna's arms, Maria went to the kitchen, shaking her head and muttering, "Doesn't like babies?"

And then it started to rain, a fierce rain that came down in sheets and pounded at the windows and sounded like bullets on the tile roof. Thunder echoed in the hills and lightning lit the room. The rain hid the terraces in the back and even Gavino's hut and his gardens. Branches of the kaki tree beat against the windows and walls.

The men could not go outside to work, but Marco had found a deck of cards and he and Francesco and Vito and Giacomo started to play. They didn't talk much, but it was a typical game, except that the cousins started yelling at each other even earlier than usual. Marco tried to lighten things up.

"Look at it this way," he said. "As long as it rains the Germans can't do much, the partisans have to stay inside, and the Allies won't be flying their planes."

"*Boh!* Play the cards, play the cards," Vito said.

The women went up to their rooms. A stack of old magazines had been left under the stairs and these became popular. Renata laughed at the "new" styles in the fashion magazines because the styles had already gone out of date.

"I really don't like magazines about the cinema," Maddelena said, throwing down *Rivesta del cinematografo* and picking up *Bella* instead.

With the rain pouring down outside their window, Rosa and Annabella lay on their beds, reading magazines and ignoring each other. Every once in a while one would glance over at the other. When Annabella got up, they had their first exchange, but it was not pleasant.

"I wish you wouldn't put your things on my side of the dresser," Annabella said as she brushed her short wavy hair.

"I didn't know we had sides," Rosa seethed. She got up and stormed out of the room.

On the third floor, Lucia went from the window to her bed to her dresser to the tower and back to the window. No one felt more constrained by the new surroundings than Lucia. She was restless and lonely and wanted to be back with her friends. With the war on, the older boys had left the village and the younger ones weren't worth talking to. She lay on her bed and wrote in her diary.

"We are stuck up here on the hilltop. Now nobody knows when we will go back. I think we will be up here forever. There's no one but old people and us and Carlotta wakes me up every morning with her crying. God I hate some of those women. They think I'm still a child. How can I ever meet someone if we stay up here forever? I'm going to be an old spinster like Fausta Sanfilippo. Or worse, Anna and me are going to be like the Spinelli sisters. Maybe we'll wear our hair funny like them and keep our jewels on all the time. That wouldn't be so bad.

"Yesterday everyone decided that we can't go out alone up here. I tried to complain but they didn't even listen to me. They think I'm a child. Why can't I just go for a walk around the house? I can take care of myself.

"Mamma's so busy with Carlotta and the others I don't have a chance to talk to her. She probably wouldn't listen anyway. We haven't talked for so long I wouldn't know what to say. I wish we would hear from Papa. Maybe he's been taken prisoner. Maybe it's something worse. I wish I was back home. I wish I could talk to Daniela and Carmella again. I don't even know where they were sent. God I wish I was home."

Lucia tucked the diary under her bed and went to the tower just off her room. It was past noon, but she didn't feel like eating. She wished she could go out but she knew she wasn't allowed. The rain was not quite so fierce now and she could see farther into the distance.

She leaned over the railing, letting the rain wash down her face and dampen her long dark hair. She thought if she leaned out far enough she might be able to see the Nero Nube farmhouse. Maybe Daniela and Carmella were there. It was too far to see.

Far off to the right, Gavino was feeding his pig in the rain. What a silly old man he was.

Up on the ridge, she thought she could see five men climbing in a single file. Could they be Germans? Maybe they were partisans.

Off to the left, she thought she saw two other shadows moving through the trees. They seemed to be coming nearer. Yes!

The shadows came closer, and then one moved out into the open for a brief moment. Then the other one followed. That one seemed to be moving slower.

"This is so exciting," she thought. "It's like watching the cinema."

Lucia watched as the figures moved closer to the farmhouse. She could see now that they were two men. Young men. They were getting very wet. Every once in a while the taller one would put his arm around the other one and help him climb over a fallen tree branch or something. Maybe that one was hurt.

The two moved closer. Their clothes looked tattered. The shorter one favored his right foot.

When they got to the open field behind the shed, the boys made a run for it, at least as fast as the one boy could run. They got to the shed, then made a dash to the back door of the house.

Why were they coming here?

Now they were directly beneath the tower. She was tempted to lean out and say something, but she didn't know who they were. They could be escaped prisoners of war. They could be some of those partisans who broke into homes and stole things. She had heard about them.

Mostly, they seemed scared.

At that moment, the taller boy looked up. Lucia didn't move back fast enough.

"Hey!" he whispered, the rain coming down on his face. It was only a whisper, but loud enough so that she heard it.

Lucia looked over her shoulder. Everyone else was downstairs.

"What?" she whispered back.

"Can you help us?"

"What do you want?"

"Paolo sprained his foot and it's getting worse. Do you have any bandages or anything?"

"Who are you?"

"We're from Montepulciano. We left the army last month. But now Paolo got hurt."

"Should I ask my mother?"

"No! No! Can't you just see if you have an old cloth or a sheet or something to wrap it in?"

Lucia remembered that the nightgown she wore yesterday was in a heap in the corner of her room.

"Want a nightgown?"

"I'd looked pretty silly."

"No. I mean for your friend."

"Perfect. Throw it down."

Lucia went back to her room, rolled the nightgown in a ball and was going to throw it down. Then she had another idea. She went back to the tower.

"Wait. I'll be right down."

Lucia put the nightgown under her arm and crept downstairs. She slid along the wall to the back door. No one could see her. The boys were standing in the rain.

"Come up on these steps and out of the rain."

"Thank you," one said.

"That's very kind," said the other.

For the first time, Lucia had a good look at the boys. Paolo was thin and sort of scraggly looking. His hair looked as though someone had cut it with rusty scissors. His shirt was soaked and pulled out of his pants.

The taller boy was stockier. He had a cap pushed back on his black curly hair and he wore a leather vest. His ears stuck out and his nose and cheeks were covered with freckles. Lucia always liked freckles.

"Why are you running away from the army?"

"It was terrible. They kept giving us orders. I'm Dino, by the way, and this is Paolo."

Paolo shook her hand. Dino held her hand longer than she thought he should.

"What are you doing here?" he asked. "We saw people inside. We thought this place was empty."

"It was until two days ago. The SS came and evacuated Sant'Antonio and some of us came up here. Other people went to other farmhouses."

"SS troops are in Sant'Antonio now?"

"Yes, they've taken over the town."

"I'm lucky," Dino said. "I was just there for two days. I was starving and these people took me in. Some German soldiers came looking for me but I hid and then I left in a hurry."

"Just you?"

"Yes. But I found Paolo right away in the hills." Dino smiled a crooked smile. "So you're the people we saw coming up the hill the other day. I thought I noticed a pretty girl in the middle."

Lucia blushed.

"Look," Paolo said. "Are you just going to chat or are you going to fix my ankle?"

"Oh, right," Dino said.

Paolo sat on a bench while Lucia tore the nightgown into strips. In a few minutes, Dino had wrapped the swollen ankle tightly.

"Does it feel any better?" Dino asked.

"Yes, but we'd better be going," Paolo said. "I want to put my foot up."

"Do you think you should go in the rain?" Lucia asked.

"We better not be seen here," Dino said. "Your friends won't like it."

"Where will you go?"

"Not very far as long as his foot is bad. We're going to try to go back to old Gavino again. He put us up a few weeks ago and he said we could come back."

Lucia suddenly realized she didn't want them to leave. "If you're that close by then maybe I can see you again?"

"Well, sure," Dino said. "We'll be around for a while."

After they turned, Dino looked back.

"Wait. What's your name?"

"Lucia."

"Lucia. Like the light in the tower."

As they hobbled off, Lucia thought Dino was more cocky than he should be. Still, he was kind of cute. And she liked his smile. And his freckles.

When Lucia went back upstairs, she found Anna playing with her doll.

"Where were you?" Anna said. "What are you smiling at?"

"Nothing. Just nothing." Lucia took her diary out from under the bed.

CHAPTER 10

▼

It was still raining the next morning, not hard but enough to keep everyone tense and worried. Rosa looked across the room when she awoke, saw that Annabella was still sleeping and went down to the kitchen. She had had a very restless night. Just as she was nodding off, she thought she heard a tiny scratching in the wall next to her. She pulled the coverlet off and leaned her head against the wall, but there was no sound.

Waiting for the noise to come back kept her awake, of course, and it wasn't long before she heard the sound again, a tiny scratch that was barely audible.

"Santa Maria!"

This time, Rosa tapped on the wall. The scratching ceased. Rosa tried to sleep. The scratching resumed. Rosa tapped the wall again. This time the noise ceased and did not continue. Rosa spent the rest of the fitful night awake and listening, and now she felt all the more cross.

"I wonder how many nights this is going to happen," she thought. She also wondered how Gatto was doing back in the village.

Standing at the sink, she watched the rain. She could see rivulets running down the terraces on the hillside and into the fields in the back. A mist covered the top of the hill behind the farmhouse and the trees glistened in the pale light. She could barely see Gavino working in his garden. There was no other sign of life, but she knew the partisans were somewhere, perhaps the Germans, perhaps others. How long would the rain last? How long would they have to stay here? She missed sleeping with Marco.

Rosa made herself some coffee. The coffee supply was already running low, but so was everything else. She wanted to see if Gavino could bring some eggs today. Rosa checked the shelves and noted that the supply of olive oil had dwindled to four bottles. She saw how Vito and Giacomo used it on everything.

Somehow, Rosa and Maria were doing all the cooking, and they had arranged a schedule on alternate days. She looked in one of the barrels of chestnut flour and found that although the level had already gone down, there was still a good supply left. She would make some polenta for *il pranzo*.

If the kitchen at the Cielo was not as well equipped or as efficient as her own in Sant'Antonio, it provided enough room for making meals for more people than Rosa had ever cooked for. A dozen iron pots and pans hung over the sink. The two *fornelli* were adequate for cooking. Rows of shelves lined one entire wall, filled with plates that did not match and bowls that were cracked.

She took some plates off a shelf. Just like my mother's, she thought, bright orange with red flowers around the rim. Rosa still had almost the complete set.

"She probably used these dishes when she was here," Rosa thought.

When she put the plates back, she noticed that there was no wall behind the shelf. Indeed, there was no wall behind any of the shelves on that side of the room.

"I forgot all about this."

She removed everything from the shelves and then tried to move the shelving itself. It was too heavy. She ran to Marco and Francesco's room.

"Marco, come quick."

Marco and Francesco had just dressed and were about to come out of their room.

"Did you sleep well?" he said as he kissed the top of her head.

"No, but I'll tell you about that later. Please come with me. I want to show you something. Oh, *buongiorno*, Francesco.

"*Buongiorno*, Rosa," Francesco said and slipped quickly out of her way. After all these years, Francesco still felt guilty when he saw Rosa.

In the kitchen, Rosa showed Marco the mysterious shelves.

"Look. There's nothing behind this."

With great effort, Marco pulled the shelves away from the wall, revealing a small dark space. It was empty except for some old wine kegs and a stool. Dirty rags littered the floor and cobwebs shone in the corners. A small window at the very top provided just a little light. It appeared to be inhabited only by some dead spiders.

"I vaguely remember this room from when I lived here," Rosa said. "I think they used it as a wine cellar."

"Where's the wine?" Marco asked.

Rosa picked up the old rags and revealed a trap door. She lifted the hinge.

"Well, whoever was here before seem to have left us with a very nice present," Marco said. He crouched down and counted forty-three bottles of wine and *grappa* in the hole. He pulled two out.

"We can have these today," he said. "Maybe that will cheer people up a little. But I don't understand why this place is so concealed."

"Maybe," Rosa said, "it was also a place to hide. Remember this farmhouse is very old. The *contadini* could have been hiding from all sorts of people. Including the landowner."

"Let's hope we don't have to use it," Marco said, taking her in his arms. Rosa told him about the scratching in the wall and her sleepless night.

"I'll get Vito and Giacomo to make some traps," Marco said.

"I wish Gatto was here," Rosa said. "He'd take care of this."

With effort, Marco pushed the shelf back into place and Rosa returned the plates and dishes. No one could guess what was behind them.

There were sounds of stirring on the second floor, and it was clear that the rain that confined the villagers to the Cielo was continuing to drain energy and increase tensions. Like any group of people forced to live together under threatening circumstances, they found that although they wanted to get along together, they still had their own needs and worries.

While they were getting dressed, Maddelena and Renata continued a discussion that had begun the night before: What happened to the silver brooch that was at their mother's bedside when she died?

"I'm sure it was there the last time I was in the room," Maddelena said.

"I'm sure it was not."

"Well, where could it have gone?"

"That's what I'm asking you."

"Are you accusing me?"

"I'm not accusing you, I'm just asking."

"You're accusing me!"

Their voices became more shrill with each insinuation.

Next door, Maria, her usual sunny but inquisitive self, tried again to get to know her new roommate, but the Contessa would have none of it.

"How did you feel when you moved into that big house?" Maria wondered, buttoning her black dress over her ample bosom.

The Contessa smiled grimly.

"Didn't it seem strange? Did your husband buy a lot of new furniture? Where did you buy them?"

The Contessa stared stonily ahead.

Maria wrapped her rosary beads around her wrist. "Do you feel that the house is empty now? Do you plan to stay there? I was so sorry to hear about your husband."

The Contessa grimaced.

"Do you make your own meals? It looks like you really should eat more pasta."

"Maria, please," the Contessa said, slamming down the book she was trying to read. "Please stop asking me so many questions! Just because you're the village saint doesn't give you a right to ask people questions."

The Contessa went back to reading *Pensione Flora,* which she had found on a shelf downstairs. Maria, flushed and embarrassed, picked up some mending.

Like most Italian widows, Maria Ruffolo wore black dresses all the time, but since she was tall with broad shoulders and a sturdy figure, she looked more elegant than dowdy in black. She wore her graying hair in long braids wound around her head, making her face look even rounder. Her cheeks were always flushed, and she had just a trace of a mustache, but she had a ready smile for everyone she encountered. The Contessa wasn't the first person to call her a saint.

For years, Maria and Davido Ruffolo were the most devoted couple in the village. Every night, they went for a walk along the river, Davido's arm around his wife's shoulder. When Angelica was born, they pushed her in a carriage, stopping often so that other villagers could admire the baby. When Angelica grew up, they hardly let her out of their sight.

Eight years ago, Davido was killed in the collapse of an iron mine in the Apuan mountains. It took three days to recover the bodies of the seven victims. Throughout it all, Maria remained steadfast, sitting in the church and praying the rosary. When friends asked her if she was angry or depressed, she said simply that it must be the will of God.

Angelica helped her through her sorrows, but then Angelica met Carlo and they were married two years later. Like most Italian brides, Angelica went to live with her husband's parents. The village of Sant'Anna di Stazzema was near the top of an Apuan hill and Maria had visited it only twice, once for Little Carlo's christening four years ago and again this last Easter. When friends asked her if she was afraid to be alone, Maria simply said such an idea never occurred to her and, anyway, it must be God's will.

As much as she missed Angelica, Maria regretted not having her grandsons nearby even more. Little Carlo was now four and Rando was two, and with Carlo off to war Angelica had her hands full. Maria wished she could be there to help.

Angelica wrote long letters and confided in her mother about everything. Maria knew how lonely her daughter was and how she was coping with the absence of her husband. Maria didn't approve, but what could she do? She wanted Angelica to be happy more than anything. She just wished it hadn't been a partisan who brought her happiness.

On the third floor, Anna played with her doll and Lucia stood in the tower, looking in vain in the direction of Gavino's farm. Roberto and Adolfo pounded each other playfully in a corner, and Gina had to say, "Boys, boys! *Statte zitto!* Be quiet! It's time for Carlotta's nap."

Gina brushed back the baby's yellow curls and smiled. Carlotta gurgled back and held on tight to Gina's finger. Gina's heart leaped. She loved that smile so much.

"Do you feel better now, my darling? You're not sick anymore? Last month, you were so sick we were afraid we were going to lose you. Yes, we did. Yes!" Gina tickled her daughter so hard Carlotta giggled and gasped.

"Now you're all better, aren't you, my darling? Oh, if only Pietro could see you. Your daddy would love you so much, too, my darling. He'd rock you to sleep, he'd tickle you, he'd throw you in the air. Pietro, Pietro…Oh, I know, my darling, you're hungry, aren't you?"

Gina opened her blouse and began to sing.

Fi la nana, e mi bel fiol,
Fi la nana, e mi bel fiol,
Fa si la nana.
Fa si la nana.

Hush-a-bye, my lovely child,
Hush-a-bye, my lovely child,
Hush, hush and go to sleep.
Hush, hush and go to sleep.

Alone in his room, Dante took more notes on *The Inferno*. He had been trying to write an analysis for twenty years and had not made much progress. Frustrated again, he read his favorite passage, the one about Beatrice, aloud. That always comforted him. He liked to think about how Beatrice was described as "a Lady so blessed and so beautiful," with eyes that are "kindled from the lamps of Heaven." And he loved the description of her voice that "reached through me, tender, sweet, and low. An angel's voice, a music of its own."

Beatrice, the woman that other Dante loved so much. A love that lasted for years and years. He opened the tattered envelope that was his marker and looked at the photo and read the note inside. He had memorized it long ago.

Fortunately, the rain still reduced the military action in the area. Artillery shelling was heard occasionally, but few planes flew overhead and the bombing had ceased. As Marco had said, the residents of the Cielo could hope that the rain would continue.

Before noon, Rosa began preparing the polenta, finding a huge copper pot and getting water to a boil. Lowering the heat, she added the chestnut flour and salt, stirring quickly with a wooden spoon. She then raised the heat and watched bubbles rise and burst on the surface. Meanwhile, Marco wiped the center of the table with olive oil.

"All right," Rosa called to everyone. "We're ready!"

"Not quite," Marco said. He went to the kitchen and brought out the two bottles of wine he found that morning.

"Where did that come from?" Vito asked, settling into his usual chair opposite Maddelena.

"Let's just say we inherited it." The wine had aged well in its secret compartment.

When everyone was seated, Rosa poured the polenta directly on the table, letting it spread and harden. She covered it with a sauce of olive oil and the tomatoes and mushrooms that Gavino had brought. Then she and Marco used a thick string to cut the whole thing into pieces.

"Magnificent!" Renata said, and everyone agreed.

"My, doesn't this look good," Gina said as she put pieces for Lucia, Roberto, Anna and Adolfo on their plates.

After one bite, Roberto said, "I think it tastes strange."

"It's made with chestnut flour," Rosa said. "Isn't that a treat?"

"I think it just tastes strange."

"If you don't eat it, you'll be hungry again tonight," his mother said.

"I like it," Anna said. Roberto stuck his tongue out at her.

Vito made an complicated gesture of giving a piece to Maddelena. Maddelena ignored him and got her own.

After lunch, Gina decided that Carlotta needed a bath. She hadn't had one since before the group left. While the women gathered around the sink and helped with the bathing, Rosa glanced out the window and saw a young man running across the fields to the back door. He seemed to be looking at the tower upstairs. There was something familiar about him, she thought. Were those freckles on his face? Then she saw Lucia come downstairs and quietly slip out the door. Rosa was tempted to alert the others, but thought better of it. She helped dry Carlotta off and tried to keep the women occupied so they wouldn't look out the window.

"Did anyone else hear a strange noise last night?" she asked. "It kept me awake all night."

"Did you hear that, too? You know what I think it is," Maddelena said.

"I know exactly what it is," Fausta said. "You don't have to tell me."

On the doorstep, Lucia whispered, "Dino! You've come back. Come up here on the steps out of the rain."

"Paolo was still sleeping so I thought I'd take a walk," Dino said.

"Isn't that dangerous? What if somebody saw you?"

"We've been running for two months now. I can't stand being cooped up."

"How's Paolo?"

"Getting better, but it will take a while before his foot is healed."

"And you?"

"Better, now that I have somebody else to talk to. Paolo is so quiet and Gavino keeps telling us the same stories about when he was in that first great war."

"I'm glad you came."

"Do you think we could go for a little walk? I can put this coat over our heads."

Lucia looked over her shoulder. "Maybe just around here. I can't go far."

As they walked close to the house, Dino told Lucia how he and Paolo had decided to flee the army when it seemed clear that they would be shipped out of Italy.

"Are you afraid to fight?"

"I'm not afraid to fight, but I just want to live. I want to see what is out there. One time Paolo and me went to Siena. Lucia, it is so beautiful! There's this big piazza in the middle of the town. And the duomo! It's magnificent! I want to see Florence, I want to see Rome."

"Don't you want to get married and have a family?"

"Well, sure, some day. But there's time for that. I want to see the world!"

Lucia held his hand as they walked in the rain.

Lucia and Dino were on the opposite side of the house when Vito and Giacomo came from the shed proudly holding the traps they had concocted with scraps of wood and wires. Maria found some cheese and bits of meat, and the cousins set the traps around the edges of rooms on all three floors.

"All the mice will be dead tomorrow," Giacomo said.

"I hope so," Rosa said.

When they went to bed that night, neither Rosa nor Annabella spoke. As they crawled into their beds they heard the rain gently beating on the window and the soft strains of Francesco's violin from the floor below. Rosa smiled and hummed along, but Annabella pulled the covers over her head. Rosa slept fitfully that night, but didn't hear any noises in the wall.

CHAPTER 11

▼

With the dawn, the rain ended and the sun slowly burned off the mist in the valley below. The hills glowed again and on a distant ridge a row of tall cypresses stood like pencils, motionless. It was as if the world was holding its breath, waiting for something to happen.

As the villagers gathered downstairs, Marco opened the window. "We need some air in here or we'll go crazy."

Immediately, birds could be heard as clearly as if they were in the olive trees nearby. The war also seemed closer. Every once in a while gunfire or shelling echoed across the hills, and Marco guessed that the partisans and Germans had found each other. Overhead, planes resumed their flights and everyone waited for the bombing in the valley as the Allies tried to drive the Germans out. The Allied ground troops still had not arrived in northern Tuscany.

"I thought I was tired of the war before," Rosa said. "Now I can't wait for it to be over."

"You'd think the Allies would be here by now," Francesco said.

"They just liberated Rome last month," Dante said. "It will take a while for them to get here."

The immediate problem in the Cielo had not been solved. Although the cheese and meat had mysteriously disappeared, the traps were still intact. Vito and Giacomo were very disappointed and, of course, each blamed the other.

"I would think," Maddelena said, looking at Vito, "that *contadini* would be able to make a simple mousetrap."

"I would think," Vito replied slowly, "that women who don't know anything would not think that they do."

"Maybe the mice ran into the hills," Giacomo said, trying to intervene.

"Then what is that along the fireplace wall?" Maddelena asked sweetly.

"There it is!" Renata screamed.

The poor little mouse looked more frightened than the women, and scurried behind the fireplace grate. Little Anna jumped up and down and shrieked, "Why is anyone afraid of a little mouse?"

Rosa and Maria grabbed brooms and chased the mouse out the door.

"There's another one!' Renata said, pointing to a shadow near the kitchen.

Maria and Rosa got rid of that one, too.

Vito and Giacomo went off to see if they could build some better mousetraps.

Maddelena, Renata and the Contessa went to their rooms. As Annabella edged by, she stumbled over a stone on the floor. Rosa instinctively reached out her hand to help and they looked each other in the eye for the first time in forty years. Then Annabella quickly let go and, her face flushed, left the room.

Lucia, hearing the commotion over the mice, took the opportunity to slip out the back door. Running across the muddy field, she kept looking back at the farmhouse and fell twice before she reached Gavino's.

"Gavino, let me in," she whispered.

"Who's there?" The old man was very deaf.

"Lucia, from the house."

Gavino pulled open the door and squinted into the sunlight. "You shouldn't have come here, little girl."

"Can I see Dino?" Lucia asked.

"He's back in the cave."

Gavino reluctantly led Lucia behind the hut and into the side of the hill. Lucia couldn't believe there was a cave there until Gavino lifted some branches and revealed an opening.

"Dino! You've got a visitor."

A sleepy Dino emerged, rubbing his eyes.

"You did come!"

"You wanted me to, didn't you?"

"Of course."

"And Paolo?"

"He's still asleep. But look, you're full of mud."

Lucia tried to brush the dirt off her blouse and skirt.

"Let me help," Dino said, wiping the grime off her shoulders.

Lucia thought he spent too much time brushing the front of her blouse.

"That's much better, isn't it?" he said. He led her to a grassy spot under a tree.

"It's so hard to sleep in that cave," he said. "And Paolo kept kicking me."

"Maybe that means his foot is getting better."

"No, it was his other foot. I'm very glad you came here, but you shouldn't have, you know. The others are going to be very upset."

"I don't care about the others. I just had to get out of that house."

"To see me?"

Lucia blushed.

"I'm glad," Dino said. "I like you, Lucia. You're a nice girl, nicer than the other girls I've been with."

"Have you been with a lot of other girls?"

"A few. You don't mind that?"

"Of course not." Lucia tried to sound sincere.

"What about you? Have you had other boys?"

Lucia didn't think Lino from Sant'Antonio counted. They had been only fourteen and they didn't actually do anything. But she didn't want Dino to think she was inexperienced. She just smiled.

"I like it when you smile," he said, kissing her lips.

"I like it when you kiss me."

The sun was high in the sky but the trees provided a cool shade as Dino and Lucia settled on the dark damp grass. He went back to the cave for a blanket for them to lie on.

At midmorning, with the men outside working and the other women upstairs, Rosa and Maria found themselves alone in the big room.

"How are you, Maria?" Rosa asked, resting her hand on her friend's. "Are you all right?"

"I'm fine, Rosa. Just worried like everyone else."

"You seem to worry for all of us."

"No, no. But I pray a lot. That helps me get through things."

"Every one of us needs prayers. I wish I had your faith in God."

"I think you do, Rosa. You don't have to say the rosary all the time to have faith in God."

For lack of anything else to do, Rosa began dusting the mantel.

"You know what is the brightest thing about this whole ordeal, Rosa?"

"Carlotta, of course."

"What a dear baby. I just love to hold her. But poor Gina. All those children. I only had one, but Angelica has two."

"Pray for Gina, Maria. Anna's sweet, but those boys…"

"They're just boys, Rosa," Maria said. "I can see Little Carlo and Rando like that soon."

"And then there's a teenage daughter."

"Lucia? Well, Lucia can't get into too much trouble here. There's no one else around."

"We don't know that, do we?"

Rosa looked away. She wanted to tell Maria her concerns about Lucia but thought she had better keep that matter to herself. Who was that boy Lucia was talking to yesterday? Was it really Dino? Was he nearby? Would she try to see him? Surely Lucia knew the rules about staying inside the house and not going out alone. If Lucia got caught up with partisans or army deserters and the Germans found out, they would all be in terrible trouble. They could be shot.

Rosa and Maria decided they could help Gina by looking after her children for a while, so they called Anna, Roberto and Adolfo into the main room.

"Let's tell stories!" Maria said.

"We'll make it a contest," Rosa said. "Who can tell the best story?"

Surprisingly, the children thought that was a good idea.

"I'll go first," Rosa said. "This is a story my father often told me before I went to sleep at night. It was my favorite story."

She began to tell the story of a kindly lizard that raised the youngest daughter of a peasant.

"A lizard raised the daughter of a peasant?" Roberto said.

"This is a story, Roberto," Rosa said. "Just listen."

The girl, Rosa said, grew up to be a beautiful woman and the king of the land fell in love with her.

"I love that part," said Maria, who knew the story well.

Rosa continued. When the girl left home to get married, she forgot to say thank you to the lizard, who promptly turned her into a goat. After many complications, the girl realized her mistake and repented. The lizard restored her beauty and the girl and the king lived happily ever after.

"That is why," Rosa said, "we must always hold lizards with much honor. We must never harm them."

"But I like to catch lizards," Adolfo said.

"Well, maybe the next time you see one, you'll let it go. Whenever our cat pounces on a lizard, I push him away."

"Do you have a cat?" Anna asked. "What's his name? I wish I had a cat."

"Gatto," Rosa said. "He's a very pretty cat, black and orange, and you could probably hear his purr a mile away."

"That's a funny name for a cat," Roberto said.

"Oh," Rosa thought, "if only we were home now Gatto could have all the lizards he wanted."

Anna was next, and she sat up straight in her chair. Unlike Lucia, who had dark hair and eyes, Anna had red hair that she wore in long braids, dimples like her brothers and a pudgy, rather awkward figure. Perhaps because her mother was always so busy, Anna lived in her own world. It was a world of princesses and witches, of dragons and enchanted forests. At ten years old, she liked to dress up in her grandmother's clothes and wear long necklaces. Even now she was wearing the long blue gown the women had found in the *armadio*.

"Anna," Maria said, "you have such a beautiful name. Do you know who Saint Anna was?"

"Um, the mother of the Blessed Mother?"

"Yes! You have someone special to pray to. And you know, I have a daughter and she lives in a little village named Sant'Anna that's quite a ways from here. There's a beautiful picture of Saint Anna and the Blessed Mother in the church there. Maybe someday you'll be able to see it. I was there last Easter and they had so many candles burning in front of the picture and…"

"Maria," Rosa said softly, "maybe Anna wants to tell her story."

Breathlessly, Anna proceeded to tell a long and very complicated story about Luciella, a beautiful but poor girl who had two evil sisters and who married a handsome man under a spell and how the sisters grew jealous and went to a witch and how Luciella was left alone with the baby…

"A baby?" Roberto said. "When did the baby happen?"

"Oh, I forgot," Anna said, and continued to complicate the story until the very end. By that time, both boys were restless.

"All right, boys," Rosa said. "It's your turn."

"We'll do it together," Adolfo said.

Anyone could tell that Roberto and Adolfo were brothers. Each had black curly hair, eyes that were almost black and ears that stuck out. Like many boys who are twelve and eight, they did not like going to school, preferring to ride their bicycles or fish in the river.

The boys stood up and Roberto began to tell of two young boys who went on an adventure in the hills.

"Two smart and very handsome boys," Adolfo giggled.

"And then, over the top of the hill, a fierce soldier came looking for them," Roberto said fiercely.

"He was going to cut them into tiny little pieces." Adolfo explained.

"And cook them and have them for dinner," Roberto said as he pounced on top of his little brother and tickled him.

Rosa and Maria thought that this was enough storytelling for one day and decided to make lunch. Leftover polenta, now fried, joined some boiled vegetables from Gavino.

"Is this all there is?" Vito grumbled.

"Be glad you have this." Rosa put the pot down firmly on the table.

Concentrating on their meals, the villagers ate mostly in silence and did not notice when Lucia quietly slipped in the back door. Except for Rosa. She followed Lucia up to her room.

"Lucia! Where have you been?" Rosa whispered.

"Out."

"Out? Out? What do you mean out? You know the rules. Your mother will be very upset."

"Please," Lucia begged. "Please don't tell Mamma. She's got enough to worry about. I had to see someone. It's fine. It's not a problem, believe me."

"Someone? Who is someone?" Rosa demanded.

Lucia was almost in tears. "There are these two boys. They're from Montepulciano. They came here the other night. Now they're staying at Gavino's. Paolo was hurt and I wanted to help them and Dino said…"

"Dino? Dino from Montepulciano? With all the freckles? He's at Gavino's?"

"Well, yes," Lucia stammered. "Do you know him?"

"He just stayed at our house for two days. He left the same day we came up here. So he found his friend?"

"Yes, but Paolo hurt his foot."

Rosa looked Lucia in the eyes. "It's not Paolo you care about, is it?"

"No."

Rosa could not help thinking of another young girl forty years ago and how she used to sneak off to see a boy and ride behind him on his bicycle. So now it was Lucia and Dino. Dino seemed like a nice boy, but they were both so young…

"Lucia," Rosa pleaded, "please be careful. Be careful in everything. You know what I mean."

"Yes, ma'am. You won't tell Mamma?"

"No."

Lucia went upstairs and took out her diary.

"I think I'm in love!!!!! He is so cute. And sweet. I think he loves me too!!!! He hasn't said so yet, but I think he wants to marry me. I would do anything for him, anything."

She drew a heart at the bottom of the page and wrote "Lucia + Dino" inside.

That afternoon, after their rest, the villagers returned listlessly to the main room. Some sat at the table, others looked out the open windows. Sporadic artillery shelling could be heard in the hills. A slight wind had come up from the valley, bringing the sounds from the other side of the hill even closer.

"Dante," Rosa said, "the war has been going on for five years now. Don't people realize that the Germans can't win? How can anyone support the Germans anymore?"

"And with Mussolini out of power," Francesco said, "how can anyone be a Fascist? I just don't understand."

Dante thought about that before answering. "I suppose people don't want to admit they are wrong."

"Or else," Marco said, "they believe so strongly in their cause that they're going to fight to the end."

"And get killed doing it," Rosa said. "And kill everyone else."

Rosa was interrupted by rifle shots, which could have been close or could have been magnified by the hills. Then there were loud, painful screams that sent shivers through the villagers. They stood terrified at the windows or sat stiffly at the table.

"*O Dio!*" Maria said.

"Must be the partisans and the Germans," Marco said. "Listen."

Then there was stillness. They another round of shots. And more screams.

"They're going to kill each other, every one of them," Dante said.

More shots. And then screams that were barely audible.

"*Santa Maria!*" Rosa whispered.

More muffled screams. And then silence.

"It's over," Marco said.

Anna and Adolfo began to cry and Gina folded them in her arms. Roberto put his head in his arms on the table and Lucia absently twirled her long hair.

"Mamma, I'm scared," Anna said. "What are they doing?"

"Hush," Gina said, holding her daughter tight. "We're going to be all right."

She led the children upstairs. The other villagers remained silent, knowing they had just heard men die. Finally, Vito said, "Well, I wonder how many Germans our heroic partisans killed."

"Now Vito," Francesco said, putting his hand on the older man's shoulder.

"What?" Vito said. "Are we supposed to cheer when the partisans kill some Germans? You know damn well what's going to happen now."

"Yes, Vito, we know," Marco said.

"Ten for one, that's the rule," Vito said. "So if the partisans just killed only one German, those soldiers in Sant'Antonio are going to go to Reboli and round up ten innocent people and shoot them."

"*O Dio!*" Maria said.

Everyone thought of the people they knew in Reboli.

"So what do you think we should do, Vito?" Francesco asked. "Let the Germans run all over us? Somebody has to fight back. The Allies aren't here. The partisans are the only ones doing it."

"The partisans have been fighting for liberty for months," Dante said.

"A lot of them are communists!" Vito said.

"So?" Francesco said. "We have to be grateful for a lot of things the communists have done."

"*Boh!*" Vito said. "We should be grateful that they come into our homes and steal our food? We should be grateful that they rape our women? We should be grateful that…"

"Vito, answer this," Rosa interrupted. "Don't you think the Germans killed some partisans, too, just now? What about them? The partisans weren't drafted. They didn't have to fight. They wanted to do this. They sacrificed their lives so that we, all of us, will live. And not all partisans are bad. Most of them are good people, I think. They're just fighting for Italy. What do you say to that?"

Vito stretched his legs and scratched his head.

"*Boh!*" he finally said.

The issue had been discussed many times in Sant'Antonio without resolution. Maria fingered her rosary beads. Renata reached over and held Maddelena's hand. The villagers were lost in their thoughts and few noticed when Fausta slipped quietly out of the room and went upstairs. The others silently followed. Marco and Dante closed all the windows.

That night, to the soft strains of Francesco's violin, Rosa and Marco washed dishes after everyone else had gone to bed.

"This makes it seem like we're back in Sant'Antonio," Marco said.

"No, not quite," Rosa said.

"At least we're together."

"For now," she said. Tears rolled down her cheeks.

"What's going to happen to us, Marco? What's going to happen to us?"

Before Marco could answer, they heard a scratching at the back door.

"O Dio," she said.

The scratching continued. This was not a mouse, Rosa thought. It was too loud. What kind of creature could it be?

While Marco carefully opened the door, Rosa stood beside the table with a broom, ready to attack the intruder.

"Well, look who's here," Marco said.

Shivering on the doorstep, the little creature was covered with dirt, its tail was mangled and it had a huge blister over one eye. You couldn't even tell that it was orange and black. But it was purring loudly.

CHAPTER 12

▼

Since he was now the only resident of Sant'Antonio, and since he certainly didn't want to talk to the Germans, Father Luigi became more and more lonely as the days went by. He took to spending more time in church, sitting in a rear pew, looking at the altar and thinking. He liked to call it meditating, perhaps even praying. There was another reason. If the British started bombing the village, which he expected at any time, they wouldn't hit the church. Or so he thought.

The church was only a little cooler than his house. The late afternoon sun streamed through the window again, just as it had last Monday. Now it was Saturday and almost a week had gone by. He read from his breviary and sat back.

"Thank you for helping me this week, God. I pray there aren't many more like this. What were those Germans doing this afternoon? I couldn't make out what was happening. It seemed like some of them went away and then a couple of hours later they came back. But they were carrying something that looked like a big black bag. *O Dio!*

"I can't worry about the Germans. I have to worry about my people in the hills. Lord, please protect them and help them to get along. I wonder how the leaders I chose are doing. They are all good men. Dante. He's a good soul, and I know the people love him. I just wish he would come to church. How can anyone not believe in God?

"I wonder when I'll be able to say Mass for the people here again. I still say Mass every morning, just by myself, but it isn't the same. I know I shouldn't say this, but I think the Mass should be said with other people. The priests at the seminary would probably disagree. They would say the mystery of the Mass is what is important. Sometimes I don't know if I agree with everything they say at the seminary.

"Today is Saturday. But no confessions today. You know, Lord, I think I miss it."

Father Luigi got up, genuflected, locked the church door and went to his study. He wiped the perspiration from his forehead, unpacked the suitcase in the chest hidden in the closet and connected his radio transmitter.

Even though it was almost dark, the humid heat had settled in the valley and enveloped Sant'Antonio. The first stars shone in the Tuscan sky and soon a half moon appeared over the steeple of the church. At another time, it would have been an idyllic scene. But three Panzers stood near the bridge, ready to be cleaned and repaired. Across one of the larger houses, a banner was now strung: 16th SS Panzergrenadier Division *Reichsfuhrer-SS*.

Sweltering in the back yard of the house they now occupied, Fritz Krieger and Konrad Schultz were absorbed in their thoughts about the day. When the sun finally set, Fritz went into the house, got two beers and handed one to Konrad. Even when they were drinking beer, they sat stiffly in their chairs.

"Shit," Konrad said. "We showed them, didn't we, Fritz? We got them Eyties."

"Our first fight, Konrad. It was good."

The soldiers were silent for a long time.

"Too bad Tommy was killed. He was a good man, Tommy was," Fritz said.

"Yeah, he was."

While patrolling, Fritz, Konrad and ten other soldiers had encountered a group of partisans in the hills. In the exchange of gunfire, their friend Tommy was shot in the chest.

Konrad took off his glasses and wiped them. "How many did we kill, five, six?"

"No more than three, probably two," Fritz said.

"Damn. We should have got more. There must have been twenty communists shooting at us."

"Poor Tommy," Fritz said. "He was always the funny guy in training."

"Don't be sorry for him," Konrad said. "He died giving the best for Volk, Reich and Führer."

"Yeah, but he's still dead."

"He fell for the Fatherland!" Konrad said.

Tommy's body was brought back by the other soldiers. Before he was buried in a field outside of the village, Fritz and Konrad had walked over to look at their friend. It was the first time they had seen a dead soldier.

"I guess I'll never forget what I saw today," Konrad said. "How his eyes bulged out. The blood all over. That hole in his chest."

"I'll never forget what we heard today," Fritz said. "The screams. The cries. But that is why we are here."

Konrad swilled another beer. "Bunch of stinking communists. Have you heard how the others are doing?"

"Franz has a bad shrapnel wound in his right leg, Ludwig was nicked by a bullet in the arm, Rudolf sprained his ankle running and Victor has some sort of neck injury. They'll be all right."

"Shit!" Konrad threw his beer bottle at the shed.

"We'd better get to bed," Fritz said. "The lieutenant says we have to get up early to go to Reboli."

"Where will we find ten Eyties?" Konrad asked. He wiped his glasses.

"Doesn't matter. The first ten we see, I suppose."

"Why don't we start with the priest? He's right up the street."

"No, Konrad. The lieutenant says we have to wait. He's useful to us now."

"Why?"

"He's communicating with the partisans. The command is monitoring it. We're waiting until he gets more information, and then…"

"And then?"

"You know what. For the Führer, Konrad."

"For the Führer!" Konrad said.

Ezio Maffini was exhausted, but he knew that he should make another entry in his journal. He needed to record his feelings at this time. Leaning back against the wall of the cave, he almost fell asleep, but then shook himself awake and found his notebook.

"This is the first time I have been able to write since Monday night. I am so tired and sad. Today we lost two of our best patriots. Owl was only seventeen years old. He was so excited about joining us, he didn't even tell his family where he was going. He couldn't wait to start fighting the Germans and the Fascists. Eagle was in his late thirties, I don't know exactly. He left the army to join us. He knew so much about how the military works and he helped us in so many ways. And he knew these hills better than anyone. I don't know what we will do without them.

"We were overpowered. We had just returned from patrolling the ridge and going to our usual hiding place in the hills. Oriole and Turkey were in the lead and Canary was at the rear. In an instant we were surrounded by maybe a dozen Germans. Owl was the closest to them and fired. He was hit in the chest. Eagle fired next and the Germans got him in the leg. Oriole, Turkey, Canary and I let loose. We got one German and the others ran. They came back to get him. We knew Owl was gone but we tried to save Eagle. He was bleeding so much he didn't last an hour.

"These were our first casualties. They died such horrible deaths. We sat and cried and then we dug their graves and buried them. We put something special with each of them. Owl had a favorite book and Eagle had a medal that he said was his good luck charm. It didn't help this time.

"So now I have only three partisans with me. They are good soldiers and it doesn't matter how many we are, it is how we feel. And this has made us more determined than ever. Oriole and Canary have some minor injuries but we are getting our strength back and we will continue patrolling and sabotaging wherever we can. Now we are doing this for Owl and Eagle. They are our heroes and we will never forget them.

"I hope we can have the support of the people. I know we killed one German so I expect the Germans will go to Reboli and find ten innocent Italians and kill them. That makes me so angry and so sad. The Germans attacked us! What were we supposed to do? We have to fight to save our country!

"I miss my angel so much! I wish I could see her again."

"*Viva l'Italia!*

Ezio was so tired that he fell asleep against the wall with his notebook still on his lap. His rifle was at his side.

CHAPTER 13

▼

Within a few days Gatto had cleaned himself up, regained his weight with the pasta and polenta that Rosa gratefully sneaked to him and was happily doing his work. He proudly guarded his pile of trophies growing neatly next to the shed.

Because mice were also inside, he had free reign of the house, finding Anna's bed a particularly good place for naps in the afternoon sun. He jumped on Rosa's lap every time she sat down.

The mice problem may have been solved, but the people at the Cielo were still finding it awkward, and at times strained, living together. It had been a week since the group arrived at the farmhouse.

Outside, the men found more things to repair but stayed close to the building. Marco noticed that a path was worn from the back door toward Gavino's hut, but assumed it was just Gavino going back and forth.

Inside, the women found more sewing to do, and spent their afternoons sitting around the large table in the main room. They had tired of the one or two dresses they had brought along and were attempting to alter the ones they found in the *armadio* by removing ribbons and lace, shortening skirts and loosening necklines.

"There," Renata said, holding up a flowered summer dress, "this should fit me just fine."

"It would be too short for me," her sister said.

To Anna's delight, Maria cut down a print cotton dress into one that would fit a ten-year-old and used the leftover material for an identical dress for her doll.

Maria was still trying to make friends with the Contessa and tried a little teasing. "I noticed Dante looked very handsome today," Maria said as they cut off the hem of a skirt.

"I think he always looks handsome," the Contessa replied and got up to get a glass of water.

At mid-morning, an explosion from the valley echoed through the hills. Everyone stopped working, and a few silently crossed themselves.

"*O Dio,*" Rosa said.

Before lunch, Rosa took Marco aside and told him how much she missed being alone with him.

"There are always so many people around," she said. "I think what I miss most is not having any privacy."

"I know. I miss it, too."

"Marco, I have an idea."

"Of course you do."

"Since you and Francesco share a room, and since Annabella and I share a room, what if we switched? I don't mean at night, because I know that's dangerous, and the men should be on the ground floor, but in the afternoon, after *il pranzo.* Just for an hour or two. It would make me feel better. Maybe Francesco and Annabella would like it, too."

"I don't know if they would or not. But I can ask."

So Marco proposed the idea to Francesco, who then asked Annabella.

"Do you really want to spend time alone with me?" she asked.

Francesco paused only a moment.

"Of course."

When she went to Marco's room after lunch, Rosa brought a tray of coffee and biscotti. "I wanted to make this special," she said, putting the tray down and holding Marco tight. "It's so good to be with you here."

"I've missed you so much," he said, kissing her.

They sat on the edge of Marco's bed, drank their coffee, ate their biscotti and smiled happily at each other. Then they pushed the two small beds together so they could both lie down. Marco took Rosa in his arms and she stroked his cheek. He had forgotten to bring a razor so now had a week's growth of salt-and-pepper beard.

"I think I like you with a beard," Rosa said.

"I don't. It itches."

"Maybe you'll keep it when we return home."

Artillery shelling could be heard distantly in the hills. They hugged some more.

"When we were playing cards yesterday," Marco said, "I was thinking how good it is for Vito and Giacomo to be with other people at this time. They may joke a lot, but I think they would be very afraid at home alone."

"And Maddelena and Renata. Can you imagine if they were at home and all this was going on? I don't think Vito is teasing Maddelena so much any more."

"Maria actually seems to be enjoying herself. She likes being with people."

"The Contessa says Maria is too nosy," Rosa said. "Can you imagine? Maria is just very interested in other people."

"She must miss her daughter and grandchildren a lot."

"She talks about those boys all the time," Rosa said.

"I feel sorry for Gina," Marco said. "All those kids."

"Isn't Carlotta the cutest baby you ever saw? When I hold her I think, well..."

"What?"

"Oh, you know. It's too bad it was too late for us to have children, Marco."

"You wanted children?"

"I never thought much about it, but holding Carlotta..."

"I'm sorry, Rosa."

"Oh, I'll be all right. Once we're back home."

Marco kissed his wife and held her for a long time. Breaking away, he said, "What do you think Lucia is up to? Sometimes she seems so happy and sometimes she seems so nervous. Is it just because she's sixteen years old? It's a good thing we never had children, Rosa. I wouldn't know what to do."

"Marco, I'm worried about her. And I have to tell you something." Rosa's voice grew softer and she looked warily at the closed door. "Nobody else knows this, and you mustn't tell anyone either. I just found out yesterday. There are two boys staying at Gavino's, and you know what? One of them is Dino."

"The boy who stayed with us?"

"Yes, and Lucia goes to Gavino's and visits him."

Marco sat up and looked down at Rosa. "Impossible! Why is she doing that? Gavino could be arrested if somebody found out. We could all be arrested."

"Shhh. Marco, Lucia really likes the boy. No one is going to find out about this, right?"

"I don't like this, Rosa."

Rosa gripped Marco's hand.

"Please, Marco. I feel so sorry for her and the boy. Imagine falling in love at a time like this."

"Maybe Dante should know."

"Dante doesn't have to know everything. And Gina doesn't either. She's got her other children to worry about. I'm sure Dino will be running away soon and this will all be over. Dino thinks war is an adventure."

"Adventure?" Marco said. "That's crazy. He's going to get killed if he takes chances like that."

"A lot of boys are going to get killed, Marco."

The artillery fire seemed to be coming nearer, rumbling and bouncing across the hills. Marco settled back down and Rosa snuggled in his arms.

"Marco, I'm still so scared."

"It's going to be over soon. It's going to be over soon," Marco insisted. "We have to keep saying that."

"How long do you think?"

"We won't be here two weeks, maybe three," Marco said, and then, reconsidering, "we won't be here a month at the most."

"Do you promise?"

"I promise."

Marco kissed Rosa on the forehead.

"You know we haven't talked about your roommate," he said.

"I know."

"Have you spoken to her since you've been here?"

"One time. She complained about something."

"And you just smiled."

"No, I can't say that I did."

"Rosa, Rosa. Are you ever going to get over this? It's been forty years. It's time to forget what happened. We may all be dead tomorrow."

"So? What difference does that make?"

"It might be good to have some forgiveness."

"I have always said this: I'll forgive if she forgives."

"If you don't talk to her, how will she know that?"

Rosa didn't have an answer.

"All right, Rosa," Marco sighed. "You've never told me what really happened. I know you were angry at Annabella because she married Francesco, but there has to be more than that."

Rosa rose from the bed and went to the window. She unfastened her hair from the back of her head and let it fall down her back. The afternoon sun shimmered through it.

"I can forgive Francesco, because I think Annabella tricked him into marrying her," she said, turning toward Marco. "She said she was pregnant. I don't believe it. She seemed to get pregnant very quickly after she started going with him, didn't she? And a month after the wedding she said she lost the baby! There was no baby, Marco. How could there have been a baby? And Francesco was stuck, and he still is."

"Did you talk to her about this then?"

"We had a big fight. She called me names and I called her names. After that we never spoke again."

"What names did she call you?"

"Many names. The worst was that she said I was an ugly *contadina*."

"What names did you call her?"

"Many names. I called her a *puttana.*"

Marco turned his head so Rosa would not see that he was smiling.

"A whore? That's all there is?" he said. "Honestly, Rosa, it sounds like you were two young girls just having a fight. You're both mature women now. Forget it."

"Marco, she said I was ugly. That's the worst possible thing someone could say about me."

"I wish you would get over this idea that you are not pretty. Doesn't being beautiful come from inside? It's not how we look. It's how we feel."

Rosa turned back to the window. "You are not a woman. You don't understand. If I had been pretty Francesco would have married me."

"You really wanted that, didn't you?"

"Then. Not now."

"I have to ask you this." Marco got up and stood behind her. He put one hand on her shoulder and stroked her hair with the other. "Would you rather be married to him or to me?"

"Oh, Marco." Rosa said, turning to him. "How can you ask that? Of course I would rather be married to you. If you had been there when I was seventeen, I would never have looked at Francesco. And now? I can't even remember what my life was like before I met you and I can't imagine what my life would be like without you."

"If you are that satisfied with your life now, why don't you just apologize to Annabella?"

"I will if she will."

They returned to the bed. The artillery fire was fading now.

"Rosa, this is so insignificant. People don't stay mad at each other for forty years became of some words."

"No? My mother didn't speak to her neighbor for twenty years because she said my mother's soup was bitter."

"So what happened?"

"The neighbor died."

Marco laughed. "My mother did the same thing. Her cousin said my mother was a bad housekeeper. Actually, she was."

"And Signora Vituchi went to her grave still not talking to Signora Pallini..."

"Because she criticized the way Signora Vituchi hung her clothes on the line."

"*O Dio!*" Rosa said. "You are making me laugh so hard I am crying."

The bed springs began to creak.

"Italian women are funny, aren't they?" Rosa said.

"But I wouldn't have them any other way."

"Marco, you don't think I'm ugly, do you?"

"Rosa, Rosa, Rosa. How many times do I have to tell you that you are the most beautiful thing in my life?"

"I love you so much, Marco."

The valley was quiet now. Marco kissed Rosa and gently unbuttoned her blouse.

In the room just above, Francesco stared out the window as the sun glinted through the trees. Occasionally, he could hear the reverberation of artillery fire.

Annabella sat on the bed and examined her nails. Pretty as a girl, Annabella had become a beautiful woman and could now be considered handsome. She wore her hair short and went to Reboli twice a month to have it waved. Her figure had filled out and so she wore dark colors but with bright scarves as accessories. She seldom laughed or even smiled in public.

Finally, Francesco broke the silence.

"How are you feeling now?"

"Worried. Sad. Afraid."

"No better?"

"No."

"We'll be out of here soon. I know we will."

"How do you know that? You don't know everything, Francesco."

"I just know that the war can't last forever. Once the Allies get to Pisa, they'll move to Lucca and it won't be long before they are here."

"If we're not all killed by the Germans first. Or the Fascists. Or the partisans will put us in the middle of everything."

There was a long silence.

"Why did you want to meet here?" Annabella finally said.

Francesco began to pace back and forth next to the window. "It's just that we do not have any privacy. There's no place to talk."

"Talk? What do you want to talk about? We never talk at home."

"I know, but things are different here," Francesco said. "Who knows what's going to happen."

"It doesn't matter. Sometimes I think nothing matters."

Francesco stopped pacing and looked at her. "'Bella, you mustn't talk that way."

"Why not? At this point in our lives what future is there?"

"Please don't say things like that," he said. "We've got years ahead of us."

"And the years ahead will be the same as the years behind. Who cares about that? You've never cared. You come home from work and you play your violin for a while and then after we eat you listen to the radio and get out the wine bottle."

"You could listen to the radio with me."

"The only thing on the radio now is war news."

"At least you could stay in the room with me."

"I'd rather go to my room. I can sew there. I can read."

Francesco waited a long time to respond, then said, "I understand."

The bright sunlight had dimmed and clouds were moving in from the west. Three planes droned overhead and gunfire sounded from the valley, breaking the silence in the room. Finally, Francesco said, "This hasn't been a happy life for you, has it, 'Bella?"

"It is what I might have expected."

"It could have been different," Francesco said.

"If we hadn't started out the way we did."

Again there was a long silence. Annabella studied her nails some more.

"Francesco, I wanted that baby so much. You've never understood that."

"I have tried to understand. Really I have."

"If we had had the baby, things would have been so much different. I would have had someone to love, and someone would have loved me."

"Are you so desperately in need of love?"

"You've never loved me. You have always hated me because I got pregnant and you had to marry me."

"It took two of us to get you pregnant, you know. I share this."

Francesco could barely remember that night. They were walking along the river, he thought, when Annabella snuggled against him. Before he could think they were under a tree in the woods. It was the tree where he and Rosa had made love only the week before.

"You didn't want the baby, did you?" Annabella said.

"I was eighteen," Francesco said. "What did I know about babies? What did I know about being a father?"

"I was seventeen, Francesco. What did I know about being a mother? We could have learned!"

Francesco's eyes filled with tears as he looked out the window. He counted the drumbeats of the artillery. One, two, three...

"We could have tried again," he said, turning to her, "but you didn't want to, ever."

"I just didn't want you to touch me, after...after that girl."

"'Bella, that was forty years ago."

"But there were other girls weren't there? From the trattoria? I don't know how many."

"There weren't many. And there haven't been any for twenty years."

"And so every night there is the wine," she said.

"Yes, and every night there is the wine."

They hadn't talked about this for a long time, but there wasn't anything else to say. Francesco turned back to the window.

"This wasn't your idea to meet this afternoon, was it?" Annabella said.

"No."

"It was Rosa's, wasn't it?"

"She wanted to spend some time with Marco, and this was just a way to do it." Francesco had his back turned to her.

"She can spend all the time she wants with Marco. It doesn't mean that you and I need to be together like this."

Again, there were minutes of silence.

"Have you two spoken at all?" Francesco asked, turning around.

"Once. She was angry at me. I don't know why."

"It's hard to believe you're staying in the same room with her and not speaking."

"We're not like you and Marco, Francesco. You men don't seem to mind when you get hurt."

"'Bella, that was so long ago."

"Not to me it isn't."

"I can't believe you are still bitter after all these years."

"I know she doesn't believe I was pregnant and that I lost the baby. She thinks I tricked you into marriage. Let her believe what she wants to believe."

"It sounds like you're too proud to forgive her."

"Maybe I am."

"What if she were to apologize? Would you forgive her?"

Annabella examined her nails again. "I don't know, Francesco, I just don't know."

Francesco turned back to the window. The gunfire had stopped.

"Shall we meet like this again?" he asked.

"It's up to you."

Late that afternoon, Gavino knocked on the back door and asked to see Dante. After some minutes, Dante came back inside and called the villagers together.

"I have some good news from Gavino," he said. "The British Fifth Army has captured Arezzo."

The villagers applauded.

"That's a big one, isn't it?" Vito said.

"They say the Germans were defending it more stubbornly than any city north of Rome," Dante said. "Some people thought it would be another Monte Casino, but the Germans gave up! And the Allies have also reached Perugia."

"Both Arezzo and Perugia are pretty far south of Florence and there are big mountains in between," Giacomo said.

"I know," Dante said. "It will take many days before they reach Florence. They could come that way, or they could come along the coast, up toward Pisa and Lucca. Either way, it will take a while."

"*O Dio.*" Maria murmured a silent prayer.

"What else did Gavino say?" Vito asked. Dante cleared his throat and waited for the room to quiet.

"As you know, Gavino is well connected in this area," he said. "He says the partisans have seen some escaped British prisoners near here. There may be only one or two, but they have found refuge in many farmhouses and it will be up to us if we want to do the same if they happen to come here. He warns us, though, that the Germans and Fascists are looking for these men and there could be trouble."

"Dante," the Contessa said, putting her hand on his, "what kind of trouble?"

"We would all be punished," he said, declining to give details.

With that grim news, everyone decided to go to bed. Francesco put his hand on Annabella's shoulder and said good night. After Rosa and Marco finished washing the dishes, she kissed and hugged him.

"Thank you for this afternoon," she said.

"Thank you, Rosa."

When she got to her room, Rosa heard Annabella crying softly into her pillow. She hesitated, then said, "Annabella, can I help?"

"Not now."

PART TWO

CHAPTER 14

▼

What Sergeant Colin Richards remembered most about the German prison camp at Laterina was the lice. Sometimes, it seemed like there were hundreds of the tiny insects crawling in his clothing, his scalp, his armpits, his chest hair and into his entire body. Scratching only made the burning worse, and the lice were virtually impossible to get rid of. On sunny days he and the other prisoners would sit outside, take their clothes off and pick the lice from their bodies. Sometimes they lined up four of five of the creatures and had races.

With little else to do, getting rid of lice became a full-time occupation, if not obsession. Each night, Richards' friend Geoff Watson would turn over the planks from under their straw mats and fiendishly squash as many of the little beasts as possible. Many days, he would take the planks, lean them against a wall and jab a burning stick into every hole and crevice he could find. He would accompany this with fierce expletives.

"You haven't talked like that since we were in the pubs in Liverpool," Richards told him.

The lice always came back, but the Italian guards just shrugged. "*Pidocchi?*" they would say. "All the prison camps have lice."

Not that there weren't other things to complain about in Campo Concentramento 82. More than four hundred prisoners from Great Britain, the United States, Canada, India and elsewhere were crowded into the camp southeast of Florence. They were grouped in three-tier bunks, each with three beds. Lice had long populated the straw mats.

Food consisted of a watery soup twice a day, a cup of coffee in the morning and a small loaf of bread several times a week. The prisoners couldn't wait for

Red Cross parcels, although even those had to be shared among five men and came only three times a week. They contained tins of cheese, stewed steak, carrots or tomatoes, biscuits, jam, tea, condensed milk, four ounces of chocolate and twenty cigarettes. A market quickly developed for trading cigarettes for meat.

Subject to dysentery as well as a lack of food, every prisoner at Laterina lost weight, some of them, like Richards, as much as forty pounds.

As members of the British XIII Corps, Richards and Watson had been captured by the German Afrika Korps in June 1942 in the brutal battle at the seaside town of Tobruk in North Africa. They were sent to a camp north of Naples for two weeks, then transferred to Laterina. As 1942 and then 1943 dragged on, friendly Italian guards reported that Mussolini was going to surrender to the Allies.

It was not until September 9, 1943, that a guard raced through the barracks waving the *Corriere della Sera* for the day. It had a four-inch headline, *"Armistizio."* The guards, who didn't like Mussolini to begin with, set the prisoners free and Richards and Watson made plans to join their unit, which must be coming north.

Then radio broadcasts gave other news. Despite Mussolini's fall, the Germans were not retreating and were engaged in heavy fighting to the south. They were also going to reclaim the Laterina prison. Most of the other prisoners chose to flee to the south while they could, but Richards and Watson decided it would be best to go north, traveling as much as possible through the rugged Apennine mountains and avoiding the Germans in the towns and villages.

"We can make it to Switzerland before winter," Watson said.

It didn't take long to pack. Richards had been able to conceal a compass though his captivity, and a knife, though blunt, found its way into Watson's kit.

With a warm sun and a gentle breeze that first day, they accomplished almost twenty miles, mainly through wooded areas, before deciding they should find a place for the night. Smoke from a farmhouse in the valley indicated that it was inhabited. An old man tending his cows saw them coming down the hill.

"We are British prisoners of war," Richards shouted, pointing to his prison clothing. After a moment, the man understood.

"Ah, *benvenuti*," he said. "Come in, come in."

At that moment, the man's wife, dressed all in black, appeared at the door. "You have *pidocchi?*"

"Si," Richards said, hoping the lice wouldn't make a difference.

"I guess we're not going to be welcome here," Watson said.

"Go to the shed," the woman pointed. "I will meet you there."

Inside the nearby lean-to Richards and Watson found that a large tank had been cut in half and turned on its side over a makeshift grate. The man filled the tank almost to the brim with water, put branches under the grate and lit them. Soon the water was boiling.

"That's nice of them," Watson said. "We haven't had a bath since Tobruk."

"They just don't want us to bring lice into the house," Richards whispered.

The woman made it clear that she wanted them to empty their pockets and take their clothes off. It was no time for false modesty. She picked up their clothes with a long stick and threw them into the fire. Then she gave Watson a bar of lye soap.

"Bagno! Bagno!" she said, poking his backside with the stick.

The water was so hot Watson could barely stand, let alone sit in it. But after months of dirt and a day's long walk, he thought it was as close to heaven as he was going to get. By the time he finally climbed out and into a huge scratchy towel that the signora provided, it was Richards' turn. When both had finished, the surface of the water was coated with tiny creatures.

"Let's hope we're finally rid of them," he said.

As they were drying themselves, the signora brought tattered shirts and pants, jackets, long underwear and shoes so worn they creaked when they were put on. Because the old man was considerably shorter than either of them, their arms hung out of the flannel shirts and their legs from the work pants.

"It's what the well-dressed *contadini* are wearing this year," Watson said when they had finished dressing.

"That's exactly what we want to look like, peasants."

"Wait," the old woman said. She found two floppy hats, one green, one blue. "You will need these."

The hats weren't only for warmth. Their heads, shaved in prison because of the lice, would be giveaways if they were seen by the Germans.

"Come," the old woman said. *"Mangiate!"*

The signora insisted they sit at the table and the old man brought out a dusty bottle of wine. Despite the language problems, everyone was soon enjoying the vegetable soup and bread, and the old man became more voluble with each glass of wine.

Richards and Watson were not the first prisoners to stop at the farm, and the couple had apparently learned from previous experiences not to let lice into the house. More important, they knew of other farmers who were willing to take in escaped prisoners.

"Tomorrow, *ingelsi,* I will show you the way," the man promised after Richards said they wanted to go north. "Tonight you stay in our barn because we have no room in our house. The hay is soft and there are no lice."

He led Richards and Watson to the barn on the other side of the field, and the two were soon settled.

"Do you believe him?" Watson asked. "What if this is a trap?"

"Why would they set us up? The Italians hate the Germans. The Nazis have taken over their country, they've killed innocent people, forced the men to join their army, pillaged their land and raped the women. Why wouldn't the Italians hate the Germans?"

"But this guy is risking his life."

"And I hear there are others willing to do the same."

"I guess I just don't understand the Italians. Would we be doing this in England?"

"Let's hope we would. Go to sleep."

Watson dug out his knife and kept it by his side through the night.

In the morning, after bread and hot milk, the farmer led Richards and Watson back to the top of the hill and pointed north. He told them to follow a narrow path through the forest, turn left when they reached a meadow, then up another hill. At the side they would find another small farm. They should tell the man that Pino sent them.

Richards and Watson tried to thank the farmer, but he disappeared down the hill. The weather was still fine, the directions good and by late afternoon the former prisoners found the farm.

"Pino sent you? Come in," the man said. "I am Tullio."

Tullio had a bigger farm and was well-connected to the partisans and farmers friendly to the Allies. He also had a wireless, and after a meal of soup and polenta and even some *grappa,* he invited Richards and Watson to listen. The news from the south was not good. Allied forces had landed at Salerno a few days ago but now the Germans were mounting a major counterattack. And although Allied forces occupied Rome, German paratroopers rescued Mussolini and flew him to Germany where he formed a token new government. Germans still occupied all of northern Italy.

"Maybe we shouldn't have come north," Watson said.

"It's too late to change our minds now," Richards said. "Anyway, it's a bloody war zone all over in the south."

After they spent a night on a haystack in the barn, Tullio led them to the base of a hill.

"You're going to have to cross the Arno eventually, but I think you should wait until you are west of Florence," he said. "People there will have better information. Be careful. There are Germans in the towns all over this area now, so stay in the mountains. I hope you can get north before winter sets in. The mountains will be even more dangerous then. For now, follow this little stream until you get to a road. Turn north on the road until you see a small shrine at the side. Turn west about a half mile. You'll see another farm. Tell him Tullio sent you. Here, you'll need this."

Tullio handed Watson something more valuable than food. It was a detailed map of Tuscany, even showing side roads and tiny villages. With Richards' compass, they should have no trouble finding their way.

In the next weeks, the routine was the same. They would get up at sunrise, walk until late afternoon, find the farmhouse to which they had been directed, get a good meal, drink some wine, sleep in the barn and, sometimes with new clothes, move on the next morning. More and more, the farmers told them that Germans were close by. Occasionally, they would hear a radio broadcast, and the news remained the same: The Germans were putting up a fierce defense, and the Allied troops were moving north very slowly.

At the end of October, Richards and Watson found themselves south of the Arno east of Empoli. Their last host had provided a guide to take them across the river but warned that there might well be Germans on the other side. They were each given knives, but no other weapons were available.

At 1 a.m., with only a sliver of a moon, they boarded the tiny boat and eased into the river.

"Stay low," their guide said.

"Don't worry, we're not going to move," Watson said as he stretched out his lanky body on the bottom of the boat. Richards crouched at his side.

Two-thirds of the way across, they heard a rustle from the other side.

"Shit!" Watson whispered.

They could see dark figures in the moonlight.

"Anschlag orer ich schieflen! Anschlag orer ich schieflen!"

"Shit! Shit! Shit!"

Before they had a chance to dive into the water, Watson was hit.

"Shit! They got my leg," Watson whispered.

When the guide was hit, the force of the bullet sent him overboard and the little boat capsized. Watson rose to the surface with Richards a few feet away.

"Grab my leg," Richards yelled, but the current drew Watson downstream. "Grab it, dammit!"

Two more bullets narrowly missed Richards' head. Watson floated farther away.

"I can't. Save yourself. See you in Liverpool."

And that was the last Richards saw of Watson. He managed to swim to underwater brush near the shore and for more than three hours he huddled in the water with his head barely above the surface. He could hear the Germans not more than a hundred yards away, swearing and calling out to each other. Finally, at daybreak, there was silence.

Soaked, cold and aching all over, Richards pulled himself to the muddy river bank. He and Watson had been traveling for two months and were still in Tuscany, nowhere near Switzerland. Now Watson was gone, probably dead. And he thought of another thing. Watson had the map. He didn't know where the hell he was.

"Just want to die…just want to die…"

Richards didn't know how long he was unconscious. He dreamed he was back in Liverpool, in bed with his girlfriend Gladys. It was warm and cozy in the little flat, hot tea on the stove, biscuits on the table. When he awoke, there was no Gladys or tea or biscuits. He was the most desolate terrain he had seen so far.

Trees were scarred with bullet holes and there was evidence of fires all over the landscape. Instead of robust farms, the fields were barren, as if they had been pillaged and deserted.

In the distance, Richards finally saw a farmer trying to dig into the thick earth. When Richards was about forty feet away, the farmer pointed his shovel at him.

"Stay back. Who are you?"

"British prisoner. Need help."

"Go away!"

"Please?"

"Go away! No stay here! *Paura!*"

"What are you afraid of?"

"Everything. The Germans, the Fascists. Partisans. Informers. Everyone."

Richards suddenly realized that he was now in a different part of the country. The Germans and Fascists must be more evident here, and the farmers more afraid to take chances. No more welcomes of hot baths and warm soup and hayloft beds. Instead, fear and horror. What Richards did not know was that the week before, Nazis had raided a farm on the other side of the valley and discovered a British prisoner hiding there. They killed not only the soldier, but also the farmer, his wife and young daughter. Then they set the house on fire.

Richards turned and headed toward a hill, thinking there might be fewer dangers in the hillsides. He was right. He didn't encounter Germans or Fascists high in the hills, but neither did he find farms, even unfriendly ones. The higher he climbed, the more wooded the hills became and the slower he traveled. Desperately needing food, he took a chance on some berries and found them edible, and then entered what looked like an old corn field. A few stalks still had ears on them and Richards almost broke his teeth eating them. He made a sack out of his extra shirt and put some stalks inside.

During the days, he continued to walk, but despite his compass was not sure where he was. He missed Watson so much that tears often streamed down his sunburned cheeks as he walked. Each night, he found some sort of shelter and attempted to sleep, knife at his side. Worse, he had developed a hacking cough that kept him awake much of the night.

Each day was colder than the one before and the nights became frigid. The blue jacket he had been given at the first farm was now threadbare. One morning he awoke to a strange stillness. When he opened his eyes he thought he must have climbed so high he was in the clouds. Everything was white. The first snow had fallen and winter had arrived.

"Shit!" he said, now suddenly even colder. "Maybe I should just roll over and let the snow bury me."

But then he heard an unfamiliar sound. Somewhere, perhaps closer to the top of the hill, a bell was ringing. It sounded like a church bell. Richards scrambled to his feet and followed the sounds of the bell. At the top of the ridge he could see a building with a cross on the top. Getting closer, he saw a majestic church at the end of a long building with gothic arches. More than four hundred years old, the monastery once housed thirty Benedictine monks known for the wine they made from nearby vineyards. Now, only four monks, all of them elderly, remained.

"Welcome, welcome," the Father Superior said as he opened the door to the bedraggled visitor. After a meal of soup, bread and vegetables, the monks assigned Richards a room, which they called a cell, near the chapel, and said it would be impossible for him to travel in the hills during the winter. Germans had come three times last summer, they said, and took away some of their wine, but they did not expect them to return in the winter. Just in case, they showed him a space down some stone steps and under the altar where he could hide if they did. It was a crypt for members of the order, and there was still room for three more.

"I will be the next," the Father Superior said, rather proudly. "And it will be soon."

When Brother Matteo lifted the heavy stone lid off one of the tombs, Richards stepped back in horror.

"Don't worry," the monk said. "Look inside."

Packed in wooden crates, dozens of bottles of wine filled the space intended for a deceased clergy.

The monks also had a good supply of food for the winter, and there were even a few English books that he could read. Richards had never been a religious man, but as the months went by he came to enjoy lying on his cot in his little cell and listening to the monks chant their morning and evening prayers. Every time he thought the weather had cleared up enough for him to leave, his cough got worse or another storm piled snow to the windows and he went back to reading *Gulliver's Travels* once again.

On December 8, the monks brought out the *presepio* set with its tiny figures of the nativity scene and spread them at the side of the altar. On Christmas, they celebrated with pasta, vegetable soup, ham, fresh bread and a delicate wine. The monks told stories of the time when people would come from all over to buy wine, before Mussolini, before the Germans. They even sang Christmas carols.

"Will we ever have those times again?" the Father Superior wondered. Everyone at the table drank another glass of wine. Richards would remember the day for the rest of his life.

When the snow finally began to disappear in the spring, he knew it would soon be time to move on. On a Monday morning he made up his mind to leave. He had put on the green coat and black pants the monks had found and had packed up his knapsack when Brother Matteo rushed in.

"The Germans! Hide!"

Richards smoothed out the bed and ran to the stairs. In the darkness, he fell headlong to the ground, ramming his shoulder against the casket where the wine was stored. He wanted to scream in pain but knew he could not. Instead, he mouthed words that had not been heard in the monastery since Brother Gregorio cut his hand sharpening a knife. It seemed like hours before Brother Matteo rescued him.

And that began another six weeks at the monastery. The monks insisted that he could not leave until his fractured shoulder was healed, and that required bed rest. The Germans made three more visits during that time, raiding the vegetable bins, but Brother Matteo made sure to escort Richards to the crypt each time.

It was June by the time Richards hugged the monks, received the Father Superior's blessing and followed their directions to a farm on the other side of the hill.

The farmers here were friendlier again, and for two months Richards again found hot soup, beds in the straw and, always, directions to the next farm.

"Go north to the next meadow and turn left. His name is Emilio."

"Go east to the fork of the road and to the other side of the hill. His name is Renzo."

"Go up the hill to the highest peak. His name is Gavino."

CHAPTER 15

▼

Gavino was up early as usual, even before his rooster. To his distress, he found that Pina, his pig, had escaped from its pen and was wandering in the old olive grove. The place was now thick with brush, and Gavino was not pleased to be chasing a pig through the sticks and the mud.

"Come here, you dirty bastard! Come here, or I'll have you for supper."

Weighing more than two hundred pounds, Pina could not outrun even the elderly Gavino. A walking stick was soon slapping its rear end and guiding it back to the pen.

Inside the hut, Gavino lit a fire in the old stove that dominated the back wall, went to the stream just outside and brought back a pail of water for his morning eggs. The hut was built into the hillside, with the stove pipe extending into the trees just above. Although he lived alone, Gavino kept the place neat and clean. He swept the dirt floor twice a day. He made his bed every morning. He dusted the table next to the chair where he read from the Bible that his father had given him. He couldn't understand much of it, but he liked some of the stories in the Old Testament.

People thought that Gavino was his given name, but in truth his real name was Giuseppe Gavino, having been honored with the name of Italy's great liberator, Giuseppe Garibaldi. Gavino was born a month after Italy was unified in March 1861, and his father loved to tell him stories of Garibaldi's victories. The family eked out a living farming on the hillside. When Gavino's parents died, his brothers and sister found homes in the valley, and Gavino was the only one of his family left. He moved to the little hut at the end of the property.

In the last year, Gavino had become more and more involved with the partisans, escaped prisoners of war and refugees from the army. He provided some food from his garden and sometimes shelter in the cave that was hidden just beyond his hut. They provided him with information that he passed on to others. He knew this was dangerous, but so far the Germans hadn't found out. When he had second thoughts, he remembered what Garibaldi had done for Italy.

The water boiled quickly and the eggs were soon ready. With prosciutto and some bread, breakfast would be sufficient until his evening meal.

Gavino was washing his plate and frying pan when he heard a knock on the door. He looked out through a crack in the wall and then untied the rope that kept the door closed.

"*Buongiorno!*" Dino called.

"Ah, *buongiorno,* Dino. Did you sleep well?"

"Until the rooster woke me up again. This place is so nice I think we'll just stay here the rest of our lives."

"I'm happy you're back, and you can stay as long as you want, but you know you should leave soon. Somebody is going to find you."

Dino rubbed his eyes and yawned. "But it is so comfortable here!"

"Of course, with that little girl coming to visit you. What more do you want?"

"That's all I want, really."

"Be careful, Dino. I see you going into the woods. Just be careful."

"Gavino, I have been with other girls. I am always careful."

Gavino shook his head. "How is Paolo?"

"He's getting better. He should get out more and use that foot."

"Of course, and as soon as he is better, then you can leave."

"Of course."

"But you are not encouraging him to walk more?"

"No."

"It seems like you want to stay here for a while."

"What do you think?"

Dino smiled and went back to the cave.

It was not five minutes later when there was another knock on the door, but this one was so soft Gavino hardly heard it.

"What does he want now?" he thought as he again untied the rope.

Before him stood the most pathetic figure he had ever seen. The man wore a jacket that was ripped at the seams and covered with so much mud that it was hard to tell it was dark green. His left pants leg was torn and his right one only went to below his knee. His boots had no laces and the soles were falling off. A grimy green hat covered matted hair and he carried a knapsack made out of an old shirt. His face was ruddy and blistered. He looked so tired that Gavino thought he might be sleeping standing up.

"Please," the man said. "British…escaped…prisoner…Renzo said I should come."

"Renzo said! Come in!"

The man collapsed into the chair and began to tell Gavino his story. He thought if he was able to keep one eye open he would not fall asleep, but he began to cough so badly his body shook. Soon his chin was on his chest.

"You need to rest," Gavino said. "Lie down here. We will talk later."

Gavino led the man to the bed and helped him take off his hat, jacket and shoes. He covered him with a light blanket and went into his garden.

Allied bombers thundered overhead and he could hear artillery in distant hills. "What am I going to do?" he thought. "An escaped prisoner? It's not enough that I have two boys running away from the army and now this? He can't stay here. I don't have a place for him. Dino and Paolo don't show any signs of leaving."

It did not occur to Gavino that he might tell the man to go away.

It did occur to him, however, that there might be another place for the man to stay. Gavino rushed to the Cielo. Fortunately, Dante was in the kitchen alone and Gavino told him about his visitor. Dante said that he could not make a decision for the farmhouse, but told Gavino to come back later with more information about his visitor.

When Gavino returned to his hut, the man was still sleeping. From what Gavino could guess, he was in his late twenties. Without his jacket, he looked thin, and his belt was loose. Gavino let him sleep but relit the fire, got another pot of water to boil and added pasta, beans, carrots, chickpeas, onions and tomatoes along with sage, bay leaf and olive oil. He found a white cloth in a drawer and spread it on the table, took some bread from the bin near the fireplace and dusted off the small bottle of *grappa* that he had saved for an occasion just like this. The soldier must be starving. He was going to have a feast.

The man, however, did not stir until the middle of the afternoon. When he finally awoke, Gavino supplied a basin of cold water and let him clean up before sitting down to eat.

"Just go slow," Gavino said.

"You don't know how grateful I am," the man said.

"I just do what we need to do."

The man had another coughing spell and gripped the table.

"Go slow," Gavino said, putting the coverlet around the man's shoulders.

"My name is Colin Richards." Every word seemed to be an effort. "I am a member of the British XIII Corps, and I was captured in North Africa in June of 1942."

After almost ten months of traveling, Richards had a working knowledge of Italian. He went on to tell Gavino about the prison camp at Laterina, how he and his friend traveled for two months but that his friend had been killed, how he spent the winter in a monastery, how he broke his shoulder and how more farmers had given him refuge in the last months.

The last leg, he said, was very difficult.

"When did you leave Renzo's?" Gavino wondered.

"Six days ago. Renzo's cousin took me across the river. Then I saw German soldiers patrolling all over. I thought I should change direction and travel at night so I wouldn't be seen. But blimey, I became horribly lost. I think I was traveling back and forth over the same territory. One time I fell down a big hill in the mud. That explains these filthy clothes. I only found the way again yesterday when I met four blokes. I guess they were partisans. They knew who you were and pointed me here."

"So how long has it been since you ate?"

"Five days."

"*O Dio!* Have some more soup. *Mangia, mangia!*"

Richards devoured his third bowl of soup.

"*Allora.* I would very much like you to stay here," Gavino said, "but I am afraid it is impossible. You see that I have no room here in this hut, and the only other space I have is a cave out in the back but there are already two boys staying there."

Gavino thought it best not to give too many details about Dino and Paolo.

"I'm sorry," Richards said. "You have already been very kind. This soup is the best thing I have eaten for weeks. I'm sure I will be fine again soon. I should go."

Richards got up from the table and, suddenly light headed, he coughed so badly that he had to grab the back of the chair to keep from falling. Gavino caught him.

"You're not going anywhere yet. There is a farmhouse across the field. I have already told them about you but they would like more information. You stay here and I will talk to them again."

Richards lay down on the bed and was soon fast asleep.

Since it was late afternoon, almost everyone had gathered in the main room at the Cielo when Gavino arrived. Only Lucia was absent, lying on her bed and writing in her diary. Rosa held Marco's hand and noticed that Annabella and Francesco were not sitting together.

"Gavino has some news," Dante said, and the room quieted down. Gavino settled on a chair at the table and described the visitor who was sleeping in his hut. He told of Richards' travels since his escape from the prison camp and the way farmers had provided refuge. He said Richards was clearly not able to travel far now and needed a place to stay for a week, maybe longer. Then he would continue on his way to Switzerland.

"Does he really think he would get that far, with all the Germans in between?" Vito asked.

"He won't know until he tries," Gavino said.

"Why is he traveling alone?" Giacomo asked. "There were others who walked out of prison when he did."

"He was with another soldier for a while and when they tried to cross the Arno the Germans shot the other man. He doesn't know what happened to him but thinks he was killed."

"*Bastardi!*" Vito and Giacomo said together.

"Does he speak Italian?"

"Yes."

There were questions about the man's health, his safety, his credibility.

"Are we agreed then?" Dante said. "He can find shelter here?"

"Wait," the Contessa said. "Where will he stay? All the rooms are filled."

"That's right."

"There's no room with us."

"Could he sleep on the floor here?"

"No, he shouldn't be out in the open."

Rosa looked at Marco.

"Come," she said to the others. "Let me show you something."

She and Marco led the group to the shelves in the kitchen. Rosa took the plates and dishes and bowls off one set of shelves and put them on the sink, the counter and the other shelves. Marco then pulled the shelves away from the wall.

"*Mamma mia!*" Maddelena said.

The little room was dark in the afternoon light. One after another, the villagers went inside to inspect it.

"I suppose it would be all right to sleep in, but I wouldn't want to stay there all the time," Renata said.

"It took you about five minutes to clear the space to open it," Vito said. "Would that be enough time if we suddenly had to hide him?"

"I don't know," Marco said. "But it's the best we can do."

"And look what's here," Rosa said, pointing to the floor. Marco lifted the cover and the villagers clapped their hands when they saw the cache of wine.

"So that's where you found those bottles!" Vito said, clasping Marco's arm.

The group returned to the main room.

"So we are agreed?" Dante said.

"Wait," Fausta said, and everyone turned toward her.

Fausta stood up and put her hands on the table. She looked at everyone in the room before beginning.

"I want to point out several things. First, I have heard that the Fascists will pay eighteen hundred *lire* for every escaped prisoner of war. Even if we have to divide that among all of us, it would still be money we could all use. Second, we are already crowded here. We are going to run out of food soon. Do we want to have another person—a stranger!—with us? Finally, and most important, the Germans have said that anyone who helps an escaped prisoner will be sentenced to death. Are we willing to risk that? Who is to say that his life is worth more than all of ours? And what do we owe the Allies anyway? They have been bombing every town around here."

Fausta sat down. There was a long silence, and then the room erupted.

"The Fascists would put a price on someone's head?" Vito asked.

"Who would even consider that?" Giacomo said. The cousins raised their fists. *"Bastardi!"* they said together.

"They are getting worse and worse," Maria said, fingering her rosary beads. *"O Dio!"*

"Other farmers take in prisoners!" Francesco said. "We have to support the people who are fighting for us."

"Assassini!" Vito and Giacomo said.

Their shouts frightened Roberto, Anna and Adolfo so much that they clung to their mother, who was nursing Carlotta.

"We can make room. We have enough, isn't that right, Marco?" Rosa said.

"Of course we can make room," Marco said. "If we don't take him in, who will?"

"Bastardi!" Vito and Giacomo said again, raising their fists again.

"They would never shoot all of us just for one man, would they?" Maddelena asked.

"No?" Fausta said. "They have. They shoot ten Italians every time a German is killed."

When the room quieted down, Rosa asked, "Fausta, why is it that you know all these things?"

Fausta smoothed her skirt and folded her hands in her lap. "I just know."

"You just know?"

"Yes."

No one in the room knew much about Fausta Sanfilippo. In fact, no one in Sant'Antonio knew much about her. She lived alone in the tiny house where she was born and where her parents had died years ago. She had no brothers or sisters that anyone knew of. She worked in the thread factory in Reboli and except for going to church and occasionally to Leoni's, she did not go out. She could sometimes be seen taking care of a small garden.

"It sounds like you have good sources," Vito said. "Perhaps we should know more about this."

Fausta refused to say anything else.

"Please let me say something," Dante said. He stood before the fireplace. "You know that I am not a religious man. I don't go to church. Some people might say that I am an agnostic."

"No, don't say that," Maria said. "Everyone believes in God."

"I didn't say I don't believe in a God. I do believe in a higher power, whether the name is God or something else. But what I want to say is that I have always remembered something from the Bible that I was taught as a child. Do unto others as you would have them do unto you. Let us think about that. How are we and Colin Richards any different? We are here together with a roof over our heads, food on the table and the comfort of each other. Yes, that could change any day now. For Colin Richards, that day has already come. He is totally alone, with no one to take care of him, with only the clothes on his back and with only the small hope of a future that could very well be denied him if he is caught by the Germans. Can we turn this man away? How will we feel if we do? I know what I believe we should do, but you must make up your own minds. I leave it to you."

There was a long silence.

"Perhaps we should put it to a vote," Vito said. "Then everyone would know how we feel."

"Is that really necessary?" the Contessa said.

"Yes, I think we should do that," Rosa said.

"Does everyone agree to a vote?" Dante asked.

There was a murmur of assent.

"All right. Let's go around the room. Who wants to allow Colin Richards to stay? Maria?"

"Yes, of course. And thank you for the beautiful speech."

"Thank you. Rosa?"

"Yes."

"Marco?"

"Yes."

"Maddelena?"

"Yes."

"Renata?"

"Yes."

"Annabella?"

"Yes."

"Gina?"

Roberto and Adolfo grabbed their mother. "Say yes, Mamma, say yes!"

Gina looked up from Carlotta. "Yes, of course."

"Fausta?"

"No."

Everyone looked at her.

"Vito?"

"Yes."

"Giacomo?"

"Yes."

"Contessa?"

"No. I'm afraid. Don't you realize what could happen to us?"

"Francesco?"

"Yes."

"And me. Yes. The majority agree. Gavino, bring Colin Richards over."

As they rose from the table, most of the villagers seemed relieved. Fausta looked around the room defiantly and strode up the stairs. Dabbing her eyes with her handkerchief, the Contessa soon followed.

"*Allora,*" Maria said. "We have to get the little room ready."

She took a broom and swept the floor while Maddelena and Renata dusted down the walls. A straw mat and extra blankets made an improvised bed over the trap door in the floor. A towel became a curtain over the little window. An empty wooden box was turned into a table and Rosa found a scarf to put over it. Annabella placed a vase of fresh poppies on top.

"That's pretty," Rosa said. Annabella smiled.

"One more thing," Maria said. She went to an old cupboard, found a *vaso da notte* and put the pot near his cot. "Now he has everything."

Pleased with themselves, the villagers waited for their new guest to arrive.

CHAPTER 16

▼

At first, Colin Richards stayed in his little room, exhausted, dehydrated and weakened by his racking cough. Rosa and Maria took turns bringing him hot soup and bread, and Marco revealed the contents of the bin underneath his cot.

"Help yourself to the wine," Marco said. "It will make you feel better. Better yet, try some *grappa.*"

Whether it was the hot soup or the wine or the *grappa,* Richards slowly began to regain his strength and spent more time in the main room. He told stories of growing up in the slums of Liverpool, getting into fights on the streets and joining the army with his chum Geoff Watson to escape his life at home. He delighted Roberto and Adolfo when he switched from Italian and used words like "bloke" and "chap."

Given new clothes by the men, he wanted desperately to continue his journey, but knew he had to wait until he was ready and when he considered it was safe. Whenever he thought he should leave, a bout of coughing brought worried looks from Rosa and Maria and he went back to bed.

As much as they welcomed Richards into the life of the farmhouse, his presence also made clear to the villagers how close the war had become. The drone of British bombers was increasing daily and the sounds of artillery fights between the Germans and the partisans seemed to be coming closer over the hills. They realized that the Germans might invade the farmhouse at any time if they knew Richards was there. And since partisans had directed Richards to the Cielo, they must be active in the vicinity.

The villagers' food supplies were also running low. Almost half of the chestnut flour and much of the pasta had been used. Rosa and Maria learned to stretch the flour when they made polenta, which was almost every day. Fortunately, Gavino brought vegetables from his garden almost daily and sometimes a rabbit or two.

As the days passed, the enforced isolation began to wear even more on the villagers. They didn't know what was going on outside and they worried about what was happening to their homes in Sant'Antonio. Unable to go far from the Cielo, they became more nervous and the bickering increased. Vito and Giacomo swore at each other with more frequency, Maddelena and Renata found more little things to argue about and the Contessa now refused to talk to Maria altogether.

Sometimes the farmhouse was in complete silence. No one talked. The men played cards but didn't say anything. The women went up and down the stairs without looking at one another. Even the children were quiet.

Although Rosa and Annabella seemed to be getting along a little better, their conversations generally consisted of *buongiorno* and *buonanotte*. When Marco asked Rosa if she and Annabella were talking, Rosa replied, truthfully, "Of course."

Only little Carlotta's giggles and coos brought smiles to the villagers' faces. Anna had the best techniques to make her little sister laugh, playing peek-a-boo behind a blanket and surprising her from behind. The women just sat and laughed when the two of them performed.

Dante knew that he should do something about the growing restlessness and irritation and he struggled to come up with a solution. Then he remembered his days in the classroom and how unruly his students became when they were not doing something. He had always kept a strict schedule for his classes so there was no time for laziness or disruptions. The same wouldn't be true for adults, of course, but he wondered if some sort of daily schedule might help ease tensions here.

"Could we discuss something, please?" he asked one night as the villagers sat sullenly in the main room. As usual, the Contessa sat close to him.

"We all know that we are getting restless because there is no sign when we will be leaving here. We are all worried about when the war will really come close to us. But we are still the people we were in Sant'Antonio. We need to continue living our lives here. We have to try to get through each day as best we can, and we all need to cooperate."

"I'm cooperating," the Contessa said, adjusting the half dozen bracelets on her arms. "I just want to be left alone."

Other villagers were also defensive and Dante tried to calm them.

"Look at it this way," he said. "There may come a time, and it might be soon, when we will all have to act together. I don't know what the reason might be. It might be a danger of some kind. We know the Germans are around, and they could very well visit us. We know the partisans are near. And now we know there are escaped prisoners in the hills."

"Colin is such a wonderful boy," Maria said, smiling at him. Richards was sitting in a corner, a light blanket on his knees even though it was very warm in the Cielo.

"We, most of us, met that situation well," Dante continued, "but we will likely face other situations, and we need to, how should I say this, be friendlier."

"We weren't all friends in Sant'Antonio," Annabella said.

"Some of us barely knew one another," Renata said.

"Well, that was then," Dante said, trying to stay calm. "This has changed everything."

"Please," Rosa said. "Let Dante talk."

"So, Dante, what are you getting at?" Vito asked.

"I think if we did some things together, we might get to know one another better."

"What kind of things?"

"I'm thinking of perhaps having a sort of daily schedule so that we don't get at loose ends."

"*Boh!* Sounds like the army," Vito said.

"Just listen to what he has to say," Giacomo told him, putting his hand on his cousin's arm.

"It won't be like that," Dante said. "Just a loose plan so that we can look forward to doing things together at certain times of the day. At other times, we would be free to do what we want. And if you don't want to participate, you don't have to."

"I like that idea," Rosa said. "I'm getting tired of looking at those same magazines over and over."

"And I'm getting tired of losing at *briscola,*" Giacomo said.

"What are you thinking of, Dante?" Rosa asked.

"For one thing," Dante said, "I wonder if Maddelena and Renata would like to teach some sewing classes for the other women. We know you're the best seamstresses in the village."

Maddelena and Renata blushed, although they knew this was true.

"Oh, I don't know," Maddelena said. "Rosa sews so well, Annabella sews so well…"

"Not like you do," Rosa and Annabella said together, then quickly looked away.

Dante called to Richards in the corner. "For another thing, maybe Colin could help us?"

"Well, of course," Richards said. "What would you want me to do? Blimey, it's the least I can do after all you've done for me."

"Well," Dante said, "you obviously know English and Italian. What if you gave us short lessons in English? After the war we're going to need it."

Dante could have taught the lessons himself, but he knew that Richards would get more attention.

"You mean it?" Richards said. "That would be fun."

"And something else," Dante said. "You've traveled through Tuscany and you've seen a lot. What if we set aside a time every day and you could tell us about your travels and the people you met and what you saw?"

"Blimey! That would be even more fun."

"Can you tell us about being locked up with the dead people?" Roberto asked. Richards smiled.

"One more thing," Dante said. "You said the other day you were an expert at poker and some other card games. Could you teach us?"

"Don't know if I'm an expert, but you learn some things when you sit around in pubs."

"I'd like to learn poker," Vito said. "Maybe then I could catch Giacomo cheating."

"And if you want," Dante told the group, "I could offer something, too. You know how much I love *The Divine Comedy*. It would please me to take you through some parts of it. It won't be difficult, I assure you, and I think you would enjoy it."

"I would love that," the Contessa said.

Rosa raised her hand. "I have another suggestion. Francesco won't admit this, but he plays the violin beautifully. Why doesn't he play for us at the end of each day? I think that would help put us all in a better frame of mind."

"How about it, Francesco?" Dante said.

Francesco looked flustered. "I only know a few pieces. You're going to get tired of them very quickly."

"We'll take the chance," Dante said.

Rosa tried to understand the look on Annabella's face. Part of it was embarrassment, she thought, but part of it also was pride.

"All right, it's settled then," Dante said. "I'll set up a schedule and post it on the wall here."

An hour or so later, the schedule was up.

9 a.m.: Card Games. Colin
      Sewing: Maddelena and Renata

10 a.m.: English lesson: Colin

3 p.m.: *Divine Comedy:* Dante

4 p.m.: Travels: Colin

5 p.m.: Music: Francesco

The next day, whenever planes were heard overhead or when artillery sounded in the distance, the villagers looked up briefly, but then went back to what they were doing. They seemed to like having a schedule of things to do.

Poker turned out to be not too much different from *briscola,* but the players couldn't use their old signals and Vito and Giacomo actually won some games. Roberto and Adolfo became the youngest members of the card-playing group.

Maddelena and Renata remembered some old sewing tricks and soon the dresses from the *armadio* were repaired once again. Rosa even convinced Lucia and Anna to join the group. For one thing, she wanted to keep an eye on Lucia. Gina mostly cradled Carlotta. The baby awakened with a fever and for the first time was a little irritable.

"Remember when we took sewing lessons from Maddelena and Renata when we were girls?" Annabella asked Rosa as they took an evening gown apart. "We learned so much."

"Yes," Annabella said. "Those were happy days."

Rosa and Annabella looked at each other and realized they were almost having a conversation. Rosa looked down to concentrate on cutting a seam and Annabella got up to find another pair of scissors.

Richards' instructions in English turned out to be amusing for all of the villagers. He said he would not go into grammar but simply give them some expressions they should know.

"The English word for '*Sì*' is 'Yes.' Please repeat after me. 'Yes.'"

"Yes!"

"For '*No*' it is "No." That is simple."

"I can remember that," Vito said.

"For '*Per favore*' it is 'Please.'"

"Please!"

"You learn fast," Richards said. "For *'Grazie'* it is 'Thank you.'"

"Thankyou!"

"No. Two words. 'Thank you.'"

"Thank! You!"

"What is the word for *grande?*" Rosa asked.

"Big. Everyone say it."

"Big!"

"And for *piccolo?*"

"Small."

"Small!"

"What about for *uomo?*" Roberto asked.

Richards thought for a moment. "Bloke!" he shouted.

They continued through greetings to be used in the mornings and evenings, the words for various foods and other basics. Richards kept the first lesson short.

"You might want to say some words in English in your conversation," he said. "That will help you to remember them."

As they were breaking up, more artillery could be heard but the villagers pretended they hadn't heard.

"How do you say *bastardi* in English?" Vito asked.

"Bastards."

"I can remember that. Bastards! Bastards!"

Dante began his discussion of *The Divine Comedy* by telling the story of Dante Alighieri's love for Beatrice, his muse and inspiration.

"The poet met Beatrice only a few times but he was hopelessly in love with her all his life," Dante said.

"An idealized love?" the Contessa asked.

"Yes."

"And a love that can never be forgotten?"

"Yes."

"Could we imagine someone else who has carried that kind of love all through his life?" the Contessa asked.

Dante's face took on a deeper tan.

"As I was saying," he continued, "The Beatrice in *The Divine Comedy* loved the poet so much that she thought his divine journey would save him from himself. And so she leaves Heaven to descend into Hell and she asks Virgil to serve as Dante's guide. Every time Dante thinks he can go no further, the promise of meeting Beatrice motivates him to continue. Finally, Beatrice leads him into Heaven and she grows in radiance and beauty as they ascend toward God."

The women exchanged glances. If the Dante in front of them loved this story so well, the rumors of his long ago love for another beautiful girl in Florence must be true, they thought.

The highlights of everyone's day were Richards' stories about his journey. They gathered around the main room, the children on the floor. Richards began by telling of his stay in the prison camp at Laterina, and he was soon bombarded with questions.

"How could you sleep with the lice?"

"Not very well."

"Did you try using gasoline?" Annabella said. "Our mother always used gasoline when I had head lice."

"So did my mother, remember, Annabella?" Rosa said. "But I don't think it did any good. The lice always came back. Perhaps they had never gone away."

Roberto and Adolfo wanted to know if anyone tried to escape.

"There was one attempt. A couple of chaps broke through the cement floor and dug out dirt every night with a spoon," Richards said, and the boys' eyes grew wide.

"What did they do with the dirt?" Roberto asked.

"They put it in their pockets and emptied it outside the next day."

"Didn't this take forever?" Adolfo asked.

"Months. They dug down three or four feet, and then they dug under the floor for maybe thirty feet until they got past the fence. Then they dug up to the surface."

"Fantastico!" Roberto exclaimed.

"One night two blighters actually went through all the way. But as soon as they got to the surface on the other side of the fence the guards saw them. They were brought back and had to sit in isolation for thirty days. Poor blokes."

"O, terribile!" Roberto said.

Dante thought this was a good time to end the session for the day.

"I think Colin is tired," he said. "Let's save more stories for tomorrow."

"Yeah, I'm knackered," Colin said, winking at Roberto.

Shortly after Francesco finished playing several selections and the women had tidied up, Gavino arrived at the back door and asked to see Dante. Dante was smiling broadly when he returned to the main room.

"Gavino had some good news from his partisan sources today," he said. "The British Eighth Army is still south of Tuscany, in Umbria, but it has not only captured Perugia, it has seized Assisi."

A cheer went up around the room.

"There's more," Dante said. "When the Allies got to Assisi they found that priests and monks had been helping Jews who had fled there. They gave them refuge and even new identifications. What a courageous thing they did. They could have been killed."

Because Sant'Antonio had no Jews and Reboli had only a handful, the Nazi extermination of Jews was something the villagers did not know much about and could not even comprehend.

"They say the Jews are being sent to camps in Germany and gassed," Annabella said.

"I can't believe the Germans are killing people like that," Rosa said. "What are they going to do next?"

"Those poor people," Maria said.

Suddenly Fausta got up and glared at Maria. "Those poor people? Well, would you want your daughter to marry one?"

"What are you talking about?" Maria said. "Who said anything about marrying? My daughter is married to a nice boy from Sant'Anna di Stazzema."

"Let me just say," Fausta declared, "that you would not want someone from an alien race in your family."

"An alien race?" Rosa said. "Who is a member of an alien race?"

"The Jews!" Fausta shouted.

Fausta's statement was so unexpected that everyone in the room sat stunned.

"Fausta," Vito said, his voice rising. "What are you talking about? Where do you get these ideas? How can you think like that?"

Before Fausta had a chance to reply, Dante intervened.

"I think we have had a long day. Let's retire now and look forward to another interesting day tomorrow."

The villagers went to their rooms, muttering among themselves. For the first time since she arrived at the Cielo, Fausta smiled.

Dante was clearly disturbed and disappointed that a day that had been so stimulating ended badly because of a few words from just one person. He went to his room and took out the letter that he kept in *The Divine Comedy*. Again, it gave him comfort.

As he prepared for bed gunfire across the hill exploded into a burst of light that whitened his room.

"Bastards!" he said. "Bastards!"

CHAPTER 17

▼

Father Luigi was so excited he had trouble dismantling the radio transmitter and putting it back in its hidden place. First, he had heard that the British Eighth Army had entered Assisi and the Germans had fled. But that wasn't the most fascinating part of the news. One of his old classmates in Greve heard it from a priest in Castiglione who heard it from a priest in Terranuova. The rumors about Assisi could finally be told. A network of priests, monks and nuns there had been giving refuge to Jews for the last eight months.

"Can you imagine?" the priest thought. "Jews? Right under the Germans' noses."

Catholics from southern Italy had been seeking refuge in Assisi for months, thinking that neither the Allies nor the Germans would bomb the beloved city of Saint Francis, the patron saint of Italy. Then Jews also began to arrive in a city where no Jew had lived throughout history.

The reports told of a family of Jews who were granted refuge in the guest house of the Poor Clares, of a young Jew who was given the identity of a monk who had just died, of Jews who were dressed in monks' robes and taught when to kneel during the Mass and how to sing hymns in Latin.

At night, under the guidance of a priest, a printer made the Jews false identity papers. Priests also taught classes on how to behave as Christians, on the catechism, on the liturgy. In turn, the priests and monks, many of whom had never met a Jew before, learned how to make kosher meals.

And there was the story of a Franciscan who led a group of Jews through a tunnel into safety in an olive grove. Up to three hundred Jews were saved because of these efforts in Assisi.

"Those priests and nuns should be declared saints right now," Father Luigi thought.

Father Luigi had never actually known a Jewish person. When he was in the seminary in Florence, he knew where the ghetto was, but seminarians weren't supposed to go there. When he saw a man he thought was a Jew on the street there, he wanted to go up and talk to him but he was too timid.

He was so pleased now that there was a painting of Saint Francis, along with Saint Clare, in his church. Saint Francis looked rather ugly, he thought, but saints aren't always pretty.

Then, as he always did, he began to compare himself with others. If he had been in Assisi in the last months, would he have been so courageous? Would he have been as skillful as these priests, thinking of ways to avoid the Germans' suspicions? Or would he have been more concerned about his own safety?

No, he thought, he was just a simple little priest in a simple little village, terribly afraid of what might happen to him and perspiring at the most insignificant thing. He could never lead people through a tunnel.

"Besides, I wouldn't fit," he thought.

No, he could never be a saint.

He finished taking the radio apart and stowed it in a suitcase in the closet.

After patrolling the hills and checking on land mines, Fritz Krieger and Konrad Schultz returned to their temporary home in the village and prepared a supper of cheese, vegetables and wurst. They shared a pack of cigarettes while working in the kitchen.

"Did you hear?" Fritz asked. "Someone tried to assassinate Hitler!"

"You're joking. How?"

"One of his officers planted a bomb in his command post. Our Führer wasn't hurt badly. He met with Mussolini the same day."

"What happened to the assassin?" Konrad asked.

"Shot," Fritz said.

Konrad put the dishes on the table. "I tell you, Fritz, God is on our side."

"Why do you say that?"

"Because our Führer now has another chance to continue the salvation of Europe against the Jews and the communists. And you know what? Now everyone will be even more determined to fight for the cause."

"Don't forget about the enemy, the British, the Americans and all the others. And the partisans."

Konrad turned away and wiped his glasses. "Bloody partisans."

"Konrad, you haven't said anything about the other day in Reboli."

"Yeah, I know."

Konrad turned around. Fritz stood in front of him and put his hands on his friend's shoulders. "That was pretty hard, wasn't it?"

Konrad looked down at the floor. "Yeah."

"We keep saying we'll do anything for the Führer, but it's hard to do some of the things, right?

"Yeah."

"But, you know, I'm glad we only hanged men. Horst and Otto tried to grab some women."

"Yeah."

"Well, that's the rule. Ten civilians for every one of us the partisans kill. But the first time was hard. I didn't like to see them hanging in the square either."

Konrad pulled Fritz' hands from his shoulders. "Fritz, stop talking about it, all right? Can't you let it alone? I don't want to think about it anymore."

Konrad turned his back and wiped his glasses again.

"Konrad, I'm sorry. But it's our job. You know that."

Konrad went to the stairs. "I'm not very hungry, Fritz. I think I'll go on up to bed."

It had been days since he had written in his journal, but Ezio Maffini knew he should add some new accounts before he forgot them. There was a lot on his mind these days.

"We still miss Owl and Eagle very much but the rest of us are trying to do as much work as before. There's so much to do now and I don't know when we'll get replacements.

"Most of our work these days has been dismantling the mines that the Germans have set up in these hills. It's hard work and very dangerous, but so far we have been successful. We found a clutch of mines near the old olive grove, just where we thought we would find them.

"Our contact told me tonight about the priests and nuns in Assisi who were saving Jews. He also told me how the *banda* there had come down from the town at night and mined the main highway and railway tracks. The Germans' supply lines are going to be wrecked. We're doing just the opposite at the bridge here. The Nazis want to blow it up when the Allies come and we're breaking down the explosives.

"It looks like these hills now have other residents. Besides us and the Germans, there are signs that escaped Allied prisoners are making their way north. We found one wandering near here the other day. He was lost and had fallen and looked terrible. He looked like he hadn't eaten in days, but we didn't have anything to give him. We were so busy with the mines that we couldn't help him much, but he knew where he wanted to go and we directed him there. It wasn't far, just a little farm near the big farmhouse on the hill. I'm sure he made it.

"*Viva l'italia!*"

Ezio leaned back against the wall of the cave. It was late at night, but still warm and humid and sleep came easily. Soon, he was back in Sant'Anna, stroking his beloved's long hair as she slept beside him.

"I have to go, my dear," he whispered.

She stirred in her sleep and opened her eyes.

"Already? Please, can't you stay longer?"

"No," he said, touching her lips. "It's too dangerous. If the Germans found out you were helping us, you'd be killed."

"But Sant'Anna is safe. The Germans will never find us."

"We don't know who they've got planted here, my darling. We can't trust anyone."

"Just a little longer?"

He kissed her eyes, her nose, her mouth. Then he moved down her body.

"Oh, my darling. My darling Angelica."

Ezio was jolted awake by the crack of thunder. He slept fitfully for the rest of the night.

CHAPTER 18

▼

Early on the morning after Fausta made her remarks about Jews, Rosa knew she had to find Dante. She went downstairs, poured a glass of water and saw him at the window overlooking the valley. His face looked haggard in the dim light, and his shoulders were stooped. Suddenly, Rosa felt sorry for Dante. Father Luigi had taken advantage of his kind nature by putting him in charge at the Cielo, and yet she could think of no one who would have been better.

"Dante, we need to talk about Fausta," she said, startling him out of his thoughts.

"What is there to say?"

"Dante, those were terrible things she said last night, and she would have said even worse things if you hadn't stopped her."

"I know, but what can we do? She has a right to her opinion."

"Opinion? What kind of opinion is that? She's the only one here who thinks like that."

Dante leaned against the wall. Rosa noticed that even with his tan he looked pale.

"Well, Rosa, what do you think we should do?" he said.

"How about locking her in her room?"

"Rosa, Rosa. You can't talk like that."

"Dante, when we were talking about whether we should have Colin Richards here, she was the only one who opposed it."

Dante ran his hand through his long hair. "The Contessa didn't want him to come either."

"The Contessa was afraid. The Contessa is afraid of her shadow. But it was Fausta who gave those arguments about how we could get some money if we turned him in, how there wasn't any room for him here, how the Germans would kill us all if they found out."

"All true, in one degree or another."

"But you got up and said how we are our brother's keeper, or something like that. And everyone else agreed with you. Why aren't you upset about what Fausta is saying now?"

"Rosa," Dante sighed, "I am upset. I'm very upset. I hardly slept last night. I was tossing and turning and I couldn't figure out what to do. I think we have only two options. One, we could confront her and tell her we don't like the way she talks and demand that she stop. In that case, she will probably get angry and say even worse things. Fausta is a very strong woman."

"You don't have to tell me."

"And then we will have all sorts of friction here. We were trying to get over that yesterday."

"And we did, until last night."

Rosa and Dante were interrupted by a squadron of British planes flying low overhead. They waited until the echoes faded.

"Or two, we could be nice to her and tell her that while we don't agree with her we respect her right to think the way she does."

"Respect her? Dante, she's a Fascist!" Rosa banged her glass on the table.

"Rosa, please be careful. That's a very strong word to use."

If Fausta was a Fascist, she would have been one of the few in Sant'Antonio. People wondered about Umberto Magnini, who seemed to go to Reboli every Thursday night for no good reason, and Coppo Famoso, who muttered about communists and the partisans more often than anyone cared to listen. But most people in the village just wanted to be left alone. They didn't even care about Mussolini. They couldn't wait for the war to end.

"Dante, she is a Fascist. Anyone can see that. Don't you?"

"I guess I don't want to put a label on it."

"Well, we have to face reality. And I'm afraid of what she might do."

Dante looked shocked, as if the idea hadn't occurred to him "Do? Rosa, what could she do? We are all confined here."

"Dante, we have an escaped prisoner of war in this house. We have partisans all around here and Gavino is talking to them. What if she got word to the Germans in the village?"

"I can't believe she would do that. And how could she?"

"I don't know, but I wouldn't put anything past her."

"You think she's that serious?

"Dante, we don't know anything about her. She works in Reboli, that's about all we know. Years ago there were rumors about her and her supervisor, maybe they're still true. He might have something to do with this. But she is not a simple little spinster who sits at home and tends her garden. I just don't believe that. I know I'm always suspicious, but in this case I think there's something we don't know."

"All right," Dante sighed again, "we will have to watch her."

Rosa and Dante stood for a long time looking out into the valley. A field of poppies shone in the sunlight halfway down the hill. Around the farmhouse, the roses and begonias and daisies softened the harshness of the worn-out olive trees. A woodpecker attacked the kaki tree. On this cloudless day, they could almost see the trees surrounding Sant'Antonio. Finally, Rosa spoke.

"*Allora.* You don't like to confront people, do you, Dante?"

"No, I never have. I wish people would get along together, be friendly toward one another."

Dante had tried to avoid conflict all of his life. As a child, he ran away when his friends started to fight. At the university he cringed when other students challenged the professors. As a teacher, he tried to get his students to see all sides of a question rather than argue about it.

"Dante, we are at war," Rosa said softly. She put her hand on his arm. "People are not getting along together, as you say. They hate each other. They're killing each other."

"This war is so terrible. I just wish it were over."

"It won't be over for a while, and when it is we're never going to be the same," Rosa said. "We don't know if Sant'Antonio will even be there when we get back. *If* we get back. We may very well die today or tomorrow or the day after that. We don't know."

Dante refused to accept that. "We're going to get back. I know we will."

"Dante, please. You don't know that." She tightened her grip on his arm. "You are a wonderful man and you have done so much for Sant'Antonio and the people and the children. But I think sometimes you are, well, naïve. You're like a little boy almost. You trust people too much."

"If we don't trust other people, what can we trust?"

They were interrupted by more people coming downstairs for breakfast. They moved to a quiet corner of the main room.

"Dante, if there was a crisis here, do you think you could take action, be our leader, as Father Luigi said?"

"I don't know, Rosa. Sometimes I doubt it."

"Sometimes we do what we have to do even though we don't think we can."

"You make it sound easy."

They were facing each other now. Dante towered over Rosa and she looked up into his eyes, which seemed to be full of tears.

"Dante, look at it this way. If no one stands up for what is right, terrible things are going to happen. Look what's happening to the Jews. Who's standing up for them? The pope? Don't make me laugh."

"Rosa, this whole situation with the Jewish people is such a big problem. Can any one of us have an effect?"

"Well, if we don't tell Fausta what we think, she's just going to be like an infection in this place. Remember the other day when you asked us how we would feel if we turned Colin Richards away? How are we going to feel if we don't confront this, if we don't let Fausta know that we violently disagree with her?"

"Rosa, Rosa, you should run for mayor. Maybe you should be pope."

"I bet I could do the job as well as he does. But I don't look good in white."

"Rosa, you are hopeless."

"Marco thinks so, too."

Rosa smiled and for the first time in days, Dante laughed out loud. Rosa reached up and hugged him. Dante was surprised. He had not had another person's arms around him in forty years. He hugged her back.

"Thank you, Rosa. You know how much I respect you. You're right, of course. We need to confront Fausta. We don't want that infection here, not now. I hope she will understand and that there won't be a big fight."

Rosa hugged him again. "Thank you, Dante."

She kept her arms around him and he held her, too. "And one more thing, Dante. I want to apologize for the way Contessa flirts with you. It must be embarrassing."

"It's a little flattering, actually. It's not a problem. I'm used to it."

Rosa looked up into his eyes. "Dante, I'm very sorry about the girl in Florence so many years ago. You've had a difficult life."

Dante pulled away from Rosa's arms. He was about to say something but then said simply, "Thank you, Rosa."

He stepped back. "I'm going to go to my room for a while. I want to do some more reading."

"More *Divine Comedy?*" Rosa asked.

"Did you have to ask? It's the only book I brought along."

"I'm glad you have it, Dante. We are enjoying the discussions. Come join us soon."

Rosa stood up on her toes and gave Dante a light kiss on his cheek. After he left, she went back to the window, mesmerized by the spectacular view. But she was suddenly alarmed when she saw a slight figure leave the back door and run across the fields toward Gavino's house.

CHAPTER 19

▼

Gina had not slept well all night. Carlotta kept waking up and crying, sometimes wanting to be nursed, sometimes wanting to be held, sometimes not knowing what she wanted. Gina didn't know what to do.

"What is it, my baby?" she said, holding Carlotta one way and then another, trying to make the child comfortable. "You're so hot. Are you getting sick again? Please, please don't get sick. We left the medicine at home."

Gina noticed that Lucia, Anna, Roberto and Adolfo were nowhere to be seen. They must have gone downstairs. Gina thought she'd better join them, but when she went downstairs, Lucia wasn't around.

"We haven't seen her at all," Anna said.

"Well," Gina said, "she must be here somewhere. Why don't you look for her? I need to take care of Carlotta."

"What's wrong with her?" Roberto asked.

"I think she might be getting sick again, like she was at home. She's so hot."

"Is she going to be all right? Should we call a doctor?" Anna wanted to know.

"We can't," Gina said. "We're stuck up here in this godforsaken place. I don't know what to do."

Anna lifted the baby's blanket and tried to play peekaboo but Carlotta didn't even notice.

"Don't we have any medicine?" Roberto said.

"We did at home, but I forgot to bring it."

Roberto stroked Carlotta's curls. "Can't we go get it?"

"I wish we could, but we can't leave here."

"Why not?"

"It's not safe. The Germans are down there."

The children stood silently around their baby sister.

"I wish Papa was here," Adolfo said, hugging his mother.

"I do, too, baby, I do, too."

"When will he come home, Mamma?" Anna asked.

"I don't know, baby, I don't know."

Coming downstairs, the other villagers stopped to console Gina and murmur to Carlotta.

"Poor little baby," Maddelena said.

"Can we do anything?" Rosa asked.

"I'm sure she's going to be all right," Maria said. "Angelica's boys get sick all the time and they get better. She told me in one letter that Nando was so sick, throwing up all over, and then in the next letter she said the only problem was that he was teething. Maybe Carlotta's teething?"

"She's only three months, Maria," Gina said. "I don't think so."

Gathered around the table in the early morning, the villagers tried to forget the unpleasantness with Fausta and anticipated another interesting day of sewing, card games and lessons. But then Rosa tapped her glass with a knife. "Please. Dante has something to say."

Dante slowly rose. "I think we should discuss something before Colin Richards gets up and joins us. Last night, Fausta said some things that raised some serious questions for all of us. I think we need to discuss this, to get it out in the open. In other words, we need to confront some issues."

He looked at Rosa, and she smiled.

"Fausta, perhaps you would like to tell all of us how you feel about certain things."

Fausta was not surprised and, in fact, welcomed the opportunity. She knew the others were upset with her, but she felt strongly about her beliefs and she was proud to talk about them. She always felt that she received her strength from her father.

Fausta's father was an early follower of Mussolini, believing in his programs to strengthen Italy, and as a child she read all of the books and newspapers and pamphlets that he had. When she grew up, she hoped to marry and have lots of children, just as Il Duce urged. Unfortunately, there were no suitors.

She did, however, attract the attention of the manager of the thread factory where she worked in Reboli. An active Fascist, he was married and the father of eight children, and he complained to Fausta that his wife was too busy with the children to take care of his needs. Somehow, he convinced her that that the best way she could serve her country would be to take care of his needs. Reluctantly, she agreed. Besides, she had wants and desires of her own.

She was happy with this arrangement until her employer's needs became his demands and his demands became shameful and offensive. Yet she felt trapped in his power. Sometimes, she wanted to quit her job and hide in her home in Sant'Antonio, but she needed the monthly pay. She always felt dirty after submitting to his obscene requests. But then he would praise her for all she was doing for the cause of Fascism. And since Fascism was all that she had to hold on to, she wore long sleeves to conceal the bruises.

Now, Fausta rose from her seat and stood in front of the fireplace. She was a study in black and white. Her face was pale and her black hair was pulled back into a bun. She wore a white blouse buttoned to the neck, a long black skirt, black stockings and flat black shoes. Although she was forty-five years old, she looked ten years older. She put on the eye glasses that hung from a chain around her neck and cleared her throat.

"First, let me say that I am a proud member of *Fasci Femminili,* the women's organization set up by the Fascist Party." She dug into her purse and held up a card for everyone to see. "Many years ago I was honored to be elected vice-secretary for this region and I continue to serve in that capacity."

Little Anna grabbed Gina's arm. "I know about *Fasci Femminili,* Mamma. Our teacher in Reboli said she was a member. Remember she told me to give up my earrings for Mussolini?"

"I remember, darling. That was a terrible thing to ask."

"Fausta," Rosa said, "wasn't *Fasci Femminili* established because women are not allowed to be full members of the party?"

Fausta ignored the question.

"*Fasci Femminili* does so many good deeds, and I wish you women would consider being a part of it. I will send you pamphlets when we return home. For example, we strive to protect and assist needy mothers and their children. We give out clothing and medical advice before, during and after childbirth. We collaborate with labor organizations for the good of the nation. We have a physical education program for girls eight to eleven. And there are so many other things that we do."

Rosa raised her hand again. "Fausta," she said, "I thought Mussolini wanted all women to get married and have children. You have not done that."

"Dear Rosa," Fausta said. "I am so pleased that you yourself finally married and it is unfortunate that you and Marco do not have children. Not all of us have the privilege to be married and have children. But, yes, you are thinking of a program called Battle for Births, which Mussolini initiated in 1927 to encourage the Italian population to grow. Because of this wonderful plan, there are substantial tax benefits for those with large families. You see how benevolent Il Duce is? The target has been five children for each family. I think it's wonderful that Gina here has met that goal."

"Fausta," Gina said, looking up from Carlotta who was still having trouble nursing, "Pietro made our children! Mussolini had nothing to do with it!"

The room echoed with laughter. Vito and Giocomo slapped each other's knees, Maddelena and Renata giggled, and Maria smiled behind her handkerchief. Anna, Roberto and Adolfo whooped. They didn't understand what their mother had said but thought it must have been very funny.

"Fausta," Marco said over the discord, "haven't you heard? Mussolini hasn't been in power since last September 8."

"Wrong!" Fausta shouted. "Hitler has established a Republican Fascist state in northern Italy, including here in Tuscany, and Mussolini is the head of it."

"It's a puppet government!"

"It's a real government! That is why we, the true Fascists, have joined with the Germans to fight the common enemy, the British, the Americans and all their Allies."

"And that's why you didn't want to give Colin Richards protection here," Annabella said.

"We are at war, Annabella. How can we give aid and comfort to our enemy?"

"And what about the Jews?" Francesco asked. "How can you possibly justify Hitler's plan to exterminate them?"

"It is very simple," Fausta said. "Let me read some things to you."

She rummaged in her purse and found a notebook. It had a swastika on the cover. Fausta had lectured on *Fasci Femminili* many times, and so her response sounded like a history lesson.

"I have been taking notes from my readings and as early as 1920 Hitler said, 'Don't be misled into thinking you can fight a disease without killing the carrier, without destroying the bacillus. Don't think you can fight racial tuberculosis without taking care to rid the nation of the carrier of that racial tuberculosis. This Jewish contamination will not subside, this poisoning of the nation will not end, until the carrier himself, the Jew, has been banished from our midst.' Now isn't that a powerful statement?"

She paused, looked around the room and continued.

"It is well known that the Jews have formed a conspiracy that includes the economic sublimation of our society and the infiltration of all of our arts and cultural institutions. The loss of the First World War was the result of a Jewish conspiracy. The Treaty of Versailles was a Jewish conspiracy designed to bring Germany to its knees. The inflation of 1923 was the result of an international Jewish attempt to destroy Germany. Look at history, and you know all these things to be true. I believe, like Hitler, that the Jews are the source of all evil in this world."

"Stupida!" Vito shouted. "How can any sane person believe that filth?"

The room turned into a battlefield. Fausta stood stonily in front of the fireplace as everyone denounced her and told her to go back to Sant'Antonio.

"You keep talking about Hitler," Rosa said over the outcry. "What about Italy? We haven't had the same policies as Germany."

"Ah, regrettably no," Fausta said, "but read what the manifesto on racial purity said in 1938. It said that, and I quote, 'Italian racial policy must be Italian in nature, and follow the Aryan-Nordic model' and at another point it said, another quote, 'The pure European physical and spiritual traits of the Italians may not be altered. The pure European character of the Italians will be changed by mixing with any other non-European race, which is the carrier of a culture other than the ancient Aryan culture.'"

"What about what happened in Rome last October?" Marco asked. "The Germans sent more than a thousand Jews to the camp at Auschwitz. Everyone knows that."

Fausta looked flustered. "That's true, and there are many Jews who are still at large but..."

"And many Italians are giving them shelter!" Rosa shouted.

"The government will find them!" Fausta slammed her notebook on the table. No one wanted to hear any more.

"There's no use talking to you," Vito said. "You don't make sense. Fausta, you are not a part of our group any more. You don't belong here."

"Yes, I think that's very clear," Fausta said. "That's fine. I would rather be in my room. I have brought some books along that I would like to read. As for you, I know you are all communists and you will all suffer under the Third Reich."

Dante tried to calm things down.

"It is probably a good idea for you to spend time in your room, Fausta," he said softly. "It would be good for you and good for the rest of us."

Fausta put her notebook back into her purse, took off her glasses and strode from the room.

"O Dio," Rosa said, "For a minute I thought she was going to say 'Heil Hitler!'"

"Good riddance," Vito and Giacomo said together.

Everyone was still in shock when Colin Richards entered the room, sleepy and a little disheveled.

"Buongiorno," he said. "You all look so serious. Have I missed anything?"

"Nothing," Vito said. "Let's play cards."

As the men gathered around a small table to learn a new card game and the women pulled out the dresses they were working on, Rosa drew Dante aside.

"Thank you," she said. "You were right. That didn't help very much, but now we know that she's even worse than we imagined."

"She certainly doesn't give in."

"I'm still afraid of what she might do," Rosa said. "I just don't trust that woman. We have to watch her, Dante. What if she runs back to the village?"

"I don't think she would do that. She's not that deranged. But, yes, we must watch her. Tell Marco. And Francesco. And tell Annabella, too."

Rosa didn't like that idea, but nodded.

"I wish we could see what is going on around here," Rosa said. "We all feel so confined. We don't know who is outside."

"Let me look around," Dante said, giving Rosa a little hug. "Thank you, Rosa."

After lunch, Dante rapped on his glass.

"Some of us," he said, "are getting more concerned about our safety. The Germans could very well visit us any moment. This morning, I looked at that little tower off the third floor and I think it would be a good lookout post. You can see the whole valley, almost to Sant'Antonio. What do you think of posting a lookout there, at least from morning until dark? Then that person can tell the rest of us if there's something strange going on in the fields around us and in the hills, and if we're going to have, let's say, some visitors."

"One person all day?" Vito asked.

"No, of course not. We could do it in, say, two-hour shifts. You, Vito, and Giacomo, Marco, Francesco and I. It might get boring, but we would know what is going on around here."

Rosa raised her hand.

"Dante, why did you only pick men? My eyesight is very good."

"Well, I…"

"And so is mine," Annabella said.

"I never thought…"

"So is mine," Maria said.

"But…well…you mean you women want to be lookouts, too?"

"Of course," the three women said in unison.

Maddelena and Renata observed that they couldn't see far anymore and they couldn't stand for long periods of time. The Contessa said she would rather not participate. Everyone agreed that Gina had enough to do with her children. And no one thought of asking Fausta, who was still in her room.

"Should I ask the men if they agree?" Dante asked.

"I don't think that's necessary," Rosa said. "You decide."

Francesco, Vito and Giacomo were too surprised to say anything. Marco reached over and patted Rosa's hand.

"All right, then," Dante said. "We'll begin tomorrow morning. Marco you can have the first shift, then Rosa, then Francesco, then…well, I'll write out a schedule and put it on the wall."

The women smiled.

Shortly after, while everyone pretended they weren't watching, Fausta emerged from her room, went to the *cesso* and then to the kitchen. She found some leftovers and took them back to her room.

With their mother busy with Carlotta, who was still feverish and crying, Roberto told Adolfo to come up to their room. Even though Roberto was twelve and Adolfo was eight, they did everything together and their stay at the Cielo had made them even closer.

"Listen," Roberto said. "I have a plan."

"So you don't have to eat polenta?"

"No, *stupido!* You know how Carlotta needs her medicine?"

"Yeah."

"And you know that it is on the shelf in the bathroom at home?"

"Yeah."

"Well, why don't we go and get it?"

"Roberto, you know what Mamma said. We aren't supposed to leave here."

"She doesn't have to know, Adolfo. It's still early afternoon. We can easily get there and be back before it's dark. No one will even notice we're missing."

Adolfo lay down on his bed, put his hands behind his head and stared at the ceiling. "I don't know, 'Berto. There are all kinds of scary things in the hills now. Mamma said there are partisans and more escaped prisoners and maybe even Germans. I don't want to go out there."

"Listen, I know the way. Maybe I should go by myself."

Adolfo jumped up. "No! You can't go alone."

"Why not? Look at Colin Richards. He went all over Tuscany by himself."

"And remember how he looked when he got here? And we're not soldiers. We don't know what to do."

"Do you want to let Carlotta die? Adolfo, she needs this medicine. Mamma will be so happy when we come back with it. Come on, Adolfo. It will be fun."

"Why don't you take Anna?" Adolfo said.

"Anna? I can't take Anna. She's a girl, *stupido!*"

His brother lay down on the bed again, put his head under the pillow and mumbled something.

"What did you say?"

"I said I wish Papa were here."

"Well, he's not. We're the men in the family now, Adolfo."

Adolfo mumbled something else.

"What did you say?"

"I said I don't feel like a man," Adolfo whispered.

"Fine. I'll go alone."

"No!"

"Then let's do it."

Having seen the makeshift knapsack that Richards had, the boys decided they would have one, too. They took one of Adolfo's shirts and tied it in a knot. They didn't quite know what to put in it, so they selected some things they thought they would need: Roberto's hunting knife in case they ran into strange animals, Adolfo's ball in case they wanted to play, some string, some biscotti they had secreted in a drawer and a little blanket in case they got cold.

"Adolfo, it's August, it's not going to get cold. And we're only going to be gone a few hours."

"I know, I just want to be prepared."

The boys crept downstairs. Everyone else was in the main room, involved in what seemed to be a very serious discussion. No one noticed when they went out the back door.

CHAPTER 20

▼

Having stayed about thirty feet from the path, even as it zigzagged down the hill, Roberto and Adolfo made it to the village without much incident. At one point, they heard some rustling and saw four men on a ridge. They seemed to be digging.

"Do you think they're farmers?" Adolfo asked.

"There wouldn't be four farmers digging, you *stupido*. Maybe they're Germans."

"They're not in uniform."

"Then maybe they're partisans," Roberto said. "I don't know."

"Maybe they're digging for treasure."

"Let's go."

At another point, they saw two men in gray uniforms. The boys hid behind a tree until they disappeared.

In a heavily wooded area two people were lying intertwined under a tree, their bare flesh reflecting the sun.

"Don't look," Roberto said as he put his hands over Adolfo's eyes.

"Who is that?"

"I think it's Lucia. I don't know who else. Come on, let's go."

"Lucia? What's she doing here?"

"I don't know, Adolfo. Come on."

"'Berto, I thought this was going to be dangerous," Adolfo said. "This isn't dangerous."

"That's because I'm leading the way," Roberto said.

As they neared Sant'Antonio, they could hear the roar of the Panzers going through the village. At the final turn they looked down on the main street.

"*O Dio,*" Roberto said.

Most of the beautiful oaks that had lined the street were knocked down. Huge ruts ran down each side and there was garbage all over. Windows in some houses were broken. Soldiers walked up and down the street, in twos and threes, their weapons at their sides. A few were sitting outside houses and looked like they were drinking beer.

Before entering the village the boys passed the church and the priest's house. As he often did, Father Luigi was watching out of the window, wondering what the Germans were doing. He was surprised to see the boys' tiny figures crawling along not twenty feet in front of his house. He knocked loudly on the window.

"Look," Roberto said. "It's Father Luigi!"

The boys ran to his door and he cautiously opened it. "What in God's name are you doing here? You shouldn't have come!"

"We had to," Roberto said. "Carlotta is real sick and we had to get her medicine."

"What's wrong with her?" the priest whispered.

"We don't know, but the medicine will make her better."

"Go quickly," the priest said. "Don't be seen. It's terrible here."

Father Luigi closed the door, mopped his brow, crossed himself and sat shaking in his chair by the window.

The Sporenzas' tiny house was just off the main street and at the opposite end of the village from the bridge. In order to get to it, however, they had to cross the street.

"Follow me," Roberto whispered.

Roberto ran down the side of the road until he was at the street. Adolfo was so close behind he stepped on his brother's heels three times. When they reached the street they could see two soldiers talking in front of Leoni's, though they saw that its sign was now on the ground.

"Maybe we should divert their attention," Adolfo whispered.

"How? Throw a rock at them?"

By running from tree to tree, crouching and crawling, they managed to get to their street. They made a dash across it and ran up the steps of their house.

"Can you believe it?" Roberto said. "Nobody saw us."

The house was not locked and they went inside.

"We'd better not tell Mamma what we saw," Adolfo said.

Dishes were piled in the sink and broken ones were scattered all over. Empty pots cluttered the stove. The chair where Gina rocked Carlotta was in pieces. The couch had big stains and a rip across the middle. Dirt and mud covered the floor.

The boys went into the bathroom to find the medicine and were almost turned away by the smell from the toilet.

"Here it is," Roberto said, finding a small bottle of red medicine on the shelf. "Let's get out of here fast."

"Wait!" Adolfo said. "Let's look at our room."

They were sorry they did. Their beds were turned over, their clothes piled in a corner. Cars for their toy trains were smashed, as if by crushed by heavy boots. Their *Pinocchio* and *Topolino* books were ripped apart. In tears, Adolfo gathered the pieces of his Pinocchio puppet and put them inside his shirt.

"Let's go," Roberto said.

The boys ran down the steps and to the main street. The two soldiers were still talking in front of Leoni's. As the boys raced across the street, one of the soldiers saw them.

"Hey! What are you doing here?"

The soldiers strode down the street and the boys had no choice but to stop. The soldiers were only four years older than Roberto, but they were very tall. One soldier pulled out his pistol.

"Is that necessary, Konrad?" the other soldier said. "They're only boys."

"They're Italian boys, Fritz. They could be working for the partisans. What are you boys doing here? Where do you live?" Konrad's Italian wasn't good but his pistol made words unnecessary.

"We're in a farmhouse up in the hills," Roberto said, shuddering.

"Where all you Eyties ran when we came here?" Konrad said. "Why did you come back?"

"Um, we had to come and get something," Roberto said. He held the bottle behind his back.

"What?"

The soldier pointed his pistol at the boys. Roberto was too scared to lie.

"Some medicine. For my baby sister. She's really sick."

"Let's see it."

Roberto held up the bottle and the soldier snatched it.

"It's only medicine, Konrad. Can't you let them have it?" the other soldier said.

"This would look great smashed on the ground, wouldn't it?"

"Please, don't," Roberto said, tears welling in his eyes. "Our sister needs it. Can't you just let us go?"

"What's that you have under your shirt, boy?" Konrad ripped Adolfo's shirt open and the pieces of the Pinocchio puppet fell out.

Fritz looked at the frightened boys. Only a few years ago, he had been like them, but as a member of the *Jungvolk* he had fun beating up other boys. These boys were sacrificing their lives for their sister.

"Konrad," he said, "just let them go."

"You're such a chicken, Fritz." He stomped on the puppet pieces but handed the medicine bottle back to Roberto.

"Now get the hell out of here and don't let us see you again."

Roberto grabbed the bottle and he and Adolfo began running up the hill. When they passed the priest's house, they didn't even see Father Luigi in the window, crossing himself again. It was not until the boys had traveled a quarter of a mile that they stopped for breath.

"Wait!" Adolfo said. "I have to pee."

"Me too."

Afterwards, they leaned against the tree.

"'Berto, that was so close. Weren't you scared?"

"Nah. They wouldn't have done anything. We're just boys."

"I was scared. Did you see their pistols? They could have shot us."

"Come on. It's getting late. Let's go."

In mid-afternoon, Gina was pleased to find Lucia was now lying on her bed but realized that she had been so busy with Carlotta, she hadn't seen the boys all day.

"Rosa," she said, "have you seen Roberto and Adolfo? I don't know where they are."

"Well, they must be somewhere around here. They couldn't have gone far."

A search of the farmhouse found no trace of the boys, but Anna discovered that Adolfo's red shirt was missing and so was a little blanket. Everyone in the house, except Fausta who was still in her room, searched for the boys.

"O Dio!" Gina said. "It's not enough that Carlotta is so sick but now the boys have run off to play."

Rosa put her arms around both Gina and Carlotta.

About a third of the way up the hill, Roberto and Adolfo were having a dispute.

"Why did you tell me to go this way?" Roberto said. "This is not the way we came."

"Yes, it is. See that tree with the broken branches? We passed that on the way down."

"Adolfo, every tree around here has broken branches. This is not the way."

The boys were exceedingly lost. After their encounter with the German soldiers they were too disoriented to follow the path they had taken down the hill. Now everything looked alike and nothing looked familiar.

"We should have put markings on trees or something," Adolfo said. "Maybe we can find those naked people again."

"They wouldn't be naked anymore. It's starting to rain."

The rain was still a drizzle, but it was enough to soak their hair and stream down their backs. They decided to wait it out under a large rock formation that jutted out from a bend in the hill.

"I'm hungry," Adolfo said, realizing that they hadn't eaten all day.

"We've only got those three biscotti."

Roberto opened the little knapsack. They each ate one biscotti and tried to split the other one but it crumbled into a hundred pieces.

"I told you we shouldn't have come," Adolfo said.

"And if we hadn't, Carlotta wouldn't get her medicine."

"Maybe it's too late anyway. She seems really sick. Do you think she's going to die, 'Berto?"

"I don't know. I just wish Papa was here. He's been gone so long. We don't even know where he is."

"Do you think he's going to come back from the war?"

Roberto hesitated. "Sure…Of course…I hope so."

The boys watched the rain as it dripped down the rocks and into the muddy ground. Eventually it stopped, although it was getting dark when they packed up their kit and moved on.

"It's this way," Roberto said.

"No, it's this way."

"All right, Adolfo, we'll do it your way."

As they started off, three planes flew low overhead and the boys clutched each other. The sounds of the engines lingered long after the planes were out of sight.

The brush became thicker as they climbed what they thought was the way back to the Cielo. They could hear rustles and sounds and could only imagine that strange animals were around. Then suddenly the brush gave way and Roberto and Adolfo found themselves falling deep into a ravine. It happened so suddenly neither had time to grab on to anything, not even each other. Adolfo landed on top of Roberto at the bottom.

"Get off of me! You're heavy!" Roberto cried.

Adolfo scrambled away. "Are you hurt?"

"I don't think so. Are you?"

"My leg hurts," Adolfo said, pulling up his pants leg. "But it looks all right."

"I don't think I broke anything." Roberto checked his arms, his legs, his backside.

"The medicine!" Adolfo said. "Do you still have the medicine?"

Roberto felt his back pocket and pulled out the bottle. It had survived unharmed.

"Mamma is going to be so mad at us when she sees these clothes," Roberto said.

"You think we're going to get back?" Adolfo said. And he started to cry.

Marco, Francesco, Vito, Giacomo and Dante went out and searched the area as far as Gavino's farm but there was no sign of the boys. It would have been too dangerous to go farther. When they returned, everyone huddled in the main room.

Gina held Carlotta, who was now very listless. "I can't believe they ran off like that," she said. "They know how I worry."

"I'm sure there's an explanation," Maria said. "And I'm sure they'll be back soon."

She didn't sound confident.

Dante was very upset. "Please. We are at war. This is not a game. No one, I mean no one, should ever leave the Cielo alone again. The *cesso* is the farthest anyone can go. Does everyone understand that? Please!"

"I'm sure everyone here understands that, don't we?" Rosa said, looking at Lucia.

When they finally climbed out of the ravine and found a trail again, Roberto and Adolfo stayed close together and walked very carefully. Since the sun had now set, the shadows were darker and the boys cowered when they heard the wind crack a branch above them. The path was muddy now and there were holes everywhere. Adolfo tripped over one of them and looked inside.

"Look, 'Berto, what's this?" Adolfo was going to kick the metal container when Roberto pulled him back.

"Don't touch it! It might be a land mine!"

"It is a mine!" came a voice from the side of the path. "Be careful!"

Suddenly a tall young man stood before them. He was wearing a dark shirt with an ammunition belt over his chest and two grenades on his belt. He pulled Adolfo away from the hole and held on to Roberto.

"Who are you?" Roberto asked.

"That's my question," Ezio Maffini replied. "Who are you? What are you doing out here at night?"

Ezio did not tell the boys his name. He had been on his nightly patrol in the area and was startled to find two young boys not far from the cave where the partisans had recently moved. Two very frightened young boys.

In minutes, the boys told Ezio how they had moved from Sant'Antonio to the Cielo, how they had gone back to the village to get medicine for their sister, how two Germans had stopped them and how they were now returning home. They omitted the part about falling into the ravine.

"So you know the way back home now?" Ezio said.

"Um, well, we could use a little direction," Roberto said.

"You're lost, right?"

"Yes, sir."

"Let me get you there," Ezio said. "I know where it is."

Ezio quickly disassembled the mine and threw it back in the hole. In less than a half hour, he led the boys to the Cielo's back door, one hand on each of the boy's shoulders. Marco opened the door and everyone, except Fausta of course, rushed to hug the boys. Gina didn't know whether to spank them or to kiss them and decided to do both. Even Lucia and Anna gave their brothers big hugs and kisses.

"Look, Mamma," Roberto said. "We have Carlotta's medicine."

Gina broke down as she took the bottle from him.

"Oh, 'Berto, my sweet 'Berto. And Adolfo. You are such good boys. I hope this helps. I hope it's not too late."

Ezio was about to slip out the door when Maria stopped him. Rosa tried unsuccessfully to eavesdrop.

"Sparrow?" Maria whispered, putting her hand on his arm. "Sparrow? Is it you? Is it really you?"

"Signora Ruffolo?" Ezio had met Maria only once, when she had visited her daughter in Sant'Anna at Easter. "Signora Ruffolo?"

"Yes, it's me. *O Dio!* Have you heard from Angelica lately? We've been here for weeks and we don't get any letters and I'm so worried about her and the boys that I'm just sick even though I don't show it. What do you know?"

"Nothing, Signora." Ezio took Maria's hands in his. "We left Sant'Anna weeks ago because it wasn't safe for us any more and it was getting dangerous for the people there. We've moved closer to here now. I haven't had any contact with Angelica since then. I'm worried, too."

"We have to pray, Sparrow." Maria wiped her eyes with her handkerchief. "We have to pray real hard."

"I have to go, Signora. I can't stay here. If I learn anything, I'll come back, all right?"

"God bless you, Sparrow." Maria kissed him on both cheeks.

Ezio slipped out the door, Rosa hurried back into the kitchen, and Maria climbed the stairs to her room and began to say the rosary.

"We should have found out more about him," Francesco said. "At least we should know his name."

"We should know where his group is staying," Vito said.

"Partisans don't give out their names," Marco said. "But I think we'll find out more about them soon enough."

Rosa knew the boys must be hungry and quickly started water to boil. By the time the boys were cleaned up, their dinner was on the table.

"Look, Roberto," Rosa said. "I didn't make polenta. You'll have to eat pasta."

CHAPTER 21

▼

Carlotta hardly stirred all night and now, as the sun rose over the Cielo, Gina tried again to get her to nurse. The baby refused. Gina then tried to give her the medicine. But whenever she put the little eyedropper into Carlotta's mouth, the baby spit it out and her face was red from the medicine. Roberto, Anna and Adolfo watched anxiously.

"I bet it doesn't taste good," Roberto said.

"I don't know, 'Berto, she took it when we were home. I don't know why she doesn't want it now."

"Maybe it's hot," Anna said. "Or maybe it's cold."

"I don't think so," Gina said. "Maybe we're just too late."

"She has to get better, Mamma, she has to." Roberto was in tears.

"Let's hope so, 'Berto. I am so proud of you and Adolfo for getting the medicine. Do you want to hold her?"

Roberto carefully took the baby in his arms and said a silent prayer. "God, please make Carlotta better, please. If you do I'll never fight with Adolfo again."

Across the room, Lucia, furious and fidgety, took out her diary and made another entry.

"I am so angry. I mean I'm glad Roberto and Adolfo went and got the medicine for Carlotta but now we are all confined to this place, maybe forever. Now I can't go to see Dino. I don't think anyone knows I have been going to see him every day. Well, Rosa does, she knows everything. But now we have to stay here. I can't even go into the tower because someone is there all the time as a lookout.

"Dino is so sweet. Yesterday we made love again under our tree. He is so gentle. I just want to be with him forever. Sometimes he scares me when he talks about all the places he wants to go and what he wants to see. When he talks like that he doesn't seem to include me. Other times he tells me how much he loves me and how much he wants us to be together. That's the Dino I like.

"I don't know how long they're going to stay at Gavino's. Paolo's foot is getting better. Dino says they shouldn't stay in one place too long. I asked him if I could go with them and he just laughed. I hate it when he treats me like a child. I'm going to be seventeen in November. A lot of girls get married when they're seventeen. Wouldn't that be something? I would have a simple little wedding. I know the dress I would wear. I saw it in Reboli. Daniela and Carmella will be my bridesmaids. Anna can be my flower girl. Even Roberto and Adolfo can be in it, maybe even Carlotta. Maybe Papa will be back by then and he can give me away. Maybe the war will be over by then and Dino wouldn't have to be running all the time.

"I don't know when I'll see him again now. He can't come here and I can't go there because someone will see us. I don't know how I can even get a message to him. I am so afraid."

Lucia put the diary back. Downstairs, Colin Richards was guiding the men through another round of poker and the women were doing the laundry. Every couple of days they would take the big terra cotta container, called a *conca*, load it with sheets and clothing and Carlotta's diapers and spread a heavy cloth over it. Then they would spread ashes from the fireplace on top and pour boiling water containing lye through the cloth.

"I think we should pour the water through one more time," Maria said.

"We've already done it twice," Annabella said.

"We want these clothes to be clean."

After the final rinse the women took all the laundry and hung it on lines on the third floor since they didn't dare go outside anymore. Sometimes, it took two days before everything was dry.

No one mentioned Fausta, who remained in her room, and the atmosphere was lighter now that the boys had returned. The villagers were certain that the medicine would make Carlotta better.

Fausta's diatribe seemed to unite the villagers against the Germans and the Fascists. Until now, most just wanted the war to be over. Now, they realized how evil the enemy was and they couldn't wait until the Allies arrived and defeated the Germans. They also wanted desperately to be freed from their captivity in the Cielo and to return to their homes and resume their lives.

There were also fewer tensions. No one would claim that Rosa and Annabella were friends, but they were speaking to each other occasionally. The Contessa had resumed talking to Maria, who tried to avoid asking personal questions. Maddelena and Renata didn't bicker as often and Vito and Giacomo argued less when playing cards.

The sun was out, and although this was August a breeze at the top of the hill kept the Cielo comfortable. The villagers were ready for another day on the schedule Dante had arranged, and Richards' English language session was again entertaining. It involved clothing.

"The English word for *"berretto"* is "cap," Richards said.

"Cap!" everyone repeated.

For *"camicia"* it is "shirt."

"Shirt!"

For *"pantaloni"* it is "trousers."

"Trousers!"

For *"abito"* it is "dress."

"Dress!"

For *"scarpe"* it is "shoes."

"Shoes!"

"I'll never remember all this," Vito said."

"You don't have to remember 'dress,'" Giacomo said.

In the afternoon, when the time came for Richards to describe his journey as an escaped prisoner, Roberto and Adolfo were most interested in how he hid from the Germans at the monastery.

"How many dead people were in that cellar?" Roberto wanted to know.

"Twelve. But, you know, it wasn't a cellar, it was called a crypt under the altar. The bodies of the monks were in tombs so I didn't actually see any dead people."

"Could you smell them?" Adolfo wondered.

"It was musty in the crypt, but not from bodies. It was just dark and damp."

"Were there a lot of bugs and spiders and things?"

"A few, but they weren't a problem."

"Did you hear anything? Like moans or anything?"

"No," Richards laughed. "No moans or anything. It was very quiet."

"Creepy quiet?"

"Just quiet."

"Were you scared?" Adolfo asked.

"Not really, not after all I'd been through before. But say, you boys had an interesting journey yesterday. Why don't you tell us about it?"

Like any boys who were twelve and eight years old, Roberto and Adolfo were excited to describe their adventure, although they exaggerated some details and left out others. Maria held Carlotta, who was still pale and listless, so they could sit close to their mother on the bench, their legs swinging.

"Well," Roberto began, "I knew Carlotta needed her medicine so I just decided to go back and get it. I asked my little brother to come along because I thought he would like to go, too."

"You said that I had to go with you!"

"So we just stayed near the path but far enough away so no one would see us," Roberto continued. "Going down was pretty easy. One time we saw some men digging. Adolfo thought they were farmers but they couldn't have been farmers."

"I bet they were partisans deactivating the land mines," Francesco said.

"Maybe," Roberto said. "Anyway, we saw two soldiers but they didn't see us."

"Mamma mia," Maria said.

"Tell them about the naked people," Adolfo giggled.

"Yes. There were two people without clothes on under a tree, but we don't know who they were." Roberto thought it best to be vague about this part of the story.

"Two naked people? A man and a woman?" the Contessa asked. "What were they doing?"

"I don't think we need to know every detail of the boys' journey," Rosa said, looking directly at Lucia, whose face had lost all color. "Then what happened, Roberto?"

"Then we got to Sant'Antonio. First we stopped at Father Luigi's house."

"You saw Father Luigi? What did he say? How did he look? Did he look all right?" The villagers were full of questions.

"He looked all right," Roberto said. "He just told us to be careful. We didn't stay there long. There were soldiers all over, maybe hundreds of them."

"Not hundreds, maybe dozens," Adolfo said.

"We hid behind one tree and then another until we got to our house and no one saw us. We just walked in and I got the medicine and we walked out."

"How did the house look?" Gina asked. "Was there any damage?"

"Um, I guess we didn't have time to look around," Roberto said.

"Everything seemed fine," Adolfo said, looking down at his hands.

"So then these two giant soldiers came up to us and wanted to know what we were doing," Roberto said. "I told them we came to get medicine for our sister and they said all right, just go home then."

"That's all they said?" Marco asked.

"Pretty much. Why wouldn't they believe us?"

"They didn't threaten you or anything?"

"Um, no, nothing like that. Anyway, we just walked away and back up the hill. Well, you know how things look different when it gets dark? I thought we were on the right path but then Adolfo said we should go this other way so we took that way and we got a little lost."

"I told him the right way but he took the wrong way!" Adolfo declared.

"I knew the right way!" Roberto elbowed his brother in the ribs.

"How did you get so muddy?" Renata asked.

"Um," Roberto said, "sometimes the path that Adolfo made us take had some holes in it."

"We stopped after a while," Adolfo said. "We were hungry and we only had a couple of biscotti with us."

"That's what you ate the whole day?" Maria said.

"Yes," Roberto said proudly. "I forget what happened next. What happened next, Adolfo?"

"That man with the rifle found us."

"Right. We were walking along and that bloke saw us and asked if he could come back with us. So that's what he did, and that's all there is to the story."

"Tell us about Sant'Antonio," Rosa said. "Did it look different? Was there any damage? Is the cemetery all right? And the church?"

"I think everything looked pretty much the same, didn't it, Adolfo?" Roberto said. "I didn't notice the church. Oh, the sign was down from Leoni's. It was on the ground. Some soldiers were drinking beer."

"The soldiers were drinking beer?" Giacomo said.

"Yes," Roberto said. "It was very scary there. We're lucky we came back alive. But we did it for Carlotta. And now she can get better."

Roberto leaned against his mother. Anna kissed him on the forehead and tickled Adolfo. Rosa clapped her hands and everyone joined in. Richards said their adventure was much more exciting than his and the boys beamed.

"I'm proud of what you did," Gina said, hugging them close, "but don't you ever, and I mean ever, leave this house again unless I know about it."

"Yes, Mamma."

The women were putting dishes on the table for the evening meal when Fausta strode into the room. She still wore her white blouse and black skirt and she carried a small suitcase in one hand and her purse in the other. Everyone stopped talking and stared at her.

"Fausta!" Rosa said. "Where are you going? You can't leave here!"

"It is time for me to go," Fausta said. "I have been reading my responsibilities as a member of the *Fasci Femminili,* and I know I cannot be silent any longer. I am going back to Sant'Antonio and I will tell the occupying forces that there is a dangerous criminal being harbored here. I am sure they will come here shortly and do what has to be done."

"Fausta, you can't! You can't do that!" everyone shouted.

Richards stood up. "Fausta, please wait! I know I'm the cause of all this. I'll leave. Right now. Please don't put these people in danger."

"You have already put them in danger," Fausta said. "You should have thought about that when you came here. And all you people should have realized what you were doing when you agreed to take him in. I told you all what the penalty would be if you harbored an enemy prisoner of war. Oh yes, I'll tell them there are partisans near here, too, and Gavino is helping them."

"Fausta," Dante said, coming toward her. "Please, think about what you're doing. These are innocent people here."

"It's too late, Dante. Don't try to stop me."

She picked up her suitcase and began to back toward the door.

"You're not going anywhere, Fausta."

From the back of the room, Marco strode forward. He held the pistol he had kept in his pocket since the day he had left home in Sant'Antonio. He pointed it now at Fausta. Maddelena and Renata screamed, the Contessa collapsed in her chair and the others looked terrified.

"Put the suitcase down, Fausta," Marco said.

"Don't try anything, Marco," she said. "I know how to shoot, too."

She dropped the suitcase and pulled a small silver pistol from her purse, pointing it first at Marco and then at the others.

Everyone plunged to the floor, hiding as best they could under the table and chairs.

Then, in a single move, Dante got behind Fausta, grabbed the hand that was holding the pistol and pointed her arm into the air. The movement caused her to pull the trigger and a bullet pierced a beam in the ceiling. Dante pulled her arm behind her back and the pistol fell to the floor. Francesco quickly grabbed it.

Now there was more screaming. Fausta struggled against Dante's strong arms, but then went limp.

"It's all right, Fausta," he said, holding both her arms behind her back. "Just give in."

Rosa found a piece of rope near the fireplace and Marco and Francesco tied Fausta's hands together. She was crying softly now and gave no resistance.

"So what should we do with her?" Francesco asked.

"Take her to her room for now," Dante said. "I think we'll have to let the group decide."

CHAPTER 22

▼

Still in shock, most of the villagers gathered silently in the main room the next day, with Fausta locked in her room and Gina taking care of Carlotta upstairs. The baby was even more feverish, still refusing to eat or take her medicine. She also had very messy diapers. Gina kept rocking her and singing lullabies.

Downstairs, around the table, Maria interrupted the long silence. "I can't believe that two people, two people we know, pointed guns at each other. That was so frightening."

"Fausta could have killed any one of us," Annabella said.

"Or Marco and Fausta could have killed each other," Maria said. "If Marco and Fausta could point guns, so could any one of us."

"So we've come to this," Rosa said. "Are we any better than the Germans? Could we really kill one another?"

"We're at war, Rosa, we're at war," Marco said.

"*O Dio!*" Rosa said. "What is happening to us?"

The group fell silent again as each person reviewed the events of last night. They didn't even pay much attention to the planes overhead or the sounds of artillery in the valley. Instead, they pondered what had happened and what was going to become of them now. Every once in awhile someone would glance at the beam above them, find the tiny bullet hole and shudder.

"Well, one thing I know," Francesco finally said. "I'm glad Marco had that pistol in his pocket."

"I didn't even know you brought it," Rosa said. "How did you take it without my seeing you?"

"Oh, Rosa," Marco replied, "you can't know everything."

"I try." Rosa teased at Marco's beard, which was now getting quite full.

"I have to ask you something, Marco," Maddelena said. "What were you thinking when you pulled out that pistol and pointed it at Fausta? Did you think you could really shoot her?"

"I wasn't thinking at all," he said. "I just knew I had the pistol in my pocket and I was sure that would stop her. I hoped she would just put the suitcase down and go back to her room."

"But when she took out her own pistol?"

"I don't know what I thought. I guess you don't think in those situations. If she had tried to shoot me, or anyone else in the room for that matter, would I have fired? I guess I would have."

"You've never shot anything other than wild rabbits and pheasants, right?" Rosa said.

"No. Maybe I could have fired it, Rosa, but I wouldn't have tried to kill her. Well, I don't know what I would have done. And that scares me. What if I had killed her and she lay there in front of us? I don't know if I could live with myself if I had done that."

"And if she would have fired, you would have been there on the floor in front of us," Rosa said. "Think about that."

Marco put his hands on the table and studied them. They were big, strong hands, and over the years they had shoveled dirt and concrete, constructed stone walls, put up windows and doors and wrung the necks of chickens. Yet now they were shaking. Marco put one hand over the other so no one else would see, but then his shoulders started shaking, too.

"Marco, Marco," Rosa said as she put her arm around him.

"I have never been so afraid in all my life," he said, tears in his eyes and his voice cracking. "Not so much afraid of Fausta's gun but afraid of myself."

Marco rested his head on his wife's shoulders as she held him tight. Everyone else tried not to notice.

"Well," Maria said, "we have to thank someone else, too. And that is Dante."

"Dante!" everyone cried.

Dante sat at the end of the table. He had not eaten any of the *castagnaccio* that Rosa had made and was staring straight ahead and running his finger around the edge of his glass. He had spent the night alternately tossing on his bed and pacing the floor. Not even *The Divine Comedy* nor the letter inside the book helped. He had never been in a situation like that before and he had no idea how he would react. He finally decided it must have been instinctive.

"Dante," Rosa said, "you saved our lives, too! You were wonderful!"

"I just didn't think you would do that," the Contessa said.

"Because you think I just sit in my room and read?" Dante said, trying to laugh. "Because you think I'm a coward? Who says I'm not?"

"You certainly weren't last night," Rosa said. "Remember what I said the other day, that sometimes we do what we have to do even though we don't think we can. Last night you did what you had to do."

"Yes, I guess so."

"Aren't you proud of yourself?"

"For knocking a woman to the floor? I don't know if that's something to be proud of."

"Dante," Rosa said, "if it wasn't for you, Fausta would have shot every one of us."

"I don't know," Dante said. "I'm like Marco. It frightens me to think of what might have happened. I felt like it was somebody else doing what I did."

"Maybe there's another Dante inside the one that you show everyone," Rosa said. "Maybe you don't give yourself credit for what you are able to do."

Dante gripped his glass and looked down at the table. "I just know that everything has changed now. We're not the same group that we were before."

"We're the same group," Rosa said. "But we've changed. And maybe now we will be more united, we will be stronger."

"I hope so," Dante said. "I just know that my arm hurts."

"Well, that will get better," Maria said.

The Contessa reached over and massaged Dante's arm.

"What we have to decide," Dante said, taking her hand off his arm, "is what to do with Fausta."

After the altercation Marco and Francesco had carried Fausta to her room, untied her wrists and left her lying on her bed. They locked the door behind them when they left. Fortunately, the tiny room had only a small slit for a window.

"Just keep her locked up in there," Vito said. "Let her rot."

"We can't do that," Maria said. "No matter how much we hate her, no matter what she threatened to do to us last night, she's still a human being. We can't sink down as low as she has."

"I agree," Rosa said. "We have to protect ourselves, but we have to take care of her. Look, I hate what she did last night as much as anyone else, but how would we feel if something happened to her?"

"*Boh!* We'd feel pretty good," Vito said.

"Well, what should we do?" Dante asked.

"I say we keep her locked in her room and take some food to her every day. That's enough," Rosa said.

"Are you going to empty her pot?" Vito asked.

"You and I can take turns, Vito."

Colin Richards came out of his little room just as the group was breaking up. He had his knapsack on his back.

"I need to say something to all of you," he said. "I apologize for being the cause of what happened last night and the only way I can make this better is for me to leave. I'm going to go now."

"No, no, don't do that," Rosa said, rising and going to him. "Fausta's no danger now. She's not going to inform on us."

"It's still a danger," Richards said. "If she doesn't inform the Germans, someone else will. I can't let you take that risk any more."

"Just stay for a few more days," Maria said, putting her hand on his shoulder. "You're still coughing."

"It's not so bad anymore." And with that Richards suddenly had another coughing spell and collapsed into a chair.

Roberto waited until he was finished. "We want to hear more stories. Please!"

"And learn more English," Vito said.

Richards agreed to stay a few more days. By then he would be better.

Giacomo returned from his lookout post and was replaced by Annabella. Maddelena and Renata cleared the table and Maria went upstairs to look in on Carlotta and Gina. Carlotta was lying in her carriage and Gina was putting damp towels on her head and chest, but there was no response.

"I've been trying and trying, but she won't come around," Gina said. "She won't eat, she won't take the medicine. I don't know what to do anymore."

Maria put her arms around her.

"You're doing all you can, Gina. Just leave it up to God now."

Maria sat on the edge of the bed as Gina tended to Carlotta.

"God!" Gina said. "I don't think I believe in God anymore."

"Gina, you've gone through so much. That's understandable. But look at all you have. Besides this beautiful Carlotta, you have Lucia and Anna and Roberto and Adolfo. And they are such wonderful boys. Can you imagine two other boys doing what they did the other day?"

"I was worried sick."

"I know, but they were only thinking of Carlotta. They wanted to make their sister better."

"I know. They're very good boys and I love them. And Lucia and Anna, too, of course."

"Lucia is so beautiful and Anna is going to be stunning, too, I just know it," Maria said. She handed Gina another damp towel.

"Poor Lucia," Gina said. "I wish I had more time to give her. She seems to need so much."

"You give her a lot, I'm sure."

"I wish we were closer. Were you and Angelica very close?"

"Oh, my, yes," Maria said. "And we still are. She tells me everything, sometimes things I don't want to know."

"I wish Lucia would."

Maria lifted Carlotta from the carriage, went to the window and held her against her shoulder. "There, there, sweet little baby," she whispered.

The valleys looked so peaceful from here. They reminded Maria of the valleys below Sant'Anna and she couldn't help but think of her last visit there and the day she met the partisan who brought Roberto and Adolfo home.

After taking the train to Pietrasanta, Maria had slowly walked up the winding path to the village at the top of the hill. She wasn't alone. Many people, some of them from far beyond, were fleeing to Sant'Anna.

It was Holy Thursday, and Maria hoped she would arrive for the service in the little church that night. She wondered why Angelica didn't meet her half way, as she had the last time Maria had visited, but it was a cool spring day and she enjoyed the walk. Of course, she soon became engaged in conversations with others who were climbing the hill with her.

"*Buongiorno, buongiorno,*" she kept saying. For a while, she held the hands of two little girls who were with their parents.

"Have you come a long way?" she asked the father.

"We live near Pisa," he said. "The Germans are all over and now the British have started to bomb. Everyone says Sant'Anna is the safest place."

"I live over by Camaiore, but north of there, a little village called Sant'Antonio," Maria said. "I'm just going to Sant'Anna for a visit. My daughter lives there. Her husband is in the army. She has two little boys and I miss them so much."

"She must be very lonely," the man said.

"Yes. Very lonely. When she first came her husband's parents were alive but then they got sick and Angelica had to take care of them all by herself and then they died and now she has the two boys to take care of and you know how active little children…"

"Yes, we know," the man said, taking his daughters' hands.

Near the top, as the path made a jagged turn, everyone naturally turned around to see how far they had come. It was one of the most spectacular views in all Italy. On this clear day, they could see for miles, past Pietrasanta, past Camaiore, almost to Lake Massaciuccoli. The little houses seemed like toys so far below.

Maria crossed herself. To live in Sant'Anna, she thought, must be like living in heaven.

Sant'Anna was not really one village but a scattering of *borgati,* or hamlets, spread across the hills between Monte Ornato and Monte Gabberi. Each of them had a name. Angelica lived in what was called Il Pero, not far from the church and school. Farther north were the *borgati* of L'Argentiera, Vaccareccia, Il Colle and Sennari. To the west was I Coletti, where Rosa's cousin Lara from Livorno was now staying.

Maria was glad that Angelica was close to the little shop run by Abramo Farnocchi and his wife Sofia Pieri. It was barely bigger than a closet, but it contained the essentials, or at least did before the influx of refugees. Abramo made the best bread Maria had ever tasted. She brought some home with her.

Maria was out of breath when she finally arrived at Angelica's, and Little Carlo and Nando bounded out to greet her before she could knock at the door.

"Nona! Nona!" they cried, both hugging their grandmother at once. Angelica joined them and there was much hugging and kissing.

In the kitchen, Maria was surprised to find a tall man buttoning his shirt and quickly brushing his hair. Angelica looked flustered.

"Mamma," she stammered. "I want you to meet...I want you to meet...Mamma, this is my friend I've written to you about. His name is Sparrow."

"Buongiorno," Maria said, too surprised to question his name.

"Buongiorno, Signora," the man said as he took her hand and bowed. "Angelica has told me so much about you. You are quite a remarkable woman and it is a pleasure to meet you. Are your tired from your long journey?"

"No, I'm just fine," Maria said, looking the man up and down. Angelica smiled as the two shook hands.

There was a long awkward silence. Angelica looked at the man. The man looked at Angelica. Maria looked at both of them, and then the man crossed the room.

"I hope you have a pleasant stay here," he said. "And now, Angelica, I must leave. I don't know when I'll be back. Perhaps in a week or two."

The man picked up an ammunition belt from a chair and slung it over his chest. Maria did her best not to watch as Angelica and the boys walked him out the door, but she couldn't help noticing that Angelica and this Sparrow had their arms around each other.

Afterwards, Angelica told her the whole story. Sparrow was the leader of a partisan *banda* who had come to her home a few months earlier looking for food. She was glad to give him some, and they soon formed a very close attachment.

"Angelica," Maria said, fearing the answer. "How close?"

"Mamma, Carlo has been gone for two years. I love Carlo very much, but I'm very lonely."

"Oh, Angelica, Angelica." Maria's eyes filled with tears.

In the long conversation that followed, Maria tried to balance what she thought was right with her deep love for her daughter. She knew that Sparrow must be a good man or Angelica would not be involved with him. Still, she was married to Carlo, and just because he was off in the war was not a reason for her daughter to be involved with another man.

Maria held her daughter by the shoulders. "Angelica, if this makes you happy, then I won't tell you anything. Just be careful. Please, be careful. But I will be praying for you."

Maria stayed until the day after Easter. Then, after a tearful farewell with Angelica and the boys, she slowly made her way back down the hill, meeting many refugees on their way up.

As she looked out the window, Maria patted Carlotta gently on her back. She couldn't help but think of the poster at Leoni's. *"Whoever gives shelter or food to a partisan group or a single partisan will be shot."*

"Please, God," Maria prayed silently. "Don't let anything happen to Angelica, to Carlo, to Little Carlo, to Nando or to the partisan, whatever his name is."

Maria's thought were interrupted when Carlotta suddenly began to cough. Maria patted her back and soon the baby quieted down. Then Maria thought she was too quiet. She held her close and hummed a lullaby.

"Gina," she suddenly asked, "You wouldn't betray Pietro, would you?"

"Betray Pietro? Why would you think that?"

"I don't know. I was just wondering."

"You know, I have never even thought of it. Not that there are any opportunities in Sant'Antonio or Reboli. But I know other women who have been involved with other men while their husbands are at war. Some women from Sant'Antonio even. Things change during a war, Maria. It's not like it was before."

"No, I suppose not."

The tears were now flowing down Maria's cheeks.

"Maria, Maria," Gina said, "What's the matter?"

"I can't tell you, Gina. I can't tell you."

Gina put her arms around Maria, realizing that now she was the one who was doing the comforting. Maria put Carlotta back into her carriage and rocked it back and forth. The baby was still lethargic.

"I don't suppose you've heard from Pietro lately?"

"Nothing," Gina said. "Not for months. I wrote him when Carlotta was born and he didn't answer. How could he not answer? He's never even seen the baby. And all the children miss him so much."

"Maybe he didn't get the letter," Maria said. "Maybe he's in a place where he can't write. Or maybe there's a letter waiting for you back home. I hope I have one from Angelica."

Carlotta was whimpering now and this time Gina picked her up. "Pietro must be dead. I just don't have any hope that he will come back."

"You mustn't think that. You don't know. We just have to keep praying that God will help us."

Both women were lost in their thoughts, and then Maria stood behind Gina and brushed her curly hair.

"You have hair just like Carlotta's," she said.

"Only hers is the natural color," Gina laughed. After weeks at the Cielo, the roots of Gina's hair were now clearly black.

"I remember when you were a little girl and how your mother and father walked you up and down the street in Sant'Antonio," Maria said. "They were so proud of you. They thought there was no other child as pretty as you were."

"Mamma and Papa always dressed me up so nice. And they gave me so many dolls. I was like a little doll to them."

"You had a pink dress that you wore at Easter one year. I still remember that. And the bonnet."

Gina laughed. "They couldn't afford a new dress for me for First Communion so I wore my cousin's."

"What's the difference? You only wore it once."

"When I was working I could bring home a little money for them. Papa hadn't been able to work for so long."

"You actually paid for everything when you were working, didn't you?"

"I was glad to do it. I was their only child," Gina said.

"I remember your mother being such a wonderful cook. She had that beautiful garden and she made such a good soup with the beans and the carrots and everything."

"You and your husband were always so good to us," Gina said. "I used to love it when he would tell me stories. I never got to know Angelica very well. She's not much older than Lucia, is she? I always thought she was so pretty."

Maria's eyes filled with tears and she turned away.

Gina rinsed the baby's towels in the basin. "I wish Mamma and Papa were here now."

"I'm sure they're looking down on you and are as proud of you now as they were when you were a child." Maria said.

Gina knew Carlotta had a fever but didn't have a thermometer to take her temperature. "Do you think I should be holding her? Will that make her even warmer?"

"I think it will make her feel better. She needs to know you're there. I'm going to go downstairs now and rest a bit. Call me if you need me, all right?"

"Thank you, Maria."

Gina held the baby and sang to her.

That night, Rosa put some leftovers together and took it to Fausta's door. "Fausta, it's Rosa. I have some food for you and I'm going to unlock the door."

With only the tiny window, the room was dark. Fausta had taken off her blouse, skirt, stockings and shoes and was sitting in a chair in her slip. Rosa was shocked to see that her neck, wrists and ankles had bruises on them, old bruises that even after all these weeks looked like rope burns. Rosa didn't say anything.

"I'm really not hungry," Fausta said.

"Well, maybe you will be later. I'll just put this on the table. But if you don't eat soon, it will get cold."

As she turned to leave, Rosa notice that Fausta's notebook lay on the floor, but that the pages had been ripped out.

"Rosa?"

"Yes?"

"Nothing. Thank you for the vegetables."

Just as Rosa locked the door behind her, Gina came running down the stairs.

"Maria! Rosa!" she cried. "Come quick!"

"What is it, Gina?" both women cried together.

"It's Carlotta! I don't think she's breathing. Come quick!"

CHAPTER 23

▼

Father Luigi awoke in a daze after a restless night. He was worried about Roberto and Adolfo coming to the village, worried if they had made it back to the Cielo unharmed and worried about little Carlotta. Thank goodness she had been baptized. He had hoped Roberto and Adolfo would be altar boys, but Gina herself didn't come to church very often. What if the baby died up there? The Germans told him he couldn't leave Sant'Antonio. What would they do for a funeral? The only thing he could do from here was to say a Mass for the baby.

It was Thursday, August 3, and although no one else would be in the church, he put on all of his vestments and looked up the saint of the day.

"Ah, St. Lydia Purpuraria," he thought. "Who in the world is she?"

He read the description: "Lydia Purpuraria (1st century) was born at Thyatira, a town in Asia Minor, famous for its dye works (hence, her name which means purple dye seller). She became Paul's first convert at Philippi. She was baptized with her household, and Paul stayed at her home there."

Father Luigi closed the book. "Well, St. Purple Dye Seller, I hope you had some good talks with St. Paul but let's say the Mass. Let's pray for poor Carlotta. And how did you sell purple dye anyway?"

The altar was covered with a white cloth and Father Luigi opened the missal. As the days had gone by and he became used to saying the Mass alone, the priest began to condense the prayers and found his mind wandering.

"*In nomine Patris, et Filii, et Spiritus Sancti*...Yes, in the name of the Father and the Son and the Holy Spirit let us say this Mass for little Carlotta Sporenza, a child of God who has become another innocent victim of this war. If Gina and her children were at home, if the Germans were not here, if the Allies had arrived, if, if, if…We don't know your plan, oh God, help us to understand it."

The priest turned the page of the missal. As often as he had said Mass he still used the book to guide him.

"*Confiteor Deo omnipotenti, beatae Mariae semper Virgini, beato Michaeli Archangelo, beato Joanni Baptistae, sanctis Apostolis Petro et Paulo*…And I confess to God almighty, to the blessed Mary, to Michael the Archangel, to blessed John the Baptist, to Saints Peter and Paul that I have not been the kind of priest my people deserve. I have been selfish, I have been weak, I have not dared to challenge the evils in this world."

Father Luigi tapped his chest three times.

"*Kyrie eleison, Kyrie eleison, Kyrie eleison, Christe eleison, Christe eleison, Christe eleison, Kyrie eleison, Kyrie eleison, Kyrie eleison*…Lord have mercy on all of us. Especially have mercy today on the people at the Cielo. Help them to understand what is happening to them and to have mercy on those who would harm them. Guard Gina and Carlotta and her other children and help them through this horrible crisis. Help the Jews and all who suffer during this terrible time. Please bring them to safety. And, yes, even bless those soldiers who are occupying our village. We are all your children."

The priest skipped the sermon. Who would listen?

"*Credo in unum Deum, Patrem omnipotentem, factorem coeli et terrae, visibilium omnium et invisibilium*…Yes, I believe in one God. I'm not sure of what else I believe in, but I know your presence. I don't understand why there is such cruelty in this world and all I can do is accept your plan."

Sanctus, Sanctus, Sanctus. The priest took a wafer from the ciborium and raised it above his head: "*Hoc est enem corpus meum*…Yes, others may doubt, but I believe this is your body, oh Lord."

Then he raised the chalice of wine. "*Hic est enem calix sanguinis mei*…And I believe that this is your blood, shed for all of us."

The "Our Father" was Father Luigi's favorite prayer and he loved to say it in Latin.

"*Pater noster, qui es in coelis. sanctificetur nomen tuum: adveniat regnum tuum: fiat voluntas tua, sicut in coelo, et in terra*…And please give us this day the bread we need for our bodies and the strength we need for our souls."

In less than a half hour, the Mass was ended. "*Missa est. Deo gratias.*"

Father Luigi took off his vestments and folded them neatly on the table in the sacristy. It was going to be another hot day and he was already perspiring. Then he went back to the altar to pray for Carlotta.

Fritz and Konrad slogged through thick mud returning to the village from the hills. The mud caked their pants and shirts and hands. Their shoes felt twice as heavy.

"Hold up," Fritz said. "I have to catch my breath."

Konrad took out a cigarette.

"Fritz, I'm getting so bored here I don't know what I'm going to do," he said. "All we do is plant mines. When are we going to have some more real fighting?"

"It won't be long," Fritz said. "The enemy is in Florence and Pisa. They should be here soon and then you can see some action."

"They're taking their time," Konrad said, throwing a match onto the path. The soldiers watched as it burned itself out. Fritz took out a cigarette and Konrad gave him a light from his.

"You know what I wish we had around here, Fritz?"

"Some women."

"Yeah, that, too," Konrad said, wiping the mud from his glasses. "No, I mean more partisans. We know they're here, they keep cutting our lines and taking our mines apart. But where are they?"

"Do you want to know what the lieutenant says?" Fritz said. "He says they're hiding in the farmhouses up here in the hills. And even if they're not, he says the people in the farmhouses know where they are."

"So what are we going to do about it?"

"Starting tomorrow, we're going to pay some visits to these farmhouses. Maybe we'll find some escaped prisoners, too. Or some army deserters."

"Good. I want some action, Fritz. I want some more action."

"You almost beat up two little boys the other day. You must have liked that."

"I was only fooling around."

"The boys didn't know that."

"Hell, Fritz, we're SS. They should be afraid of us."

"Let's get going, Konrad. It's getting dark."

Ezio Maffini had time for only a short entry in his journal.

"A very strange thing has happened. I have encountered my angel's mother again. She is staying in a farmhouse near here with other people from her village. I remember meeting her last Easter at my angel's house. Seeing her made me ache for my angel even more.

"This is the same farmhouse where I returned two young boys who were lost. When I was coming back, I met two young men. They are from Montepulciano and have been running away from the army. One of them had a bad foot but it is mostly healed now. I talked to them about joining our *banda* and they are interested. They say they want to see the world, but I told them they can't see the world unless we defeat our enemies first. I hope they will join us. We need them!"

"*Viva l'italia!*"

CHAPTER 24

▼

Early in the morning Rosa, Maria and Annabella went outside and picked the roses and oleanders, the poppies and begonias, the sunflowers and wildflowers that were growing around the house. They filled every vase and jar and pot they could find and covered the long table in the main room, leaving a space in the middle.

Carlotta's little body didn't need a big casket so Vito and Giacomo took a small dresser drawer, cut it down to size and made a cover. Maddelena sewed a cushion out of a blanket and Anna relinquished the long blue velvet gown she had been wearing so that Renata could make a lining. Vito put the improvised casket on the table.

Gina and her children came down from upstairs and almost everyone gathered around as she placed little Carlotta in the box. Colin Richards had volunteered to be the lookout so the others could be together. Fausta, of course, remained locked in her room.

Rosa and Maria stood next to Gina, looking down at the tiny child. "She looks so pretty," Rosa said. "Like she's sleeping," Maria said. Carlotta's curls were tight against her head and she wore her pink dress with white lace. Around her neck was a gold chain with a tiny cross, a gift from the Contessa.

"She's at peace now," Annabella said, wiping away tears.

Lucia hugged her mother. "I'm so sorry, Mamma. I should have helped you more. I was so wrapped up in myself. I really loved Carlotta, I did. I should have shown it more."

Gina wiped the tears from her daughter's face. "It's all right, it's all right. You didn't know. And I know how you feel. I was sixteen once, too, you know."

Gina held her for a long time.

Rosa put her arm around Gina. "How are you, Gina? This is so terrible."

"I can't get used to this," Gina said. "I cried all night, but now I don't have any more tears left."

"They'll come," Rosa said, "and they should. We need to cry." Rosa's eyes were filled with tears.

Anna, Roberto and Adolfo stood together in the corner of the room, holding hands. Gina went over to them.

"Come and say goodbye to your sister," she said. "You need to do that."

"Do we have to?" Adolfo said.

Gina took their hands and led them to the table. The three children began to sob uncontrollably.

Anna gently placed her doll inside the coffin. It was almost as big as Carlotta.

"Are you sure you want to do that?" Gina asked.

"Yes, Mamma, I do."

Because the children were crying so hard, Gina took them into the kitchen. She knelt and put her arms around them. "I know it's hard," she said, "but we did everything we could. Anna, you were so good with Carlotta. You made her laugh so much. You boys. I never thought you could actually get to the village and bring back the medicine, but you did. You are very very brave and I'm so proud of you."

"But the medicine didn't work!" Roberto cried.

"No, no," their mother said. "'Berto, I don't think any medicine would have helped her. Her little body just couldn't fight the sickness off any more. Maybe it was an infection, we don't know. But she put up a big fight for such a tiny baby. I'm proud of her, too."

"If we didn't come up here to the Cielo, if we had stayed at home, she wouldn't have gotten sick again," Anna said through her tears.

"Carlotta must have been sick before we even got here," Gina said. "We don't know what would have happened, and we can't think about 'what ifs' any more. We had her for three months and we can be grateful for that. Remember how she used to smile at you? How she grabbed your fingers? She knew each of you by your voices."

"I called her my little Carlottina," Roberto said.

"She was my little Tina," Adolfo said, wiping his nose with the back of his hand.

Gina held them close. "Always remember that when you think about her."

"I wish Papa could see her," Roberto said. "He doesn't even know she's dead."

"He may not even know she was born," Gina said.

She was about to say that Pietro would find out when he returned, but she doubted now that he would ever return and didn't want to let the children think that he would.

"Do you think that God took her because he wanted her in heaven?" Anna asked.

Gina didn't know how to answer that question. She didn't know what she believed about God and heaven but didn't want to discourage Anna if she believed.

"Perhaps, perhaps. That's a nice way to think about it. We don't know."

Rosa interrupted them. "Gina, I think it's time."

Gina and her children joined the others as they stood around the table. Maria said that perhaps the villagers would like to say some prayers.

"Let's start with the 'Our Father,'" she said.

Padre Nostro, che sei nei cieli,
sia santificato il tuo nome,
venga il tuo regno,
sia fatta la tua volontà,
come in cielo cosí in terra...

"Did you hear that?" Maria said. "Our Father who art in *cieli*—in Cielo, in heaven, where we are. God must be with us. Now let's say the 'Hail Mary.'"

Ave, Maria, piena di grazia,
il Signore è con te.
Tu sei benedetta fra le donne
e benedetto è il frutto del tuo seno, Gesú...

"*O Dio,*" Maria said.

Gloria al Padre e al Figlio e allo Spirito Santo.
Come era nel principio, è ora, e sempre
nei secoli dei secoli.
Amen.

The villagers crossed themselves.

Nel nome del Padre, del Figlio e dello Spirito Santo.
Amen.

Francesco stepped toward the table, carrying his violin. The Corelli "La Folia," which always brought contentment and serenity to the villagers in the evening, now only sounded mournful.

"I want to do one more thing," Gina said when he had finished. She put her hand on Carlotta's head and began to quietly sing.

Fi la nana, e mi bel fiol,
Fi la nana, e mi bel fiol,
Fa si la nana.
Fa si la nana.

Dormi ben, e mi bel fiol,
Dormi ben, e mi bel fiol,
Fa si la nana.
Fa si la nana.

Soon all the villagers were singing the lullaby and everyone, even Vito and Giacomo, wiped away tears. Some villagers began to hold hands. Francesco, standing next to Annabella, took her hand in his. Maddelena and Vito stood next to each other but they did not join hands.

Hush-a-bye, my lovely child,
Hush-a-bye, my lovely child,
Hush, hush and go to sleep.
Hush, hush and go to sleep.

Sleep well, my lovely child,
Sleep well, my lovely child,
Hush, hush and go to sleep.
Hush, hush and go to sleep.

"Sleep well, my darling," Gina said, and leaned down to kiss the baby's forehead. The children also kissed their sister and the family went out the back door. The others also bade farewell to the infant. Rosa noticed that Francesco put his arm around Annabella and that she was crying. Then Marco nailed the cover on to the coffin and carried it out, followed by the others, with Gatto trailing behind. Everyone took as many flowers as they could carry. They would be safe in such a big group. Just then, it started to rain.

Vito and Giacomo had dug a grave under a huge chestnut tree about thirty feet from the house. After placing the coffin, they covered it with dirt and then a layer of sod. The flowers made a huge pile on the little mound. Marco had created a cross out of white birch.

Carlotta Sporenza
1944–1944
Our Little Angel

When they returned to the Cielo it was time for *il pranzo*, but no one felt like eating. Now the rain was beating against the windows. Thunder mixed with the roar of airplanes and lightning could not be distinguished from the anti-aircraft firings from the valley.

"I wish Father Luigi had been able to come up here for this," Maria said, putting her hand on Gina's shoulder.

"I understand," Gina said. "I know the Germans won't allow him to leave Sant'Antonio."

"And I feel so bad that we couldn't have buried Carlotta in the cemetery in Sant'Antonio," Maria said.

Gina held Maria's hand. "When the war is over this will be a nice peaceful place and that's a lovely spot under the chestnut tree. Carlotta will like it there and we can come and visit her."

There was a long silence. Everyone wondered whether they would even leave the Cielo.

"If the war doesn't end soon, I think we will all go crazy," Annabella said.

"I'm getting to feel the same way, Annabella," Rosa said.

Maria looked at both of them and smiled. Rosa and Annabella seemed to be talking more.

"What can we do?" Marco said. "What can we do besides wait?"

Francesco got up and paced back and forth in front of the window. Lightning flashed and thunder echoed across the hillsides. "I don't know," he said, "but there must be something we can do besides sitting here."

"We can't put ourselves in more danger than we are already," Maddelena said. "We have an escaped prisoner in the kitchen and a Fascist locked in her room. That makes me very nervous."

"You don't want Colin here?" Maria asked.

"Of course I do. It's just a worry, that's all. And as for Fausta, well, who knows what she will do?"

"Let's just try to all get along together," Dante said.

Rosa put her hand on his arm. "Dante, Dante, you just want everybody to be at peace."

"Yes, I do."

Francesco returned to the group and pounded the table. "Well, I just think we need to do something, anything."

A worried frown crossed over Annabella's face.

"Francesco," Rosa said, "why do you suddenly feel so strongly about this? You didn't seem angry before."

"I don't know," he said. "It's just that with everything that's happened in the last few weeks, Colin Richards, Fausta, now Carlotta. The war seems so much closer now and we are so helpless."

Annabella went to her husband and put her arm around his shoulder. "You don't think we're going back soon now, do you?"

"No."

While everyone else retired to rest, Francesco went to his room and took out his violin.

Lucia was looking out the window when she saw the two figures running from Gavino's hut. It was raining just like when they first arrived at the Cielo weeks ago. With her mother resting and her sister and brothers trying to nap, Lucia ran over to the tower. Fortunately, Rosa was on duty as the lookout.

"Rosa! It's all right! It's only Dino and Paolo!"

Rosa didn't have a chance to reply before Lucia turned, ran down the steps and opened the rear door.

"Come up here on the steps," she said.

"Are you all right, Lucia?" Dino said. "You look sad."

"My baby sister died yesterday."

"Oh, Lucia, I'm so sorry."

"It's all right." Lucia turned her head so Dino wouldn't see her tears.

"Lucia," Dino said. "I wanted to see you again before we left."

"Before you left? Where are you going?"

"You knew that we couldn't stay here forever. Paolo's foot is better and we need to go."

Paolo walked back and forth in the rain, exercising his foot. "Hey, it feels good," he yelled to Dino.

"But where are you going?" Lucia asked.

Paolo looked down at the ground.

"We weren't going to tell you," Dino said.

"Why not?"

"Because we're joining the Garibaldi brigade."

"The partisans?" Lucia shouted. "What do you know about fighting? You ran away from the army because you didn't want to fight. You'll be killed in a minute."

"No, we won't," Dino said. "We know how to fight. We just didn't want to fight for the Germans. And anyway, there are lots of things to do besides fighting."

"How do you know?"

"We met a partisan the other night. He told us all about it. They really need more people now. They need them to find the mines. They need them to harass the Germans. And Lucia, we're going to see so much!"

"This is so laughable. You're a lover, Dino, not a fighter."

"Well, I'll learn to be a fighter!"

Dino dropped the pack from his back, took Lucia in his arms and kissed her forehead.

"I'm going to miss you," he said.

"Dino, please take me with you. The partisans have women."

"Lucia, you know we can't."

"I won't be a bother, I promise. I can run fast. I won't get in the way."

"Lucia, it would be too dangerous. We can't risk it. We can't put you in that danger."

Lucia broke away from his arms and sat crumpled on the steps. She was sobbing.

"Oh, Lucia, please don't make this harder than it already is. We had some good times, you know that. Let's be glad about that."

"You make it sound like it's over."

"Lucia, you know me. You know how I want to travel, how I want to see the world."

"Without me."

"I have to do this alone. I'm sorry."

Paolo nudged Dino. "We'd better go. This rain isn't letting up."

Dino lifted Lucia from the steps and held her. "I'll always remember little Lucia, the light in the tower."

"Stop calling me little Lucia!" she hissed. "I'm a grown woman. Almost. I'm old enough to…to…"

"To what?"

Lucia pounded her fists against Dino's chest. "Never mind."

Paolo tugged at Dino's arm. "Let's go, Dino."

"Can I have a kiss, Lucia?" Dino said.

"You've always wanted more than that." Lucia tears flowed freely now.

"I wish we had time," Dino said. He tried to kiss her but she pulled away.

"Dino, you don't know anything about women!" Lucia said. "You say you've had so many girls but you treat them all the same way. You only care about yourself! Goodbye, Dino!"

She ran into the house, slamming the door behind her.

"Let's go, Paolo," Dino said as he put his pack back on. "She was a nice girl, wasn't she? But she sure was stubborn. Most girls would have liked to kiss me goodbye."

Lucia raced up the stairs, encountering Rosa returning from lookout duty.

"Lucia! What happened? Why are you crying?"

"It's over, Rosa, it's over. Let me alone!"

Rosa reached out to stop her, but Lucia ran to her room, threw herself on her bed and buried her face in the pillow. When the tears finally stopped, she took out her diary.

"Dino just left. Good riddance, I'd say. He was so mean to me just now. He didn't even care how I felt, he just wanted to get going. He's going to join the partisans! I can't believe it. He's not a fighter. He's going to be killed, I know it.

"What do I care? All he thinks about is himself. He wanted to kiss me but I wouldn't let him.

"Oh God, it's only been an hour and I miss him so much already. I miss his strong arms around me. I miss his gentle hands when he makes love to me. How can I live without him?

"I wonder if he really loved me. He said he did. He probably tells that to all the girls. He'll probably find another girl on the other side of the hill, and another one after that.

"I wish I felt better. I'm so tired and I don't know why. I just want to die. Like Carlotta. They could bury me here, too. I guess there won't be a wedding like I thought. I'm going to be an old spinster like Maddelena or Renata. I'll never have anyone to love me, no one like Dino anyway.

"Oh, God, I am so afraid. The war is coming closer and closer. Dino was the only good thing I had in my life. Now he's gone."

Gina, exhausted, had fallen asleep on the other side of the room. When she awakened she found Lucia sleeping, her diary still in her hand. Gina put the diary away, covered her with a light blanket and told Anna and the boys to be quiet when they played with Gatto. Then Gina crept back into her own bed. Her breasts hurt from stopping nursing so quickly. She missed Carlotta so much. And she felt so bad for Lucia. Except for the frequent flashes of lightning, the room was dark even in the middle of the afternoon.

CHAPTER 25

▼

Before her children awakened the next morning, Gina folded up Carlotta's carriage and put it in a corner. She found a cardboard box and put the baby's things in it. Her yellow dress, her tiny white shoes, her stuffed bear, her rattles and rings, a little box that Lucia had given her and the pictures that Anna, Roberto and Adolfo had drawn. Last was a white envelope containing a lock of the baby's yellow hair. Gina closed the box and tied it with a pink ribbon. She would show these things to Pietro when he returned. If he returned.

She looked around at her children. The boys were curled up on their bed, Adolfo's arm over Roberto's head. Anna lay on her back and appeared to be having a pleasant dream. But Lucia was sleeping fitfully and seemed to be moaning a name. Gina couldn't make out what it was. The girl looked so peaceful with her long brown hair strewn over the pillow. Her cheeks seemed to glow from underneath. Her figure had begun to blossom, tiny breasts and full hips.

"Such a beautiful child," Gina thought. "What did I do to deserve her?"

Gina and Lucia had not had a good relationship since the girl turned thirteen. Until then, she had been like little Anna was now, with a powerful imagination and a cheerful nature. She liked to sit at Gina's side when she sewed and stand on a stool when Gina made pasta. She loved to sit on her father's lap when he told stories. She even liked to go to church, and her First Communion day had been the biggest event of her life.

But then came the war and Pietro Sporenza was drafted into the Italian army. At first he was assigned close to home, but then was sent to the front lines and he didn't say where. His letters became less and less frequent and contained little information. At home in Sant'Antonio, Gina let her imagination run wild. He was taken prisoner and so he couldn't write, she thought. Or perhaps he was assigned to a dangerous and secret duty. Or he was having an affair with a beautiful nurse. Even though Pietro had never been unfaithful to her, Gina became obsessed with that scenario.

Preoccupied with her worries about Pietro and taking care of her younger children, Gina spent less time with Lucia, and Lucia spent more time with her friends Daniela and Carmella even though Gina didn't approve. The girls were the daughters of Bruna Manziano, a woman who as far anyone knew never had a husband. Gina didn't like the way they talked and twice she caught them smoking in Lucia's bedroom.

"Stay away from those girls," Gina told Lucia. "They're only interested in boys."

"Oh, Mamma," Lucia replied, "we're all interested in boys but there aren't any boys around here."

"I've seen you talking to boys at the well," Gina said, "and how you flirt with them. Be careful, Lucia. You know you can get into trouble."

"I know what to do," Lucia said.

"No, you don't," Gina said, and proceeded to tell her daughter how to protect herself. Lucia didn't want to listen.

As for Lucia, she had begun to criticize the way her mother dressed, low-cut outfits that showed her figure, the way she dyed her dark hair blond and frizzed it, the way she put heavy rouge on her cheeks.

"No one else in the village looks like you," Lucia shouted at her mother one day.

"That's fine," Gina said. "I don't want to look like all those other women."

At the Cielo, Lucia maintained a stony silence with her mother, not even much interested when Carlotta got sick, and she certainly didn't tell her mother about Dino. Her mother would have a fit and forbid her to leave the Cielo. Gina, of course, suspected something was going on and wondered where Lucia was going. But she just didn't want to know.

"It's best to let her sleep," Gina thought as she looked at Lucia. "Maybe with Carlotta gone she'll talk to me more. When she's ready to tell me about what's going on, she will. I'm not going to ask."

Gina hugged the box with Carlotta's things and put it in a corner. Wiping away tears, she tucked blankets around Roberto, Adolfo and Anna and then went downstairs.

The women there rushed to embrace her.

"How are you, Gina?" Annabella asked.

"Did you sleep all right?" Rosa asked.

"We are all praying for you and Carlotta," Maria said. "We're going to miss Carlotta so much. Such a beautiful baby, such a happy baby. And you are such a wonderful mother." Maria enveloped Gina in her strong arms and kissed her.

"Is there anything we can do?" the Contessa offered.

Even Maddelena came up and held Gina's hands. "I'm so sorry, my dear. I'm so sorry."

Gina thanked the women for their kindness and said she would be all right. She urged them to get back to what they were doing.

What they were doing was trying to make Colin Richards' last day at the Cielo a memorable one. His cough had finally subsided and he knew it was time to go. Gavino decided to spend the day with the villagers, and when he saw how little food they had left he went back to his farm and brought back two rabbits and sacks of tomatoes, beans and peas.

"Now you have enough for a few days and I will bring you more later," he said. "Maybe a chicken, too."

When Richards came out of his room he went first to Gina and said again how sorry he was. He said his mother had lost a baby girl when he was five, and he still remembered how everyone felt such a loss. He said he hoped she would find some peace. Gina hugged him.

To avoid thinking about the war, about Carlotta and about what was happening to them, the villagers tried to keep their regular schedule. When the time came for the English lesson, Vito and Giacomo had a little scene prepared in Richards' honor. They stood before the fireplace.

Vito: Good morning, Mr. Tassara.

Giacomo: Good morning, Mr. Tambini.

Vito: How are you?

Giacomo: I am well. How are you?

Vito: I am well. I want buy shoes.

Giacomo: What color?

Vito: Black.

Giacomo: Here shoes. Beautiful?

Vito: Yes, beautiful. How much cost?

Giacomo: Many *lire*.

Vito: No buy.

Giacomo: Goodbye, Mr. Tambini.

Vito: Goodbye, Mr. Tassara.

Everyone cheered, Vito and Giacomo bowed and Richards shook their hands.

"That's very good," he said. "You'll have no trouble when the Americans and English come and thank all of you for what you've done. And I would like to thank you personally. You don't know how much this has meant to me. You've made me feel a real part of your family. And that's how I feel you are, a real family. I've seen how you are all helping Gina now. You must have been very good friends in Sant'Antonio or you wouldn't be so kind and friendly with each other here."

There were some odd looks around the room, but mostly the villagers nodded in agreement. Now that they had been at the Cielo for a month, life in Sant'Antonio seemed far in the past, and unpleasant memories were mostly forgotten.

"Except for Fausta, of course," Rosa said.

"Perhaps," Richards said, "this time alone in her room will allow her to think about what she believes. People have been known to change."

"I don't think there's much chance of that," Annabella said.

"You never know. She has a lot of time on her hands now," Rosa said.

"Well, I still want to thank the rest of you for your great hospitality," Richards said. "I will always remember you."

"Will you write to us?" Vito asked.

"I certainly will. You can expect a letter as soon as I get back to England."

"Will you write about your adventures getting there?" Roberto asked.

"In great detail, Roberto."

The group broke up after lunch and Rosa took a plate of cooked vegetables to Fausta, who was still sitting in her chair in her slip. Books were thrown about on the floor.

"I've brought you a little lunch," Rosa said. "Gavino brought us some vegetables."

"I appreciate it, Rosa. But I'm not very hungry these days."

"Colin Richards will be leaving tomorrow."

"Oh."

"I thought you'd like to know that."

"It doesn't matter."

"Gina seems to be doing all right."

Fausta straightened the books on the floor with her feet. "I started to cry yesterday when I heard you all sing the lullaby. Poor Gina. Those poor children, too."

"You feel sorry for them?"

"Well, of course."

Rosa was about to say something but decided against it.

"I know what you're thinking, Rosa."

"What?"

"That if I had gone down to the village and informed the Germans about Richards being here, those children, like everyone else, would have been killed."

"Exactly right," Rosa said. "You know, I suppose it wouldn't matter for some of us. Maddelena and Renata. Vito and Giacomo. Dante. Even Francesco and Annabella and Marco and me. We're old, or at least getting older. But what about Gina and her children? How would you feel if the Germans had come in and gunned them all down? Lucia? Anna? Roberto? Adolfo? Carlotta, rest her soul. How would you feel about those children when you were sitting safe in your house in Sant'Antonio, Fausta? Have you thought about that? Have you?"

Rosa's voice grew more shrill as she became agitated. Fausta began to cry.

"Please, Rosa," she said. "I've been sitting here for days and that's all I've been thinking about."

"And?"

"Rosa, I'm so confused I don't know what to think. For so many years I believed so much in one thing. It gave me comfort. The *Fasci Femminili* group was so understanding. The women were so nice."

"Nice? You call them nice?"

"Yes, nice. We held our meetings in Reboli twice a month and I looked forward to them so much. They were all I had. I didn't have friends in Sant'Antonio and at work, well..."

"You had a cruel employer, didn't you?"

Fausta turned away. "I can't talk about it, Rosa."

"It has something to do with those marks all over, doesn't it"

Fausta nodded, but her back was still turned. Rosa said a swear word under her breath.

"I'm sorry, Fausta," she said. "I'm sorry you have had such a miserable life. But don't you see? Italy can't survive under the Fascists. Look what happened under Mussolini, how he brought us into this war and now the Germans have occupied Tuscany and everyone is fighting and we are all so afraid. The only way we're going to get out of this is when the Allies finally arrive and liberate us all."

"Mussolini was my hero. Hitler was my hero."

"*Was,* Fausta, *was.* Not any more."

Fausta turned back to Rosa. "And I have been thinking about what the Germans and the Fascists have said about Jews. They are an inferior race, aren't they, Rosa? Aren't they?"

Rosa looked at her grimly. "Fausta, do you believe in God?"

"Of course."

"Do you think He would make some people better than others, some people superior to others?"

"No." Fausta looked away. "Well, I don't think so."

"Well, think some more about that."

Fausta rubbed the marks on her wrists.

"The burns still hurt, don't they?" Rosa said.

"Yes. But the hurt inside is worse."

"I'm going to go back downstairs, Fausta. Perhaps tomorrow we can talk some more."

"Rosa, how can you ever forgive me?"

"During a war, Fausta, we have to forgive a lot of things."

As Rosa locked the door behind her and returned downstairs she couldn't help but think of what she had just said. Yes, during a war we had to forgive a lot of things. Some things just weren't as important as they had seemed before. Maybe something that happened forty years ago wasn't important any more. Maybe she had been unjust and unkind. Lately, she thought that Annabella had been kinder to her. Rosa would have to think more about this.

For his last tale of his journey from the prison camp to the Cielo, Richards described his brief encounter with the Germans at the river and how his friend Geoff Watson had been shot as they crossed the Arno in a tiny boat.

"Was he killed?" Roberto asked.

"I don't know, but I think so."

"The Germans are bastards," Vito said. "Every one of them."

"Now we can't say that," Maria said. "There are probably many soldiers who are just doing this because they have to. Colin, if you were on that river bank and German soldiers were coming across, would you have shot at them?"

Richards didn't take a moment to answer. "Yes, of course. We're at war. We don't like to think about the things we have to do, but sometimes, we just have to do them."

"I can't help thinking that those soldiers have mothers, too," Maria said.

"Oh, Maria, you always want to think the best about people," Rosa said.

"Santa Maria," the Contessa said.

"If you think the Nazis are so kind," Francesco said, "think about the Jews they're killing in the camps in Austria, think about the Italians who were killed in the Ardeatine cave!"

The story of the Ardeatine cave massacre was well known throughout Italy even before the villagers went to the Cielo. In Rome only four months earlier, on March 24, German troops had rounded up 335 Italians, at least 255 of them civilians, took them to a cave and shot them. The massacre was ordered in retaliation for the partisans' killing of 35 German soldiers and was part of Hitler's policy to kill ten Italians for every German that Italians killed.

Francesco pounded on the table. "And think about all the terrible things they're doing around here! We have to remember what they're doing, for God's sake!"

The villagers were surprised by such passion from someone who had said very little since they arrived at the Cielo. Annabella closed her eyes.

"The war," Rosa said. "When will it ever be over?"

That evening, Gavino returned to the farmhouse, out of breath and perspiring. His face was ashen.

"The Germans…" he began.

"What?"

"The Germans raided two farmhouses today. Nero Nube and Vino Rosso."

"O Dio!" Giacomo said. "Those places are near here. Did they find anything?"

"No," Gavino said, taking off his hat and wiping his forehead with his red handkerchief. "They were looking for partisans and deserters and escaped prisoners of war. But there weren't any at either place."

Gavino didn't tell the group that the Germans had roughed up some of the men and took a pig from one of the farms and food from another. Both farms had almost run out of food.

The villagers sat stunned.

"This means that we are likely to have visitors soon, maybe even as early as tomorrow," Dante said. "We will need to be prepared. Let's start the lookout earlier. Marco, please be in the tower at 5 tomorrow morning. Colin, you should leave here as early as you can."

"I'm packed and ready," Richards said. "Maybe I should leave now?"

"No," Marco said. "You won't find your way in the dark. Wait until early morning."

"You'll want to go to Fernando's," Gavino said. "It's the first farm next to the stream on the other side of the hill."

"Fernando's, right. I don't know what I would have done without you, Gavino," Richards said, giving him a hug. Tiny Gavino seemed lost in his arms.

"I don't know what any of us would do without Gavino," Maria said. She kissed him.

"What about Fausta?" Rosa asked. "If the Germans do come here, won't they think it strange that we have a woman locked up in a room?"

"Rosa, can we ask a big favor from you?" Dante asked.

"I know what you are going to say. Yes, I will stay with her. The Germans will think we are just two woman talking."

"About your secret recipes for making ravioli," Marco said.

"Of course," Rosa said.

As they rose to go to their rooms, the villagers realized that if Richards left early in the morning they would never see him again. Roberto and Adolfo shook his hand very seriously, the women kissed him and Richards himself seemed about to lose control.

"Blimey, I'm going to miss you all," he said as he went back into his little room. Marco and Francesco pushed the shelves back and replaced the dishes, bowls and pots.

As Rosa and Annabella prepared for what would be a restless night for both of them, Rosa said, "Annabella, I think we should have a good talk. What do you think?"

"Yes, Rosa, I think so, too. Let's talk before it's too late."

PART THREE

CHAPTER 26

▼

Fritz Krieger and Konrad Schultz could remember exactly where they met. When they were ten years old, they lived just a couple of streets apart in Munich but didn't know each other until the night of November 9, 1938. Hearing a mob of people on the streets, the boys slipped out of their homes, unseen by their parents. A little later, they found themselves standing side by side on a nearby street as Nazi storm troopers and the SS swept by, shouting and smashing windows in every shop that was owned by Jews. Fritz and Konrad got caught up in the frenzy and ran after the mob. Soon they too were chanting "For the Führer! For the Führer!" A venerable old synagogue stood at the end of one street and Fritz and Konrad jumped up and down as they watched the crowd set it afire.

As the flames turned their faces red, they grinned at each other.

"They got those hymies, didn't they?" Konrad said.

It was not until later, after their parents had punished them for going out at night, that they learned that what happened in Munich occurred throughout Germany in an event called *Kristallnacht*. Besides all the destruction, more than 25,000 Jewish men in Germany were shipped off to concentration camps.

That night was so exhilarating that after that the boys went to each other's houses just to talk about it. They joined the *Jungvolk*, the junior branch of the *Hitlerjugend*, and at night they recite the oath they had taken: *"In the presence of this blood banner, which represents our Führer, I swear to devote all my energies and my strength to the savior of our country, Adolf Hitler. I am willing and ready to give up my life for him, so help me God."*

Every Wednesday afternoon and on weekends, they met at a local school. They liked the hikes, the songs and the stories and they also marched in parades, participated in swimming contests and, best of all, took part in the *Wehrsport*, military training, in the nearby forest. Fritz and Konrad were always on the same team, seeking out the opposing team and sometimes ending up fighting violently.

"We beat up those kids good, didn't we, Fritz?" Konrad would say.

"We're bigger and tougher," Fritz would reply.

"You know what I was thinking, Fritz? I was thinking those boys were hymies when I beat them up."

Their parents despaired when the boys came home with their brown shirts and black shorts muddy and torn. But the parents knew better than to complain. Neither family paid much attention to politics or what was going on in Berlin. They missed celebrating Christmas and didn't think the Yule observance was a good substitute. They tried to look the other way when their Jewish friends disappeared. But they realized that under Hitler, their lives were so much better than during the devastation that followed the bloody war that was supposed to end wars.

Fritz was an only child, and his parents doted on him. His father, who managed a popular beer garden, took him hiking in the Bavarian Alps. His mother made apple strudel for him every Saturday. Fritz liked to read, even the works of Schiller when he was not yet a teenager.

Konrad's father was a gentle man who worked in a print shop and his mother was busy with three girls. Konrad didn't like school, and kept getting into trouble with his teachers for fighting. He said he didn't like to read because it hurt his eyes. His parents got him glasses. Konrad said he still didn't like to read.

The parents were stunned but remained silent as their sons became fascinated with Hitler, studying his life at school and listening to his speeches on the radio. When Hitler invaded Russia in 1940, the boys declared that they couldn't wait for the day when they could join the army. They were twelve at the time.

In 1942, the boys joined the *Hitlerjugend*. Fritz always teased Konrad about their first day at camp. After indoctrination, they sat across from each other in the cavernous dining room, a gigantic swastika hanging at one end. They had just finished saying the Hitler Youth prayer:

Führer, my Führer given me by God,
Protect and preserve my life for long.
You rescued Germany from its deepest need.
I thank you for my daily bread.
Stay for a long time with me, leave me not.
Führer, my Führer, my faith, my light.

Hail my Führer.

Then, because he was so excited and nervous, Konrad dropped a pile of hot mashed potatoes in his lap. His face beet red and perspiring so much that his glasses steamed up, Konrad managed to finish his meal while Fritz tried desperately not to giggle as their youth leader stared at them sternly.

In the *Hitlerjugend,* the boys learned even more about Hitler, how he saved Germany after the world war and how the Jewish/Communist conspiracy had to be defeated. They were taught that Jews were both subhuman and evil. And they believed that the war was a great adventure that would ensure Germany's place as the leader of the world.

They liked to recall an incident involving a friend.

"Remember Heinz?" Konrad would often say at night before they fell, exhausted, into their bunks.

"Yeah, his father called Hitler a crazy man," Fritz would say.

"So when Heinz told his platoon leader what he said, the father was sent off to Dauchau and Heinz got promoted."

"Do you think you could do that, Konrad?"

"Sure," Konrad would say proudly. "If I got a promotion."

The boys would laugh, but wondered what they would really do.

As the war progressed, Fritz and Konrad and other members of the *Hitlerjugend* took on more homefront duties. At first they went door to door to collect scrap metals and they cleaned up after bomb attacks. Then they were trained in handling infantry weapons and how to man anti-aircraft batteries. But they couldn't wait until they were seventeen and could join the army.

Instead of the regular army, Fritz and Konrad decided to join the Waffen-SS. Late at night, they would look at books showing SS insignia, weapons and uniforms, imagining how they would fire the P-08 Luger, how they would wear the field-gray uniform with the jagged S-rune on its collar, how they would proudly wear the buckle with the "My Honor Is Loyalty" inscription.

Since they suddenly were more than six feet tall, they met the SS height requirements, and they certainly could trace their Aryan ancestry back to 1800. At first, Konrad feared that his eyesight might prevent him from joining, but the physical restrictions had been relaxed.

"I can see a hymie better than anyone," Konrad would boast.

As soon as Fritz and Konrad were accepted, they began to hear the widely circulated stories of the arduous training exercises inflicted on SS recruits. Some were exaggerated. Some were not.

There were reports of thirty-six hour shifts with only three half-hour breaks in which the young soldiers could eat.

There was the story of a line of soldiers in full battle gear ordered to march into a water-filled trench until the water reached their necks.

There was the account of soldiers cowering in a ditch while tanks rolled over their heads.

One story, which was true, was that all recruits had to load 220 pounds of gear on their backs, then run two miles in battle uniform in twenty minutes.

One night, Konrad ran into the barracks and accosted Fritz.

"I just heard," he said, out of breath and almost in tears, "that we have to stand at attention and balance a hand grenade on our helmets while it goes off! Fritz I won't be able to do that! I'll pee in my pants."

"Settle down, Konrad," Fritz said, putting his hand on his friend's shoulder. "That story's been going around for years. It's never happened."

Konrad wiped both his glasses and his eyes.

It was true, however, that live ammunition was used in Waffen-SS exercises and that some negligent soldiers died.

"This is just to get us to work together," Fritz explained to Konrad after one particularly grueling day. "If we don't do it now, we won't do it in battle. We have to learn to obey orders, no matter what."

"I just want to die right now," Konrad said as he collapsed on his bed. "Every bone in my body hurts."

"Better to hurt now than to be killed later. That's what the lieutenant always says. We always have to do what the lieutenant says."

Near the end of their training they went to a beer hall to celebrate getting their tattoos—gothic lettering signifying their blood group—on the underside of their left arms.

"Now everyone will know we're members of the SS!" Konrad shouted, downing another beer.

Fritz swallowed another draft. "We're never going to be ashamed of this, will we, Konrad?"

"Ashamed? We're going to be heroes after the war, Fritz! Heroes!"

Whatever they felt about their training, Fritz and Konrad had the utmost admiration for their lieutenant. They didn't always remember his name but, like all soldiers in the Waffen-SS, referred to him by his title, *Obersturmführer,* rather than "sir." At twenty-seven, the lieutenant wasn't much older than most of his troops and he often ate meals with them. Unlike the traditional Prussian discipline that separated officers from other ranks, the Waffen-SS encouraged comradeship and equality. Officers were to earn their troops' respect.

That was difficult for this young lieutenant to accept. At home in Stuttgart, he stood when his father, a minor police official, entered the room, waited for his father to begin eating before he ate and followed behind him when they went for walks.

Officer training at Bad Tolz, in the heart of the Bavarian Alps, gave him a new perspective on military life and Germany. Besides the long marches, the gun training and the weapons drills, cadets studied Hitler's *Mein Kampf* and developed a sense of mission. They learned who Germany's enemies were and how to forge a fierce hatred into the souls of their soldiers.

The lieutenant joined the 16th SS Panzergrenadier Division *Reichs führer-SS* in March 1943. He would have preferred being assigned to a more dangerous duty but accepted his role to root out partisans from sleepy Tuscany. Now, as he straightened his crisp uniform jacket on the hanger, he thought about the skirmish with partisans a few weeks ago. It had gone well enough, even though the bastards killed one of his soldiers. Facing civilians in the farmhouse raids would be different. But if they were helping the partisans they were the enemy and had to be treated like the enemy. He thought the execution of the ten civilians in Reboli would teach them a lesson.

The lieutenant also wondered how tough his men would be. He wondered how tough he would be.

"For the Führer!" he kept repeating. "For the Führer!"

One hot night in early August, the lieutenant ordered his troops to stand formation on the street in Sant'Antonio. Having risen to the rank of corporal, *Rottenführer*, Fritz and Konrad were next to each other.

"Tomorrow," the lieutenant announced, "we will begin going to the farmhouses in the hills. We believe these people are harboring dangerous criminals, including partisans. And who are the partisans?"

"Communists!" the men shouted back.

"And what happens to communists?"

"We shoot them!"

"And what happens to people who help communists?"

"We shoot them!"

"Good. Be in battle gear at 4 a.m."

"Heil Hitler!"

CHAPTER 27

▼

The sun hadn't yet risen when Marco climbed to the tower, but the moon and stars cast an eerie light over the hills. Mist covered the valley below and from the third floor of the Cielo, he could not see any signs of the village. The trees on the hillsides dripped with dew and the vines glowed in the moonlight. In the quiet before dawn, the world seemed at peace.

"Who could believe there's a war going on?" Marco thought as he scanned the horizon. He wished he had brought his binoculars from the village.

But off to the right, he suddenly saw, there was suspicious activity at Gavino's hut. Marco could see perhaps a dozen dark shadows surround the hut and then three of them disappeared into it.

Marco ran into the Sporenzas' rooms on the third floor.

"Gina! Get up! Get up! The Germans are coming!"

Then, downstairs, he woke Maddelena and Renata in their room, Maria and the Contessa in theirs and Rosa and Annabella in theirs.

"The Germans! Rosa, go to Fausta's room!"

On the first floor, he quickly awakened Vito and Giacomo, Dante and Francesco and then ran to the kitchen.

"Colin," he yelled into the little room. "Are you in there?"

"Yes, I just woke up."

"Stay there. Don't make a sound. The Germans are coming!"

"Shit!" came the muffled cry. "Shit, shit, shit!"

Francesco and Dante, who had managed to pull on their pants, were now at Marco's side.

"Francesco! Throw Fausta's pistol in to Colin," Marco shouted. "They'll be looking for weapons." Marco threw his own pistol to Richards, who quickly tossed the weapons into the wine cellar under his cot. Marco ran back to the tower. He heard a loud noise from Gavino's hut, like a firecracker, then another and another. The shadows emerged from the hut and Marco could see the glow of a flame. The flame became bigger and brighter, and Marco knew the hut was on fire. At the same time, all of the men were running toward the Cielo.

Marco, Francesco and Dante were standing in the kitchen when the lieutenant and the dozen soldiers stormed into the room. The lieutenant was a tall man, thin and with a narrow mustache. He pointed his submachine gun around the room. All of the others aimed their rifles at the frightened villagers. One of the soldiers seemed to be trying to look fierce through his thick glasses.

"What do you want?" Marco said, his arms folded across his chest. "We're just people from Sant'Antonio staying here for a while."

"Yes, we're letting you use our houses in the village," Francesco said.

"Use them! Use them!" the lieutenant shouted, his faulty Italian mixed with German. He swung his fist into Francesco's face, knocking him to his knees. "You people should be glad we're here and protecting you from those Americans and British. And you should be glad we let you stay up here. We could have sent you on the trains to Germany."

Francesco mumbled something and the lieutenant was about to strike him again when Annabella ran down the stairs and into the room.

"Please," she cried, "he's my husband. Please don't hit him. He didn't mean to say anything."

"We've got too much to do to worry about him," the lieutenant said as he pushed Francesco to his knees. Annabella sank to the floor and cradled her husband's head in her arms.

"What do you want? What are you going to do?" Marco asked.

"We're looking for people who don't belong here. Partisans. Prisoners. Men who should be in the army or the work force. Weapons. Radio transmitters."

"There's nothing here," Dante said. "There's no one you want here."

"That farmer in the hut said the same thing. But he just had some people there. Two men who deserted the army. And we know he helped escaped prisoners and the partisans. But he won't help them any more."

"What did you do to him?" Dante cried.

"What do you think? He wouldn't answer our questions."

"So you killed him?"

"We'll do the same to you if we find anybody here we don't like."

"I told you, there's no one like that here," Marco said.

"We'll see for ourselves. Come on, let's start at the top."

Followed by the other soldiers, the lieutenant charged up the stairs, their steel heels echoing on the stone steps. Some scattered to the rooms on the second floor. Fritz and Konrad went to the top. They found Gina cowering in a corner with Lucia, Anna and the boys. The soldiers ripped down the sheets that enclosed their room and threw the beds and dressers around.

"Please," Gina cried, "please don't harm my children."

"We're not doing anything bad," Anna said.

"What's this?" Konrad said as he picked up a leather-bound book.

"It's just my diary," Lucia cried. "Please don't touch it."

"All your secrets in here," Konrad said.

"Come on, Konrad, let her keep her diary," Fritz said.

"She can keep it, Fritz, she'll just have to put the pages back together." And with that the soldier tore the pages out of the book and scattered them on the floor. Lucia burst into tears.

"Say, you're not so bad looking for an Eytie," Konrad said. "Too bad we don't have time to stay here longer."

Then he noticed Carlotta's carriage in the corner.

"What's this?" he said. "Looks like you have a baby. Where is it?"

"She died! She died last week!" Gina cried.

"One less Eytie to worry about then."

Fritz looked at the two boys.

"Say, haven't I seen you before? Weren't you the boys in the village last week?"

"Yes," they mumbled in tiny voices.

"You were stealing medicine for your sister," Konrad said. "But she died. Lots of good you did, right?"

The boys were sobbing now. Gina stood up and was about to slap Konrad but he grabbed her arm and threw her to the floor.

"Maybe you want to join your daughter."

Roberto and Adolfo put their arms around their frightened mother.

"Come on," Fritz said, "let's see what they're finding downstairs."

On the second floor Gatto stood at the door to Rosa's and Annabella's room, his back arched, his tail straight up, his green eyes menacing.

"Look, Konrad," said Fritz, "it's the pussycat from our house. He came all the way up here."

"Hey. Here, Kitty, Kitty." Konrad reached down to pick up Gatto, a clear indication that he knew nothing about cats. Gatto slashed at Konrad's hand, tearing a deep gash into his wrist, and then, making a horrible guttural sound, flew at the soldier's throat.

"Why you…" Gatto had fled down the stairs and was hiding behind the woodpile next to the fireplace before Konrad, his right hand bleeding, could ready his rifle. The bullet bounced off the steps and into the wall.

In the next minutes there was considerable shouting and crying. Finally, the lieutenant took control.

"Schultz, forget about the damn cat and be careful with your rifle. The rest of you stop your yelling and screaming!"

When four soldiers went into Maddelena's and Renata's room, they found the sisters in their nightgowns and with curlers in their hair. They sat together on Renata's bed, holding each other.

"Just you two old biddies in this room?" one asked.

"Please leave us alone," Maddelena cried. "We're just old ladies. We're not a harm to anyone."

One soldier opened the wardrobe and tore the rack of dresses from their hangers and threw them on the floor. He looked around the room to see what other damage he could do and turned over the dressing table.

"Why are you doing this?" Renata screamed.

"Looks like good places to hide transmitters," the soldier said.

"Well, there aren't any here," Maddelena said calmly. "You can clearly see that."

Fritz and Konrad rushed into Maria's and the Contessa's room. The Contessa fluttered with her necklace and Maria stood stolidly beside her bed.

"I am sure you will find nothing here," she said. "Now please just go back to the village. You're just young boys, you shouldn't be doing this. *O Dio,* what did you do to your hand?"

Konrad had wrapped a handkerchief around his hand but not before blood had splattered onto his shirt and pants.

"It was," he mumbled, "it was an accident."

"Let me look at it," Maria said, removing the handkerchief. She took a sheet from her bed, ripped off a long strip and wrapped it tightly around his hand.

"There," she said. "That should hold until you get back to the village. I think you should go there right now and have this looked at. Take your friends with you."

Konrad was about to say something but Fritz gave him a warning look. "Let's go next door," he said.

Rosa's and Annabella's room was empty. The soldiers tore the beds apart and turned over the dresser and chair. Across the hall, the lieutenant and three soldiers confronted Rosa, who was sitting on the bed, and Fausta, who was in the chair. Both women were in their nightgowns.

"Two ladies just talking?" the lieutenant said.

"Yes, of course," Rosa said.

The lieutenant grabbed Rosa by the shoulder. "Before sunrise?"

"My friend had something she wanted to ask me," Rosa said, breaking free.

"What about?"

"Just woman talk. Cooking."

The lieutenant noticed Fausta's books on the floor, along with her notebook with the swastika on the cover and Fausta's *Fasci Femminili* card.

"Are you a member of the *Fasci Femminili*? What are you doing here if you're a Fascist?"

"Well, I…," Fausta began, trying to cover the marks on her wrists.

"Well, what? Why are you here with all these communists?"

"I live in Sant'Antonio," Fausta said simply.

"And you've been here for weeks. So you must know how many partisans and prisoners and deserters have come here. How many?"

The lieutenant was shouting now. Rosa looked at Fausta, a pleading look in her eyes. Fausta looked down at her hands and smoothed her skirt.

"Come on, lady. You're a member of the *Fasci Femminili*. You're supposed to tell us these things."

"None that I know of," she said softly.

"No partisans or prisoners or anyone else have come while you have been here?"

"No."

"And no one is here now?"

"No."

"You're sure of that? I will report you if you're lying."

Fausta looked the lieutenant in the eye. "No, no one."

"No partisans or deserters are in this building now?"

Fausta again looked him in the eye. "No, lieutenant. I told you. No one has come here and no one is here now."

"What are those burns on your hands and neck and ankles? Where did you get them?"

Fausta's face reddened. Rosa rose and whispered in the lieutenant's ear. "Fausta has a lover who likes to play games."

The lieutenant smiled. "Oh, she likes to play games, does she? Maybe she'd like to play some games with me."

The lieutenant rubbed his hands around Fausta's neck. Fausta looked terrified. Rosa whispered again in the lieutenant's ear. "Her lover is…" and she said the name of Fausta's employer in Reboli. "I'm sure he wouldn't like to share her."

"Mr. Fascist himself?" the lieutenant said. "The one with all the children? Well, I hope you have a lot of fun, lady."

The soldiers left the room without disturbing anything and went downstairs. They went from room to room, finding Marco's and Francesco's and Dante's rooms empty but still tearing everything apart.

Across the hall, four soldiers found Vito and Giacomo playing cards on Vito's bed. If they had looked closely, they would have seen their hands shaking.

"You always play cards this early in the morning?" one said.

"Oh, hello, sir," Vito said. "Actually we started playing last night and we just couldn't stop. My cousin is beating me. Do you play *briscola*, sir?"

"No, I don't play *briscola!*"

"It's a good game. Sit down, we'll teach you. It's easy."

"Stop talking like that! Do you expect us to believe that story?"

"Believe what you want," Giacomo said, putting down the ace of hearts.

The soldiers threw the cards on the floor and searched under the bed.

"What are you guys, some sort of comics?" one of the soldiers said.

In the main room, Annabella and Francesco still sat on the floor. Annabella hugged her husband and he leaned against her. Marco and Dante stood at the door to the kitchen. But they were frozen. Colin Richards was in the midst of a coughing attack. Hearing the steel heels on the steps, they began to talk loudly.

"Did you find anything, lieutenant?" Dante shouted.

"We told you no one else was here." Marco declared.

"Are you finished now?" Francesco asked.

"We don't harbor dangerous criminals," Annabella said.

"I still think there is something suspicious going on," the lieutenant said. By this time, Richards' cough had subsided. "People sitting around talking, people playing cards. You think we're fools?"

He looked in every corner of the room, then pushed Marco and Dante aside and went into the kitchen. Konrad and Fritz followed.

"Konrad, look," Fritz said as he examined the shelves, "they have dishes just like we have in our house."

"Not any more," Konrad said, taking the plates and bowls with his one good hand, smashing them on the floor and exposing the dark space where Richards crouched in a corner. The villagers were terrified.

Dante stepped in front of the shelves. Since he was so tall, it was difficult to see anything behind him. "Can't you leave the dishes? We need them."

"What's so important about a few dishes?" Konrad asked.

"Well," Dante said, "we know that your victory may soon be near but we would like to have something to eat on as long as we are here."

Konrad smashed another plate on the floor.

"Come on, men," the lieutenant said. "Let's look in the shed back there and we've got two more farmhouses to visit this morning. Maybe we'll have better luck there."

As the soldiers left the Cielo and disappeared into the shed, the villagers gathered at the windows, clinging to one another. Then they watched as the invaders went down the hill. There were no screams, no shouts, just utter silence.

"It's all right to come out now," Dante told Richards as he pushed the shelves aside. Richards emerged, carrying his knapsack.

"I'm going," he said as he rushed toward the back door. "I'll be fine. Thank you! And thank Gavino, too!"

Richards had not heard the soldiers' conversation about what happened at Gavino's farm.

"God bless you, Colin Richards!" Maria called, and all the others repeated it. Not one of them believed that Richards would make it to Switzerland.

Marco went back to the tower to make sure the Germans had indeed disappeared from the hillside. It was only 6 o'clock and the sun was just starting to rise. The attack had taken less than an hour.

"Let's see what happened at Gavino's," Marco said on returning to the main floor. "I'm afraid of what we'll find."

Marco, Francesco and Dante, with Vito and Giacomo running after them, hurried to Gavino's hut. The fire had gone through the roof and was still simmering in the walls. The men tore open what was left of the door and entered the smoky hovel.

Gavino was in his chair, his arms tied behind his back. His head rested on his chest. He had been shot three times.

"Bloody bastards!" Vito shouted. "Bloody bastards!"

"He wouldn't talk so they tied him up," Francesco said. "Good man, Gavino!"

They untied Gavino's hands and gently laid him on his sooty bed. They wiped his face and beard and placed his charred Bible on his chest. Then they wrapped all his blankets around him and tied them together. Vito and Giacomo found a shovel and dug a grave near the cave in the back. In a few minutes, Gavino joined the earth he had loved all of his life. Marco put up a little cross: "Gavino, a friend to all who needed him." The men took off their caps and crossed themselves. They had no time for more than that.

When the men returned to the Cielo the women had already straightened out much of the furniture, remade the beds and picked up the clutter. No one said a word.

CHAPTER 28

▼

With the cleanup at the Cielo completed, there was little to do. The SS raid hung like a heavy dark cloud over the farmhouse, but the villagers reasoned that if they didn't talk about it, they wouldn't have to think about it. Rosa and Annabella sat at the main table, saying little. Vito and Giacomo tried to play cards but lost interest. Maria and the Contessa shared a room but not their thoughts. Gatto stayed cowered behind the woodpile.

Dante picked up *The Divine Comedy* and tried to find comfort in the story of Dante Alighieri and Beatrice, the love of his life. Again, he read the letter that was his marker and wiped his eyes. But he soon put the book down and stared out the window.

The only conversation was in the Sporenzas' room on the third floor. When Gina returned from helping with the cleanup, she found Lucia putting the pages of her diary back in order.

"O, *cara mia*," Gina said. "I'm so sorry. That soldier was so cruel. Here, let me help."

"No!" Lucia cried, gathering up the pages. "Mamma, no. I can do it myself."

Then she burst into tears.

"Lucia, Lucia, what's wrong?"

Lucia just shook her head.

"Please tell me, I just want to help you. Are you sure you want to save this diary? The pages are all torn."

Through her tears, Lucia nodded her head.

Gina sat on the floor with Lucia, picking up the few remaining pages of the diary. "You wrote so much!"

Lucia snatched the pages away. "Mamma, please don't read it."

"I wasn't reading, honestly. I was just picking up the pages."

Lucia was still crying.

"Lucia, do you want to talk about it? I know you've been up to something. I haven't said anything because I didn't think you'd want to tell me. And, yes, I guess I didn't want to hear about it if there was a problem. But I'm feeling better now. I still miss Carlotta so much, but I'll get used to it. I would like it so much if you would talk to me, Lucia. Such a terrible thing happened today. We need to be closer. We don't know what's going to happen to us."

Lucia wiped the tears from her cheeks with the back of her hand.

"Oh, Mamma…"

"Tell me, Lucia, tell me."

"It's just…"

Gina put her arms around her daughter. "What, my darling?"

"I didn't want to tell you. You seemed so busy with the others. And then Carlotta got sick. But I knew you wouldn't let me. Anyway, it's over now so it doesn't matter."

"What's over? What wouldn't I let you?"

"Dino."

"Dino? Who's Dino? Have you been involved with a boy here? Where? How could you be? There's no one else here but us."

Lucia blew her nose and leaned back against the wall. She couldn't keep her secret any longer.

"Dino was running away from the army. He was with another boy, Paolo. They were from Montepulciano. They were staying at Gavino's."

"That's incredible," Gina said. "How did you meet this Dino?"

"I was in the tower the week we first got here. They were coming across the field. Paolo was limping. I tore up that nightgown from the *armedio* and they used that to wrap around his foot.

"So that's where that nightgown disappeared. I wondered."

"Dino and I started talking and we got to like each other. Once or twice he came here but mostly I went over there."

"You went over there? Lucia, you could have been killed! You know we aren't supposed to leave the Cielo."

"I know, I know. But I never saw anyone, Mamma, and no one saw me. And Gavino was very kind. He never told anyone."

"So no one here knew about this?"

"Rosa knows. She knows everything."

Gina remembered now about Rosa's questions to Dante. Why didn't she figure out that Rosa was talking about her daughter? She wished she had paid more attention. She couldn't use her other children as an excuse.

"So Gavino was present when you were with this boy?" Gina asked.

"No. Dino and Paolo were staying in a cave behind his hut."

"In a cave? You went to this boy in a cave? Oh, my darling."

"I didn't go in the cave. We went for walks. We went into the woods."

"You spent a lot of time with him?"

"Yes."

Gina was afraid to ask the next question, but she knew she must. "Lucia," she took her daughter's hands. "Did you and Dino make love?"

Lucia was silent for a long time while her mother looked at her. Finally, she closed her eyes and whispered, "Yes."

"*O Dio!*"

"Mamma, I loved him! And he loved me! At least he said he did."

Gina didn't know how to react because so many thoughts were tumbling through her mind. First, she blamed herself for not paying more attention to Lucia, not just at the Cielo but for all these years in the village. Then she remembered herself as a teenage girl, how she loved to be with boys. And, no, Pietro was not the first boy she had made love with. And she and Pietro had made love many times before they married. Suddenly, she thought of something.

"Lucia, last week when Roberto and Adolfo were talking about going to the village, they said something about seeing two naked people under a tree. That was you and this boy, wasn't it?"

Lucia's face became very red. "Yes," she whispered.

"*O Dio!*"

"Mamma, it doesn't matter anymore. Dino is gone. He and Paolo joined the partisans."

"The partisans!"

"So it doesn't matter anymore," Lucia repeated. "Nothing matters anymore." And she burst into tears again. Gina took her in her arms and smoothed her hair. They were silent for a long time. Then Gina spoke.

"Lucia, a long time ago I was a girl like you. I know what it means to want a boy and to have a boy want you. I had boyfriends, too, before your Papa. I thought I loved them so much. But then I met your Papa and I knew I would never love anyone else. As much as I don't like what you've done, I have to say I'm happy that you found a little love in this terrible time. Whatever happens, you can remember that."

"Oh, Mamma, I loved him so much."

"I know, *cara mia,* I know." Gina kissed the top of Lucia's head. "But you'll get over it. The war is going to end soon, we'll be going back to Sant'Antonio and all the soldiers will come back. Maybe even your Papa."

"Do you really believe that?"

Gina knew that she didn't, but it was what a mother was supposed to say, so she said it.

"Mamma, I don't know how I'm going to live through this." Lucia blew her nose again.

"You will, my darling. You don't think you can now, but you will. When we go back to Sant'Antonio the war will be over and you'll be with Daniela and Carmella again. Maybe you can get a job in Reboli and you will meet other boys. You will forget about Dino, I promise."

"I don't see how I ever will, Mamma."

Gina helped the girl to her feet. "You're going to be all right, my darling. Let's go downstairs and see what Anna and the boys are doing."

Lucia put the remnants of her diary under her bed, wiped her face and brushed her hair. Gina thought Lucia looked unusually pale and tired.

In the late afternoon, some of the villagers were sitting in the main room. They had begun talking again and were reminiscing about Gavino. Such a good man. So kind. So generous.

"And he knew everyone around here," Rosa said. "The partisans, the prisoners. How did he know everyone?"

"It was because he liked everyone and they liked him," Marco said.

"But why would he risk his life for them?" Francesco asked. "He didn't have to do that."

"You know what I think," Dante said. "Gavino wouldn't have the words to express this, but I think he was doing it because he loved Italy so much. He told me once that he was named for Giuseppe Garibaldi. In a way, Gavino was a great liberator, too. We can all be grateful for that."

The villagers fell silent. Maria fingered her rosary beads.

"I imagine those bastards raided Due Stelle and Olivio this morning, too," Rosa said.

"I hope they didn't find anything," Maria said. "I hope no one was hurt."

The villagers thought of their friends in the other farmhouses and wished they could all be together again.

"You know," Rosa said, "when I lived here many years ago my mother always used to say that no one could harm us because the Cielo was so high in the hills. Now I know that's not true."

"No place is safe any more," Annabella said.

"I know a place," Maria said. "It's where my daughter Angelica lives. Sant'Anna. Has anyone been there?"

No one had visited the place, but Maddelena and Renata said they had cousins from San Miniato who had fled there.

"And my cousin Lara," Rosa said, gripping Marco's arm. "She and her husband moved there when the British started bombing Livorno."

Maria reminded Rosa that Angelica and Lara had become good friends in the little village.

"Hundreds of people are going there now because it is so isolated and safe," Maria said. "It's only about thirty miles from here, but it's up a steep winding path through the forest and at the very top of a hill. You have to walk from Pietrasanta to get there. Its real name is Sant' Anna di Stazzema. My daughter's husband's family has always lived there so when she got married she moved there. Now they have two little boys."

"And the Germans will never find it?" Giacomo asked.

"Never."

The other villagers smiled. They didn't believe any place was safe any more.

Dante stood up before the fireplace. "I have to say this. I think all of you were just magnificent today. Maddelena and Renata, how you pretended to be just little old ladies…"

"But we are little old ladies," Maddelena said, stretching her arm around her sister and giving her a hug.

"Vito and Giacomo, how you pretended to be playing cards…"

"We weren't pretending," Vito said. "Giacomo was beating me."

"Anyway, all of you stood up to them extremely well and we should all be proud of one another."

Dante paused and cleared his throat. "And then, of course, Fausta. I think we should be proud of Fausta, too. If she wanted to, she could have told the Germans about Colin Richards. They would have shot him, they likely would have shot the rest of us, and they would have taken Fausta back to the village and given her a reward."

"I can't believe she didn't say anything," the Contessa said.

"Why do you think she didn't, Rosa?" Annabella asked.

"I think she has thought about what she said and what she did the other night, and I truly think she's sorry," Rosa said. "But I think what finally got to her was the children. She would have been responsible for the deaths of your children, Gina."

"*O Dio,*" Gina said, trying to put her arms around all four of her children.

"Maybe it's like a deathbed conversion," Maria said.

"Conversion!" the Contessa said. "I don't believe in such a thing."

"Well," Dante said, "what are we going to do about her now? Should we allow her to come back with us?"

"I don't think so," the Contessa said. "She scares me to death. I don't see how she could have changed her mind in just a few days."

"I still say we should let her sit in her room and rot," Vito said, and Giacomo seconded his cousin.

The group started to talk loudly to one another and Dante called for order.

"Look at it this way," he said. "We've just been through a terrible thing where we all had to unite against the Germans. Can't we be forgiving and allow her to come back into our company?"

There were murmurs of dissent around the room, but also nods of agreement.

"Shall we take a vote then?" Dante asked. "Does anyone object to letting Fausta come back?"

There were still some complaints, but when Dante asked the villagers to raise their hands if they disagreed, no one did.

"Good," Rosa said, "I'll go and tell her."

Rosa got up and was about to go upstairs when there was a loud knock on the back door.

"*Mamma mia,*" Maddelena said, ready to flee back upstairs. "They've come back."

Marco looked out the window but saw only a tall young man wearing a strange hat and with an ammunition belt over his chest.

"I think it's the partisan who brought Roberto and Adolfo back last week," Marco said, opening the door. Rosa wondered why Maria suddenly stiffened and stared straight ahead.

Ezio Maffini entered and quickly closed the door behind him. He looked tired, as if he hadn't slept in a couple of nights.

"I heard the Nazis were here this morning, and I just wanted to make certain everyone was all right," Ezio said.

"That is very kind of you," Dante said, shaking Ezio's hand. "Yes, we are all right. A bit shaken, but except for Francesco, no one was injured."

Ezio looked at Francesco, whose eye had now swollen and whose cheek had turned an impressive shade of blue.

"It could have been worse," Francesco said.

Rosa saw Ezio and Maria look at each other and then look away. She remembered that when Ezio brought Roberto and Adolfo back, he and Maria had a conversation. How do they know each other? she wondered. How could they possibly know each other?

Ezio took off his ammunition belt and sank into a chair. "I saw what they did at Gavino's," he said quietly. "Terrible thing, terrible. He was a good man. He helped us so much."

Maria brought him a glass of water.

"Gavino always had some food on hand when we needed it and he knew everything that was going on. I don't know how he found out, but he certainly was connected."

"We wouldn't have had Colin if it wasn't for him," Maria said.

"Colin left this morning after the raid," Rosa said. "Only the good Lord knows where he is now."

"God help him," Ezio said.

Vito stood in front of Ezio's chair. "So Mister Partisan," he said. "How many Germans did you kill today?"

Ezio looked confused. "Germans? We didn't see any Germans today."

"Good," Vito said. "Then no Italians will lose their lives today."

Ezio was about to say something when Dante intervened. "What can you tell us about what is going on? We don't know anything."

"We have some contacts," Ezio said, declining to be more specific. "They are able to tell us what the Allies are doing, what the Nazis are doing. Florence is liberated now but there's still some fighting in the streets. Most bridges have been destroyed, but not the Ponte Vecchio. And the great works of art have mostly survived intact."

"Oh, thank God!" Dante cried.

"Around here, there's been much more action in the last weeks. The SS is patrolling the hills now so we've run into them. Our *banda* has been lucky and we haven't lost anyone for three weeks. But we're short-handed. We've been working day and night. I've got two new boys to help in my *banda* but they just joined us this week."

"Your new boys," Gina said. "Would they be from Montepulciano?"

She put her arm around Lucia, who suddenly started to pay attention to the conversation.

"Why, yes," Ezio said. "They were running away from the army and they stayed at Gavino's for a couple weeks. Do you know them?"

Lucia and Gina didn't know how to answer that, but Lucia said, "Are they all right?"

"They're all right. They just have a lot to learn."

"Will you take care of them?" she asked.

"Partisans always take care of each other."

That didn't seem very comforting to either Gina or Lucia.

"We really need more help," Ezio said. "We've got so much work to do. We have to find the mines the Germans have planted. We have to save some bridges. We have to cut the telephone lines. We have to harass and confuse the Germans. So much. I wish we had someone who knows these hills better than we do."

Francesco started to say something but he looked at Annabella and decided against it. When Ezio got up to leave, Rosa noticed that Maria helped him put his ammunition belt back on and that he smiled at her.

"Can we ask your name?" Francesco said.

"You can call me Sparrow."

Ezio shook hands with most of the villagers. Vito turned his back and went into the kitchen.

"Buona fortuna, Sparrow!*"* the villagers cried as Ezio left.

Francesco went out the door with him and whispered, "How can we contact you? Can you give me directions?"

"Follow the path to the stream, take it to the right about a half mile, then look for a thick grove of olive trees. We're in a cave deep in the back."

CHAPTER 29

▼

Rosa and Annabella were unable to sleep that night after the tumultuous events of the day. The Germans' terrifying raid. The murder of Gavino. Colin Richards' departure. The visit by the partisan. Coming so soon after the threats by Fausta and the death of little Carlotta, it was almost too much to bear. Both of the women dwelled on one thought after another but just as they slipped into sleep other images woke them.

Unable to cope with all the feelings that tumbled through her mind, Rosa reached into the past where it was safe. With the moonlight streaming onto the bed where she slept as a child, she took herself back to a childhood warmed by her parents' love. As though she was at the cinema, she watched her mother cooking in the kitchen just below. She heard her father cutting wood outside. She relived the joys of Christmas and Easter. For some reason, she especially remembered the time at night before she went to bed. It was the most comforting part of her day and she always fell right asleep afterwards. Her mother would be reading in a corner and her father would hold her on his lap, making up stories. Rosa pulled the covers tight, disturbing Gatto, who had, as usual, spread himself over the entire bottom of the bed.

A few feet away, Annabella folded her hands across her chest and stared at the dark ceiling. Annabella was not thinking about the past. She was worried about Francesco. He seemed to be changing before her very eyes. Normally he was quiet and sad, never telling her how he felt about anything. Now he was suddenly outspoken. Even more worrisome, it looked like he wanted to take some sort of action, though she had no idea what that might be.

Today, he had confronted the Germans soldiers, something unthinkable a few weeks ago, and now had a black eye to show for it. This afternoon, he was very much interested in the partisan and where he was hiding. What was Francesco thinking? Annabella had rarely been very interested in Francesco's thoughts before. She preferred to leave him alone just as long as he left her alone.

In the semi-darkness Annabella saw Rosa reach down and adjust Gatto so that she could move her feet.

"Are you still awake?" she whispered.

"Yes," Rosa said. "I haven't been able to sleep at all."

"Neither have I."

"Maybe we shouldn't even try," Annabella said. "I was going to get up but I didn't want to disturb you."

"Funny, I thought the same thing."

The women threw off their covers. Annabella carefully lowered herself into the chair that had been badly damaged by the Germans. Rosa stood at the window, looking at the star-filled sky. Neither said anything for a long time.

"How is Francesco?" Rosa said at last. "He has quite a bad bruise."

"At least nothing's broken," Annabella said. "He'll be all right."

"Francesco seems so…I don't know…different lately."

"He's on edge. He wants to do something, just doesn't know what."

"We all do," Rosa said. "What do you think he'll do?"

"I don't know. I've never seen him like this."

Rosa was about to ask Annabella if this worried her, but felt it wasn't her place to ask such a question. Instead, she said, "You were so gentle and kind to him this morning. He must have liked that."

Annabella just shrugged and the two women were lost in their thoughts again. Perhaps she should have hugged him more, Annabella thought. Perhaps she should have stayed with him longer after the Germans left. Perhaps she should have told him how proud she was of him. It was too late now.

"I keep thinking about Gavino," Rosa said.

"I do, too," Annabella said. "Such a kind and wonderful man."

Again, there was a long silence. Finally, Annabella said, "Rosa, what did you say to Fausta so that she didn't tell the Germans about Colin Richards? We were all so surprised when we heard that. Was it really about the children?"

Rosa turned toward Annabella and leaned against the wall next to the window. "I didn't say anything, not much anyway. She has just been sitting in her room thinking and I suppose she came to her senses. She said she cried when she heard us singing at Carlotta's funeral."

"Well, it was amazing. If she had said something, we'd all be dead now."

"I know. I couldn't believe it either when the soldiers asked her and she just said, 'No, no one here.'"

"'No, no one here,'" the two women said together, laughing as they recalled how Fausta had stood up to the Germans.

"Do you think she's really changed?"

"I don't know," Rosa said. "When I told her tonight that she could come downstairs now, she said she wanted to wait. Maybe tomorrow, she said. I think she's embarrassed."

"Francesco says he still has her pistol," Annabella said. "He said he was sorry he didn't have it when the Germans came this morning."

"He would have shot at them?"

"The way he's feeling now, I think he would have. And then they would have killed him and all the rest of us. Thank goodness Marco told him to give it to Colin."

The women were silent, thinking of how narrowly they had escaped death. Rosa turned back to the window again.

"Rosa," Annabella said suddenly, "are you still in love with Francesco?"

Rosa whirled around. "What? Annabella, please, that was forty years ago."

"Yes, but you could still be in love with him. Maybe you just don't realize it. I've tried to see something in your eyes when you look at him, but I don't see anything different."

"That's because there isn't anything there. Annabella, yes, I was in love with Francesco once. He was the biggest love of my life for so long. And, yes, I suppose I was still in love with him after you two got married. I don't know for how long. That was so long ago."

It was so long ago, Rosa thought, that it was difficult now to even remember the times she spent with Francesco. For a moment she relived a picnic near the river. It was a hot August day, much like now. They had brought prosciutto and cheese and apples. They talked about how many children they would like. She wanted two, he wanted more. She remembered his dimples when he laughed and how his dark curly hair tumbled down his neck. She knew she wasn't pretty, at least not pretty enough for him. But he said he liked it when she smiled and she made him laugh. They were so young, Rosa thought, as if the girl in the memory was someone else. They didn't have a thing to worry about.

Annabella broke the daydream. "You had other men," she said. "I know you had other men."

Rosa seemed surprised that Annabella knew about Sergio and Franco. Did the entire village know?

"Annabella, I didn't love either of them. I can tell you that."

"So when did you stop loving Francesco?"

"I told you I just don't know, Annabella. I know that when I started going out with Marco I never thought about Francesco. And I never have since. Marco is my life now and he always will be. He tells me stories about Francesco and how they hunt together and how he's such a good card player. I find the stories interesting, but nothing more. Marco says Francesco never mentions you. I've wondered about that, but Marco says it's not our business."

Annabella studied her nails in the moonlight. They were chipped and split. She wished she had remembered to take some polish along. She ran her fingers through her hair. The wave had gone completely out and after weeks at the Cielo, her hair felt stringy. She wondered if she would ever see her hairdresser in Reboli again.

"Rosa?"

"Yes?"

"I really was pregnant. I didn't lie. I didn't force Francesco to marry me. His father did."

"Annabella, I don't want to talk about it."

"Well, I do, Rosa! We've got to get this straightened out. And I don't blame you. I've been at fault, too. We're two silly old women who are too stubborn to talk to each other."

Rosa was too surprised to answer.

"I *was* pregnant, Rosa, I was. I guess I got pregnant one of the first times Francesco and I made love. And I'll tell you another thing. I wanted him to make love to me. He didn't want to at first, but I coaxed him into it."

"So, Annabella, you did want to take him away from me, didn't you?"

"I wasn't thinking about that. I was only thinking how much I wanted him. I didn't think about you. I didn't think about our friendship. I didn't think about getting pregnant. I didn't think about getting married. Rosa, we were seventeen years old. We didn't think about what would happen next."

"No, we didn't."

"So when I got pregnant and I told my parents, they were upset but they said they would help me take care of the baby. But then my father told Francesco's father and all hell broke loose. Francesco's father beat Francesco up. He said he didn't deserve to be his son. And he said he would disown him if he didn't marry me."

That would have meant that Francesco wouldn't inherit the family trattoria in Reboli.

"So we had this big church wedding. You weren't there, I know that because I looked for you. But it was a farce. Francesco didn't love me. We spent the first week not even talking to each other. Then we mainly just talked at meal times, just a little. Four weeks later I had the miscarriage."

Rosa felt embarrassed at learning this and ashamed that she had thought Annabella had made up the pregnancy.

"Annabella, you don't have to tell me all this."

"I want to. I know you never believed I was pregnant and you thought I tricked Francesco into marrying me by telling him I was. That's right, isn't it?"

"Yes."

"Well, it wasn't a trick."

Gatto stirred on the bed, rising, arching his back, stretching first his front legs and then his back legs before settling down to a new position. The women watched him as if they had nothing else on their minds. It was a good fifteen minutes before Annabella spoke.

"Sometimes I wish he had married you, Rosa. I think he's still in love with you."

"Annabella, please. That can't be."

"You don't know our marriage, Rosa. We're like two strangers living in the same house. Francesco is always sad and I just want to be by myself."

"I'm so sorry, Annabella. I'm so sorry."

Annabella didn't think it necessary to bring up Francesco's affairs or his drinking. The affairs ended years ago and she noticed that he always refused the wine and *grappa* when it was offered at the Cielo.

"I look at you and Marco and see that you're so happy and I know what I've missed. I suppose everyone in Sant'Antonio thinks we're such a happy couple. What rubbish."

"It's not too late to do something about it, you know," Rosa said. "This war has made all of us look at things differently."

"I know. When I heard Francesco say that he wanted to do something, anything, rather than just sit here, I was surprised and now I'm worried. He has never shown that kind of passion about anything."

Then Annabella recalled one other time. His father had treated one of the girls at the trattoria badly, for no reason. Francesco was furious and confronted his father who told him to mind his own business. Francesco came home that night and drank heavily. He didn't bring up the subject again. But Annabella wondered if Francesco contained more passion than he revealed.

"You do love him, don't you?" Rosa said.

"Yes. Deep in my heart. I don't show it, but I do. When that officer hit him this morning I was so angry. I wanted to do more than put my arms around Francesco but I was afraid to. I was afraid to show him how I feel."

"You still can, you know."

"It may be too late."

Rosa went behind Annabella's chair and touched her shoulder. Annabella grasped her hand and kissed it.

"We've all changed, Annabella. Look at us. We don't even look like we did forty years ago. But you're still beautiful, and I'm still, well, you know."

"Rosa, I wish you wouldn't demean yourself like that."

"Well, it's true. I'm so short, my face is so homely. You are so tall and dignified. You dress so well. I've always admired that. And Francesco is still handsome too, though not of course as handsome as Marco."

"I've always thought Marco was so good looking," Annabella said. "So tall. Still so, well, robust! And so much hair!"

The women laughed. Francesco may have lost his hair but he was still lean and wiry and looked at least ten years younger than he was. Rosa was always pleased to see that he still had his dimples when he smiled.

"Francesco is a good man, isn't he?" Rosa said.

"He's a wonderful man. He would help anyone. And I know I haven't done my part. I've been cruel and spiteful to him. We both have been angry at each other for all these years and now there's a big black pit separating us. And neither of us wants to take the first step to cross it."

"I'm sorry, Annabella. I never knew."

"I'm so worried, Rosa."

"We all are, Annabella."

"What's going to happen to us?"

"I don't know, Annabella. I don't know."

The two women went back to their beds and Gatto reluctantly made room for Rosa. Rosa and Annabella were still staring at the ceiling when the sun started to rise.

CHAPTER 30

▼

It was barely light the next morning when Marco, Francesco and Dante, followed by Vito and Giacomo, slowly made their way back to Gavino's farm. They darted between trees and crouched low, fearing that they might be seen. Marco and Francesco carried the pistols they had retrieved from the wine cellar.

Marco was surprised to see how fast Francesco could run. At fifty-six, Francesco was fourteen years younger than Marco and seemed to be in excellent condition.

Marco and Dante stayed about twenty paces behind and Vito and Giacomo, both in their eighties, did the best they could considering that the path led through the Cielo's old fields, ancient olive groves, tangled vineyards and heavy brush.

"I don't know how Gavino made it through this mess," Marco said.

"He was small," Dante said, "even smaller than Giacomo and Vito."

They traveled more than a half mile before reaching Gavino's little farm.

About half way they found leaflets sticking to the branches of the olive trees and gathered around. Apparently, the leaflets had been strewn by a German plane. Written in Italian, the leaflets warned that anyone who gave shelter to partisans or knew where they were hiding would be shot and their houses blown up.

Francesco threw a leaflet down in disgust. "These are the same messages that are on that poster in the village. The Nazis think that these kinds of threats will stop people from helping the partisans? They must be more stupid than I thought."

Dante was more concerned. "I'm sure some people will be more afraid now that there has been more shooting. Think of all the old women who are living alone, maybe with children. Do you think they're going to let partisans into their homes after they've seen this kind of message?"

"Let's hope there are still enough people who aren't afraid. If it weren't for the partisans, we'd all be dead," Francesco said, storming ahead.

Marco and Dante looked at each other.

"Why do you think Francesco is so angry lately?" Dante asked.

"I just don't know," Marco said.

"*Boh!* Partisans!" Vito said, out of breath.

About a quarter mile farther, other leaflets were found in the ancient vineyards. These had been dropped by Allied planes. These urged everyone to sabotage the Germans' communication lines, to refuse to report to the army and to organize because "the moment for decisive action is near at hand."

"*O Dio,*" Dante said. "Now we get instructions from the other side. They want to recruit us to join the partisans. What are we supposed to do?"

"I know what we're supposed to do," Francesco said. "We're supposed to support the partisans. We're supposed to fight the Nazis. We can't wait for the Allies or this war is never going to end."

"*Boh!*" Vito said.

Francesco led the way as they neared Gavino's hut, now just a heap of charred timber and stone. The remaining walls had caved in and it was more forlorn than yesterday.

The men paused briefly before Gavino's grave and then inspected all sides of the ruins. A garden contained beans, peas, tomatoes and zucchini ready to be picked and potatoes that were nearing a harvest. They were pleased to find four rabbits in one pen and three hens and a rooster in another.

"If we can get these back to the Cielo, we won't go hungry for a while," Marco said, putting vegetables into a sack.

"And we can come here every few days to get more vegetables," Dante said.

"That's assuming we don't run into partisans and Germans fighting on the way," Francesco said.

Dante heard something moving in the brush. Marco and Francesco pulled out their pistols and all five men crouched down.

"Who do you think it is?" Vito whispered.

"It must be somebody short or we would see him," Giacomo said.

The brush gave way and a black form could be seen.

"It's a German," Vito whispered to Marco. "Shoot him!"

"No, wait," Dante said.

The dark form pushed its way through the brush.

"It's a pig!" Vito shouted. "It's Gavino's pig!"

Pina was covered with mud and obviously in distress.

"Poor pig," Giacomo said. "It probably misses Gavino. Look, it's limping."

A closer inspection revealed that the pig's right hind leg was badly mangled.

"I think we have to make a decision," Marco said. "We could somehow get the pig to the Cielo and try to take care of it, but it's not likely to survive."

"What do you think Gavino would want us to do?" Francesco said.

"I think he'd want us to have some good meals," Vito said.

Both Marco and Francesco were expert hunters and knew how to make a quick kill. It was accomplished in minutes.

"Let's get going," Marco said. "Those shots could be heard all over."

Marco and Dante tied Pina's body with rope and, with Francesco taking the lead, the men slowly dragged it back to the Cielo, a tiring effort through the vineyards and olive groves. When they reached the farmhouse they were greeted with mixed emotions by the women.

"Oh, you killed that sweet pig," Maria said.

"Oh, look at that face," Maddelena said.

Rosa was more practical. "Look, would you rather leave it to die at Gavino's? How merciful would that be?"

Everyone set about making use of Pina. Besides providing food, the pig allowed the villagers to take their minds off the Germans' raid, the bombers overhead and the artillery in the valley. Marco and Vito and Giacomo had butchered pigs many times, so they took charge, with Francesco doing the heavy work.

First, they rigged two hooks to the beams of the shed. Then they tied the pig's rear hoofs with ropes and Francesco raised it to the ceiling. Marco put a large pan under its head, took a knife and slit the pig from rear to front. The men gathered all the entrails that fell out and put them in pots. Blood dripped into the pan; the flesh would become clean and white.

"All right," Marco said, "we'll leave the rest until tomorrow. It will take a while for the blood to stop."

Understandably, after slaughtering the pig, no one was much interested in eating and the villagers again became silent, aware of the sounds of war that were coming closer. In the afternoon, Fausta came downstairs. She wore her white blouse and black skirt and her hair was pulled back as usual. But her face was flushed and her eyes red. Everyone looked at her but no one said anything. Fausta moved awkwardly toward the fireplace.

"I, I just want to say something," she said.

The villagers looked up and waited expectedly.

"I, I just want to say I'm sorry. I did a terrible thing. Please forgive me." Fausta burst into tears, covered her face with her hands and turned toward the wall. Rosa smiled, but no one made a move until Maria went up to her.

"It's all right, dear," she said, putting her hand on Fausta's shoulder. Fausta collapsed in tears on Maria's generous bosom.

The rest of the villagers silently went back to what they were doing and Fausta went to a corner, sat down and idly turned the pages of a magazine.

Long after the others had gone to bed that night, Marco and Francesco sat alone at the long table, going over the events of the day and cleaning their pistols. Francesco seemed very nervous.

The two men had shared many confidences over the years, but they knew when they should not ask questions of the other. For Marco, that meant giving Francesco privacy about his marriage. Whatever arrangement Francesco and Annabella had, Marco reasoned, it was their business. Like many men, they did not talk much at all, sometimes hunting all day and exchanging only a dozen sentences. But they felt a strong bond of friendship and there was nothing either of them would not do for the other.

Marco and Francesco had met thirty years ago when Marco was hired to make repairs at the Sabbatini family trattoria in Reboli. Francesco helped him with the work and they quickly became friends. Marco was married to Emilia at the time and he sometimes wondered why Francesco never talked about Annabella. But Marco was not the kind of man to ask questions about that.

Although Marco was only fourteen years older, Francesco found in him the kind of father he wished he had and Marco found a son he never had. But they also regarded each other as equals, and they liked to hunt and, especially, to play cards together. Every afternoon, Francesco escaped from the trattoria to join the other men at Leoni's.

Tonight, Marco sensed that Francesco wanted to tell him something.

"You seem tense lately," Marco said, putting down his pistol. "Are you feeling all right?"

"I think I've made up my mind about something, Marco."

Marco waited. Francesco hesitated for only a moment.

"I want to join the partisans."

If the two men had not been such good friends for so long, this would have come as a surprise. But Marco had watched Francesco over the last few days, noticing how upset he was about the Germans' raid and how interested he was in the partisans. He had put a few things together.

"I thought that was it," Marco said.

"You did? You knew that?"

"Francesco, I know you too well and you know me too well not to know what's going on in our minds. Am I surprised? No. Am I worried? Yes."

"Well, so am I."

The two men grew silent, as they often did when they were discussing something besides hunting and *briscola*. And just as he did when he had the long conversation with Annabella, Francesco went to a window. He didn't want to let Marco see the fear in his eyes. Marco sensed it anyway.

"What are you worried about, Francesco?"

"Well, obviously I'm not a young man anymore."

"You're a lot younger than I am."

"And a lot older than that partisan who called himself Sparrow and probably every one else in the Garibaldi *banda*."

"But you're in good shape," Marco said. "You were running ahead of us when we went to Gavino's today. You did the major work in bringing that pig back. And you hoisted it up on those hooks. That pig must weigh more than two hundred pounds. You weren't even sweating or out of breath like the rest of us."

"I think I can still do some things a younger man does. And after all the hunting we've done here, I know every inch of these hills. Sparrow said they need someone like that. So I have something to offer."

Marco told him about two of his friends from the construction line, both in their fifties, who had joined the partisans.

"What happened to them?"

"I don't know," Marco said, neglecting to add that there were reports that both men had been killed.

"What else are you worried about?" Marco asked.

"Well, if I leave, there will be only four men here at the Cielo. I'm not saying I have contributed much, but it might be important to have another older fellow here."

"You mean if the Germans come again?"

"No. You saw I wasn't much good this time. My eye is still bloody. No, I meant if we suddenly had to pack up and leave, I wouldn't want to leave all that work to Annabella."

"You're worried about Annabella, too, aren't you?"

"Yes," Francesco sighed. "Marco, things have changed between us since we've come here. I can't say everything is perfect. It certainly isn't. But I think we've started to talk a little more. Maybe she won't agree, but that's what I feel. If I leave now, well…I don't know."

Marco got up and stood behind Francesco. He put his hand on his shoulder. Outside, it was such a clear night that they could see lights in the valley and bonfires on distant hills.

"Why do you want to do this, Francesco?"

There was a long silence. Marco remembered a day in 1935 when they were coming down the hill to Sant'Antonio after hours of futile hunting. Mussolini had just invaded Ethiopia and authorized the use of mustard gas to destroy civilian villages. Both Marco and Francesco had opposed Mussolini from the start, and this act was contemptible. Marco was upset, but Francesco was furious and belligerent. He shouted and cursed like he never had before. Marco had never seen him like that. By the time they reached Sant'Antonio, however, Francesco had become his usual self, quietly taking his rifle apart before going home to Annabella.

Francesco attempted to answer Marco's question. "Because, Marco, I finally want to do something on my own that is good."

"What are you talking about? You're a good man, you know that."

Francesco turned to him. His voice was cracking and his words came slowly. "Let me finish. All my life I've done things because I was forced to. I went to work for my father in that tiresome trattoria. I took over the business when my father died and I've hated every day of it. I married Annabella. You know I didn't want to, but my father made me. And I've been unhappy ever since. And so has she. Nobody knows better than I do that I haven't been a good husband."

"Francesco, Francesco," Marco interrupted. He stood helplessly in front of his friend and didn't know what to say.

"There's more. I know I haven't told you this before. But I've had affairs. Five of them actually in the first twenty years we were married."

"Francesco, please, you don't have to tell me this."

"I want to, Marco. No, I don't do that any more. So now I drink. Every night."

"You haven't touched a drop here."

"Funny how the war can change even those habits," Francesco said.

"But you haven't answered the question," Marco said. "Why do you want to join the partisans?"

"Marco, for just once in my life I want to do something because it is the right thing to do. I want to be proud of myself for a change."

Neither man spoke. They both knew that although Francesco might be a hero, he could be a dead hero.

"What do you think Annabella is going to say when you tell her?" Marco asked.

"I don't know. But I'm going to tell her tomorrow and I want to leave right then. Sparrow told me where to find him."

"You would leave right away?"

"Yes."

The two men had been friends for thirty years, but they had never been closer. Each had tears in his eyes.

"Marco," Francesco said. "I'm worried about Annabella. I know she seems like a strong independent woman, but she's really delicate and vulnerable."

"Francesco, you don't have to worry about Annabella. First, nothing is going to happen to you. But if by God it does, Rosa and I will take care of her."

"Rosa?"

"Yes, Rosa. She told me today that she and Annabella had a good talk last night. I think they're going to be all right."

Francesco wiped his forehead. "Marco, you don't know how much that means to me. Now I can go and not worry so much."

Marco held Francesco by his shoulders and looked him in the eyes.

"Francesco," he said, "I want to tell you this. I will worry about you. We both know the dangers and we both know you could get killed. But I think what you're doing is very brave. I wish I had your courage. I don't. When you're out there, just remember that I will be next to you all the time. No, not next to you, I'll be behind you. I'll even be pushing you on."

"Don't push too hard, Marco," Francesco laughed. "I'm not a young man anymore."

CHAPTER 31

▼

Pina was ready to make her contribution to the villagers' sustenance. Fortunately, the last inhabitants of the Cielo must have had pigs because their equipment was still on shelves in the shed, although by now much of it was dusty and rusty. Starting early in the morning, the men needed two hours just to clean the saws, the cleavers, the butcher knives, the grinders.

Then they took down the pig and laid it on the long bench in the shed. Donning aprons, they got a tub of water boiling and scraped the skin until it was pink. Then, using saws, cleavers and knives, they cut away the sections for hams, the flesh from the head and neck for head cheese, the shoulder pieces for sausages, the spinal meat for salami.

"Poor pig," said Vito, running his fingers down the edge of a meat cleaver, "but lucky us."

Every once in a while Marco looked at Francesco, wondering if he had changed his mind. Francesco kept his head bowed over his work, but Marco thought he looked worried every time artillery fire was heard in the valley or Allied bombers droned overhead.

In the house, the women prepared to make sausages, cutting the chunks into even smaller pieces and cleaning the pig's intestines. They knew the job would be dirty and messy, so they had put on men's shirts and pants they found in a closet. Even the Contessa had traded the silk dress she wore every day and was wearing a red flannel shirt and bib overalls.

"Do I look like a *contadina*?" she asked, turning around. The women smiled. The Contessa still had her yellow hair in tight ringlets, sparkling rings on her fingers and heavy rouge on her cheeks.

Rosa put small pieces of the pig's head into boiling water. She added garlic, salt and pepper. After it was sent through a grinder, the mixture was stuffed into large pieces of the intestines to make blood sausage. "I always hated *biroldo*," she said.

Meanwhile, Maria selected lean meat for salami and pushed it through a grinder.

"I'll need smaller intestines for this," she said, and they were quickly supplied by Maddelena and Renata.

The children, Roberto, Adolfo and Anna, were assigned the task of tying up the sausages with strings. It was a gooey job and they made it clear that they hated it.

At the end of the table, Gina placed meat from the hind legs in a barrel and added salt, pepper, garlic and wine for prosciutto.

"It's too bad all this is going to take weeks to cure," Gina said. "Surely we'll be back home by then."

"We're going to have enough for all of Sant'Antonio," Maddelena said. "We can take what we don't use back with us."

The women looked at each other, knowing that no one could even hope they would return. Before they could say anything, Fausta came down the stairs and stood awkwardly at the table.

"Can I help?" she asked.

No one else looked up, but Rosa put a bowl of unpleasant looking portions of Pina's backside in front of her.

"Well, I'm sorry, but someone has to cut this up into little pieces. Would you mind?"

"Not at all," Fausta said, taking the bowl into the kitchen as three Allied bombers swooped low over the hill and toward the valley. The Cielo's walls reverberated for a long time.

Chopping the meat into small pieces, Rosa said, "It's hard to believe that we're here making sausages when the world is falling apart outside the door."

"We have to keep busy," Maria said. "Otherwise we'll go crazy."

"Francesco says we have to do something," Annabella said. "I don't know what he means. But I don't think he means chopping up a pig."

Putting down her knife, Rosa cornered Gina. "Where's Lucia? Is she all right? I think she's been looking tired lately."

"She's resting. And she would get sick with all the smells here."

"Gina, you don't think?"

"Rosa, I don't think, I know."

Rosa put her hand on Gina's arm. "I'm so sorry, Gina. Please tell me if I can do anything."

"I will. But there's nothing any of us can do now. Rosa, you know what she's been up to."

"Yes," Rosa said. "I tried to stop her, but she wouldn't listen."

"Nobody can stop Lucia, Rosa," Gina said. "You did what you could."

At the table, Maria looked up from chopping a hind quarter. "I just thought of something. Next week is *Ferragosto*."

"*Ferragosto!*" Maddelena and Renata shouted together.

Since the 1880s the Catholic Church had celebrated the Blessed Virgin's Assumption into Heaven on August 15 and it had become a secular holiday as well. Some people always declared that the feast could trace its way back to the days before Christ when the Emperor Augustus proclaimed that August would be dedicated to a series of festivals and celebrations, with one on August 13 in honor of Diana, the goddess of fertility. Others noted that the gods of the harvest were also honored during August.

Whatever its origins, August 15 was a day in which Italians could try to forget the heat of the month and celebrate with parades, dances and, especially, feasts.

"Let's have a feast next Tuesday!" Maria said. "We have the food now and Lord knows we need a celebration."

"A celebration?" Annabella said. "What are we to celebrate about? The Germans have invaded us, the partisans are fighting outside and the Allies are nowhere near to rescuing us. We're besieged in here."

"That's all the more reason to celebrate," Maria said. "We're alive, we're together, we have each other. And we're going to get through this, pray God we will."

The other women merely nodded. There was no use arguing with Maria.

"I don't know if we can plan things a week ahead," said Rosa. "Who is to say that any of us will still be here then? Who is to say we'll still be alive?"

"We will," Maria said, fingering the rosary beads in her pocket. "I just know we will."

"Maria," Annabella said, "don't you ever get angry? Don't you ever get discouraged?"

"No, she doesn't," the Contessa said. "She's a saint."

"I guess I don't get angry very often," Maria said. "I do get discouraged. I wonder why God allows bad things to happen. But then I think of everything that is so good in this world. I look at little children mostly, and I see so much hope for us."

"But your husband was killed in that awful accident," Rosa said. "Your daughter has moved away. You're all alone."

"Yes, but I hear from Angelica regularly, or at least I did until we came up here. And I know she's safe in Sant'Anna. And I think about Little Carlo and Nando. I have to smile every time I look at their picture."

At that moment, presumably because he had been sniffing so vigorously at what was spread on the table, Gatto sneezed.

"See!" Maria said. "Even Gatto believes that we're going to be all right."

"Maria," Rosa said, "that's just an old wives' superstition. Nobody really believes that a cat sneezing will bring good luck."

"Well, we can believe what we want to believe," Maria said, sneaking Gatto a choice chunk of Pina's liver.

Caught up in plans for the celebration, Maria described what they could prepare for the feast.

"We're going to stew some vegetables. We'll have sliced tomatoes. A nice lettuce salad. And now, pork chops! My mouth is watering just thinking about it. It's too bad the prosciutto won't be ready."

"Remember last *Ferragosto,* Renata?" Maddelena said. "We went to Reboli and watched the procession."

The Chiesa di Saint Ignazio sponsored the biggest festival in Reboli. The highlight was a procession with little girls strewing flower petals before the statue of the Virgin that six strong men carried on a platform down the main avenue.

"We're never going to have a *Ferragosto* like we had," Renata said. "It's all in the past now."

Rosa took the opportunity to take Maria aside. "Maria," she whispered, "do you know that partisan who came here the other night? That Sparrow? I couldn't help wonder…"

"Shhh," Maria said. "Yes, I know him."

"How? How could you know him? Are you helping him? Is that why you were so upset in church before we came here?"

"No, no, I'm not helping him."

"But then?"

"It's Angelica." Maria whispered even more softly. "She knows him. Please don't tell anyone."

"I won't," Rosa said, putting her hand on Maria's arm. "But how does Angelica know him?"

"That's all I can say now, Rosa. Please don't ask any more questions."

Maria's eyes filled with tears and she turned away.

Marco, Francesco, Dante, Vito and Giacomo came in from the shed just as the women finished their work. The men's aprons were so soaked with blood they looked like they had fought the Germans. Everyone was exhausted and ready for the afternoon rest.

It was then that Francesco asked Annabella if they could meet alone in her room. Annabella was both eager and apprehensive. The meeting did not start well.

At first, Annabella was angry with Francesco for wanting to join the partisans.

"Francesco, this is stupid!"

Then she seemed concerned about her own safety.

"How could you even think of leaving me now?"

Then she worried about him.

"Francesco, you're fifty-six years old! You can't do this!"

But then she listened as he pleaded.

"'Bella, please," he said, as she sat slumped on the bed, her face buried in her hands. He had never seen her look so old and tired. He had never felt so young and strong.

"We've been here almost a month and the war is still going on and we're not doing anything about it. Just outside, there are people who are fighting for our cause. We need to support them. I need to join them. I know you're surprised that I would want to do this. Well, let me tell you, you're not as surprised as I am. I can hardly believe this. It's not like me, I know. But people change. Don't you see, Annabella, it comes down to what each of us can do. And I think I have to do something."

"Such as leaving me alone here?"

"Annabella, I'm sorry. My mind is so confused now. But I really feel that this might be good for us. When I come back…"

"If you come back…"

"*When* I come back. I know I will, 'Bella, I just know I will."

"Just like you knew we would be out of here in three weeks."

"Well, maybe if more people had joined the partisans a month ago we would have been out of here in three weeks. But listen, 'Bella, please understand why I want to do this."

"I don't think I'll ever understand."

"I tried to explain it to Marco last night and I didn't do it very well then, either. All I know is that for once in my life I need to prove something to myself. I can't go on like I have been. For years, my life hasn't had any meaning. I work at a job I hate, I come home and I'm sullen and withdrawn because I hate myself, too. And, yes, that's why I drink every night. I want to do something good and honorable."

Francesco was pacing now, and his voice grew softer.

"And there's something else. I know I haven't been a good husband to you. I'm not asking you to love me. That's too much to ask. But maybe if you saw me doing something good you could get to like me."

Francesco had tears in his eyes as he stood over his wife. She raised her head.

"It's not just you, you know," she said. "It's been my fault, too."

"Let's not talk about who's at fault, 'Bella. That's in the past. Let's see what we have right now and then maybe what we might have in the future."

"I haven't been able to believe in a future for years," she said.

"The war has changed everything, 'Bella. We have to think about now, and then we can think about what might happen later."

Annabella wiped tears from her eyes and took his hands in hers.

"I know you're not asking my permission, Francesco. I don't think I could, or even would, give it. I'm terrified that you're doing this and I wish I could say I am proud of you. I can't right now. Forgive me. I just pray that you won't get hurt. Be careful, Francesco. Please. I want you to come back, I really do."

Francesco pulled Annabella to her feet and put his arms around her. After a moment, she put her arms around him and they remained in a tight embrace for minutes. They had not held each other like this since before their wedding and yet somehow it did not seem strange.

"I'll be careful, 'Bella," he said softly. "I'll be fine."

He kissed her on the forehead and she slumped back down on the bed, hugging herself. Then he went downstairs to finish packing.

Marco and Rosa were just coming out of the kitchen. Rosa couldn't believe Marco when he revealed Francesco's plans and she bombarded him with questions for which he had no answers.

"I'm very worried," she said. "I have very bad feelings about this."

"He'll be all right, Rosa. And anyway, we can't stop him."

For a moment, Rosa wondered if perhaps she really was still in love with Francesco, at least a little. No, she wasn't going to think about that.

Francesco emerged from his room carrying a knapsack. He had Fausta's pistol in his pocket and Marco had given him a compass.

"Do you know how to find them?" Marco asked.

"Yes, I'm sure of it. I'll be there before dark."

"Do you have everything? The pistol? Bullets? The compass?"

"Yes, yes. I've got everything."

There was an awkward silence.

"Wait," Francesco said. "I forgot something."

He went back into his room and returned with his violin case. "Here. I won't need this where I'm going."

"We're going to save it for you," Rosa said.

Francesco and Marco embraced, patting each other on the back.

"So this is it?" Marco said.

"Yes."

Francesco turned to Rosa.

"Goodbye, Rosa. Take care of Marco. And please look after Annabella."

"I will. Don't worry about Annabella. And you take care of yourself," she said, kissing him on both cheeks and hugging him. They both had tears in their eyes. Rosa put her arm around Marco as they watched Francesco slip out the back door and run down the path before anyone else noticed.

Naturally, his departure became the topic of conversation for the rest of the day. Everyone found reasons for Francesco to join the partisans, none of them accurate. Vito made his expected comments about partisans but he didn't seem as angry as usual. Now he knew a real partisan and he also knew that Francesco was a good man. Maybe the partisans did some good, maybe they weren't all bad.

That night, the villagers didn't want to go to bed, afraid of what might happen during the night and what the next day might bring. So they remained sitting around the table and huddled on the floor until well past midnight.

"I'm just grateful that Angelica is in Sant'Anna," Maria said as the room became even more dark and gloomy. "At least one of us is safe. But we can't dwell on what might happen. We have to think about other things. We can think about *Ferragosto!*"

When Rosa went upstairs to check on Annabella, she found her lying on the bed fully dressed, her hands across her chest.

"Annabella, are you awake?"

"Yes."

"Can I get you anything?"

"No."

"Annabella, I'm sure Francesco will be all right."

Rosa was glad the room was so dark that Annabella could not see the fear in her eyes.

"You know something?" Annabella said. "I miss the sounds of the violin. I was getting to like 'La Follia.'"

CHAPTER 32

▼

Exhausted and not very hungry, Dino and Paolo collapsed at the entrance to the partisans' cave beyond the olive trees. They had spent four days in hard work, cutting telephone lines so the Germans in Sant'Antonio could no longer communicate with the unit in Reboli and helping disconnect the land mines the Germans had placed in the hills.

More important, they had learned to take part in combat, helping the more experienced partisans in skirmishes with the Germans. The others would lead the way and Dino and Paolo would follow them with more ammunition, or they would play cat-and-mouse with the Germans to flush them into the open. In the last four days, the *banda* could claim eight Germans killed, with no partisan casualties except a broken arm.

Now, Dino and Paolo were glad to be in the relative coolness of the cave after spending the day under the steaming August sun. They had been given new names, Robin and Owl, but despite Sparrow's urging, they usually didn't use them when they talked to each other. After a long silence, Paolo asked, "What are you thinking about, Dino?"

"Lucia."

"Lucia? Why are you thinking about Lucia? You don't think about Elisa. Or Sofia. Or Ottavia."

"I know, but Lucia was different. She had a mind of her own. I've never met a girl like her. Why wouldn't she kiss me when I left? Why would any girl not want to kiss me?"

Paolo had several answers to the question but decided to keep them to himself.

"After the war is over, Paolo," Dino said. "I'm going to go to Sant'Antonio and find Lucia."

"After the war is over, Dino," Paolo said, "Lucia will probably be married to somebody else."

"No! She wouldn't do that, she wouldn't."

Dino and Paolo were so involved in the argument over Lucia that they didn't see the shadowy figure at the entrance to the cave.

"Permesso?" the man said. "Is anyone here?"

Aiming his rifle, Dino went to the entrance. "Who are you? What do you want? What are you doing here?"

"I want to see the man in charge. He said his name is Sparrow. He told me how to get here."

Dino looked the man up and down. He was a short fellow, wiry and bald-headed. He had a bloody right eye and a badly bruised cheek.

"What did this Sparrow look like?" Dino asked.

Francesco gave Dino a good description of Ezio.

"Why do you want to see him?"

"Take me to him and I'll tell him myself."

"No. Wait here."

Dino reluctantly went into the back reaches of the cave. Like many caves in the Apuan mountains, the partisans' hideout stretched back through labyrinthine tunnels and crevices. Some parts were used to store ammunition, some for supplies, some for shelter. All were dark and dank. Sparrow's headquarters were near the end of the longest tunnel.

At length, Ezio emerged. He recognized Francesco immediately because of his bruised eye.

"Buonasera," Ezio said. "Why did you come here? What do you want?"

"Sparrow." Francesco waited a moment. "I want to join your brigade."

Ezio's surprise was evident. The partisans were a motley group, farmers, students, army deserters, communists, factory workers. But all of them were relatively young. Eagle, who was killed in the German ambush a month ago, was in his late thirties and the oldest in the group. The man in front of him looked to be in his mid-forties.

"I know what you're thinking," Francesco said. "That I'm too old. I'm fifty-six."

"You're fifty-six?"

"Yes, but that shouldn't prevent me from joining you. I'm stronger than I look. I've got energy. And I can offer something important. I've been hunting with my friend for twenty years and I know these hills like the back of my hand. You said you needed someone like that."

It was true. In more times than Ezio liked to remember, the partisans had wasted time getting from one place to another because they didn't have a map showing direct routes. Or they didn't know about bridges that didn't exist anymore or streams that suddenly appeared. They could use someone who knew every inch of the region. Ezio looked intently at Francesco. The man looked muscular and he had strong hands. That would be useful.

"Tell me this," Ezio said. "Why do you want to join us? This isn't some adventure, you know."

"I want to join," Francesco said, "because I am tired of sitting in that farmhouse while the war is raging outside. We can hear the bombers and we can hear the artillery and the shelling. I just want to do my part."

"Why are you doing this now? The war has been going on for sometime."

Francesco's eyes were pleading. "Because it's getting worse every day. The bombing, the shelling. And I'm worried that the Germans are going to finally win. We can't let that happen, can we?"

Ezio still seemed doubtful.

"Please," Francesco said. "Try me out. If it doesn't work, send me back."

Knowing that the partisans desperately needed more men, Ezio agreed and led Francesco back to his part of the cave. Ezio was much taller than Francesco, but he kept telling him to watch his head as they made their way through the tunnels. Stones suddenly jutted out from the top and sides and the dripping water made the ground slippery. The tunnels were dark except for occasional candles.

Ezio suddenly stopped.

"You should know something first," he said. "This is a very dangerous time. The Germans have gone mad in these parts and are killing and burning without reason. At first they said they would kill ten innocent people for every German we killed. Now it's worse than that. They're killing many people, mostly women and children because the men are either with us or in hiding. They say they're doing it because the people are helping us, the partisans. But it's not just that. They've gone crazy. So we have to be very careful."

"Scorched earth?"

"Exactly."

"Then it's even more important that I join," Francesco said.

"Then I'm glad you came. But first, you need a new name. Mine is Sparrow. Those two young men at the entrance are Robin and Owl. How is Hawk for you?"

"Fine. I feel like a hawk."

The two men shook hands. Francesco looked at the young man who was spreading out a map on a makeshift bench and remembered another young man thirty years ago. He'd been married eight or nine years by then and his only worry was whether Annabella would find out about the affair he was having with the clerk in the shop next to the trattoria. Francesco suddenly felt the pangs of a wasted life.

Putting rocks on the four corners to hold down the map, Ezio looked up at Francesco and also had memories. He thought Francesco, with his bald head and beard, looked like a shorter version of his father. His father had schooled him on the history of Italy and told him that it was sometimes necessary to give up everything to fight for what was right. At times, there would be terrible consequences. His father was now somewhere near Florence, working in the Resistance and helping the partisans. Ezio hadn't heard from him in months.

"Let's look at this map and I'll show you where we are working," Ezio said.

The map showed the northern part of Italy and Ezio traced the Apennine mountains from the Mediterranean across to the east and down the spine of the peninsula.

"Now here," he said, moving his finger from west to east, "is what we call the Gothic Line."

"I know about the Gothic Line," Francesco said. "I've just never seen it on a map."

"Here it is. It runs from coast to coast, from here on the west, south of La Spezia, then southeast through the Apuan mountains, then here north of Florence, then through the River Foglia and then to the Adriatic."

"Is it as strong as the Germans claim?"

"The strongest. It was built by Italian labor, you know. Forced labor. They built steel shelters, they spread deep mine fields, they dug tunnels and ditches. The Germans are even using old castles. It's about twelve to fourteen miles deep and they say it is impenetrable. We'll find out."

Ezio then traced the area south of the Gothic Line, from Pisa to Florence.

"Here is where the battles are raging now. The Allies are moving north and they've liberated Pisa and Florence, but they haven't gotten farther. At first, the Germans were fighting hard but now they seem to be retreating and blowing up bridges on the way."

Francesco remembered that the Germans were in Sant'Antonio because of its crucial location at a bridge.

"And this is where we are," Ezio said, pointing to the area farther north of Pisa and Lucca. "Here's Camaiore, here's Stazzema, here's Pietrasanta. And this isn't on the map but the little village of Farnocchia is here. Just five days ago, the Germans came here and ordered the village evacuated. The partisan band there fought the Germans and eight Germans were killed. So the Germans burned many homes. Now many people from there have gone to another village, Sant'Anna di Stazzema, which is at the top of this mountain over here to the west. People from all over have gone there because it's one of the safest places around here."

"Have you been there?"

Ezio hesitated. "Yes, but our *banda* left a few months ago. We knew we were putting the people in danger because they had been helping us."

Francesco told Ezio that a woman from Sant'Antonio had a daughter who lives in Sant'Anna. He wondered why Sparrow wasn't surprised by this.

As Francesco looked at the map and continued to ask questions, Ezio's thoughts took him back in Sant'Anna. What was Angelica doing at this moment? Was she safe? Was there a threat from the Germans?

He remembered the day that he and Angelica met. Ezio's *banda* had been patrolling the hills near the village and were running out of food. With so many evacuees arriving in Sant'Anna, the partisans hesitated about asking people there for food, but there was no one else to ask.

Some of the villagers flatly turned them down. Even the priest said that he had too many people living in his house to be giving food to partisans. But he gave Ezio the names of others who might help. One was Angelica Marchetti.

Ezio had been involved with a couple of other women at the university in Pisa, but he never saw anyone as lovely as the tall, slender woman who answered the door. With her long hair, her luminous skin, her full breasts and narrow waist, she didn't look old enough to be the mother of the two young boys who clung to her skirt.

Yes, she said, the partisans could have some vegetables from her small garden, some fruit she had preserved, some fresh pasta and some bread she had baked that morning.

"Why are you doing this?" Ezio had asked.

"I guess it's something I learned from my mother," Angelica replied. "It's what she would do."

Ezio took to coming back to Angelica's, but not for food. He and Angelica had long talks and he often stayed to play with the boys. Sometimes he and

Angelica took them on walks in the hills. The younger boy, Nando, hardly remembered his father and thought that Ezio might be his "papa."

One night, after the boys were asleep in their room, Ezio stayed the night with Angelica. Then there were more nights. Ezio knew that Angelica's husband was a soldier in the war, but he was deeply in love.

Then, for a moment, Ezio pictured Angelica waving goodbye from her doorstep as he left for the last time two months ago. His *banda* was going to move to another hideout because it was becoming too dangerous near Sant'Anna now that the Germans were moving north. People who had helped the partisans would be killed.

Francesco interrupted Ezio's thoughts. "Did you hear me? Do you know people in Sant'Anna?"

"We have some very good friends in Sant'Anna," Ezio said, folding the map.

"But there is no one is protecting Sant'Anna now?"

"There's another *banda* near there now. They're a rough bunch. I don't trust them."

"Why not?"

"Did you ever hear of Barbano?"

"No."

"One of the worst criminals around. Now he's leading these hoodlums and deserters. They goad the Germans and get in fights with them. They're good at that. But they put the civilians in danger. They take too many risks. They think they're more powerful than they are."

"I thought all partisans got along together."

"Hah! We're just people. There's a lot of infighting. But we are all clear about one thing. We want to get those damn Germans out of our country. No, we're just men, and some women, who are trying to sabotage what the Germans are doing and then getting into gun battles with them whenever we can. We're just doing what we can, we're not trained fighters, most of us. We're students, laborers, young and old…"

"Some of us really old," Francesco interrupted.

Ezio put his arm around Francesco's shoulder. "No, not so old, my friend. Let's go back to where you will stay."

Ezio led Francesco to the corner that would be his and he introduced him to the twenty or so partisans who were now part of his *banda*.

Lying on the rough floor of the cave that night with his knapsack as a pillow, Francesco thought about his wife at the Cielo. He was sorry he had to leave

Annabella, but he knew he had made the right decision. When the war was over, she would know that, too.

Early the next morning, Ezio gathered all the partisans and explained the day's mission. They were to go to friendly farmers in the area and try to get more food. Ezio put together four groups of partisans and brought out his map to show them where each would be going. When he told the third group that it should cross a stream to the west of Nocchi, Francesco interrupted him.

"Wouldn't it be safer to cross the stream east of Nocchi?" he asked. "The woods are thicker there."

"Good point," Ezio said. "Cross it east of Nocchi."

At another point, Francesco suggested a more direct route to Loppeglia than the one Ezio had shown. Ezio agreed.

As the groups left the cave, Ezio clasped Francesco's hand. "Thank you," he said.

In the first three farmhouses, the partisans received fearful welcomes. They were quickly led inside and told that they should leave as soon as possible. But the women pressed bread, cheese and vegetables into their hands.

"Buona fortuna," they whispered.

At the fourth, an elderly woman came to the door. It was clear that she could hardly see, but she led them inside where five children, dressed in rags, stood around the table, their eyes wide. Francesco and the other six partisans explained who they were and the woman said her husband had left a sack of food in the shed in the back. They could pick it up there.

As the partisans were leaving the shed with the food, one of them, Oriole, told the others to stop. "Three Germans just came to the door," he whispered.

Incredulous, the men watched as three soldiers forced their way into the hut. After a minute, there was a gunshot, then another and another and so many more that the partisans could not count them all. The soldiers ran from the hut and in another minute smoke poured from the door and windows. Then flames burst through the straw roof.

"Let's go," Oriole said.

The seven partisans ran from the shed and confronted the Germans. Oriole, Thrush and Francesco each fired twice. The Germans didn't have a chance to fire. All three lay sprawled in front of them. One managed to raise his rifle and aimed it at Francesco. Francesco had to fire only once.

The other partisans attempted to rush into the hut but it was engulfed in flames. They could only watch as the walls collapsed. The partisans quickly confiscated the soldiers' weapons.

On their way back. Francesco was shaking.

"Your first time, right?" Oriole said.

"Yes."

"It won't be your last."

"I've never killed a man before. Do you ever get used to it?"

"No, you never will."

Dino and Paolo and the other partisans had already returned, and they put their weapons in one pile and the food they had collected in another. Ezio stood before the group and praised them for their efforts. Later, he took Francesco aside.

"Now you have seen the enemy."

"Yes. And now I know I'm glad I came."

For the second night in a row, Annabella lay quietly on her bed, still fully dressed and staring at the ceiling. Rosa, on the bed next to her, was aware that Annabella was awake and therefore was unable to sleep herself. Around 2 a.m., Rosa attempted to break the silence.

"Annabella?"

"Yes."

"You can't sleep?"

"No."

"Do you want to talk?"

"I don't know what to talk about, Rosa. I'm just so sad. I feel like dying."

"No, Annabella, no. We can't talk like that."

The words that Annabella had been saying to herself now poured out. "Why not? Are you going to be like Maria? 'Everything is wonderful, everything is great.' Well, I don't think everything is wonderful. My husband has left me and the fighting is getting worse. He's going to be killed, I know it, and I'm going to be left alone. Sometimes I wish that the Germans would just come and kill us all and then it would be over."

"Annabella, Annabella, please," Rosa cried. "I'm not going to tell you to think about the good things, like Maria does. But I think we need to have some patience. Marco says the war is coming to a crucial point. I know we've been saying for weeks that the Allies are on their way, but now they really are. And there are signs that the Germans are retreating. Once they leave Sant'Antonio, we can go back there."

"We?" Annabella said. "It's not 'we' anymore for me, Rosa."

"Francesco will come back, I know he will." Rosa's voice was not reassuring and the two women lay quietly for a long time.

"Annabella," Rosa said, "can we be friends? At a time like this, we can't hold old grudges. We have to start over. I'm sorry for not believing you, I'm sorry for not trusting you and I'm sorry for not talking to you all these years. I would really like us to be friends again."

Annabella swung her legs to the floor and sat on the edge of the bed.

"Rosa, of course," she said quietly. "I'm sorry, too, for the way I treated you. We've been silly and stubborn, haven't we?"

Rosa also sat on the bed and the women faced each other. Rosa reached for Annabella's hands. "We still have much to look forward to when we get back, Annabella."

"Let's hope so, Rosa. God, let's hope so."

Since both women were crying, neither did very well in consoling the other.

CHAPTER 33

▼

Father Luigi pushed back the radio transmitter and rested his head in his arms on the desk. The news from Sant'Anna was so alarming that he felt sick. Normally, the little village of Sant'Anna di Stazzema was so isolated that Father Luigi rarely heard a report. With people from other parts of Italy seeking refuge there, the biggest problem was taking care of the burgeoning population. Somehow, the village was coping.

For several months, the residents had given food, supplies and shelter to a partisan group, but that band had moved to another hillside and so Father Luigi had not heard anything from Sant'Anna in weeks.

Now, he had learned that the Germans had ordered the village evacuated but that another partisan band had told the villagers to stay. *Mamma mia!* Those partisans couldn't protect all those people!

Father Luigi feared that the Germans would do what they did at Farnocchia a week ago, burning many houses after the partisans had killed eight soldiers. Father Luigi's friend, Father Ignazio Lanzano, had fled from Farnocchia to Sant'Anna to see if he could prevent more bloodshed and terror.

Poor Father Ignazio, the priest thought. He remembered first meeting Father Ignazio at a Confirmation service in Versilia before the war. Father Ignazio, who was then in his late twenties, was much younger than Father Luigi, but they discovered they shared a passion for chestnut ravioli and went to a popular trattoria in Versilia. They had visited one another occasionally since then.

As usual, Father Luigi thought of his own shortcomings. He couldn't imagine being in Sant'Anna at this time. He was just a simple parish priest. He would be terrified.

Then he thought of something else.

"*O Dio.* Maria Ruffolo's daughter lives in Sant'Anna. Maria's whole life revolves around that daughter. What if something happens to her?"

Everything was happening at once. Outside, in the streets of Sant'Antonio, the soldiers were boarding trucks. Were they evacuating? If they were, it was in a hurry because Father Luigi could see that the banner proclaiming the 16th SS Panzergrenadier Division still hung on a house near Leoni's. Where were they going?

He had to warn Sparrow. With his hands trembling so much, he could barely reassemble the radio transmitter. He was on it for only a couple of minutes when the door behind him opened. With the noise from the trucks, no one heard the gunshots.

On the street a half mile away, Fritz and Konrad loaded gear onto a truck and went back into the house for the rest of their equipment. Konrad was plainly nervous.

"Have you seen Horst and Karl?" Konrad asked, pacing between the rooms. "They should be here now."

Fritz smiled. "They went with the lieutenant to the priest's house. They had a job to do."

"Oh yeah?"

Fritz pointed an imaginary pistol. "The lieutenant just got the message. They had to take care of it right away."

"Serves him right. I bet he was a communist," Konrad smiled, too. "How long do you think it will take us to get to that village?"

"You heard what the lieutenant said," Fritz said, buttoning his camouflage field jacket. "We'll be going by roads until maybe midnight and then it's on foot because there is no other way to get there."

They checked each of the rooms to see if they had forgotten anything.

"What do you think is going to happen?" Konrad asked, so jittery that he wiped his glasses for the third time in a half hour. He was having difficulty because his right hand was still bandaged from Gatto's attack.

"I don't know. When we get there, we will do what the lieutenant orders. Remember, we have to obey his orders. Settle down, Konrad. It's not going to help us if you're so nervous."

"I can't help it. This is going to be the day we prove ourselves to the lieutenant, I know it."

They put on their steel helmets, left the door open behind them and went to the street.

"Will there be partisans in this village? Shit! I hope there are partisans."

"From what the lieutenant said, this is a village filled with people who have helped the partisans, so if there aren't partisans there now there have been in the past. We need to teach these people a lesson, Konrad. It's for our own safety. If these people keep helping these communists and the communists keep killing us, where are we then? We have to show them, Konrad. We have to show them."

"I'm ready, Fritz. This is what I've been waiting for."

"Are you sure? This is the big test for both of us. We have been trained to obey orders, no matter what they might be."

"Fritz, of course. I know that. I'll do anything the lieutenant says."

"Remember that, Konrad. He may order you to do something you aren't ready to do."

"I will, Fritz, I will."

The two soldiers went out to the truck.

"It's for the Führer, Konrad. It's for the Führer!"

Deep in the partisans' cave, Ezio called an emergency meeting. He had just talked to his source in the valley and received just a little information before the line suddenly went dead. Perhaps the radio transmitter broke down, he thought, not daring to imagine that something worse had happened.

"We expect there's going to be trouble soon in Sant'Anna," he said. "The Germans posted a manifesto saying that the village had to be evacuated by tomorrow. If not, the Germans would come in and clear the village out."

"Evacuate?" Oriole said. "Where could they go? There must be five hundred people there now. Are they all going to flee to the forests?"

"I don't know," Ezio said. "But Barbano's band tore down the manifesto and put up one saying the villagers should stay, that the men should fight and the partisans would protect them."

"*Stupido!* There aren't many men there now. And how can that small band of partisans protect all those people?"

"What are we going to do?" Francesco said. "Can't we help them? We've got to do something!"

"What do you suggest we do?" Ezio asked, trying to be calm and realistic at the same time.

"Let's go down there!" one partisan said.

"We can help fight them!" another cried.

"We have enough arms," said another.

"I know a direct way," Francesco said.

Ezio quieted the uproar.

"Wait," he said. "I know we desperately want to do something. But look at us. Twenty of us against, what, a couple of hundred Germans, maybe more. What chance do we have? What good would we do if we all got killed. We'd be martyrs, yes, but dead martyrs. There's no point in that."

The men grumbled and argued among themselves. Dino and Paolo huddled together in a corner, afraid of whatever was going to happen.

"So we just sit here?" Oriole said. "Is that what it means to be a fighter?"

"Look," Ezio said, pounding his improvised table. "I'm so angry I want to take my machine gun and run over there and shoot every damn Nazi I see. I don't want something to happen to Pietro or Antonio or Carla or Augusto or all the others who have helped us. But I know I'd be dead before I got a shot off."

Ezio didn't mention Angelica. He couldn't bear to think of something happening to her.

"Isn't anyone going to help those people?"

"Father Ignazio Lanzano from Farnocchia has moved there now and will try to intercede."

"A priest? What is a priest going to do? The Germans aren't going to listen to him. They're going to kill him, too."

"Look, we have to be reasonable," Ezio said. "We can't win this one."

As the men, some of them grumbling, some of them silent, drifted to other parts of the cave, Ezio stood alone, shaking. He never prayed, but now he said a silent prayer for Angelica Marchetti. Once this damn war was over he hoped he would see her again.

The scream seemed so real that Rosa bolted upright in bed, only to find that Annabella was also wide awake.

"Did you hear that?" Annabella said.

"I thought I was dreaming," Rosa said. "Was that really a scream?"

"I think it was."

The women looked at their watches. It was almost 3 a.m.

"Somebody must be hurt," Rosa said.

Then they heard voices coming from the next room. Rosa went out into the hall and knocked on Maria and the Contessa's door.

"Maria? Contessa? Is something wrong?"

Wearing a long silk nightgown and with a matching scarf protecting the curlers in her hair, the Contessa came to the door. "Maria must have had a bad dream," she said. "She started screaming. But now she won't say anything."

Sitting on the edge of her bed, Maria wore a cotton nightgown, light blue with tiny flowers and a ribbon around the neck. Rosa thought it must have been a gift from Angelica because Maria would never buy something that she would call "girlish." Maria seemed frozen and Rosa put her arm around her.

"What's wrong, Maria? Did you have a nightmare?"

Maria stared straight ahead.

"Maria, it's all right. It's all right."

Rosa rubbed Maria's back. Annabella poured a glass of water from the nightstand. "Drink this, Maria. It will make you feel better."

Maria's breath was uneven and the words came slowly.

"*O Dio.* I was dreaming about Angelica and the boys. They were on a picnic in the forest. Suddenly there was this terrible storm. It was so loud. The lightning! The thunder! Then there was a fire. Red flames all over. And then just black earth. Black! They were gone! And I couldn't do anything. I was watching, but I couldn't do anything!"

"It was just a dream, Maria," Rosa said. "We have been through a terrible time and we are all imagining things."

"This wasn't imagination, Rosa," Maria said. "It was real. Something very bad is happening. I know it. I have to go to Sant'Anna."

Maria darted from the bed and was almost out the door before Rosa, Annabella and the Contessa gently guided her back to the bed.

"You can't go there," Rosa said. "You know we have to stay here."

"Stay here?" Maria said. Her eyes were glazed. "Where are we?"

"You're here with friends," Rosa said. "You'll be safe."

Rosa looked at Annabella and the Contessa and shook her head.

CHAPTER 34

▼

Like almost everyone else in Sant'Anna di Stazzema, Angelica Marchetti had hardly slept all night. At 4 a.m., she finally got up and untangled Little Carlo and Nando, who were, as usual, intertwined in the small bed next to hers. She wiped the sweat from their foreheads. Even now, warm sultry air engulfed the little room.

She leaned out of the window to see the hamlets in the hills. The moon hovered over Monte Lieto, shedding its light on the tops of the trees in the hillsides and illuminating the facade of the little white church across the square. There were no sounds, just a peaceful silence. Waiting.

Then a light went on in the priest's house and she wondered why Father Ignazio was awake. Poor Father Ignazio. So many homes were burned in Farnocchia a week ago and now he was trying to help the people here.

"How are you, Father?" she had asked him when they crossed paths in front of the church two days ago.

His face was ashen. He looked much older than thirty-three. "Very worried. Fighting everywhere. Partisans all over. Germans may raid. Don't know what to do."

"What can we do, Father?"

"Pray, pray, pray." And he hurried back into the priest's house.

Angelica went into the church, empty except for the tiny bent woman in black who was always there praying for her son, killed in Russia. Angelica lit a candle before the statue of Saint Francis, then turned to kneel before the painting of Saint Anna and the young Virgin Mary. Sometimes she thought her mother looked like Saint Anna but she herself had no resemblance at all to Mary.

Angelica didn't pray as much as her mother. She didn't carry a rosary around her wrist. Instead, she wore a bangle that Sparrow had given her. It was made of twisted pieces of copper wire they had found on one of their walks in the forest. Angelica supposed she was a sinner, but she didn't feel like a sinner.

She looked up at Saint Anna. "What am I going to do? I love my husband and I love Sparrow. Can God ever forgive me?"

In three days, it would be the feast of *Ferragosto,* but the village wouldn't celebrate. There wasn't enough food. Angelica supposed that her mother was preparing for *Ferragosto,* one of her favorite days in the year. Angelica hadn't heard from her for more than a month. She wondered what was going on in Sant'Antonio now, if German soldiers were threatening the villagers. She wondered if her mother was alive.

From her window, Angelica could see that some lights up in the hills and down in the valley. Other people must be worried, too. Today was the day the village should have been evacuated. A few men had left, although the majority were already gone from the village and Sant'Anna was now mostly the home of women and children.

Somehow, housing had been found for all the refugees from other parts of Tuscany and beyond, first in the school and the priest's house and then in homes. Angelica had taken in a family of eight from Montecino and they were staying downstairs, sprawled now in corners in every room.

Angelica hugged herself. She liked wearing Sparrow's scarf around her shoulders and over her nightgown. She had never washed it since he put it on her the morning he left, and she imagined that it still held his scent. She wondered if she would ever see Sparrow again.

Angelica loved Sant'Anna now, but it had taken her a long time to get used to it. She had arrived in the village five years ago, when Carlo brought her here as a young bride, only eighteen years old. With about four hundred people, the village was much larger than Sant'Antonio, where she had grown up, but it didn't seem big. Unlike Sant'Antonio, where the houses were all lined up along one street, Sant'Anna was spread out in the hills. She hadn't even been to some of the hamlets yet.

Angelica hadn't wanted to leave her mother alone in Sant'Antonio, since her father had died only a year earlier, and she was especially troubled when Carlo told her how remote Sant'Anna was. But her mother told her she had to go where her husband was and make her life with him.

When Carlo took his bride home after their wedding, Angelica was worried as the path from Pietrasanta led higher and higher, first through olive groves and then through deep forests of beeches, chestnuts and oaks. They stumbled over the sharp stones and once Angelica almost slipped down a cliff as they turned a corner. Carlo grabbed her just in time. For the last miles, they had to walk along a mule path and when they got near the top they turned around to see the great valley spread before them. The houses looked like toys.

"This is like a fairy tale," Angelica told Carlo, out of breath and gripping his arm tightly.

"And you will always be my princess," Carlo had said, kissing her on the forehead.

"We're going to have a wonderful life here, aren't we, Carlo? Aren't we, Carlo?"

"I'm afraid it's going to be a very hard life, my darling."

He explained that the village dated back to the 16th century and the church was built in 1560. For centuries, inhabitants had eked out meager livelihoods from farming, working in the nearby mines and chopping wood in the forests. They thought nothing about carrying loads of wood down to Pietrasanta on their backs. Each way took two hours.

Their house in the *borgato* of Il Pero was tiny, but she and Carlo were happy living with his parents. They had three rooms upstairs and they could come and go as they pleased. Soon, Angelica and Carlo welcomed Little Carlo and, two years later, Nando.

Then Angelica's world turned upside down. Carlo was drafted into the army and sent to the eastern front. His father and then his mother became ill. Soon she was not only caring for her two young sons but also for her husband's parents. She had to cook for them, bathe them, empty their pots from the night. But she was like her mother. God gave her this burden to bear, and so she would bear it. And then Carlo's mother died, and then his father. Now Angelica devoted all her time to her sons.

With the war dragging on, Angelica became increasingly tired and lonely. She hadn't heard from Carlo in almost two years and assumed he was killed along with so many other Italian soldiers in Russia. Then one day, about six months ago, four partisans came to her door looking for food. She was struck by their leader, who was taller than the others, had blue eyes and black wavy hair. She thought he looked a little like Carlo. He said his name was Sparrow.

Angelica had been shopping at Serina and Adamo's *bottega* in Sant'Anna five days ago when SS soldiers raided the village and posted a sign on the church in big bold letters: *Evacuate! You have five days to leave!* A flood of customers had rushed into the shop.

"What are we going to do? Where are we going to go? We thought it was safe here! We didn't think the Germans would ever come here!"

"Boh!" Adamo said, calmly wiping his hands on his apron. "Don't pay attention to them. The partisans will take care of us. They took care of those people in Farnocchia last week, didn't they? They'll protect us, too."

"But the Germans burned houses in Farnocchia!" said an old woman holding the hand of her young grandson."

"Boh!"

"And this is not the same band of partisans who were here before," Angelica reminded Adamo.

Adamo winked at Angelica. "You liked the ones who were here before?" Angelica blushed. Did everyone in Sant'Anna know that she was involved with Sparrow?

"I just don't think those partisans will be able to protect us," she said. "Look at how many refugees are here now."

"We've got people from Lucca sleeping on the floor of the kitchen," Serina said, looking up from wrapping some cheese in stiff white paper.

Adamo put a slab of prosciutto into the slicer. "Anyway, we don't have to worry. No German soldier has been killed around here. There isn't any reason for reprisals."

"Do you really believe that?" his wife said as Adamo concentrated on slicing the prosciutto. Angelica looked at him skeptically.

The next day before Angelica went to the shop she stopped at the church and found that the SS poster had been torn down. Instead, the partisans had put up their own hand-written sign:

"Do not obey the Germans!

"Women, children and old people, do not leave your homes. Offer passive resistance.

"Men who are able to fight must try to find every kind of weapon from guns to hay forks. The partisan formations are ready for action and ready to fight the Germans.

"Get ready to fight. Your freedom, your salvation is in your hands."

"The men are supposed to fight?" Angelica asked Serina. "How many men are here now? We're only women and children here now. And how is Barbano's *banda* going to protect us? They don't have enough men to fight hundreds of Germans."

Serina began to cry.

When she went to the shop the following day Angelica found that Adamo had fled into the hills.

"He said I would be fine," Serina said. "He said I shouldn't worry. He said the Germans wouldn't kill women and children. He said the Barbano band will protect us. Do you think that's true?"

Serina's eyes were frightened and filled with tears. Angelica gave her an extra hug before she left the shop.

Now when she leaned out of the window Angelica found that there was also a light at the Benottis. Maybe Elisa Benotti was going into labor. Elisa was due to have her baby today and Angelica would go over to help. Elisa was her best friend. She was the only one in the village she had told about Sparrow.

It was now almost 5 a.m. Maybe she could get some sleep before Little Carlo and Nando woke up.

CHAPTER 35

▼

When the sun finally banished the moon from the heavens, August 12 began as a beautiful day in Sant'Anna. The sky was a brilliant blue and cloudless. The chestnut trees and oaks glowed with dew. The flowers around the square in front of the little church sprang to life.

Because it was Saturday, women rose to bake enough bread for both Saturday and Sunday. Some tended to the pigs and cows in the sheds behind their houses. In one house, Elisa Benotti was about to give birth. In another, the Pierini family prepared to butcher the cow they had killed on Friday. In another, Bruna Parisi nursed the baby she had borne less than three weeks earlier.

But there was a clear sense of foreboding. All of the doors and windows remained closed, as if that would ward off whatever harm might be coming. The villagers had not obeyed the order to evacuate.

On Monte Lieto, just north of the village, about forty partisans hid in the chestnut trees. Nunzio Barbano, the ruffian who was their leader, paced back and forth. If the Germans were stupid enough to come today, the partisans were ready to fight.

5:30 a.m.: The lieutenant gathered his exhausted troops in a clearing to the northeast of the village. They had come on foot for four miles after their trucks could no longer get through the gnarled trees and broken branches of the forest.

For the last miles they were guided on the mule tracks by fifteen local collaborators who showed them the way and carried their ammunition. All wore masks. Among them was Augusto Garritano. Everyone in Sant'Anna knew he was a Fascist. The day before, he had moved his wife and two sons to Pietrasanta.

The lieutenant stood on a boulder and ordered his troops to stop talking.

"Now listen to this," he shouted. "You may be tired but we're just starting this operation. We have received orders from battalion headquarters. This is the most important operation we have had since we came here. Understand this. We will be one of four companies that will arrive simultaneously in the village. One will come from the northwest, one from the north and we will come from the northeast. The fourth will come from the valley to the south."

The lieutenant was getting hoarse, and after the long hike, he was sweating. He paused for breath and took a swig out of his canteen.

"The people here are traitors. They are helping the enemy, the partisans who are fighting us. They cannot claim innocence. We have warned them over and over. We told them five days ago to evacuate. They have refused. Now it's time to teach them a lesson."

Fritz and Konrad looked at each other. "Hell, yeah," Konrad said, and Fritz nodded.

"Our aim in this operation is to stop these people from helping the communists. And we have to do it in a way that other people will take notice. If they see what happens here, they will stop helping the partisans, too."

Fritz and Konrad jabbed each other in the ribs.

"In Farnocchia two weeks ago, there were other people who were helping the partisans. You know what happened to them. We burned their houses. I am ordering you to take the same action here. Other commanders today may give different orders. They may tell their soldiers to shoot and kill the people who live here. That is their right. I am not ordering you to do that. My order is to burn."

Konrad looked disappointed. "Why won't he let us kill?" he whispered out of the side of his mouth.

"The lieutenant never did like killing," Fritz said. "He thinks burning is enough."

His voice ragged, the lieutenant continued to shout. "This is the plan. The village has been divided into four quadrants. Each of our companies will be responsible for one quadrant. Ours is the northeastern quadrant. When we arrive you are to split up in groups of three or four. Go immediately door to door. Tell the people to come out. Search the house for partisans. If you find partisans, you can kill them. Then when everyone else is out of the house, set it on fire. Do you understand that?"

"What if someone shoots at us?" Konrad asked.

"Then you have the right to shoot back, but not until you are forced into that position."

Konrad grimaced.

"Soldier, you better obey my command!" the lieutenant shouted. He wiped his face with a white handkerchief.

"Yes, Sir!" Konrad said, getting to his feet.

The other soldiers lined up, adjusted their camouflage jackets, put on their steel helmets and secured their weapons.

"All right," the lieutenant said. "Get your supplies and let's move out. For the Führer!"

6:00 a.m.: Angelica had just drifted off to sleep when she was roused by bright flashes that lit her room like a midday sun. The flares came from four directions.

From her window, she could see a few men coming out of their houses into the deserted streets and she could barely hear their whispered conversations. "That was a signal…Germans…maybe looking for men to go work in Germany…better go to woods to hide…wives and children can stay here…they'll be safe."

She saw the men rush off into the woods. Frozen, she stayed by the window and soon made out scores of soldiers in the hills all around. She knew even more would be deeper in the forests. She pushed herself away from the window and closed the shutters tight. Then she roused Little Carlo and Nando.

"Wake up, my darlings. Oh, I hate to wake you."

The boys rubbed their eyes.

"What's happening?" Carlo whimpered.

"Don't be afraid. Just be quiet. Very very quiet. I'll be right here. All right, my baby?" She pushed them into a closet and returned to the window.

6:15 a.m.: The *borgata* of Il Colle was considered the poorest in Sant'Anna. The houses were small, with straw roofs, and close together. The Turrini family had lived in their hut for generations, going back to Andrea Turrini's great-grandfather. This morning, Andrea had fled into the woods with the other men of the village even though, at sixty, he was too old to serve in the army or be sent to Germany.

Having arisen when her husband left the house, Emilia Turrini had lit the fire in the small stove and pulled down a skillet to fry some eggs. Then she shuffled to the crib where her youngest child, born only three months ago, was sleeping. She wanted to nurse the baby before she made breakfast.

Before she got to the crib, three soldiers battered down the door and stormed into the room.

"*O Dio!* What are you doing!" She grabbed the skillet from the stove. "Get out of my house!"

The first soldier fired and Emilia crumpled to the floor, the skillet beside her.

"See what's behind that sheet!" one soldier shouted.

The soldiers pulled aside a sheet aside from the corner of the room and found eight children huddled together. One by one, each was shot. The oldest was sixteen, the youngest was the three-month-old.

"Start the fire!" another soldier yelled.

The soldiers poured gasoline on the straw roof, lit a match and ran to the next hut.

6:20 a.m.: Elisa Benotti had been in labor for three hours and the contractions were increasing. This was her first child and she was screaming in pain. She wished her friend Angelica Marchetti would come to help, but her mother and older sister took turns wiping her forehead and massaging her back.

"Oh-oh-oh-oh-oh!" she moaned.

"Almost there," her mother whispered. "Push! Push!"

Suddenly, four soldiers burst into the house. Elisa's mother cried out and picked up a broom as her only weapon. A soldier raised his rifle and with a single shot, the woman lay dead. The sister put her arms out trying to protect Elisa and was killed in an instant.

Elisa screamed. "No! No! No! No!"

A soldier raised his rifle and shot her.

"Look, she was about to deliver," he said. "Well, one more Eytie."

He took his bayonet, sliced the baby from the womb and held it in the air by its feet.

"Look at this!" he shouted. Another soldier shot it in the head and threw it on the bed. The baby was still connected to its umbilical cord. They rushed outside and set the house on fire.

6:30 a.m.: With everyone screaming and crying, Father Ignazio tried to calm the refugees who filled his house to overflowing. He had locked and bolted the doors and closed all the shutters. Perhaps if the people couldn't see what was happening outside...or perhaps the Germans would think that no one was inside...

"Pray, pray, pray," he whispered as he went from room to room.

Still, the walls were not thick enough to keep out the sounds of machine guns and shouts from the streets. And they were getting closer.

"Hide, hide, hide," he called as he made his way back through the rooms.

6:40 a.m.: In the *borgata* of Vaccareccia, the soldiers forced more than a hundred women and children from their homes

"Raus! Raus!" the Nazis shouted.

Prodding the screaming victims with their guns, the soldiers shut them up in three stables. In the corner of one of them, Maria Pieri stretched her arms around her sons, three, ten and twelve, and her daughter, eight. They were all wailing.

"What's happening to us? What are the soldiers doing?" the children cried.

"Don't worry," Marissa said, fighting back tears but trying to be calm. "The soldiers just want to make sure we are all here. They will let us go back home very soon."

Then two soldiers came in. They held bombs in their hands.

"See what presents we have for you?" one shouted.

"What are they going to do, Mamma, what are they going to do?" the twelve-year-old, Marcello, cried.

The soldiers ran from the stable, threw the bombs inside and locked the door. The bombs exploded. Marissa and three of her children were killed instantly. Marcello climbed up a beam and escaped through the roof before the Germans returned with straw that they spread on the bodies and then set afire.

Among the dozen people in a nearby stable were Gianna Bianchi Marsano, her elderly parents and young son, Marco. They had fled to Sant'Anna from Lucca a week before.

"Hide behind this door," Gianna told Marco. "Quick!"

A soldier burst into the stable and began shooting. Gianna was hit in the head.

"Mamma! Mamma!" Marco shouted.

The soldier whirled around and aimed his gun at the boy. Even though blood flowed down her back, Gianna took off her shoe.

"Get away from him!"

She slammed the shoe on the back of the soldier's head and kicked him in the legs. The soldier whirled back.

"You whore!" Gianna crumpled to the ground. The soldier was still firing as Marco ran out the door and into the woods. The soldier set the stable ablaze.

6:50 a.m.: In the *borgata* of Franchi, Antonio and Filomena Pierini were known for their hospitality. They took in evacuees from other villages and they welcomed neighbors to join them at a dining room table that was always laden with food.

On the evening before, Antonio had killed a cow and the family was waiting for the butcher to come today. Suddenly the *borgata* was filled with soldiers who pounded on the doors and yelled *"Raus! Raus!"* A woman next door who refused to come out was immediately shot.

Six Germans stormed through the door, killing Antonio, Filomena, who was four months pregnant, and two little girls. Then they threw straw on the bodies and flames surged through the house. A boy and a neighbor girl managed to run out the back door and hide in the garden for the rest of the day.

6:55 a.m.: The refugees huddled at the windows in the schoolhouse, hearing the gunshots that were coming closer and closer, watching as the black smoke from the distant *borgati* rose in the air. More than fifty refugees from all over Tuscany had been housed in the building for weeks.

"Why did we come here?" a woman from Uzzano cried. "Why did we think this was such a safe place?"

"That's what everyone told us," said another, holding her whimpering little daughter. "Maybe it was a trick. Maybe the Germans wanted us all here so they could kill us all!"

"Don't say that! They won't kill us! Why should they kill us?"

7:05 a.m.: Fritz and Konrad stormed into a house in the *borgata* of Sennari.

"Raus! Raus!" they shouted and two women and three children fled out the front door and stood screaming next to a stable.

It didn't take long to search the closets, under the tables and beds, behind the chairs. No one else was there.

"The others are shooting, Fritz," Konrad said. "Why are the others shooting?"

"Their commanders told them to," Fritz said. "Ours did not. That's our orders. You heard what the lieutenant said."

At the stable, Konrad pushed the women with his rifle, knocking them down as he threw gasoline on the side of the house and lit some matches.

Forty-five minutes after the onslaught had begun, Sant'Anna was in ruins. The soldiers were in a frenzy, yelling to each other as they ran from *borgata* to *borgata,* setting everything on fire. Almost every house was aflame and dense smoke shut out the dazzling morning sun. In the barns behind the houses, cattle bellowed and horses and pigs shrieked in terror as the walls around them burned down. The crackling of the fires drowned out the sounds of the machine guns. With their houses burning, and the village filled with smoke, many people crawled, coughing and screaming, into the square in front of the church. Surely the Germans wouldn't harm them at the church. Some huddled against each other, others were so terrified they lay crumpled on the stones. Screams and cries echoed throughout the village. The smell of burning flesh permeated the air.

7:45 a.m.: All eleven members of the Parisi family had been at home early in the morning, but then the father, two daughters and two sons went down to Valdicastello where they had some land. Bruna Parisi was nursing her daughter Anna, only twenty days old, when she heard noises next door. Then gunshots.

"Quick!" she told the oldest son, "Throw everything out in the back!"

"Why?"

"Because the Germans might do what they did in Farnochia. They burned all the houses. We want to save some things."

A daughter threw herself on her mother. "Are they going to kill us? Mamma, are they going to kill us?"

"No, no, my darling. Just be quiet."

When the Germans arrived they took Bruna Parisi and her five children out and pushed them against a wall.

"Please don't kill my children!" Bruna screamed, holding Anna against her bosom. The soldier aimed his gun at the baby, then the mother, then the other children. All died instantly.

7:50 a.m.: Huddled in the closet with her two sons, Angelica did not hear the Germans storm through the door downstairs. She did, however, hear them order the family from Montecino out of the house. In seconds, the door to the closet was flung open and she looked into the barrel of a gun.

"*Raus! Raus!*" Fritz ordered.

With a force she didn't know she possessed, Angelica pulled Little Carlo and Rando out of the closet, down the stairs and into the crowd in the square in front of the church.

"Don't cry, my darlings," she told her sons. "We're going to be safe here with all these other people. See, your little friends are here."

The boys clung to their mother's skirts.

Outside Angelica's house, Fritz was shaking. He had seen the faces of the women and children he had forced into the square. He had watched as fire consumed their homes after he poured the gasoline. He had observed his fellow soldiers turn into a frenzied mob. Yet he was a member of the SS and this was his duty.

"For the Führer! For the Führer!" he kept saying to himself.

Konrad was shaking, too. He was so nervous that when he started to pour gasoline on the house he spilled some of it on his trouser legs.

"Konrad!" Fritz shouted. "Watch it!"

"Shit! Shit! Shit! Fritz, help me! Help me!"

It was too late. The flames from the house circled and spread to his legs. Fritz dragged him into the street. Konrad was writhing on the ground and screaming.

"Help me, Fritz! Help me!"

Fritz tore off his own shirt and tried to smother the flames. It was no use. He tried to tear Konrad's trousers off but flames seared his hands. Soon Konrad's entire body was on fire. He couldn't scream any more, but his eyes pleaded for Fritz to help.

"No! No! No! No! No!" Fritz cried.

Fritz crouched and watched helplessly as the flames engulfed his friend.

"No! No! No! No! No!"

Fritz bent so low that his helmet touched the ground. The lieutenant put his hand on Fritz' shoulder. He didn't say anything, but at the next house he and a sobbing Fritz were met by an elderly couple, a mother and her two young sons.

Raus! Raus! the lieutenant said. "Away, away!"

Pointing his machine gun at their backs, he ordered them to flee into the forest.

8:15 a.m.: Bands of German soldiers went to the priest's house and the school, forcing the people inside into the square in front of the church. When all of the surviving villagers—more than 130—were in the square, the soldiers surrounded them on three sides and blocked off the fourth. Twenty soldiers went into the church, threw a grenade on the christening font, riddled the ancient organ with machine gun bullets and dragged pews into the square, surrounding the villagers. Then the soldiers raised their rifles.

"No! No! No!" the villagers cried.

"*O Dio,* help us! Help us!"

"Please! No!"

The screams echoed through the distant hills. Disoriented and disheveled, Father Ignazio stumbled into the square and pushed his way to the front, blessing the people on his way. Angelica and the boys were at his side. The priest grabbed Nando and held him over his head.

"Please," he cried, striding toward the soldiers. "In God's name, please spare these innocent people."

A single shot killed the priest, another the boy in his arms.

"Fire!" a commander shouted and raised his Luger. The sound of dozens of rifles echoed from one hill to another. Like a deck of cards, the villagers fell to the ground, one on top of another.

On the opposite side of the square soldiers soaked the church pews with gasoline. Matches were lit and soon the fire engulfed the square, burned the bodies and blackened the front of the church.

The soldiers, choking from the smoke, retreated to the far corners of the village. Exhausted, they took out their canteens and ate their lunch.

One of them had a harmonica. They began to sing.

8:30 a.m.: Hidden in the chestnut trees on Mount Lieto, Nunzio Barbano and his men watched in horror. "God damn you to hell!" he shouted over and over and slumped to the ground.

12:30 p.m.: Word of the massacre spread quickly and when Ezio and the other partisans heard about it they set off for Sant'Anna. Overcome with grief, they made their way through the hills. As they came nearer, they could see the cloud of black smoke rising overhead. They went from *borgata* to *borgata*, picking through the smoldering ruins of the houses. At Il Pero, Ezio ran to Angelica's house, but almost missed it. Nothing remained in the smoldering fire. Lying on the ground in front was the charred body of a young man. His uniform had been burned away, but his belt was still on. Ezio read the words on the buckle: "My Honor Is Loyalty."

When the partisans finally reached the carnage in the square, the stench was unbearable. With Francesco at his side, Ezio started to dig through the bodies, trying to find Angelica, but it was useless.

"Do you think you want to do this?" Francesco said. "What if you find her?"

"I can't, Francesco," Ezio sobbed. "I can't."

Francesco put his arm around Ezio's shoulders and together they collapsed in front of the church.

People from other villages arrived in the days to come, finding the bodies of 560 victims, mostly women and children. Some were never identified. They were buried in a mass grave in front of the church.

CHAPTER 36

▼

On the feast of *Ferragosto*, the villagers at the Cielo were attempting to have the celebration that Maria had planned, if only for her sake. Maddelena and Renata spread a white sheet on the table and Rosa and Annabella filled pots with roses and begonias and spread them around the room. The Contessa put on more makeup and jewelry, and Dante, who had worn work clothes since the group had arrived, donned his white suit and red ascot. British bombers still flew overhead, but there was a strange stillness in the hills and from the valley.

"Maybe the Germans have left," Marco said as he brought five bottles of wine from Colin Richards' former hiding place.

"Oh, Marco, do you think so, do you really think so?" Rosa stopped slicing the zucchini and tomatoes she was preparing for a vegetable plate. She took the wine bottles and kissed him.

"You know what I think?" Maria said. "I think the fighting is over. I think we're going to be able to go home very soon."

Maria had never mentioned the nightmare she had three mornings earlier.

All of the villagers gathered around the table. As Maria had predicted, there were indeed pork chops, more pork chops than anyone could have imagined.

"Let's say a prayer before we eat," Maria said. "I think we should thank God for all his goodness."

None of the other villagers thought that God had been good to them, but they closed their eyes, as if in prayer.

"And for Pina," Vito added.

"And for everything God has given us," Maria continued. "I think we should also thank the Blessed Mother on her glorious feast day."

The villagers were about to start passing the food when Maria decided there was someone else to thank.

"And thanks to Santa Anna," she said. "Without her, there would be no Blessed Mother, now would there?"

"Can we eat now?" Vito asked.

"Yes, yes, of course," Maria said, picking up a heaping plate of pork chops and handing it around. "You know, they don't celebrate *Ferragosto* in Sant'Anna because they've just had the solemn novena to Santa Anna. Her feast day is July 26. I wish I could have been there this year. The little church is so pretty and..."

"Could you pass the vegetables, Maria?" Rosa said.

The villagers soon tired of the conversation about saints and asked that more wine be passed around. Soon, all of the pork chops had disappeared. And the vegetables. And the wine. At the end of the meal, when everyone was too stuffed to move, Vito started singing old Italian songs and was soon joined by others. Rosa saw how Maddelena smiled at him and hummed along.

Mamma, son tanto felice
Perché ritorno da te
La mia canzone ti dice
Che'e il più bel giorno per me
Mamma, son tanto felice
Viver lontano perche?

The children were induced to tell stories and everyone noticed how Dante was smiling, his eyes glistening. Given too many scraps of pork chops, Gatto sprawled in front of the fireplace.

"I can't believe it's the middle of August already," Maddelena said, fanning herself with her handkerchief.

"We've been here more than a month," Renata said, grasping her sister's hand. "I never thought we'd be here this long."

They almost didn't hear the soft knock on the back door. Because he was so distraught about his loss and the tragedy at Sant'Anna, it had taken Ezio three days to have the will and the stamina to come to the Cielo. He was alone, although he had asked Francesco if he wanted to accompany him. Perhaps he'd like to see Annabella?

Francesco thought it over, but decided against it. He and his wife might have an argument or she might ask him to stay or he might even have second thoughts. Better to wait. Despite what happened at Sant'Anna, the Germans were fleeing north. Perhaps it would be only a few more days before all action would cease around here.

At the door, Marco quickly let Ezio inside. Ezio's face was ashen and his shoulders stooped.

"Sparrow!" Maria cried. Rosa grew wide-eyed.

Annabella rushed forward. "It's Francesco, isn't it? He's been killed, hasn't he? *O Dio.* I know he's been killed." She started to cry.

"No, no," Ezio said. "Francesco is fine. He was so busy he didn't want to come with me."

"Then why have you come?" Dante asked.

When he climbed down the hill from the cave, Ezio had kept rehearsing what he would say but none of it made any sense. And nothing could be comforting. It would be better just to tell the truth.

"I have some terrible news," Ezio said.

"Here," Maria said, handing him a glass of water. "Sit down. Drink this."

As the villagers gathered close to him, Ezio remained silent for long minutes, then began to sob. Maria put her arm around him. "There, there, just tell us. We've been through so much, how terrible can it be? God will protect us."

Ezio wiped his eyes and in the next minutes poured out the terrible story, barely pausing for breath. When he had finished, there was no sound in the room. Marco and Dante went to the windows. Rosa clutched Annabella's hands. The children held on to Gina. Maddelena, Renata, Vito, Giacomo and the Contessa sat solemnly, holding on to the table as if to support their very lives.

The story was incomprehensible.

Shootings?

Killings?

Burning?

Destruction?

Hundreds of people slaughtered?

At Sant'Anna? The safest place? Thirty miles from here?

They had heard of other massacres, like the one at the Ardeatine caves in Rome, but this one was so near, this one was so horrible.

And there was Angelica and her two little boys. And Rosa's cousin and Maddelena and Renata's cousins and who knows who else.

Everyone looked at Maria, who sat slumped in a chair next to the table. Her fingers rested on her rosary beads. Her eyes were closed. No one knew what to say.

"Signora Ruffolo…" Ezio began.

"Don't talk to me!" Maria's eyes flashed. "Don't say a word! Why didn't you protect her? Why did you leave Sant'Anna? Why..." She burst into tears and buried her face in her hands.

"No!" Ezio cried. "It's not my fault! We had to leave! We left in order to protect the people there! The Germans would have killed everyone there!"

Ezio was also sobbing again.

"And now they've killed everyone anyway!" Maria cried. "Why did this happen! God in heaven, why did this happen! *O Dio! O Dio! O Dio!*"

Rosa put her arm around Maria. "There, there, Maria." She didn't know what else to say.

Maria brushed Rosa's arm from her shoulder, stood up and struggled up the stairs to her room. The villagers could hear her door slam shut.

Ezio went to the stairs after her. "I loved Angelica, Signora!" he shouted after her. "I loved her!"

Ezio flailed his arms in the air and strode around the room, not looking where he was going. "Damn! Damn! Damn! Damn!"

Rosa went up to him and put her arms around him. Slowly, he quieted down.

"Dear Sparrow," she said. "It seems like you have suffered a terrible personal loss. I'm so sorry, I'm so sorry."

Ezio hugged her. The other villagers were now angry, anguished, bitter, terrified and terribly confused.

PART FOUR

CHAPTER 37

▼

Allied bombers had awakened Rosa, Marco and Dante in the early morning and the three stood close together in the main room of the Cielo. They would have liked some coffee, but the last had been used days ago. The best they could do was water from the well, which, fortunately, was still abundant.

"There are more planes today, aren't there?" Rosa said. "It sounds like there are more."

"I think so, too," Dante said. "I don't know what that signifies."

"Perhaps we're getting closer to the end," Marco said, looking wearily out the window.

"We've been here almost two months now," Rosa said as she joined him. "We should be getting closer to the end."

The first rays of the sun had broken through the clouds but heavy mist still covered the valley and there was no sign of Sant'Antonio. In the last few days the lookouts could see activity in the distant hills, and of course they thought of Francesco and Sparrow and all the other partisans. But there had been no contact with the partisans since Sparrow's visit.

"Do you think we should do something about Maria?" Marco asked. "It's been more than two weeks and she hasn't left her room."

"What can we do?" Rosa said. "She just doesn't want to come out yet."

"I think we have to let her take her time," Dante said. "What a horrible thing! Incomprehensible. I still can't believe it." He shook his head and wiped his glistening eyes.

The Contessa reported each day that Maria spent her days and nights lying on her bed. Occasionally, she drank water when it was offered but seldom the soup that Rosa or the Contessa brought.

The other villagers were still terrified. No one wanted go to bed at night, afraid that they would be awakened by Nazis, shot to death and the Cielo burned to the ground. During the days, they stayed close together, occasionally hugging one another as they wandered from room to room.

Dante tried to begin a daily schedule again, but no one seemed interested in sewing or *The Divine Comedy* and he dropped the idea. He found himself putting down his favorite book and staring out the window. Maddelena and Renata mostly sat on Renata's bed, holding hands. Roberto, Adolfo and Anna tried to play together, but ran to their mother when a bomber flew overhead or there was an explosion in the valley. Gina tried to comfort Lucia, who now threw up everything she ate. Lucia told her mother that she didn't care if the Germans came, she just wanted to die.

Annabella refused to talk about Francesco, and Rosa feared that Annabella was trying to adjust herself to the possibility that he would never return.

Neither Vito nor Giacomo wanted to play cards, but Vito returned to a childhood hobby. He gathered a pile of sticks near the back door and, using his pocket knife, began to make small whistles. At first, they were only for the children, but then he made one for everyone at the Cielo and these provided the only happy moments in the farmhouse now. Occasionally, Roberto would start playing his whistle on the third floor and Marco or Rosa or Giacomo or someone downstairs would join in and there would be a short concert. Francesco's violin lay untouched on his bed.

Mostly, the villagers felt trapped, waiting for the worst and unable to do anything to prevent it.

"We're just like those people at Sant'Anna," Rosa said as she returned to the table. Sunshine now lit the entire room. "They had no idea this was going to happen. It may even be worse for us because we know what happened to them."

Marco and Dante had no response. As the sky grew brighter, other villagers gradually came into the room, rubbing their eyes because no one had slept well again. As usual, Fausta sat in a straight-back chair in a corner of the room.

"How is Maria today?" Rosa asked the Contessa. "Is she any different?"

"She's the same. She just lies there."

Rosa shook her head, then headed for the kitchen.

"Does anyone want eggs for breakfast?" she asked.

Vito and Giacomo were the only ones who nodded. Gina said that Roberto and Adolfo would like some, though the boys made faces. Gina knew Lucia would refuse anything to eat.

Marco and Dante had made one hurried trip to Gavino's garden for more vegetables, and brought back the rabbits and chickens, too. But no one felt like eating, and Rosa had to prod them to eat even the smallest bowls of soup.

"I wonder where Colin Richards is now," Rosa said, trying to make conversation as she brought a plate of fried eggs to the table.

"Who knows?" Vito said. "Now if I were Maria I would say that he's in a fancy hotel in Switzerland and having eggs and sausages for breakfast."

The mention of Maria cast another cloud over the room. Finally, Annabella broke the silence.

"What I want to know," she said, "is why God would allow this terrible thing to happen. I thought God was good. Now I don't know what to believe."

"I don't know either," Maddelena said. "I never thought much about it before. Now I'm just angry. And I'm angry with God."

"I am, too," Rosa said. "And now I'm more worried and frightened than ever before."

Marco put his arm around his wife.

"Maybe Father Luigi would have an explanation," Maddelena said, but the mention of Father Luigi brought another cloud to hover over the villagers.

"Poor Father Luigi," Rosa said. "I wonder what the Germans have done to him."

"Don't think about it," Marco said, kissing Rosa's hair.

"We'll have to figure this out for ourselves," Rosa said. "Why would a God who is supposed to be so good permit this evil thing to happen? How there be so much evil in the world? How can God let people be so cruel? How can…"

"I know why."

Everyone looked up. Maria stood at the bottom of the stairs. Her hair, normally wrapped in braids around her head, hung loosely down her back. She was still wearing her light blue nightgown with the ribbon around the neck. It looked far too big and her skin fell in folds under her arms. Her face was pale and large black circles surrounded her eyes.

"Maria!" Rosa said. "Come, sit down!"

Rosa and the Contessa helped Maria to a chair at the table while Annabella brought her a glass of water.

"Here, dear," she said. "You should drink this."

Maria looked around the table. It was as though she were seeing a group of strangers and she wondered why they were here. Rosa found a large towel and draped it over her shoulders.

"Take your time, Maria," Dante said. "It's so good to see you again."

Maria took a sip of water and looked around the table again. She seemed to recognize her friends now.

"I heard your question, Annabella," she said. "It's something I've been thinking about, too. And I know the answer now."

The villagers leaned forward.

"It's God's punishment for Angelica," she said.

"What?"

"What are you saying?"

"Maria, don't talk like that."

Maria raised her hand. "Yes, that's what it is. You see, Angelica was involved with another man. It was with that partisan who has come here, Sparrow. I didn't want everyone to know that I knew him because I couldn't admit to myself that Angelica was seeing him."

"Maria," Rosa said, "what difference does it make if Angelica was seeing him?"

"What difference? Rosa, Angelica was married! Yes, her husband was off to war and she hadn't heard from him in a couple of years. But she was still married! She took vows to be faithful. 'Till death do us part.' I don't blame the partisan. He wasn't married. But Angelica was. And something else. I knew they were involved and I didn't say anything. I thought, well, she deserves some happiness. But it was wrong. It was a sin on her part and it was a sin that I never said anything!"

Maria started to cry so hard that her entire body shook. The villagers were at a loss to respond. They wanted to console her but they also wanted to say that she was horribly mistaken. Dante tried to be reasonable.

"Maria," he said gently. "You know I don't believe in God, but let's just grant that there is a God and that He does punish evil. Would this God let hundreds of people be killed just because one person was committing a sin?"

Maria had to think about that. "I don't know the answer to that. All I know is that six years ago, when Davido was killed in the mine, I thought my life was over. He was everything to me. But then Angelica had Little Carlo and Nando and I had something to live for again. Now I have nothing, no daughter, no grandchildren, no one. It's God's punishment, I know it is."

Maria put her face in her hands and sobbed uncontrollably.

"Maria," Rosa said, "sometimes we think that God is like a father who punishes a child for doing wrong. Maybe the church tells us to think that way, I don't know. But would he send Nazis to kill innocent people just because someone sinned? That's not right. That's not the God I believe in."

"Rosa," Annabella said, "who is the God you believe in? A God that would take my Francesco from me?"

"I believe in a God who is just but allows us to make our own decisions," Rosa said. "We're human. We make mistakes. We do bad things. And then we have to live with them. We're responsible for what we do."

"Wait," Vito said. "You mean Hitler and all the Nazis can be forgiven because they're human? Is that what you're saying?"

"I want to answer that."

From her corner of the room, Fausta raised her hand. She had rarely spoken since she was permitted back into the villagers' company.

Fausta stood up. "The reason the Germans are raping and killing people and looting and burning houses is that Hitler is an evil man."

Rosa and Annabella looked at each other.

"And," Fausta continued, "he has gotten other evil people to follow him. Maybe some of these people, like the soldiers at Sant'Anna, don't think what they're doing is wrong. They probably don't think about what they're doing at all. They only do it because Hitler or Kesselring or someone ordered them to. They think they have some great cause, but they're still responsible, each one of them. Look at how mean they were when they came here. And they are evil. Evil! And I don't think they can be forgiven."

Everyone of course agreed with Fausta.

"Fausta," Vito said, leaning over to look at her. "For once in your life you said something right."

Fausta sat down. She looked relieved, as if she had finally said out loud what she had been thinking for weeks. After a long silence, Dante stood up next to the window.

"Here's what I think," he said. "What good does it do to try to figure this massacre out? It was so enormous, so terrifying, we can't even begin to understand why it happened. The more we try, the less we will understand. Some people say there is a reason for everything, but how can we find a reason for this? So while you were talking, my mind took me to *The Divine Comedy*."

"Dante," Rosa said, "you can't find all the answers in a book!"

"I know that, Rosa. But *The Divine Comedy* does have some answers. I don't mean to act like a professor now, but hear me out."

A few people murmured, and Vito groaned, but most seemed eager to listen to a man they had respected all their lives.

"Remember when we talked about the *Inferno* and how fearful everything was? The next part, the *Purgatorio,* contains some less fearful images. I know it's common to think of Purgatory as a place where we are punished for our sins until we get to Heaven. But Dante says it's also a place to purge our sins, and that is done by suffering. Do you understand?"

The villagers looked confused. "You'd better explain, Dante," Vito said.

"Think of it this way. In the *Purgatorio* the spirits there are given examples of Mary and others to help them with their suffering. And there's something else. Dante depicts the spirits as a community of penitents, moving together toward the common goal of salvation. So the lesson for us, I think, is that we are all suffering here together in this farmhouse, on this hill, in this war. This is our purgatory. We have faced many things together and we need each other now more than ever. Let's think about that rather than trying to find answers to a question for which there are no answers."

Dante sat down, and again there was silence. The villagers tried not to listen to the planes overhead, the artillery and shelling in the hills. Then, from the back of the room, a dainty figure stepped forward.

"Excuse me," the Contessa said as she went to the fireplace and stood in the very spot where Fausta had made her speech weeks ago. Unlike Fausta, the Contessa was so small and frail she looked like she would blow away in a strong wind. Her hair was in small ringlets but the bleach had worn out, and the black and gray blended together. As usual, she had too much rouge on her cheeks. Her pink silk dress, which she wore daily, was now torn and tattered at the edges, but the rings on her fingers shone. Looking at her, Rosa was reminded of the porcelain dolls in the antique shops in Reboli. But now the Contessa seemed strangely determined.

"I would just like to add something to what Dante said," she began.

The villagers smiled. What could the Contessa possibly add?

"I know what you are thinking. You think that I am this silly old woman who reads romance novels and doesn't have a deep thought in the world. Well, let me tell you about myself."

Rosa and the other women sat up straight in their chairs. People in the village had wondered about the Contessa for years, but they never really learned much about her. All they knew was that her husband brought her to Sant'Antonio about twenty years ago and he died soon after. She was left in the big house at the end of the village and rarely went out. Rosa and Annabella were talking about her one recent night and concluded that the Contessa must be in her late sixties.

"I know I'm something of a mystery and there are a lot of stories," the Contessa continued. "I'm sure most of the stories are false. First, I'm not a contessa. I don't know why people started calling me that. My husband owned a clothing shop in Lucca and he had a little money, yes. But he was certainly not a count or any royalty. I suppose I got the name because I like to wear jewelry, especially in my hair.

"My name is actually Gabriella Valentini. I don't mind being called the Contessa, but it would be please me greatly if you would call me by my real name sometime."

The villagers whispered her real name among themselves.

"As you probably know, Nino, my husband, died of a heart attack twenty years ago shortly after we moved here. Nino loved me so much, he treated me like a doll. There was nothing he wouldn't do for me, and I still miss him very much. After he died, I just wanted to stay at home. I like to read, I play the piano and I have this wonderful doll collection that has given me so much pleasure. When we get back home I'm going to give the dolls to little Anna. Maybe that will help replace the one she gave to Carlotta."

Gina hugged Anna, who beamed. But even Anna knew that the dolls might not be there when they returned to Sant'Antonio. She also knew that they might not return to Sant'Antonio.

"But that isn't what I'd like to talk about. In the last weeks, since that terrible happening at Sant'Anna, I've been thinking about us here at the Cielo. And I've been so overwhelmed. You have such courage! Every one of you. Think about it. Gina and her wonderful children. Roberto and Adolfo going to the village to get medicine for Carlotta. Little Carlotta and the battle she went through. Maddelena and Renata trying to teach us sewing amidst all this. Francesco giving up everything to fight for us. Annabella, Rosa, Marco, Vito, Giacomo, all of you. Yes, even you, Fausta. You may have been wrong at first, but you stood up to those Germans when they came here."

In the corner, Fausta looked most uncomfortable.

"And Colin Richards, escaping the Germans and now having to travel through the very hills they occupy. Gavino, who gave his life. Father Luigi, surrounded by the Nazis in the village. All the partisans who are fighting for us. And now Maria. Oh, Maria, Maria! Now you have this great burden and you are so strong. We have shared the same room since we came here and I know I was very cruel to you. And you just suffered my insults. I'm so sorry. Please forgive me."

Maria smiled a little and whispered, "It's all right."

"And I need to apologize to someone else," the Contessa said, shyly looking at Dante. "I know I've made a fool of myself, flirting with you all the time, and I'm sorry."

Dante's face turned red and he looked down at his hands.

"I know this is a long speech and already I'm worn out. But what I mostly want to say is this. You have all shown so much courage. Not me, I don't include myself in this. But we have all suffered together as Dante said. And I think we have formed a sort of community right here at the Cielo, just as Dante and that other 'Dante' said. This purgatory has brought us together. If I may say so, I think we are even something like a family. I just hope we can keep that, no matter what happens here and after we get back to the village. Somehow, I firmly believe we're going to get back there."

The Contessa was shaking. She had never given such a speech before. Rosa put her arms around her. "You are courageous, too, *Gabriella*." Then Annabella and Maddelena and Renata and the other women took turns hugging her. When Maria enfolded her in her arms, both women began to cry.

The men shook her hand awkwardly, except for Dante. He stood a foot over her and could have patted her head. Instead, he leaned down and kissed the top of her hair and whispered something in her ear. She smiled.

Then all the women gathered around Maria, hugging and kissing her.

"Maria," Rosa said. "You must know that you still have a family. We are all here."

Maria didn't say anything, but she smiled through the tears that streamed down her face.

CHAPTER 38

▼

On a cloudy morning in the second week of September, the lieutenant gathered the remnants of the 5th Company of the 2nd Battalion of the 35th SS Regiment of the 16th SS Panzergrenadier Division *Reichsfuhrer-SS* of the X1V Panzer Corps of the 14th Army stationed in Sant'Antonio and prepared to move out. More than forty of his men had been killed or wounded in the last few weeks in their battles against the partisans. Three, including Konrad, had died at Sant'Anna and the others as the Germans continued their "scorched earth" policy, ransacking and burning more villages. The lieutenant kept telling his men that their efforts to eradicate these communists would be successful, but now, as they prepared to abandon the village, few of the soldiers believed that. They were discouraged and afraid.

"Now listen to this," the lieutenant shouted when the troops stood in formation on the main street. "These are our orders. The enemy is approaching Reboli from the south. They will be coming here shortly so we have to destroy the bridge. Twenty of you are going to the bridge immediately."

At the front of the line, Fritz wondered if the destruction of one bridge could stop the enemy.

"Then you are to return and we will evacuate this village and move to the north. It will be dangerous. The communist bands are thick in this area. We will probably encounter heavy fighting."

Fritz wiped his forehead as he put on his helmet. This is it, he thought. The approach of the Allied armies meant that the Germans would be forced back to the Gothic Line. Short of supplies and now lacking in troops, the army could not hope to win this war, he thought.

He missed Konrad so much. Many nights he had nightmares in which Konrad was screaming as the flames soared around him and Fritz was powerless to help him

"No! No! No! No! No!" Fritz would cry. Trembling, he would wake up in a cold sweat and turn on the light. He could not get used to seeing the empty bed beside his.

Then Fritz remembered the horror of the massacre at Sant'Anna and the carnage that followed in other villages. More murders, more houses burned. He just wanted to go home.

Home. He hadn't thought much about his father and mother lately. He wondered if they had survived the Allied bombing raids in Munich. For a moment, he thought of the hikes in the Bavarian Alps he had shared with his father. Then he thought of the good times he and Konrad had had in the *Hitlerjugend,* of the rigors of training for the SS, of their first days in Sant'Antonio. This all seemed so long ago.

What if he hadn't joined the SS? What if he had fled, like some of his friends, to Sweden when the war was about to start? What if he had not believed in Hitler so strongly? Was that a mistake? He remembered how he and Konrad used to talk about their friend Heinz' father, sent off to Dachau. Maybe the father was right after all. Maybe Hitler was a crazy man.

"All right," the lieutenant said, "complete the tasks. Remember: For the Führer!"

Even the lieutenant was trembling.

This morning, Rosa tried to make the day seem as normal as possible. She had convinced Maria to return to sharing the cooking duties with her, though they both struggled to get the others to eat. With the little chestnut flour that was left, they made a batch of *castagnaccio.*

"Look what we made for breakfast," Rosa said, passing the plate around. "Doesn't this look good?"

"Would anyone like some water?" Maria said, trying to smile but with tears in her eyes. "It's all we have to drink now."

A few villagers raised their hands.

The order had been given. Twenty soldiers went to the bridge. Half went to the Reboli side. They cleared away the brush to expose the explosives they had installed weeks ago. In minutes, the dynamite was lit and the soldiers fled.

Perfectly, the dynamite at each end exploded and the bridge dropped into the river with a roar that echoed throughout the valley and into the hills. For a minute, the sky was obliterated and a heavy layer of dust and debris covered the village.

The sounds could even be heard deep in the partisans' cave in the hills. Ezio ran to the front and found Francesco cleaning his pistol.

"Hawk!" he shouted. "The Germans have blown up the bridge over the Maggia! That means they're coming north. We have to warn the people at the Cielo."

"All right, let's go."

"We should take some men with us. I'll find Robin and Owl. You get Oriole and some others."

The men made their way out of the cave.

"Hawk," Dino cried. "Not so fast. We can't all run like you."

The villagers heard the explosion and ran to the windows.

"They did it," Vito said. "The bastards, they did it."

Then the roar of Allied bombers could be heard coming from the north. The planes flew over the Cielo and suddenly there were explosions in the valley. One after another, pounding the little town that wasn't even on the map.

"They're bombing Sant'Antonio!" Dante cried. "They want to get the Germans before they leave."

Then a bomb exploded across from the Cielo, near the ruins of Gavino's hut. The blast reverberated through the hills and the walls of the Cielo shook.

"We don't have to wait for the Germans to kill us!" Vito shouted. "The Allies will do it!"

Maria took out her rosary beads. The villagers knelt around the table and began to pray.

Francesco was the first to arrive at the Cielo. When Marco opened the back door he couldn't believe that his friend was standing in front of him again, with other partisans behind him.

"The Germans!" Francesco said breathlessly. "They're on their way. Hide!"

And with that, he turned and was about to leave.

"Wait!"

Annabella pushed Marco aside and ran out on the steps. She didn't say a word, but grabbed her husband and hugged him to her. They kissed for a long time.

"Bella…"

"I know, my darling, I know. You have to go. Be careful, please!"

"I will. I will be back soon. This is going to be over very quickly."

From the tower, Lucia cried out, "Dino! Dino!"

Dino looked up, just as he had the first time they met. "Lucia! Don't worry! I'll be back!"

The partisans ran into the olive grove.

The only place to hide in the Cielo was the tiny room that had been used by Colin Richards. Marco and Dante hurried the women and children into the space and the room was full. They left the shelves loose so that the women could escape if they had to. Rosa swept Gatto into her arms as she rushed inside. Dante ran up the stairs to the tower lookout while Marco, Vito and Giacomo stood by windows downstairs. Except for Marco's pistol, they had no weapons.

In the late afternoon, the sun burst through the clouds and the Cielo's golden walls glowed. Except for the trees swaying in a soft breeze, there was little movement. The partisans crouched in the olive grove, knowing the Germans would be coming this way. They had been waiting for hours.

In the tower in the Cielo, Dante shaded his eyes so that he could see into the distance. At first, the movements at the eastern end of the farm could hardly be detected, and Dante squinted into the sunlight. Then it was clear that these were German soldiers, a couple of dozen. He watched in astonishment as fifteen partisans emerged from the olive grove, ready to confront their enemy.

Dante ran downstairs to tell the others. The women refused to stay hidden, but gathered at the windows, terrified by what they might see but wanting to witness what they hoped would be their salvation.

Ezio and Francesco were at the front of the group, their rifles ready, Dino and Paolo stationed themselves at the ends of the olive grove and the others were between them.

The Germans were surprised. Before they could make a move, the partisans made theirs. Ezio, Francesco and the others emerged from the gnarled trees and fired. Three soldiers fell. Fritz and the lieutenant fired back.

"Dino! Watch out!" Paolo shouted.

But Dino was struck in the neck and fell to the ground. Paolo tried to get to his side but too many bullets prevented him and he saw his friend lying motionless.

"Dino!" Paolo screamed, then quickly returned to his position.

At a window of the Cielo, Lucia saw what happened and sank to the floor, limp. Gina cradled her in her arms.

Behind a bush, Ezio crouched and fired at Fritz. The soldier's arm was raised and the bullet entered his right side.

"Shit!" Fritz cried as he crumpled to the ground. He tried to look up but the bright blue sky faded quickly before his eyes. In seconds, the war was over for the soldier who just wanted to fight for the Führer. Then three more Germans also fell to the ground.

Then the lieutenant noticed a small, bearded man under a withered tree and fired. Francesco didn't have a chance to raise his gun, but collapsed onto the tree's hard roots.

Looking out the window, Annabella saw what had happened and screamed.

"I have to go to him!" she cried, pulling open the door.

"No! No! You can't!" Rosa grabbed Annabella from the door.

But while Rosa and Annabella scuffled, a tall strong woman ran out past them.

"Stop the shooting! These are not communists! Stop the shooting!" Fausta screamed as she ran across the fields, her arms in the air.

"Fausta, stop!" Dante cried, running after her. Midway, he overtook her and threw her to the ground. The big man was an easy target. The lieutenant fired first and then there was a rain of bullets from all of the Germans. Dante fell on top of Fausta, shielding her from the bullets.

Marco ran into the fields, readied his pistol and fired. The lieutenant fell.

It was all over in five minutes. Ezio and the other partisans quickly captured the remaining Germans as they tried to flee. Annabella broke free from Rosa's grasp and ran into the fields. When she found her husband, Francesco was holding his hands over his chest and blood oozed to the ground.

"'Bella, 'Bella," he whispered. "I'm sorry. I'm sorry for everything."

"There, there, my darling. Don't talk. We'll get you inside and take care of you."

"I'm sorry, 'Bella. I love you. I've always loved you…"

"I've loved you, too, Francesco…"

Francesco tried to speak, but blood oozed from his mouth and his eyes glazed over. His hands fell to his side. Annabella's tears streamed down on his face. Rosa and Marco stood silently and then gently raised her to her feet. Ezio came over from where the other partisans were taking care of Dino's body.

"Signora," he said, "your husband was the bravest man I ever knew."

Annabella clasped his hand.

"The bravest man I ever knew, too," she said.

Maria made her way to Ezio. She hugged him. "I'm sorry for what I said about you," she said. "You are so brave. Thank you for all you have done."

Then Vito came forward and shook Ezio's hand. He could only say "Thank you." There were tears in the old man's eyes.

Vito helped Giacomo and Marco carefully lift Dante's body and lay it on the ground. Oddly, he had a smile on his bloody face. Fausta was bruised and muddy, but otherwise unhurt.

"He gave his life for me," she said, dazed. "Why did he do that?"

Gina had brought Lucia to their room on the third floor and gently laid her on the bed.

"I want to go to him, Mamma," Lucia whimpered. "I want to go to Dino."

"No, no, stay here," Gina said. "It will be all right, *caro mio*. We're going to have a baby, remember?"

CHAPTER 39

▼

At first, some villagers thought they should bury Dante and Francesco near Carlotta's little grave, but Annabella wanted to return her husband's body to Sant'Antonio. Since they were certain the Allies would be arriving soon, they decided to prepare the bodies and wait.

While Marco, Vito and Giacomo found lumber to make coffins, the women lovingly washed the bodies. Annabella took charge of Francesco's, talking to him softly as she cleaned the deep wounds in his chest. She washed his head and beard and Maddelena and Renata helped her dress him with the shirt and pants that he had left in his room. The sisters couldn't hear what Annabella was saying to her husband, and they didn't want to listen. When they were finished, Annabella kissed his lips.

Then they turned their attention to Dante, whose body was so battered by the bullets that some parts were in shreds. But Rosa found his cream-colored suit and red ascot in his room and Dante looked not too much different than he did at their nightly meetings. The smile was still on his face.

"Oh Dante," Fausta said, breaking into tears as she touched his chest, "how can I ever thank you?"

"Such a wonderful man, such a good man," Maria said. She rested her hand on his forehead.

Rosa and Marco held each other as they looked at the bodies of their dear friends. Rosa sobbed so hard she began to shake.

"Dante, Dante...Francesco, Francesco..."

Marco held her close. He was shaking, too. It was then the Contessa's turn to pay respects. She placed a small pearl necklace on Dante's folded hands.

"Just a little gift from a foolish old lady, but it's all I could think of."

Curtains were used to line the coffins and the bodies were carefully lifted inside. Vases of flowers and the Cielo's last remaining candles were on the table nearby. Just as Vito and Giacomo were about to nail down the covers, Marco thought of something and asked the group to wait. He went to his room and brought Francesco's violin to Annabella.

"Do you think he'd like this?" he asked.

"Yes, of course," Annabella said. She placed the violin next to her husband.

Then Rosa thought of something. She went into Dante's room and found *The Divine Comedy* at his bedside.

"He'll want this with him," she thought. As she dusted the book off, a battered envelope fell out. She had seen Dante look at the envelope a few times when he talked to the group and was surprised when he hurriedly put it back. She knew she shouldn't open the envelope but could not resist. The edges of the letter were torn and the script, in a fine hand, was barely legible. It was dated 6 May 1896.

"*Caro* Dante,

"I was sorry to leave in such a hurry last night, but I needed to catch the last train to Rome. I am settled in my room here now, and will begin work on Monday.

"Beloved Dante, you know how much I love you and I will always carry you in my heart. You taught me so many things about life and about myself in our months together. You taught me to laugh when I didn't think I could even smile any more. You taught me that it's all right to cry sometimes. You showed me the beauties of Michelangelo and Fra Angelico and Raphael and so many others. You helped me understand *The Divine Comedy*. (Remember how we laughed when I got things wrong?) You made me see the beauty in the flowers and the trees and the birds. I will always remember watching the sunsets with you and then the glorious sunrises after we had spent our passion. (The next sentences were smudged and Rosa couldn't read them.)

"I know, though, that we could not preserve our love in the society we are in. We would always have to be secretive, and afraid that people would find out. So it is best that I leave. I will attempt to find a new life in Rome, and you must find a life there.

"But, *caro* Dante, know that I will always love you. Think of me when you read *The Divine Comedy*. Think of me when you see flowers and trees and birds. Remember me when you see a sunset and when you see a sunrise. I will always do the same.

"Your beloved,

"Raffaello"

A photograph, faded and frayed, fell out of the envelope. Two young men, wearing white shirts and black pants, had their arms around each other's shoulders and looked like they were about to burst out laughing. Both appeared to be about twenty-two. The taller one was clearly Dante.

"Your Beatrice," Rosa said. touching the face of the other man. "The love of your life."

She returned the letter and photograph to the envelope and placed it back into the book. "Well, Dante, your secret will always be safe with me. I will tell no one."

Rosa carried the book back into the main room and put it next to Dante in the coffin.

"I thought he should have his great love with him forever," she explained.

"He always loved that book," Maria said.

With the two coffins side by side in front of the fireplace, the villagers felt it would be awkward to hold a prayer service as they had for Carlotta. While Francesco was a churchgoer, Dante always said that he didn't believe in God. Maria silently fingered her rosary beads and Annabella whispered a prayer.

Rosa suggested that perhaps some people might like to share memories of Francesco and Dante. She began by talking about Francesco as a young man, recalling his laughter and how he loved to ride his bicycle. As for Dante, she remembered how he always thought the best of people and just wanted everyone to get along together. She said the entire group should be grateful for his kindness and patience during their ordeal. Gina remembered being a pupil in Dante's classes when she was a little girl and how he always made her laugh. Marco told stories about hunting with Francesco, describing the wild rabbits and pheasants that he shot and saying he would miss him very much. In tears, Fausta thanked Dante for saving her life. Giacomo said Francesco was the best *briscola* player he ever met. To everyone's surprise, Vito also said he was proud of Francesco for joining the partisans.

After others had spoken, Rosa said, "I think we should sing something, What about '*Bella Ciao*'?"

The song of the partisans was well known in Tuscany and sometimes at night the villagers could hear it from the hills. They joined hands in front of the coffins.

Let my body rest in the mountains
Bella ciao, bella ciao, bella ciao ciao ciao
Let my body rest in the mountains
In the shadow of my flower.

This is the blossom of those that died here
Bella ciao, bella ciao, bella ciao ciao ciao
This is the blossom of those that died here
For land and liberty.

Rosa looked around the room at the circle of villagers, everyone holding hands. Marco stood next to her on one side, Annabella on the other. Then Renata and the Contessa and Gina and Lucia and Anna and Roberto and Adolfo and Fausta and Giacomo and Vito and Maddelena. She could hardly believe that Vito was holding Maddelena's hand. "We have to try to get along together." That's what Dante had said. "We're like a family." That's what the Contessa had said.

For the rest of the day, Annabella sat next to her husband's coffin, her hand resting on the top. With Gatto on her lap, Rosa joined her for a while, holding her other hand, and then the other women took turns.

After yesterday's destruction of the bridge, the Allied bombing and the battle with the Germans, the countryside was strangely quiet. Now, the villagers waited. In one corner, Maria found a dozen ways to fix Anna's long hair, though sometimes it was difficult since Maria's tears still flowed freely. In another, Fausta and the Contessa were getting to know each other, two women who had been so private and who had revealed so much about themselves to the group.

Roberto and Adolfo played in their room, staying close to Gina. Ever since the Germans' raid, the boys had frequent nightmares and were always tired during the day. Gina sat with Lucia, who was stretched out on her bed, holding her stomach.

"Mamma, I don't know if I can go through with this," Lucia cried. "It's only the beginning and it's so long yet."

"I know, my darling, but the time will go by fast. Once we get back home there will be so much to do."

"It's going to hurt, isn't it?"

"Yes, I can't tell you it won't hurt. But millions of women have gone through this before and millions of women will still go through it, and every one of them has been glad she did."

Lucia turned over on her side. "I can't imagine being glad. Why should I be glad?"

Gina stroked her daughter's back. "Because, my darling, you're going to have a precious baby that is all your own."

"I never thought I'd be a mother," Lucia cried through her tears.

"And I never thought I'd be a grandmother." Gina hummed a lullaby while she continued to stroke Lucia's back.

In the late afternoon, a loud knock on the back door startled the villagers out of their thoughts. Rosa went to the window and told Marco, "Don't open the door. I don't think they're the Allies."

Marco looked out the window, too. Four soldiers, with dusky skin and wearing dark green uniforms and steel helmets, were waiting. They had rifles in their hands.

"Well, they're not Germans," Marco said, opening the door.

"Buongiorno, Signore,*"* the first soldier said. "Let me introduce ourselves. We are members of the *Forca Expedicionaria Brasileira.* We are Brazilians attached to the Fifth Army."

By now, many of the villagers had gathered around the door.

"Come in! Come in!" Marco said. "We thought we would see the British or Americans."

"We hope they will be coming soon. We were sent to the Arno and Serchio valleys to do reconnaissance and patrolling."

The soldiers saw the coffins laying in front of the fireplace.

"I'm sorry," the first soldier said. "There has been a battle?"

"Thank you," Marco said. "Yes, there has been a battle. We have lost two great men."

The soldiers took off their helmets and bowed their heads.

"Why are you here?" Marco asked.

"We are liberating villages from the Germans. The Germans thought they could stop us by blowing up some bridges, but we found others that were safe."

"And you have been to Sant'Antonio?"

"Yes," the soldier said, pausing because he knew he had an important announcement, "we have come to tell you that the Nazis have left Sant'Antonio. You can return home!"

A moment of stunned silence and then shouts and cheers and tears spread through the room.

"We're free!"

"We can go home!"

"Can you believe it?"

"Thank you, God in heaven!"

The soldiers grinned. They could not understand everything these crazy Italians were saying, but they knew what the reaction would be since they had already stopped at three other farmhouses.

When the room settled down, Rosa tugged at the soldier's sleeve. "We should know this," she said. "What is the village like? Are our homes all right? How much damage is there?"

The soldiers looked at one another, not wanting to reply.

"It may be better, Signora," the first soldier said, "if you find this out for yourself."

The soldiers said they had to inform other farmhouses and they left bearing a dozen sausages that Rosa and Maria stuffed into their backpacks.

Although the villagers were extremely anxious to return home, they decided to wait until morning. That would give them time to clean the Cielo and pack what little belongings they had. Most went right to their rooms. When they kissed good night, Rosa and Marco couldn't help smiling despite all that had happened.

"Tomorrow night, we'll be sleeping together again," Rosa said.

"Let's hope it's in our own home," Marco said

"Marco, remember when we left home two months ago and you promised that we would come back?"

"And now we are."

"And I told you how much I loved you and you said how much you loved me."

"I remember."

"You know something, Marco? Now I love you even more. You have been so strong here, like a rock. I don't know how I could have gotten through this without you."

Marco took his wife in his arms. "*Cara* Rosa. You are the one who has been so strong. You've held everyone together here."

He kissed her again. Before they went to their rooms, they stopped by the coffins. Rosa kissed the lids and Marco held his hands on the covers for a long time.

In bed, Rosa looked out at the star-strewn sky for the last time. She doubted if she would ever come back to the Cielo and wanted to remember this moment. But she was also aware that Annabella was wide awake in the next bed.

"You can't sleep, can you?" Rosa asked.

"No. So many thoughts are going through my head."

"Do you want to talk about it?"

"When we first got here I dreaded going back to the village because I thought that life would be the same with Francesco and I was so tired of that. Then, when

Francesco and I started talking together here, I thought perhaps we might have a future together after all. Now, it's all ruined. Francesco is gone, and I'm going to be alone. Rosa, I am so very very sad."

Rosa turned on her side so she could look at her friend.

"Annabella," she said, "you can't keep thinking about what might have been. Francesco is dead but you can be so proud of him. I feel terrible, too, not because I was still in love with him but because I realize how much I care for you and I feel so bad for you. At least now you know that Francesco loved you and that you loved him. You didn't know that when you came to the Cielo."

Annabella raised her head. "Are you trying to say that God allowed all this to happen so that Francesco and I could get together? I don't believe that."

"No, I don't either. But if we hadn't come here, and we hadn't suffered through all this, you wouldn't have known of Francesco's feelings, would you?"

"No, I guess not. Oh, Rosa, it's just too complicated. I just want to go home, bury Francesco, and sit in my room."

"*Allora*. You're going to have a frequent visitor if you do," Rosa said, reaching between the beds to clasp Annabella's hand. "And you know, we wouldn't be friends again if this hadn't happened."

"I know."

"Let's go to sleep now. We don't know what to expect tomorrow."

CHAPTER 40

▼

The villagers could not have asked for a better day for their return to Sant'Antonio. The sky was cloudless, the sun bright and the air cool for the middle of September. As they gathered in the main room, each had a small sack or bundle. Annabella went directly to her husband's coffin and sat by its side. Maria sat next to her, holding her hand.

"Let's have a good breakfast before we go," Rosa said, readying the pans and dishes. "We don't know when we're going to eat again."

For once, everyone had a healthy appetite, and since there wasn't much food left, the plates soon were clean. Afterwards, as the women washed the dishes, Marco came in from the shed, but he was not alone.

"Look," he said, "I found these people wandering in the fields."

A tall man stood at the door, holding a young boy in his arms. A woman held a girl by the hand. An elderly woman dressed in black crouched behind them, surrounded by four other children. Their faces were dirty and their clothes torn and muddied.

"Please," the man said, "we have been traveling for seven days and haven't eaten anything for two. Do you have anything to spare?"

Everyone pulled them into the room and Rosa and Maria quickly fried the rest of the eggs and boiled some vegetables. There was still a little *castagnaccio*.

The man saw the two coffins in the middle of the room and took off his cap.

"We have lost two of our dear friends," Rosa said. "We will tell you later, but come, sit down."

As the visitors devoured the meal, the man introduced himself, his wife, her mother and their children. They had been bombed out of their home in a village on the other side of the mountain and hoped to find an abandoned shed or somewhere to stay until they could find something permanent. They had been sleeping in the forests.

"Are you saying that you are looking for a place to live?" Rosa asked.

"Yes," he said. "I don't know where we'll find one. Many places are bombed and in ruins now."

The villagers looked at one another.

"Well," Rosa said, "what do you think of this place?"

"It's wonderful, but it doesn't look like you have room for anyone else."

"There's room," Rosa smiled. "We are just about to leave!"

Rosa told the visitors about the gun battle that occurred just outside, that two of their men had been killed and that all the people there were returning to Sant'Antonio. The Cielo would be empty.

"It's in good condition," she said. "No, it doesn't have plumbing, but there is a *cesso* just outside."

"And," Marco added, "there's a vegetable plot across the field and a few chickens and rabbits in the pen next to the shed."

All of the newcomers, even the man, burst into tears. Maddelena and Renata took everyone on a tour of house and the children promptly staked out places on the third floor.

"This is even too big for us," the man said when they came back downstairs.

"With all those children, you won't find it big at all," Rosa said. "I lived here when I was a child and it would be wonderful to have children living here again."

After Marco had given the man a short tour of the shed and the *cesso,* the villagers prepared to leave. First they stopped at Carlotta's grave, where Gina and the children knelt and said a silent prayer. Adolfo placed his favorite ball next to her marker. Marco looked to see if everyone was ready and then shouted, *"Andiamo!"* Everyone, of course, remembered how Dante had said that when they started up the hill two months ago.

When they started down the path to the village, Rosa stopped and looked back one last time. The brilliant green leaves on the kaki tree set off the Cielo's golden walls and the red tile roof shimmered. So much had happened since they had arrived more than two months ago. She clutched Marco's arm.

"The Cielo!" she said. "Was it heaven?"

"Purgatory, like Dante said."

All of the new residents were standing outside, waving.

"Arrivederci!" they shouted. *"Mille grazie!"*

"Buona fortuna!" Rosa shouted back.

Vito and Giacomo led the group, pushing a mule cart with the coffins of Francesco and Dante. Rosa and Marco, guiding Annabella between them, came next. Every once in awhile, Annabella sobbed quietly. Maddelena and Renata followed, avoiding all the stones. Maria and Gina held Lucia's hands, careful that she wouldn't stumble. Anna carried the box with Carlotta's things and Roberto and Adolfo pushed Carlotta's carriage, now loaded with pork chops, sausages and vegetables. Twice, the boys got out the whistles Vito had made and played a little tune. Fausta and the Contessa came last, arm in arm, while Gatto trotted happily along at the side, pouncing on lizards and swatting butterflies.

Large stones and tree branches often obstructed the path, forcing the villagers to edge around them. Huge craters where bombs had fallen lined either side. In some areas, heavy shrapnel had destroyed the trees. In one section, fires had scorched acres of olive groves and vineyards. The small shrine to an unknown saint lay scattered on the ground. Even under the bright sun, the countryside looked desolate.

The villagers stopped at the bend in the road where they had witnessed the scene of the battle on their way up the hill. It was now even more barren and only white bones remained of the carcass of the mule.

At the last turn, they could see the village spread out before them. There weren't any trees left standing to conceal it.

"O Dio!"

Women began to cry and men swore. From this distance, it seemed as if no home had been spared by the Allied bombers. Some looked slightly damaged but others appeared ruined and a few leveled. Huge pieces of concrete, twisted pieces of metal and heavy tree trunks littered the streets. The villagers stood immobile for many minutes, unable to comprehend the destruction before them.

"O Dio!"

"It can't be!"

"Our lovely village!"

"The Allies may have rescued us, but they did this bombing first," Rosa said.

Marco helped his wife over a tree branch. "If they hadn't, the Germans would still be here."

Before going to the village the group stopped at the church. The doors had been blasted open and shafts of sunlight fell through a huge hole in the roof. Heavy dust covered everything. The painting of Saint Francis and Saint Clara, its frame broken, tilted crazily behind the side altar.

Vito and Giacomo placed the coffins before the altar. Tomorrow there would be a burial in the cemetery. Annabella kissed her husband's coffin before following the others out of the church.

The group stopped in front of the priest's house. No one wanted to go in, afraid of what they might find.

"Come," Rosa told Marco. She took him by the hand and they went up the stairs. The door was battered down and a breeze swept through the hall. Chairs and cabinets were tipped over and papers cluttered the floor. With no sign of the priest in his little parlor or office, they went to his study.

"Father Luigi?" Rosa called. "Father Luigi?"

The priest was slumped over his desk. The blood had dried on the back of his head and around the numerous bullet holes in his back. He had been dead for a month and the summer heat had not been kind. Then they saw his radio transmitter.

"*Bastardi!*" Marco cried.

"*Bastardi!*" Rosa said. "*Bastardi!*"

"We will need help," Marco said. "We will have to come back."

When they told the other villagers waiting outside, there was a universal cry of *"Bastardi!"*

Because people from the other farmhouses were also returning, the streets were filled with cries of joy as old friends met one another and screams of anguish when they saw what had happened to their homes. From everywhere came cries of *"Bastardi!"*

At his butcher shop, Guido Manconi muttered and cursed as he tried to get through the debris to open the door. Nino Leoni struggled in front of his *bottega,* trying to prop its damaged sign against the front of the building.

"We'll be open tomorrow," he shouted to Marco. "We won't have anything to sell, but we'll be open!"

Marco picked his way to Leoni's and told Nino about Francesco and Dante, little Carlotta and Father Luigi. Not usually an emotional man, Nino started to tremble. Soon, word spread throughout the village.

"Dante is dead."

"Francesco is dead."

"Little Carlotta is dead."

"Oh no!" *"O Dio!"*

"And Father Luigi was murdered."

"O Dio!"

The other villagers described the Nazi raids on their farmhouses and how frightened and defenseless they had been. Another person had died. Old Gustavo Lugano had suffered a heart attack and was buried near the Due Stelle. Everyone knew about the massacre at Sant'Anna but no one mentioned it.

When Lucia saw Daniela and Carmella, all three girls shrieked and hugged each other. Then Lucia began to cry.

"What's wrong? Lucia, what's wrong?" her friends asked.

"I can't tell you."

"Is it because of Carlotta? Is your Papa dead?"

"No, no." Lucia turned her back. "I can't tell you."

Daniela and Carmella let Lucia go. They knew she would eventually tell them whatever horrible news she had.

Rocks and branches of trees covered the torn red banner of the 16th SS Panzergrenadier Division in the middle of the street. Vito and Giacomo gathered it up and tore it to shreds.

Rosa and Marco agreed that they would stay with the others in their group to make certain that everyone had a home. The tiny cottage where Maddelena and Renata had spent their entire lives looked intact from the outside and when everyone crowded through the narrow front door they found that, except for inches of dust everywhere, the sisters could move back in.

"I suppose this house was too small for those big Germans," Maddelena said, looking into a closet. "Lucky for us."

The bombing seemed indiscriminate. Across the street, Vito's portion of the double house was leveled, nothing more than a pile of rubble, but the same bomb spared Giacomo's house next door.

Vito was in tears. "Everything I own was in there."

"You're going to live with me," Giacomo said, grabbing his cousin's shoulders. "We're going to be all right."

Maria's house suffered little damage but at the edge of the village the west side of Gina's house had collapsed, leaving the living room and bedroom exposed.

"You're all going to stay with me until it can be repaired," Maria said, as Gina, Lucia and Anna and the boys stumbled through the rubble. "We'll get someone from Reboli to build a new wall there and it will be fine. Don't you worry. Come with me. My house is big enough for all of us."

They went into Maria's house. Dust covered everything here, too. Soldiers had occupied it, but did not destroy anything.

"I want to find something," Maria said, going to her bedroom and returning with a large photograph from her dresser. She showed it to Gina.

"This is Angelica, and this is Little Carlo and Nando. They took this picture last year, so the boys are bigger now. I mean…

Maria couldn't finish. Gina put her arms around her shoulders and Anna reached up and hugged her.

"I still can't get used to the idea that they are gone," Maria said. "I keep thinking I'm going to get a letter from Angelica…"

Gina held Maria for a long time. Breaking away, she said, "Did you know we're going to have a baby?"

"How could you think I didn't know?" Maria said, putting her arm around Lucia. "You're going to be just fine, my darling. We're going to take care of you."

The Contessa would also have a new house guest. Fausta's little house was severely damaged and the Contessa insisted that since her own home, always too big for her, was relatively intact, Fausta should live with her.

Finally, Rosa, Marco and Annabella arrived at Annabella's house. She burst into tears. Part of the roof had collapsed into the upstairs bedrooms. They didn't want to go inside.

"Oh, Annabella," Rosa said. "I'm so sorry."

"All I wanted to do was return home and stay in my house, and now I don't have a house," Annabella cried.

"There, there." Rosa hugged Annabella close and looked at Marco over her shoulder. Marco nodded.

"We have an extra room," Rosa said. "Would you like to stay with us?"

Annabella hugged her friend. "Just for a while," she said. "Until my house is fixed."

Rosa and Marco found that their own home had escaped serious damage. The back terrace contained huge holes but Gatto settled in under the bench as if he had never left. When they went inside, Rosa and Annabella found that the soldiers had left dirty dishes in the sink and had torn the beds apart. But it was in better condition than they expected.

"I hope they didn't take anything," Rosa said ominously.

She went to the chair near the window, unwrapped the blankets in the chest behind it and found the photo of her mother and father on their wedding day. She returned it to its place on the wall next to the door, put her fingers to her lips and touched her parents' faces.

"We'd better go back to the priest," Marco said.

Marco, Rosa and Annabella found Nino again and asked him to come along. At the priest's house, Marco and Nino put handkerchiefs around their mouths and carefully lowered Father Luigi's bloated body to the floor. Rosa and Annabella found towels and sheets and soaked them thoroughly in the sink in the kitchen. Then they wrapped the body as well as they could.

"A saint," Rosa said. All of them crossed themselves. There would be another burial tomorrow.

That night, Marco started cleaning the house and Rosa and Annabella washed dishes.

"The bastards broke some of my nicest dishes, the ones I got from my mother," Rosa said.

"Well, the bastards broke my heart," Annabella said with a small smile.

"Oh, Annabella, I'm sorry. I shouldn't be worrying about dishes when you've lost so much."

"My husband lies dead in the church and my house is in ruins and I'm here washing dishes."

Even though her hands were wet with dishwater, Rosa held Annabella close. They left the dishes for another time and went outside to sit on the bench. As soon as Rosa sat down, Gatto jumped up on her lap.

From the nearby streets came the sounds of boards being ripped from houses, dirt being shoveled, nails being pounded. From the hills, they could hear the partisans singing:

Let my body rest in the mountains
Bella ciao, bella ciao, bella ciao ciao ciao
Let my body rest in the mountains
In the shadow of my flower.

"Look at those stars," Rosa said. "I've never seen them so bright."

"You wouldn't know there is still a war going on," Marco said, sitting down next to Rosa.

"When do you think the other Allies will come through, the British, the Americans?" Annabella asked.

"Soon, I hope," Marco said. "We're going to need food, water, everything. That food we brought from the Cielo won't last long."

"Well, at least we're home again," Rosa said.

For a long time, the three sat quietly. Marco reached over and held Rosa's hand. Rosa held Annabella's.

"Can you see the Cielo from here?" Annabella asked.

"Not at night," Rosa said, "but sometimes, if the day is very bright, you can see just a speck on the hillside."

"It's nice to know that it's there. Do you think you'll ever go back to visit the new people?"

Rosa thought for a minute. "I don't think so."

CHAPTER 41

▼

EPILOGUE

Rosa turned the ravioli over again on the counter so they could thoroughly dry and be ready for tonight. Ninety-five should be enough, she thought. She would have to go to Leoni's for olive oil, but she could do that after visiting the cemetery. The house was clean and the back yard looked pretty. Looking out the back window, she saw Gatto under the bench. Gatto didn't run around much any more and when a lizard hopped by, he opened one eye, scrutinized it and then went back to sleep.

"Poor Gatto," Rosa thought, "we are all getting old."

It was Rosa's idea to have the party. In early September she told her husband, "Marco, I have an idea."

"Of course you do."

"In two weeks," she said, "it will be one year since we all returned home from the Cielo. I think we should get together and celebrate the fact that the war is over and we are back home."

"Those of us who are still here," Marco said.

"I know, Marco, but many of us are still here."

So Rosa talked to the others and the meal was planned. Rosa would make the ravioli, Marco would prepare rabbits and chickens and others would bring various dishes and desserts.

After gathering sunflowers from the terrace, she walked up the street and toward the cemetery. The ordeal last year had taken its toll, and a number of people, most of them elderly, had died. The cemetery expanded into the next field.

The white marble tombs shone in the sunlight. Almost every one had a photograph of the deceased and fresh flowers in small vases. Rosa placed her flowers on her parents' graves, throwing away the ones she had brought yesterday. She said a prayer, then made the rounds of others she knew.

FRANCESCO SABBATINI

Fresh flowers were already on the vault. Annabella must have been here already. She was glad the picture on the headstone showed Francesco when he was young, when he had hair.

DANTE SILVA

Dear Dante. There was no photo on his headstone. Rosa liked to think of him now as the smiling young man in the photograph from his book. "I will always keep your secret," she whispered as she touched his tomb. She left some flowers for him, too.

MADDELENA SPINELLI

Poor Maddelena. She had always looked tired after they had come down from the Cielo and she died soon after getting influenza last winter. She must not have had the strength to fight off the illness.

RENATA SPINELLI

Renata collapsed at her sister's funeral and stayed inside their house after that. She died a month later.

VITO TAMBINI

Poor Vito. He died of a heart attack while cutting down a tree in the back yard. Giacomo missed him very much but still played *briscola* at Leoni's every day.

DON LUIGI MAMMOLITI

The entire village missed Father Luigi. They had suspected he was working with the partisans but they never knew how much. As Maria kept saying, "He was a saint." Father Luigi was especially missed now that a new priest was pastor. Father Filippo Filice had been ordained last June and already practiced his hell-and-damnation sermons on the congregation. Rosa found her mind wandering during Mass now.

She glanced over at the church, still shrouded with scaffolding. The church couldn't pay for repairs, so men from the village and the hills did the work whenever they had a chance. Inside, women had thoroughly cleaned the pews, the altar and the floors, and they raised the painting of Saint Francis and Saint Clara.

Rosa closed the cemetery gate, touching the new bronze plaque dedicated to the six soldiers from Sant'Antonio who died in the war. She turned the corner and walked toward Leoni's. Each day, Rosa found some changes in the village, walls being fixed, doors and windows replaced, roofs repaired, painting being done. Some homes were covered with green canvas while repairs were made inside. Little was accomplished while the war was going on, and the winter had been hard, but when the war ended in May, there was a new life for the village. It would never look the same, but trees and shrubs could hide some of the damage from the bombs.

Some houses had been torn down and only empty lots remained, like teeth missing from an old man's mouth.

"I wish young people would move here and build some new houses," Rosa thought.

Rosa liked the way Annabella had put a new roof over her porch and started flowers growing in front. The Contessa's house also had a fresh coat of paint. Rosa was amazed that the Contessa and Fausta were still getting along in the big house.

Rosa waved to Roberto and Adolfo playing cards on the grass outside the Sporenzas' house. The family had moved from Maria's only two months ago. On the porch, Anna was helping Lucia rock Little Dino.

"Every time I see him he's so much bigger," Rosa told Lucia, tickling the baby's chin.

"No wonder," Lucia said. "He wants to nurse all the time."

The baby was almost four months old now, chubby and constantly smiling.

"You love your baby, don't you, Lucia?"

"More than love, Signora. I adore him!" She hugged him close and kissed his forehead.

Rosa put her hand on Lucia's arm. "How are you, my darling?"

"I'm all right," she said softly.

"Do you ever hear from Paolo?"

"Yes. He's working in Montepulciano. He says he'll come to see me sometime. He wants to see Little Dino."

"That would be nice for both of you." Rosa paused. "You miss Dino a lot, don't you?"

Lucia burst into tears. Rosa put her arm around her.

Sometimes, Lucia wheeled Little Dino in his carriage up the hill to the Cielo and visited Dino's grave, next to Gavino's. Lucia let the baby play on the grass that had grown around it.

Two weeks after Little Dino was born, Lucia wrote an entry in her diary.

"Dear Dino,

"I wish you could see our baby. He looks just like you. He has black curly hair and big ears and I think he's going to have freckles.

"I'm sorry we parted so angry. I have thought of you every day since then and I'm so sorry I said such awful things to you. I know now that you wanted to see so much more of the world than just our little village and I should have understood that. I wish we could have talked again.

"It's too late now. Wherever you are, I hope you can see Little Dino and know that he is the joy of my life now, just as you were for me for such a few short weeks. Know that I will love you always."

Lucia tied the diary in a pink ribbon, put it at the bottom of a dresser and never looked at it again.

After helping Lucia dry her tears, Rosa turned to her sister.

"Anna, how's your Papa? Any better?"

"I think so," Anna said. "Yesterday he smiled at me."

Rosa could see their father through the window. Much to Gina's astonishment, Pietro had hobbled home one day in June, a month after the war ended. A land mine had shattered his right side, knocking out an eye and making his right arm and leg useless. On many days, Pietro stayed at the window, staring into the street. He rarely talked, no matter how much little Anna tried to coax him and no matter how much Lucia tempted him with Little Dino.

Every Sunday, Gina, Anna and the boys walked up the hill and visited little Carlotta's grave. Lucia and Little Dino stayed home with Pietro.

In front of Leoni's, Franco Deserto, Leandro Magno, Danilo Falone and Renzo Papia no longer sat in their customary chairs. Leandro and Danilo had died, Franco suffered a stroke and was confined to bed and Renzo was in the final stages of the *brutto male* at his daughter's house.

Now, the places were occupied by four former soldiers. One was blind, another had had his left leg shot off, the third could not use his right arm. Their crutches lay beside them. The fourth man was in a wheelchair, having lost both legs. They never talked about the war. They hardly talked at all. They were all in their twenties.

"During the war," Rosa thought, "we only had old people and young children in Sant'Antonio. Now we have crippled young men, too."

Inside, Marco was playing *briscola* with Giacomo and two other men. Without Francesco or Vito, there were no regular players anymore and sometimes it was difficult to find a fourth person.

"It's not the same game," Marco said every day when he returned home.

"*Allora*. Then why do you go?' Rosa always asked.

"Where else is there to go?"

Rosa bought two large bottles of olive oil and told Marco he should come home soon to get ready for the party. The game was about to end anyway.

As soon as she returned home, Rosa prepared the sauce for the ravioli, and when Marco returned he brought Giacomo with him. They set up two long tables between the apple tree and the orange tree and strung paper lanterns overhead.

"How are you, Giacomo?" Rosa asked as she brought out plates and silverware and napkins.

"The same," he replied. "Always the same."

"The house is still pretty quiet?"

"Sometimes, I think I hear Vito. He's swearing at me."

"No! Really?" Rosa said.

"You know Vito. He never means it."

Rosa wondered how long Giacomo could go on without his beloved cousin. He always wore one of Vito's whistles on a chain around his neck.

"*Permesso?*" Annabella was at the door. She brought a bean soup.

"I had trouble with the new stove so I don't know if this is even cooked," she said, putting the pot on the counter.

Annabella had sold the trattoria in Reboli and used some of the money to buy new furnishings for her house. She never talked about Francesco, but Rosa noticed that Corelli's "La Follia" was the only recording Annabella had to play on her new Victrola.

"I'm so glad you're doing this," Annabella said, hugging Rosa. "We need to be together again."

Marco hugged Annabella, too. Rosa knew Marco missed Francesco terribly. Sometimes he woke with a start in the middle of the night, went to the window and stared at the hills. Rosa always got up and stood at her husband's side, trying not to notice the tears in his eyes. He rarely went hunting anymore.

They looked up when they saw Maria being escorted by a tall young man who looked familiar.

"You remember Ezio," Maria said

"Also known as Sparrow," he said, shaking hands.

"When he called and asked what I was doing today," Maria said, unwrapping a huge torte, "I told him to come over."

Ezio was now a law student in Pisa and continued to write his account of the partisans' activities. Every month he came to visit Maria and they talked, and cried, about Angelica and the boys. Once, they traveled to Sant'Anna, but they turned around before they reached the village.

"I don't want to see," Maria had said.

"I don't either," Ezio had replied.

Gina and Pietro arrived, followed by the boys carrying vegetables.

"Oh, look," Maria said, "here comes my baby."

Lucia pushed Little Dino in the carriage once used by Carlotta. Anna walked proudly by the side while Gina guided Pietro over the terrace stones with his crutches. Maria swooped down to pick up the baby and started to make gurgling noises. Roberto and Adolfo giggled.

"Don't you dare laugh," Maria scolded the boys. Little Dino was passed around, just as Carlotta had been a year ago.

The Contessa and Fausta were the last to arrive. Fausta found a place in a corner, which was fine with some of the other villagers.

"You know I can't cook," the Contessa said, "so I bought some gelato at Leoni's."

"That was sweet of you, Gabriella." Rosa tried to use the Contessa's real name whenever she could, at least whenever she could remember what it was.

With everyone there, the neighbors gossiped. Someone was sick, someone was working again, someone was pregnant, someone was getting married. Gina said that when she was at the Cielo on Sunday the new family thanked everyone again for letting them stay at the farmhouse.

"Have you been back to the Cielo?" Gina asked.

"No, not yet," Rosa replied. "Maybe someday."

Rosa wanted to remember the Cielo as it was when she was a child, not the refuge from the war.

The sun was setting by the time everyone had found a place at the table. Gina helped Pietro to a chair at the end, kissed the top of his head and put his crutches at his side. Little Dino had been nursed and was sleeping in his carriage. Marco lit candles in old Chianti bottles. Gatto sat under Rosa's chair, awaiting scraps.

"Oh, I almost forgot," Rosa said, rushing back into the house. She returned with an envelope.

"You won't believe this. Colin Richards wrote a letter to us in July and it just arrived. It was addressed to Dante, and I imagine they didn't know where to deliver it, so they left it at Leoni's. I just got it yesterday."

The letter was passed around.

"Dear good people at the Cielo,

"I want to thank you again for taking care of me and putting up with me for so long last August. I have worried every day about you and wonder if you have survived. I have a feeling that you have.

"I managed to get through a lot of the region after leaving the Cielo. There were a few times when I thought I wouldn't make it, but somehow I did. At least, I did until I was almost at the Swiss border. I turned a corner on the path and ran right into three German soldiers. I was kept in a prison camp until the war ended. And then I returned to England. (Roberto, I can write a long version of this if you want.)

"Life is pretty much the same here in Liverpool. I miss my friend and wish he was here to go to the pubs with me. You remember how I talked about my girl-friend Gladys? Well, I came back to find that she married someone else. But then I met a really nice girl at a dance hall and we plan to be married next year. I am very happy.

"I hope you are all well. I think of all of you every day and thank God for everything you did for me.

"*Arrivederci!* (Tell Vito and Giacomo I still know a little Italian!)

"*Salute!*

"Colin"

"Oh, that is so nice," Annabella said. "Did he give a return address?

"Yes, it's right here," Rosa said. "Who wants to write to him?"

"I do!" Roberto shouted. "Mamma, can I write to him? Can I? I want to tell him everything we did."

Gina hugged her son. "Of course."

Before they started passing plates, Marco opened a bottle of red wine.

"I think we should give a toast to those who aren't here," Rosa said.

"Dante!" she began.

"Angelica!" Maria said.

"Father Luigi!" Rosa said.

"Francesco," Annabella whispered.

"Carlotta," Gina, Anna and the boys said together.

"Vito!" Giacomo said.

"Maddelena!" the Contessa said.

"Renata!" Fausta added.

"Little Carlo and Nando!" Ezio said.

"Gavino!" Marco said.

"And Dino," Lucia murmured.

"And all the others who died in the terrible war," Rosa said quietly.

For a few minutes, there was silence. Then Rosa said, "All right, shall we start with Annabella's soup? And then my ravioli."

ACKNOWLEDGMENTS

Any author has many people to thank. For me, those people include, first, my wife, Barbara, and our daughter, Laura, for their invaluable editing services; our sons, Jim and Jack, for their support; Larry Baldassaro, Don Pfarrer, Kurt Chandler and Martha Bergland for their constructive suggestions, and in Italy, Marcello Grandini, my indefatigable driver/interpreter; Enio Mancini, the director of the Sant'Anna di Stazzema Museum, and, especially, my cousin Fosca, whose stories of her family's experiences in World War II and whose personal courage inspired this novel.

For more information about *The Cielo: A Novel of Wartime Tuscany* please visit

www.thecielobook.com

ABOUT THE AUTHOR

The son of Italian immigrants, Paul Salsini was a writer, editor and writing coach at *The Milwaukee Journal* for many years and now teaches writing courses at Marquette University. His travel articles about Italy have appeared in *The New York Times* and elsewhere. He and his wife, Barbara, have three children and four grandchildren and live in Milwaukee with their cat, Bella.

978-0-595-40697-5
0-595-40697-1

Printed in the United States
63520LVS00005B/1-90